好讀出版

王爾德
短篇小說集I

Selected Works of
Oscar Wilde

王爾德

Oscar Wilde

劉珮芳＝譯

CONTENTS

王爾德的童話世界

文／劉珮芳

初讀王爾德的童話令人振奮；再讀王爾德的童話令人沉思；三讀王爾德的童話令人撫卷長嘆，久久不能自已。

這位愛爾蘭裔的英國文學家以其喜劇作品、無礙的辯才、似是而非的雋語和「為藝術而藝術」的主張，為自己在文壇上奠下不朽的地位。事實上，才華橫溢的王爾德還有一片純淨有趣卻較不受世人青睞的天空——他的童話創作。

在他為數不多的童話作品中，沒有「公主與王子從此過著幸福快樂的日子」或「風平浪靜的美好生活」，只有醜陋貪婪的現實世界和讓人能夠忍受這世界的主要因素——愛。

在〈快樂王子〉中，王子和小燕子為了幫助一群素不相識的人而犧牲自己；在〈夜鶯與玫瑰〉裡，小夜鶯不吝惜地欲助「天下人愛其所愛」的情操足令人類汗顏；〈自私的巨人〉更為愛和自私做了最好的註解。

王爾德不斷藉由不同的故事來探討「愛」這個主題。情人之間的愛是霸道、獨占、容不下一粒沙子的；父母子女之間的愛是寬容的，而朋友之間的愛在他看來卻彷彿是虛偽狡詐的（也許和他個人的交友經驗有關）。他提供讀者一個廣袤的思想空間，要讀者從不同的角度來探討人類這最複雜也最獨特的感情。他對愛的多面探討豐富了讀者的感情，他的童話故事不是一個靜止的夢幻樂園，而是波濤起伏、精采有趣、與社會脈動相連接的有情世界。

　　除了愛這個主題，王爾德童話故事的另一個主題是「智慧」。在〈年輕的國王〉、〈星星男孩〉和〈驕傲的爆竹〉中，他藉由身份顯貴或自以為身份顯貴的不同角色，來傳述缺乏智慧的人生是多麼可悲的人生。不具備生活中的智慧，面對一堆金銀財寶，只能帶來貪慾而無法拓展生活境界；缺乏認清自己的智慧只能枉度光陰，到頭來還落得被人訕笑的結局。在王爾德拿手的諷喻本領下，世間百態清清楚楚地呈現在讀者眼前，他在〈一個忠實的朋友〉中，對小個子漢斯缺乏智慧的作為及磨坊主人仗著犀利的言詞扭曲真理，卻哄得旁人服服貼貼的描述，讓人覺得，若缺乏智慧、魯莽行事，那麼一切的作為都只好以悲劇收場了。

　　有人說「生活是一門藝術」，然而藝術的生活卻非得有智慧帶領不可。若不具智慧之眼，如何能看出生活之美呢？

　　王爾德的童話故事想和讀者分享的，往往不是美好、寧靜、祥和以及其他順利安穩的人生，而是充滿挫折、試煉和痛苦的體驗，因為在勞苦磨難之後，所得的報償是珍貴至極的愛和智慧。

　　王爾德是一位善於說故事的人，就讓我們一同探訪他的童話王國，細細品味他的精采作品吧！希望讀者朋友在進入這座寶山之後，都能滿載而歸。

快樂王子

快樂王子的雕像內突然傳出一陣碎裂聲，
好像有什麼東西破掉似的。
原來，快樂王子那鉛做的心已經破碎了。
這一天，天氣嚴寒得叫人想哭。

城裡一根又高又大的圓柱上屹立著一座快樂王子的雕像。他的
身上綴滿了金子作成的亮片，兩眼鑲著昂貴的藍寶石，腰間的佩劍
有顆閃亮的大紅寶石嵌在劍柄上。

在一般民眾的心目中，他真是備受尊崇。

「他像風向標一樣漂亮，」一個很希望有人誇獎他極具藝術品
味的市議員如此說道：「只是，好像不怎麼實用。」為了怕有些人
說他這人性格不切實際，他又趕緊補上這句話。事實上，他做人最
講究實際了。

「你為什麼不跟快樂王子學學呢？」有位睿智的母親如此開導
她那哭鬧著要摘取天上明月的兒子。「快樂王子從來不會這樣哭鬧
要這要那的。」

「我真高興，這個世界上還有這麼快樂的人。」有個鬱鬱寡歡
的人抬頭凝視著雕像，口中喃喃地說道。

「他看起來好像一位天使。」一群披著明亮的紅色斗篷、繫著潔白圍兜的育幼院院童在踏出教堂大門時，齊聲說道。

「你們怎麼知道天使長什麼樣子？」數學老師問他們，「你們沒見過天使啊！」

「啊！可是我們在夢裡看見過天使呢！」孩子們答道；然而，數學老師卻皺著眉頭，一臉嚴肅的表情，因為，他覺得這些孩子只是在童言童語罷了。

有天晚上，一隻小燕子飛掠過城市的上空。牠的伙伴們早在六個星期之前就飛往埃及過冬去了，這隻小燕子因為忙著和最美的蘆葦小姐談戀愛而延誤了行程。它們相識於初春時節，那時，小燕子追逐著一隻大黃蛾來到河邊，牠一看到蘆葦那苗條的身影便立刻被她吸引，情不自禁地停下來和她聊天。

「我可以愛上妳嗎？」小燕子問道，牠說話從來不拐彎抹角的。蘆葦小姐聽完牠的話，優雅地欠了欠身。於是小燕子便在她身旁飛繞著，還用翅膀拍點著水面，撩起一波波閃耀的漣漪。這就是小燕子的羅曼史，而且這段感情持續了一整個夏天。

「這真是一樁可笑的戀情，」另一隻燕子笑道，「她不但身無分文，親戚還一大堆。」沒錯，河邊確實長滿了蘆葦。秋天一到，其他的燕子便都飛走了。

自從伙伴們離開之後，小燕子不免開始感到有些寂寞，而且對於牠的戀人也有些生厭了。

「她從不開口說話。」小燕子說道，「而且我還真怕她是個水性楊花的女人，因為她老愛隨風搖曳，對著風賣弄風情。」當然啦，風怎麼吹，蘆葦就怎麼擺動啊。

「我承認她是很顧家，」小燕子繼續說道，「可是我喜歡遊山玩水，所以我的妻子也該喜歡遊山玩水才是啊！」

「妳要跟我一塊兒走嗎？」小燕子終於開口問道；可是蘆葦小姐卻搖著頭，因為她離不開她的家。

「原來妳一直在耍我，」小燕子叫道，「我要到埃及的金字塔去了。再見！」說完，牠便飛走了。

牠飛了一整天，到達快樂王子的城裡時，已經是晚上了。「我該在哪兒落腳歇息呢？」牠說道，「希望可以在這兒找到棲身之處。」

不一會兒，牠便瞧見了圓柱頂上的快樂王子雕像。「我就在那兒歇息一下好了，」牠高興得大叫，「視野廣闊，空氣新鮮，真是個好地方。」於是牠在快樂王子的腳下降落。

「這可是間黃金打造的臥室哪！」小燕子環視四周，輕聲地自語著，然後準備就寢；就在牠把頭埋進臂彎即將入睡之時，突然有一大滴水珠落在牠身上。「開什麼玩笑！」牠大叫，「天空晴朗，萬里無雲，而且星光燦爛，竟然還會下雨。看來北歐的天氣還真有些奇怪。蘆葦是比較喜歡雨水沒錯，可是那也只是基於她個人的私心啊！」

正說著，一滴水珠又落了下來。

「哎，這雕像若不能擋風遮雨還有什麼用呢？」小燕子說道：「我還是找個好的煙囪頂管避避雨好了。」牠決定起飛，另尋棲身之處。

就在牠展翼高飛之前，第三滴水珠落下，牠順勢往上一瞧──啊！牠看到什麼呢？

快樂王子的雙眼飽含淚水，而這些眼淚正順著他的黃金臉頰流下。在月光的映照下，他的面容如此美麗，以致於小燕子心中充滿了憐憫之情。

「你是誰？」小燕子問道。

「我是快樂王子。」

「你為什麼要哭呢？」小燕子問道，「我都被你淋濕了。」

「當我還活著，有著一顆人類的心時，從來不知道什麼是淚水，因為我住在無憂無慮、悲傷哀愁不許入內的宮殿裡。白天，就和我的伙伴們花園裡玩，一入夜，便在大廳和一群紳士淑女們狂舞。那時，在花園的四周圍著一堵高牆，但是，我卻從來沒有問過牆外的世界是什麼樣的光景，只因我周圍總是充滿了美好的事物。因此，我的朝臣們都稱我為『快樂王子』；如果縱情享樂就可以稱為『快樂』的話，那麼，我當時的確很快樂。我就這樣過了一生。死後，他們把我放在這麼高的地方，我也因此得以看盡這城裡一切的醜惡與悲淒。我的心雖然是用鉛作成的，但我仍忍不住要悲傷落淚。」雕像耐心地說著。

「什麼！這傢伙竟然不是純金打造的？」小燕子低聲自語著，因為牠不好意思大聲發表牠個人的意見。

「在遠方，」雕像繼續以低緩而富節奏感的聲音說道，「在遠方的一條小巷中住著一戶貧苦的人家。他們有一扇窗沒有關，透過這扇窗，我看到一位婦人坐在桌前，她的臉色憔悴，雙手既粗糙又紅腫，而且滿是被針頭扎傷的痕跡。婦人是個裁縫，正為一襲絲緞禮服縫製著西番蓮繡花，那是皇后身邊一名最美的女伴在宮廷舞會上要穿的。可是婦人的兒子病了，正躺在角落邊的木床上喘息。小男孩發著高燒，嘴裡不斷央求媽媽買橘子給他吃。而身無分文的母親卻只能餵他喝河水，所以他一直哭個不停。親愛的小燕子，你能幫我把劍柄上的紅寶石挖出來，送給那位可憐的母親嗎？我的雙腳都黏在底座上，無法離開呀。」

「可是我要去埃及呀！」小燕子說道，「我的朋友們正沿著尼羅河飛行，和一大群蓮花談天說地。而且牠們不久就要飛到埃及國王的墳墓上睡覺去了。那埃及國王躺在彩繪著自己畫像的棺材裡，身上纏著黃色的亞麻布，還塗著香料，頸上繫著碧玉串成的項鍊，可是雙手卻有如乾枯的樹葉。」

「親愛的小燕子，」快樂王子說道，「你就留下來陪我一夜，當我的信差好嗎？那個小男孩又病又渴，而且他的媽媽很悲傷啊！」

「我不怎麼喜歡小男孩，」小燕子答道，「去年夏天，我在河邊玩的時候，有兩個粗魯的男生，也就是磨坊主人的那兩個兒子，老是拿石頭丟我。當然，我的飛行技術高超，他們是打不到我的，而且我來自以動作迅捷靈敏著稱的家族，要想打到我，根本連想都別想。不過，再怎麼說，這都是很失禮的行為。」

然而，快樂王子臉上悲傷的表情卻讓小燕子心裡很難受。「這裡好冷。」小燕子說，「不過，我還是決定留下來，陪你一個晚上，當你的信差。」

「真是謝謝你，小燕子。」快樂王子說道。

於是小燕子從快樂王子的劍柄上取下那顆珍貴的紅寶石，用牠的喙銜著這顆寶石，飛掠過城裡建築物的屋頂。

牠飛過有著大理石天使雕像的教堂尖塔。牠飛過傳出陣陣歌舞笑聲的皇宮，還看見一位美麗的少女和她的戀人走上皇宮中華麗的陽臺。

「這些星星真美，」少女的戀人對少女傾訴著，「而愛的魔力更美！」

「真希望我的禮服能在舞會來臨前做好，」少女說道，「我特別吩咐裁縫師，要在禮服上繡上美麗的西番蓮花朵，可是這些裁縫師老是偷懶。」

小燕子飛過河流，看到船隻的桅杆上掛著閃亮的燈籠。牠飛過猶太人聚居的地方，看見幾個猶太人正在做生意，忙著用銅秤在算帳。最後，牠終於抵達目的地，降落在那戶窮人家的窗邊。牠探頭往裡面瞧，發高燒的孩子正在床上不斷地翻來覆去，而母親則疲憊得趴在桌上睡著了。於是，牠把寶石放在桌上，就在這位裁縫師的頂針旁邊；然後再飛到小男孩身旁，用牠的翅膀搧著小男孩的額頭。

「好涼快啊，」小男孩說道，「我的病一定是快好了。」說完，小男孩便甜甜地睡著了。

於是，小燕子飛回快樂王子身旁，並將牠所做的事告訴他。「好奇怪，」小燕子說道，「雖然天氣很冷，我卻覺得自己的身體好暖和。」

「這是因為你做了一件好事。」快樂王子說道。如此，小燕子陷入了沉思之中，不久後也就睡著了。沉思，總是讓小燕子昏昏欲睡。

天一亮，小燕子便飛到河邊去玩耍，還洗了個澡。

「太不可思議了，」有位鳥類學家剛好經過河邊，看到小燕子不免大吃一驚。「冬天竟然還有燕子！」於是他便寫了一篇關於此事的大幅報導，投到當地的一家報社去。文章刊出後，人人都引用了其中的語句，只不過，鳥類學家的用字艱澀深奧，很多字詞都是人們所不懂的。

「我今晚就要到埃及去了，」小燕子說道，而且牠對這個計劃興奮得很。所以，前往埃及之前，牠盡情地參觀此地的風景名勝，遊玩了不少公共紀念堂，還在教堂的尖塔上消磨許多時光。小燕子每到一處就惹來麻雀們羨慕的眼光，麻雀們甚至還竊竊私語道：「看！多麼優秀的陌生鳥兒啊！」小燕子真是得意極了。

當夜幕低垂，月亮升起時，小燕子飛到快樂王子身旁。「要不要我到埃及的時候順便幫你辦些事？我今晚就要出發了。」小燕子大聲說道。

「親愛的小燕子，你就再多陪我一個晚上，好嗎？」快樂王子說道。

「我要去埃及哪！」小燕子答道，「明天，我的伙伴們就要飛到第二個瀑布了。那裡有許多河馬蹲臥在蘆葦叢中，而且有一位馬蒙神坐在一塊巨大的花崗岩寶座上，這位神祇整夜守望著星星，一旦晨星閃爍上升，馬蒙神便歡欣地大叫一聲，然後歸於沉默。中午時分，獅子會來到河邊飲水。這些獅子的眼睛好像綠寶石，而且牠們的吼聲比瀑布的聲音還要響亮。」

「親愛的小燕子，」快樂王子說，「我看到遠處的閣樓上，有一個年輕人正埋首於堆滿稿紙的桌上，他的玻璃杯裡放著一束乾枯的紫羅蘭。他的頭髮蓬亂乾燥，嘴唇紅得像石榴，眼睛則大而充滿夢想。這個年輕人正趕著寫劇本，可是他冷得幾乎無法下筆。壁爐裡已經沒有炭火，而且他也快餓昏了。」

　　「我再留下來陪你一晚好了。」小燕子說道。牠真是一隻好心的燕子。「我要再送一顆紅寶石過去嗎？」小燕子問道。

　　「唉！我已經沒有紅寶石了，」快樂王子回答道：「現在就剩下我這雙眼睛是值錢的東西了，我的眼睛是兩顆珍貴稀有的藍寶石，原產於印度，已有千年以上的歷史。你挖出我其中一顆眼睛，拿去送給那個年輕人吧。他可以把藍寶石拿去賣給珠寶商，然後就有錢買食物和炭火，也就有力氣寫完劇本了。」

　　「親愛的王子，我不能這麼做！」小燕子哭道。

　　「親愛的小燕子，照我說的去做吧。」快樂王子說道。

　　於是，小燕子只好啄下快樂王子的一隻眼睛，準備將寶石送到那個年輕人的住處。這閣樓的屋頂上有個洞，所以小燕子不費吹灰之力便來到年輕人身旁。此時，年輕人正把頭埋進雙手間，對於小燕子的來到全然不知；然而，他一抬起頭，就在枯萎的紫羅蘭上發現那顆晶亮閃爍的寶石。

　　「我就要轉運啦！」他興奮地叫道，「這一定是哪個賞識我的人送來的禮物，我終於可以完成我的劇本了。」年輕人說著，臉上滿是喜悅。

　　第二天，小燕子飛到碼頭附近去玩，看著工人們辛勤地搬運貨物，牠大聲說道：「我就要去埃及了！」可是沒人理牠。晚上，牠又回到快樂王子身邊。

　　「我來跟你說『再見』，我要去埃及了。」小燕子說道。

　　「親愛的小燕子，你就再多陪我一個晚上，好嗎？」快樂王子說道。

「冬天到了，」小燕子答道，「這兒就快下雪了。我得到陽光和煦的埃及去啊，那兒有綠色的棕櫚樹，還有一群在泥地上玩耍的鱷魚。我的伙伴們正在神廟上築巢，而且周圍還會有粉紅色、白色的鴿子看著牠們，並且和牠們嘰嘰咕咕地交談呢！親愛的王子，我真的得走了，我會永遠記得你的。明年春天，我再回來看你，而且我會帶回兩顆寶石給你，補償你送出去的那兩顆寶石。我會給你一顆比紅玫瑰還要紅的紅寶石，和一顆與大海一樣湛藍的藍寶石。」

　　「在底下的廣場上，」快樂王子說道，「有一個賣火柴的小女孩，她不小心把全部的火柴都掉到水溝裡去了，那些火柴全都不能用了。如果她就這樣空手回家，她父親會狠狠地揍她的。她現在正傷心地大哭呢！而且這個小女孩既沒有鞋襪可穿，也沒有帽子可戴。小燕子，把我的另一隻眼睛挖出來送給她，這樣，她父親就不會打她了。」

　　「我再留下來陪你一晚好了，」小燕子說道，「可是我不能再挖你的眼睛了，你會變成瞎子的。」

　　「親愛的小燕子，」快樂王子說道，「照我說的去做吧。」

　　於是，小燕子只好啄下快樂王子的另一隻眼睛，帶著這顆珍貴的寶石，迅速地往下俯衝。牠飛快地飛過小女孩身旁，把寶石丟進她的手掌中。

　　「好漂亮的玻璃珠啊！」小女孩低頭一看，高興地叫嚷著跑回家去了。

　　然後，小燕子飛回快樂王子身邊。

　　「你現在什麼都看不到了，」小燕子說道，「我會留下來陪你，永遠都在你的身邊。」

　　「不，小燕子，」快樂王子說道，「你得趕快到埃及去。」

　　「我要永遠陪在你身邊。」小燕子說完便在快樂王子的腳邊睡著了。

　　當朝陽升起，新的一天又開始時，小燕子便飛上快樂王子的肩頭，整天陪著他，講述自己在各地旅遊時見到的奇聞異事。牠告訴快樂王子，牠曾在尼羅河的河岸看到朱鷺用長喙捕捉金色的魚；也在沙漠裡看過和這個世界一樣古老、且事事皆知的獅身人面雕像；還有那些跟在駱駝旁邊漫步、手上戴著琥珀珠鍊的商人；以及那皮膚像黑檀木一樣黑，禮拜大水晶球的月之山國王；更有那需要由二十個祭司以蜂蜜蛋糕餵養、盤在棕櫚樹上的巨大綠蛇；而且還有那駛著大葉片橫渡大湖、老是和蝴蝶打仗的矮人族。

「親愛的小燕子，」快樂王子說，「你告訴了我許多令人嘆為觀止的景象，然而，這世間最叫人感到嘆為觀止的事，卻是世人的苦難，這世界最深奧的事莫過於悲苦。小燕子，你沿著這城市飛一圈，然後把你所看到的景象告訴我。」

於是，小燕子繞著這座城市飛了一圈。牠看到富人在他們富麗堂皇的家中縱情享樂，而乞丐卻只有在門口呆坐的份。牠飛進暗巷中，看到一群面黃肌瘦的貧窮孩童，目光呆滯地瞧著黑漆漆的街道。而在拱橋的下面，則有兩個小男孩瑟縮在橋墩旁，互相擁抱試圖取暖。

「我們肚子好餓！」兩個小男孩說道。

「你們不可以睡在這裡！」巡夜人大聲喝斥著他們，兩個小男孩只好站起來，在雨中蹣跚而去。

小燕子飛回快樂王子身邊，並把牠所見到的一切景象都告訴快樂王子。

「我的身體鑲有金子作成的亮片，」快樂王子說道，「你把它們一片一片剝下來，送給窮苦的人民。活著的人總喜歡金子，覺得擁有金子便擁有快樂。」

於是，小燕子便把快樂王子身上的金子片一片片剝下來，失去金片的快樂王子看起來顯得灰撲撲又髒兮兮的，實在不怎麼好看。小燕子把剝下來的金子一片片分送給窮苦的人家。面黃飢瘦的孩子開始有了紅潤的臉頰，而且開始在街道上嬉戲、歡笑，高聲地說：

「我們有麵包吃了。」

不久，開始下雪了，下過雪之後便開始降霜。於是，整座城市有如粉雕玉琢，街道似乎閃閃發光，屋簷下掛著的冰柱就像水晶作的短刀一般。行人全都裹著厚重的皮裘，小男孩們則戴上紅色的帽子，到冰上溜冰。

可憐的小燕子，牠覺得愈來愈冷了，可是卻又不想離開快樂王子，牠太愛他了。

小燕子飛到麵包店門口，趁店家不注意時撿拾麵包屑充飢，並且不斷鼓動翅膀以保持身體的溫暖。

但是，小燕子終於撐不下去，牠快凍死了。牠用僅有的一絲力氣再度飛上快樂王子的肩頭。

「親愛的王子，再見了。」小燕子輕輕地說著，「讓我親吻你的手，算是道別，好嗎？」

「你終於要去埃及了，真是太好了。」快樂王子說道，「你在這兒耽擱了不少時間。謝謝你的幫忙，來，跟我親吻道別，我真喜歡你。」

「親愛的王子，我不是要去埃及，」小燕子說道，「我要去死神之殿報到了，死亡和睡眠是兄弟嘛，可不是嗎？」

於是，小燕子在快樂王子的唇上輕吻一下，便摔到王子腳邊，死去了。

此時，快樂王子的雕像內突然傳出一陣碎裂聲，好像有什麼東西破掉似的。原來，快樂王子那鉛做的心已經破碎了。這一天，天氣嚴寒得叫人想哭。

第二天早晨，市長和市議員們在廣場上散步，他們經過快樂王子的雕像下面，抬頭往上瞧時，市長驚叫道：「我的天哪！快樂王子怎麼變成一尊破銅爛鐵呢！」

「啊！真是一尊破銅爛鐵！」市議員們立刻附和著市長的話。他們總和市長有著相同的見解，並湊上前上去仔細看看雕像。

「王子劍柄上的紅寶石掉了，兩隻眼睛也不見了，身上鑲著的金片也不知跑哪兒去了，」市長說著，「其實，現在的他真的比乞丐好不了多少！」

　　「真的比乞丐好不了多少！」市議員們立刻贊同市長的批評。

　　「嘿，而且他腳邊還躺著一隻死鳥！」市長繼續說道，「我們真該貼個公告，宣佈鳥類不可以死在這裡才是。」市長一說完，旁邊立刻有工作人員把這項重要宣佈記下來。

　　不久，快樂王子的雕像被拆了下來，因為有位美學專家說：「既然他已經不再光彩美麗，也就沒有什麼用處了。」

　　於是，被拆下來的快樂王子便被送進鎔化爐去了。而市長也忙著召開市政會議，討論一下該如何解決鎔化雕像後所得的鉛。「這樣好了，我們就用這些鉛再塑一尊雕像吧。而且，就塑一尊我的雕像吧。」

　　「塑我的像！」「塑我的像！」這回，每位市議員都有自己的主張了。而且，他們還為了堅持自己的主張爭吵個不休，我離開會場時，他們還在吵呢！

　　「真奇怪，」工廠的監工看著快樂王子的雕像鎔化時，說道：「這顆破裂的心怎麼沒有被火鎔掉呢？把它扔掉好了。」於是，他們便把快樂王子的心，扔到小燕子被丟棄的那堆廢棄物上。

　　「幫我把城裡最珍貴的兩樣東西找來吧。」上帝如此吩咐著天使。於是，天使便將那顆破裂的鉛心和死去的小燕子，帶到上帝面前。

　　「做得好，」上帝說道，「這隻小燕子，將在我天堂的花園裡為眾人歡唱；這位快樂王子，則將在我以黃金打造的城市中頌讚於我。」

The Happy Prince

High above the city, on a tall column, stood the statue of the Happy Prince. He was gilded all over with thin leaves of fine gold, for eyes he had two bright sapphires, and a large red ruby glowed on his sword-hilt.

He was very much admired indeed. "He is as beautiful as a weathercock," remarked one of the town councilors who wished to gain a reputation for having artistic tastes; "only not quite so useful," he added, fearing lest people should think him unpractical, which he really was not.

"Why can't you be like the Happy Prince?" asked a sensible mother of her little boy who was crying for the moon. "The Happy Prince never dreams of crying for anything."

"I am glad there is some one in the world who is quite happy," muttered a disappointed man as he gazed at the wonderful statue.

"He looks just like an angel," said the charity children as they came out of the cathedral in their bright scarlet cloaks and their clean white pinafores.

"How do you know?" said the mathematical master, "you have never seen one."

"Ah! but we have, in our dreams," answered the children; and the mathematical master frowned and looked very severe, for he did not approve of children dreaming.

One night there flew over the city a little swallow. His friends had gone away to Egypt six weeks before, but he had stayed behind, for he was in love with the most beautiful reed. He had met her early in the spring as he was flying down the river after a big yellow moth, and had been so attracted by her slender waist that he had stopped to talk to her.

"Shall I love you?" said the swallow, who liked to come to the point at once, and the reed made him a low bow. So he flew round and round her, touching the water with his wings, and making silver ripples. This was his courtship, and it lasted all through the summer.

"It is a ridiculous attachment," twittered the other swallows; "she has no money, and far too many relations" ; and indeed the river was quite full of reeds. Then, when the autumn came they all flew away.

After they had gone he felt lonely, and began to tire of his lady-love. "She has no conversation," he said, "and I am afraid that she is a coquette, for she is always flirting with the wind." And certainly, whenever the wind blew, the reed made the most graceful curtseys. "I admit that she is domestic," he continued, "but I love travelling, and my wife, consequently, should love travelling also."

"Will you come away with me?" he said finally to her; but the reed shook her head, she was so attached to her home.

"You have been trifling with me," he cried. "I am off to the Pyramids. Goodbye!" and he flew away.

All day long he flew, and at night-time he arrived at the city. "Where shall I put up?" he said; "I hope the town has made preparations."

Then he saw the statue on the tall column.

"I will put up there," he cried; "it is a fine position, with plenty of fresh air." So he alighted just between the feet of the Happy Prince.

"I have a golden bedroom," he said softly to himself as he looked round, and he prepared to go to sleep; but just as he was putting his head under his wing a large drop of water fell on him. "What a curious thing!" he cried; "there is not a single cloud in the sky, the stars are quite clear and bright, and yet it is raining. The climate in the north of Europe is really dreadful. The reed used to like the rain, but that was merely her selfishness."

Then another drop fell.

"What is the use of a statue if it cannot keep the rain off?" he said; "I must look for a good chimney-pot," and he determined to fly away.

But before he had opened his wings, a third drop fell, and he looked up, and saw - Ah! what did he see?

The eyes of the Happy Prince were filled with tears, and tears were running down his golden cheeks. His face was so beautiful in the moonlight that the little swallow was filled with pity.

"Who are you?" he said.

"I am the Happy Prince."

"Why are you weeping then?" asked the swallow; "you have quite drenched me."

"When I was alive and had a human heart," answered the statue, "I did not know what tears were, for I lived in the Palace of Sans-Souci, where sorrow is not allowed to enter. In the daytime I played with my companions in the garden, and in the evening I led the dance in the great hall. Round the garden ran a very lofty wall, but I never cared to ask what lay beyond it, everything about me was so beautiful. My courtiers called me the Happy Prince, and happy indeed I was, if pleasure be happiness. So I lived, and so I died. And now that I am dead they have set me up here so high that I can see all the ugliness and all the misery of my city, and though my heart is made of lead yet I cannot chose but weep."

"What! is he not solid gold?" said the swallow to himself. He was too polite to make any personal remarks out loud.

"Far away," continued the statue in a low musical voice, "far away in a little street there is a poor house. One of the windows is open, and through it I can see a woman seated at a table. Her face is thin and worn, and she has coarse, red hands, all pricked by the needle, for she is a seamstress. She is embroidering passion-flowers on a satin gown for the loveliest of the queen's maids-of-honor to wear at the next court-ball. In a bed in the corner of the room her little boy is lying ill. He has a fever, and is asking for oranges. His mother has nothing to give him but river water, so he is crying. Swallow, swallow, little swallow, will you not bring her the ruby out of my sword-hilt? My feet are fastened to this pedestal and I cannot move."

"I am waited for in Egypt," said the swallow. "My friends are flying up and down the Nile, and talking to the large lotus-flowers. Soon they will go to sleep in the tomb of the great king. The king is there himself in his painted coffin. He is wrapped in yellow linen, and embalmed with spices. Round his neck is a chain of pale green jade, and his hands are like withered leaves."

"Swallow, swallow, little swallow," said the Prince, "will you not stay with me for one night, and be my messenger? The boy is so thirsty, and the mother so sad."

"I don't think I like boys," answered the swallow. "Last summer, when I was staying on the river, there were two rude boys, the miller's sons, who were always throwing stones at me. They never hit me, of course; we swallows fly far too well for that, and besides, I come of a family famous for its agility; but still, it was a mark of disrespect."

But the Happy Prince looked so sad that the little swallow was sorry. "It is very cold here," he said; "but I will stay with you for one night, and be your messenger."

"Thank you, little swallow," said the Prince.

So the swallow picked out the great ruby from the Prince's sword, and flew away with it in his beak over the roofs of the town.

He passed by the cathedral tower, where the white marble angels were sculptured. He passed by the palace and heard the sound of dancing. A beautiful girl came out on the balcony with her lover. "How wonderful the stars are," he said to her, "and how wonderful is the power of love!"

"I hope my dress will be ready in time for the state-ball," she answered; "I have ordered passion-flowers to be embroidered on it; but the seamstresses are so lazy."

He passed over the river, and saw the lanterns hanging to the masts of the ships. He passed over the Ghetto, and saw the old jews bargaining with each other, and weighing out money in copper scales. At last he came to the poor house and looked in. The boy was tossing feverishly on his bed, and the mother had fallen asleep, she was so tired. In he hopped, and laid the great ruby on the table beside the woman's thimble. Then he flew gently round the bed, fanning the boy's forehead with his wings. "How cool I feel," said the boy, "I must be getting better" ; and he sank into a delicious slumber.

Then the swallow flew back to the Happy Prince, and told him what he had done. "It is curious," he remarked, "but I feel quite warm now, although it is so cold."

"That is because you have done a good action," said the Prince. And the little swallow began to think, and then he fell asleep. Thinking always made him sleepy.

When day broke he flew down to the river and had a bath. "What a remarkable phenomenon," said the professor of ornithology as he was passing over the bridge. "A swallow in winter!" And he wrote a long letter about it to the local newspaper. Every one quoted it, it was full of so many words that they could not understand.

"Tonight I go to Egypt," said the swallow, and he was in high spirits at the prospect. He visited all the public monuments, and sat a long time on top of the church steeple. Wherever he went the sparrows chirruped, and said to each other, "What a distinguished stranger!" so he enjoyed himself very much.

When the moon rose he flew back to the Happy Prince. "Have you any commissions for Egypt?" he cried; "I am just starting."

"Swallow, swallow, little swallow," said the Prince, "will you not stay with me one night longer?"

"I am waited for in Egypt," answered the swallow. "To-morrow my friends will fly up to the second cataract. The river-horse couches there among the bulrushes, and on a great granite throne sits the god Memnon. All night long he watches the stars, and when the morning star shines he utters one cry of joy, and then he is silent. At noon the yellow lions come down to the water's edge to drink. They have eyes like green beryls, and their roar is louder than the roar of the cataract.

"Swallow, swallow, little swallow," said the Prince, "far away across the city I see a young man in a garret. He is leaning over a desk covered with papers, and in a tumbler by his side there is a bunch of withered violets. His hair is brown and crisp, and his lips are red as a pomegranate, and he has large and dreamy eyes. He is trying to finish a play for the director of the theatre, but he is too cold to write any more. There is no fire in the grate, and hunger has made him faint."

"I will wait with you one night longer," said the swallow, who really had a good heart. "Shall I take him another ruby?"

"Alas! I have no ruby now," said the Prince; "my eyes are all that I have left. They are made of rare sapphires, which were brought out of India a thousand years ago. Pluck out one of them and take it to him. He will sell it to the jeweller, and buy food and firewood, and finish his play."

"Dear Prince," said the swallow, "I cannot do that"; and he began to weep.

"Swallow, swallow, little swallow," said the Prince, "do as I command you."

So the swallow plucked out the Prince's eye, and flew away to the student's garret. It was easy enough to get in, as there was a hole in the roof. Through this he darted, and came into the room. The young man had his head buried in his hands, so he did not hear the flutter of the bird's wings, and when he looked up he found the beautiful sapphire lying on the withered violets.

"I am beginning to be appreciated," he cried; "this is from some great admirer. Now I can finish my play," and he looked quite happy.

The next day the swallow flew down to the harbor. He sat on the mast of a large vessel and watched the sailors hauling big chests out of the hold with ropes. "Heave a-hoy!" they shouted as each chest came up. "I am going to Egypt" ! cried the swallow, but nobody minded, and when the moon rose he flew back to the Happy Prince.

"I am come to bid you goodbye," he cried.

"Swallow, swallow, little swallow," said the Prince, "will you not stay with me one night longer?"

"It is winter," answered the swallow, "and the chill snow will soon be here. In Egypt the sun is warm on the green palmtrees, and the crocodiles lie in the mud and look lazily about them. My companions are building a nest in the Temple of Baalbec, and the pink and white doves are watching them, and cooing to each other. Dear Prince, I must leave you, but I will never forget you, and next spring I will bring you back two beautiful jewels in place of those you have given away. The ruby shall be redder than a red rose, and the sapphire shall be as blue as the great sea."

"In the square below," said the Happy Prince, "there stands a little matchgirl. She has let her matches fall in the gutter, and they are all spoiled. Her father will beat her if she does not bring home some money, and she is crying. She has no shoes or stockings, and her little head is bare. Pluck out my other eye, and give it to her, and her father will not beat her."

"I will stay with you one night longer," said the Swallow, "but I cannot pluck out your eye. You would be quite blind then."

"Swallow, swallow, little swallow," said the Prince, "do as I command you."

So he plucked out the Prince's other eye, and darted down with it. He swooped past the matchgirl, and slipped the jewel into the palm of her hand. "What a lovely bit of glass," cried the little girl; and she ran home, laughing.

Then the swallow came back to the Prince. "You are blind now," he said, "so I will stay with you always."

"No, little swallow," said the poor Prince, "you must go away to Egypt."

"I will stay with you always," said the swallow, and he slept at the Prince's feet.

All the next day he sat on the Prince's shoulder, and told him stories of what he had seen in strange lands. He told him of the red ibises, who stand in long rows on the banks of the Nile, and catch goldfish in their beaks; of the Sphinx, who is as old as the world itself, and lives in the desert, and knows everything; of the merchants, who walk slowly by the side of their camels, and carry amber beads in their hands; of the King of the Mountains of the Moon, who is as black as ebony, and worships a large crystal; of the great green snake that sleeps in a palm tree, and has twenty priests to feed it with honey-cakes; and of the pygmies who sail over a big lake on large flat leaves, and are always at war with the butterflies.

"Dear little swallow," said the Prince, "you tell me of marvellous things, but more marvellous than anything is the suffering of men and of women. There is no mystery so great as Misery. Fly over my city, little swallow, and tell me what you see there."

So the swallow flew over the great city, and saw the rich making merry in their beautiful houses, while the beggars were sitting at the gates. He flew into dark lanes, and saw the white faces of starving children looking out listlessly at the black streets. Under the archway of a bridge two little boys were lying in one another's arms to try and keep themselves warm. "How hungry we are!" they said. "You must not lie here," shouted the watchman, and they wandered out into the rain.

Then he flew back and told the Prince what he had seen.

"I am covered with fine gold," said the Prince, "you must take it off, leaf by leaf, and give it to my poor; the living always think that gold can make them happy."

Leaf after leaf of the fine gold the swallow picked off, till the Happy Prince looked quite dull and grey. Leaf after leaf of the fine gold he brought to the poor, and the children's faces grew rosier, and they laughed and played games in the street. "We have bread now!" they cried.

Then the snow came, and after the snow came the frost. The streets looked as if they were made of silver, they were so bright and glistening; long icicles like crystal daggers hung down from the eaves of the houses, everybody went about in furs, and the little boys wore scarlet caps and skated on the ice.

The poor little swallow grew colder and colder, but he would not leave the Prince, he loved him too well. He picked up crumbs outside the baker's door when the baker was not looking and tried to keep himself warm by flapping his wings.

But at last he knew that he was going to die. He had just strength to fly up to the Prince's shoulder once more. "Goodbye, dear Prince!" he murmured, "will you let me kiss your hand?"

"I am glad that you are going to Egypt at last, little swallow," said the Prince, "you have stayed too long here; but you must kiss me on the lips, for I love you."

"It is not to Egypt that I am going," said the swallow. "I am going to the House of Death. Death is the brother of Sleep, is he not?"

And he kissed the Happy Prince on the lips, and fell down dead at his feet.

At that moment a curious crack sounded inside the statue, as if something had broken. The fact is that the leaden heart had snapped right in two. It certainly was a dreadfully hard frost.

Early the next morning the mayor was walking in the square below in company with the town councilors. As they passed the column he looked up at the statue: "Dear me! how shabby the Happy Prince looks!" he said.

"How shabby indeed!" cried the town councilors, who always agreed with the mayor; and they went up to look at it.

"The ruby has fallen out of his sword, his eyes are gone, and he is golden no longer," said the mayor in fact, "he is little better than a beggar!"

"Little better than a beggar," said the town councilors.

"And here is actually a dead bird at his feet!" continued the mayor. "We must really issue a proclamation that birds are not to be allowed to die here." And the town clerk made a note of the suggestion.

So they pulled down the statue of the Happy Prince. "As he is no longer beautiful he is no longer useful," said the art professor at the university.

Then they melted the statue in a furnace, and the mayor held a meeting of the corporation to decide what was to be done with the metal. "We must have another statue, of course," he said, "and it shall be a statue of myself."

"Of myself," said each of the town councilors, and they quarrelled. When I last heard of them they were quarrelling still.

"What a strange thing!" said the overseer of the workmen at the foundry. "This broken lead heart will not melt in the furnace. We must throw it away." So they threw it on a dust-heap where the dead swallow was also lying.

"Bring me the two most precious things in the city," said

God to one of His angels; and the angel brought Him the leaden heart and the dead bird.

"You have rightly chosen," said God, "for in my garden of Paradise this little bird shall sing for evermore, and in my city of gold the Happy Prince shall praise me."

夜鶯與玫瑰

快樂起來吧！你會得到你的紅玫瑰的。

我會在午夜時分用歌聲培育它，

而且用我心臟裡的血液澆灌它。

我不要你任何的回報，只希望你做一位真心的有情人。

「她說，如果我能送她一朵紅玫瑰，她就答應當我的舞伴！」年輕的大學生大聲說道：「可是，我的花園裡沒有紅玫瑰啊！」

一隻在橡樹上的窩休息的夜鶯，聽到年輕人的樹下獨白，便好奇地探出頭來。目光穿過層層的樹葉，她仔細地看著年輕人，也打量著他的話。

她聽到年輕人再度叫嚷著：「我的花園裡沒有紅玫瑰！」而且看到他那美麗的雙眼正飽含著淚水。「唉！我的幸福竟取決於這麼微不足道的東西。我遍讀聖賢書，洞悉宇宙哲學的奧祕。然而，只因為沒有紅玫瑰，我一輩子的幸福就要毀了。」

「哇，終於出現一個真心真意的有情人了，」夜鶯自言自語著，「我曾在數不盡的夜裡，歌頌著這樣的人；在數不盡的夜裡，向群星傳講這類人的事蹟，現在，我竟然真碰上了這樣的人。哇！這個年輕人的髮有如風信子花一般深沉，雙唇如同他想要的紅玫瑰般鮮麗；只是，他對愛情的執著令他的臉色蒼白，眉宇間淨是憂鬱的神色。」

「王子將於明天晚上舉辦一場舞會，」年輕人繼續喃喃自語，「如果我能送給她一朵紅玫瑰，她就答應當我的舞伴，和我跳一整夜的舞。如果我能送給她一朵紅玫瑰，我就可以擁她入懷，讓她的頭倚在我的肩上，而且還能緊握她的手。可是，我卻沒有紅玫瑰可以送給她，明天晚上，我只好枯坐在旁，看著她從我的眼前走過。她連看都不會看我一眼了，唉！我的心都快碎成一片片的了。」

「他真是個有情人。」夜鶯說道，「當我在歌頌愛情的時候，他卻為愛情所苦。我心中最美麗的戀愛，竟是他痛苦的根源。不過，愛情當然是可貴的東西，它比翡翠還要珍貴，價值更勝寶石。即使用珍珠和石榴也買不到，而且也不會被當成商品出售，它的份量更是用黃金也無法秤起。」

「樂師們會坐在演奏席上彈奏樂器，」年輕人繼續說道，「而我鍾愛的人兒會隨著豎琴和小提琴的樂聲婆娑起舞。她將曼妙輕盈地舞著，彷彿腳尖從不曾著地，而衣著光鮮的王公貴族們會像蒼蠅般圍繞在她的身邊。唉，唯一不能跟她一起跳舞的人就是我，只因為我沒有紅玫瑰可以送她。」年輕人說著便撲倒在草地上，雙手掩面，哭了起來。

「他在哭什麼？」一隻綠色的小蜥蜴，翹著尾巴跑過學生身旁時，問道。

「是啊，他怎麼了？」一隻在陽光下翻飛的蝴蝶開口道。

「是啊，這到底是怎麼回事？」一朵小雛菊輕柔地對它的鄰居耳語道。

「他為了一朵紅玫瑰而哭泣。」夜鶯回答了大家的問題。

「為了一朵紅玫瑰？」大夥兒齊聲叫道，「這真是滑天下之大稽！」愛挖苦人的小蜥蜴誇張地笑著。

然而，夜鶯再明瞭年輕人心中的憂愁不過；她靜靜坐在橡樹下，細細思索著愛情的奧祕。

突然間，她伸展開棕色的翅膀，躍進天際。像一抹影子飛掠過小樹林，像一抹影子穿過花園。

花園中央的草叢裡有一株美麗的玫瑰，飛行中的夜鶯瞧見了，便飛下來停在樹枝上。

「請給我一朵紅玫瑰，」夜鶯大聲說道，「我會為你唱一首最好聽的歌作為報償。」

然而，這株玫瑰卻搖搖頭。

「我是白玫瑰，」它回答道，「潔白如浪濤中的泡沫，潔白勝山頂的積雪。去找我弟弟吧，它就繞著老日晷生長，也許它可以給你一朵紅玫瑰。」

於是，夜鶯飛到繞著老日晷生長的那株玫瑰那兒。

「請給我一朵紅玫瑰，」夜鶯大聲說道，「我會為你唱一首最好聽的歌作為報償。」

然而，這株玫瑰也搖搖頭。

「我是黃玫瑰，」它答道，「顏色亮麗如琥珀王座上那美人魚的秀髮，顏色亮麗更勝草場上未割刈的水仙花。去找我弟弟吧，它就生長在那個年輕人的窗戶下，也許它可以給你一朵紅玫瑰。」

於是，夜鶯來到年輕人的窗戶底下，找到那朵玫瑰。

「請給我一朵紅玫瑰，」夜鶯大聲說道，「我會為你唱一首最好聽的歌作為報償。」

然而，這株玫瑰搖搖頭。

「我是紅玫瑰沒錯，」它答道，「顏色豔紅如鴿子的雙腳，顏色豔紅賽過海中珊瑚的觸手。然而，隆冬的嚴寒凍僵了我的葉脈，冰霜凍壞了我的花苞，暴風雨打傷了我的枝椏，我看，今年我是開不出花來了。」

「我所求的只是一朵紅玫瑰而已，」夜鶯哭喊道，「只要一朵紅玫瑰就好！難道沒有什麼方法可以讓我得到一朵紅玫瑰嗎？」

「是有一個辦法，」這株玫瑰說道，「不過太可怕了，我不敢告訴妳。」

「說吧，」夜鶯答道，「我不怕的。」

「如果妳想要一朵紅玫瑰，」這株玫瑰說道，「妳得在午夜時分用歌聲培育它，而且用妳心臟裡的血液澆灌它。妳必須邊唱歌給我聽，邊把妳的胸膛插進我的刺中。妳必須整夜唱著歌，讓刺撕裂妳的胸膛，使妳的血液流進我的葉脈中，變成我的血液。」

「為了得到一朵紅玫瑰，必須以死亡為報償，這代價真大，」夜鶯說道，「對所有生物來說，生命都是最寶貴的。能夠坐在綠意盎然的樹林裡，看著駕駛金馬車的太陽和駕駛珍珠馬車的月亮相互追逐，是多麼有趣的事。山楂的味道那麼香，山谷中潛藏的風鈴草和山上的石南是如此的美。然而愛情卻比生命還可貴，況且鳥類的一顆心怎麼比得上人類的一顆心呢？」

於是，她伸展棕色的羽翼，飛入天際。像一抹影子飛過花園，像一抹影子似地掠過樹林。

那個年輕人仍然躺在剛剛那塊草地上，美麗的雙眼仍浸潤著未乾的淚珠。

「快樂起來吧，」夜鶯大聲說道，「快樂起來吧！你會得到你的紅玫瑰的。我會在午夜時分用歌聲培育它，而且用我心臟裡的血液澆灌它。我不要你任何的回報，只希望你做一位真心的有情人，因為愛情比哲學更具智慧，比權勢更具力量。愛情，有著絢爛斑斕的翅翼，五彩燄火般的身軀。它的雙唇甜美如蜜，氣息似最高貴的香料。」

年輕人抬起頭來往上瞧，仔細地聆聽著，但卻聽不懂夜鶯的話，因為他只懂得寫在書本上的東西。

然而，橡樹卻明白了，而且為此深感悲傷，因為橡樹非常喜歡這隻住在它枝椏上的夜鶯小姐。

「請為我唱一首道別曲，」橡樹輕輕說道，「妳離開之後，我一定會非常寂寞的。」

於是，夜鶯為橡樹吟唱了最後一首歌。她的歌聲婉轉輕妙，有如從銀壺中流瀉出的水聲。

當夜鶯唱完時，躺在草地上的年輕人站了起來，從口袋裡掏出一隻鉛筆和一本筆記簿。

「這隻夜鶯長得真漂亮，」學生穿過樹林時自言自語道，「那是無庸置疑的。不過，她有感情嗎？大概沒有吧。其實她就像大部份的藝術家一樣，外表絢麗，內心卻一點也不真誠，她根本不可能為別人而犧牲自己，在她的心裡大概只惦記著歌唱這件事吧！眾所皆知，藝術是很自私的。然而，不可否認的，她的歌聲的確不錯。只不過，非常可惜，她的歌聲既沒有任何意義也不具任何實用價值。」年輕的大學生說著，之後便走進自己的房間，躺在簡陋的床上，開始思念起他的夢中情人，不一會兒便睡著了。

當月亮升上中天，夜鶯便來到玫瑰花叢前，用自己的胸膛抵著樹叢的荊棘。她一整夜都對著玫瑰花叢唱歌，並用自己的鮮血澆灌它，清冷晶瑩的月亮也斜掛在天際傾聽著。夜鶯整夜不停地歌唱，胸前也被棘刺愈插愈深，血液汩汩地湧出。

她先是歌頌男孩和女孩心中萌發的初戀情意，唱到最高潮處，一朵大而美麗的玫瑰隨之綻放，一片片的花瓣也隨著一首首的歌曲展開。起初，玫瑰花的顏色蒼白，有如徘徊河上的霧靄，有如清晨時泛白的天際，有如破曉時的銀光；有如銀色鏡面中玫瑰花的倒影，也似水池中玫瑰花的身影。這株玫瑰花叢正在最好的狀態下綻放著這朵花。

不過，玫瑰仍舊呼喊著夜鶯，要她將胸膛再刺得深一些。「刺深一些，夜鶯小姐，」玫瑰花叫道，「不然的話，在花長成之前，天就要亮了。」

於是，夜鶯將自己深深地扎入刺中，並且愈發賣力地歌唱著，此時她正歌頌著萌生於紳士與淑女靈魂中的熱情。

於是，蒼白的花瓣上開始出現細緻迷人的粉紅色光澤，就像新郎親吻新娘的雙唇後，雙頰上所浮現的紅暈一樣。然而，刺尚未插入心窩，所以玫瑰花的花心仍是一片白，因為，只有夜鶯心臟裡的鮮血才能染紅玫瑰花的花心。

於是，玫瑰再次要求夜鶯將胸膛插得更深入些。「夜鶯小姐，再刺深一些，要不然在花朵長成之前，天就要亮了。」

於是，夜鶯更用力地將自己插入刺中，讓刺觸抵心窩，一陣錐心刺痛貫穿夜鶯全身。痛楚愈發加劇，夜鶯的歌聲也就愈發激昂，此時她正歌頌著愛情的完美無缺，連死亡也無法阻絕。

大而美的粉紅色玫瑰開始變得豔紅嬌麗，就像東邊天際裡的一朵玫瑰花。葉瓣閃耀如一條紅色的腰帶，而花心之燦爛炫目彷彿一顆紅寶石。

然而，夜鶯的歌聲卻愈來愈微弱，她小小的翅膀開始掙扎拍動，雙眼逐漸變得模糊。她的歌聲逐漸瘖啞，而且她覺得喉嚨裡似乎有東西梗著。

終於，她唱出了最後一個音符。蒼白的明月聽見了，忘了黎明時刻已到，猶在天空裡躊躇。紅玫瑰花聽見了，全身上下如癡如醉地顫動著，在早晨寒冷的空氣中熱情地綻放每一片花瓣。音符的回音飄進山間那映著粉紫光輝的洞穴，喚醒睡夢中的牧羊人；也飄到河邊的蘆葦叢中，蘆葦花則將它傳給大海。

「看哪，快看哪！」玫瑰花叢叫道，「玫瑰花已經長成了！」然而夜鶯卻毫無反應，因為她已倒在草地上，胸口還扎著刺。

正午時分，年輕的學生推開窗戶，朝外望去。

「哇，太幸運了！」他高興地叫道，「這兒有一朵紅玫瑰哪！我這一生從未看過這樣的玫瑰花啊！它是如此的嬌豔美麗，我想它必定有一個很長的拉丁文學名。」於是他俯下身，摘採下玫瑰花。

然後，他穿戴整齊，手中握著這朵玫瑰花，火速趕到教授家去。

教授的女兒正坐在門廊上，將藍色的絲線纏繞到捲絲軸上，腳邊伏臥著她的小狗狗。

「妳曾經說過，假如我送妳一朵玫瑰花，妳就答應當我的舞伴，」學生氣喘吁吁地說道，「喏，這是世界上最嬌豔的一朵紅玫瑰。今晚，妳可以把它別在妳的胸前，當我們一塊兒婆娑起舞的時候，這朵花會告訴妳，我有多麼愛妳！」

然而，女孩卻皺了皺眉。

「我想這朵花可能和我的禮服不配，」她答道，「而且，內廷大臣的侄子送了我一些珍貴的珠寶，大家都知道，珠寶要比花兒貴重得多了。」

「啊！妳真是不知感恩。」年輕人憤怒地說著。之後，他便將手中的玫瑰花扔到路旁，一輛急駛的馬車輾過它，它掉進了路旁的水溝裡。

「不知感恩？」女孩說道，「我告訴你，你才是粗魯無禮。況且，你以為你是誰？不過是一個學生罷了。我就不信，你也會和內廷大臣的侄子一樣，在皮鞋上裝飾著銀製的帶扣。」說完，她從椅子上站起來，轉身走進屋內。

「愛情真是愚蠢不堪的東西，」年輕的大學生離開教授家時，一邊自言自語著，「它的實用程度不如邏輯學的一半，因為它無法證明些什麼，又老是講些不會發生的事，而且總是叫人相信一些不真實的事。事實上，在這個講求實際的年代裡，愛情是非常不實用的東西，我還是回去唸唸哲學，研究研究抽象論好了。」

於是，他回到房間裡，抽出一本沾著塵埃的厚重書本，開始讀了起來。

The Nightingale
and the Rose

"She said that she would dance with me if I brought her red roses," cried the young student; "but in all my garden there is no red rose."

From her nest in the holm oak tree the nightingale heard him, and she looked out through the leaves, and wondered.

"No red rose in all my garden!" he cried, and his beautiful eyes filled with tears. "Ah, on what little things does happiness depend! I have read all that the wise men have written, and all the secrets of philosophy are mine, yet for want of a red rose is my life made wretched."

"Here at last is a true lover," said the nightingale. "Night after night have I sung of him, though I knew him not: night after night have I told his story to the stars, and now I see him. His hair is dark as the hyacinth-blossom, and his lips are red as the rose of his desire; but passion has made his face like pale ivory, and sorrow has set her seal upon his brow."

"The prince gives a ball tomorrow night," murmured the young student, "and my love will be of the company. If I bring her a red rose she will dance with me till dawn. If I bring her a red rose, I shall hold her in my arms, and she will lean her head upon my shoulder, and her hand will be clasped in mine. But there is no red rose in my garden, so I shall sit lonely, and she will pass me by. She will have no heed of me, and my heart will break."

"Here indeed is the true lover," said the Nightingale. "What I sing of, he suffers - what is joy to me, to him is pain. Surely love is a wonderful thing. It is more precious than emeralds, and dearer than fine opals. Pearls and pomegranates cannot buy it, nor is it set forth in the marketplace. It may not be purchased of the merchants, nor can it be weighed out in the balance for gold."

"The musicians will sit in their gallery," said the young student, "and play upon their stringed instruments, and my love will dance to the sound of the harp and the violin. She will dance so lightly that her feet will not touch the floor, and the courtiers in their gay dresses will throng round her. But with me she will not dance, for I have no red rose to give her" ; and he flung himself down on the grass, and buried his face in his hands, and wept.

"Why is he weeping?" asked a little green lizard, as he ran past him with his tail in the air.

"Why, indeed?" said a butterfly, who was fluttering about after a sunbeam.

"Why, indeed?" whispered a daisy to his neighbor, in a soft, low voice.

"He is weeping for a red rose," said the nightingale.

"For a red rose?" they cried; "how very ridiculous!" and the little lizard, who was something of a cynic, laughed outright.

But the nightingale understood the secret of the student's sorrow, and she sat silent in the oaktree, and thought about the mystery of love.

Suddenly she spread her brown wings for flight, and soared into the air. She passed through the grove like a shadow, and like a shadow she sailed across the garden.

In the centre of the grass-plot was standing a beautiful rose tree, and when she saw it she flew over to it, and lit upon a spray.

"Give me a red rose," she cried, "and I will sing you my sweetest song."

But the tree shook its head. "My roses are white," it answered; "as white as the foam of the sea, and whiter than the snow upon the mountain. But go to my brother who grows round the old sundial, and perhaps he will give you what you want."

So the nightingale flew over to the rose tree that was growing round the old sundial.

"Give me a red rose," she cried, "and I will sing you my sweetest song."

But the tree shook its head. "My roses are yellow," it answered; "as yellow as the hair of the mermaid who sits upon an amber throne, and yellower than the daffodil that blooms in the meadow before the mower comes with his scythe. But go to my brother who grows beneath the student's window, and perhaps he will give you what you want."

So the nightingale flew over to the rose tree that was growing beneath the student's window.

"Give me a red rose," she cried, "and I will sing you my sweetest song."

But the tree shook its head.

"My roses are red," it answered, "as red as the feet of the dove, and redder than the great fans of coral that wave and wave in the ocean-cavern. But the winter has chilled my veins, and the frost has nipped my buds, and the storm has broken my branches, and I shall have no roses at all this year."

"One red rose is all I want," cried the nightingale, "only one red rose! Is there no way by which I can get it?"

"There is a way," answered the tree; "but it is so terrible that I dare not tell it to you."

"Tell it to me," said the nightingale, "I am not afraid."

"If you want a red rose," said the tree, "you must build it out of music by moonlight, and stain it with your own heart's blood. You must sing to me with your breast against a thorn. All night long you must sing to me, and the thorn must pierce your heart, and your life-blood must flow into my veins, and become mine."

"Death is a great price to pay for a red rose," cried the nightingale, "and life is very dear to all. It is pleasant to sit in the green wood, and to watch the sun in his chariot of gold, and the moon in her chariot of pearl. Sweet is the scent of the hawthorn, and sweet are the bluebells that hide in the valley, and the heather that blows on the hill. Yet love is better than life, and what is the heart of a bird compared to the heart of a man?"

So she spread her brown wings for flight, and soared into the air. She swept over the garden like a shadow, and like a shadow she sailed through the grove.

The young student was still lying on the grass, where she had left him, and the tears were not yet dry in his beautiful eyes.

"Be happy," cried the nightingale, "be happy; you shall have your red rose. I will build it out of music by moonlight, and stain it with my own heart's blood. All that I ask of you in return is that you will be a true lover, for love is wiser than philosophy, though she is wise, and mightier than power, though he is mighty. Flame-colored are his wings, and colored like flame is his body. His lips are sweet as honey, and his breath is like frankincense."

The student looked up from the grass, and listened, but he could not understand what the nightingale was saying to him, for he only knew the things that are written down in books.

But the oak tree understood, and felt sad, for he was very fond of the little nightingale who had built her nest in his branches.

"Sing me one last song," he whispered; "I shall feel very lonely when you are gone."

So the nightingale sang to the oak tree, and her voice was like water bubbling from a silver jar.

When she had finished her song the student got up, and pulled a note book and a lead-pencil out of his pocket.

"She has form," he said to himself, as he walked away through the grove - "that cannot be denied to her; but has she got feeling? I am afraid not. In fact, she is like most artists; she is all style, without any sincerity. She would not sacrifice herself for others. She thinks merely of music, and everybody knows that the arts are selfish. Still, it must be admitted that she has some beautiful notes in her voice. What a pity it is that they do not mean anything, or do any practical good." And he went into his room, and lay down on his little pallet bed, and began to think of his love; and, after a time, he fell asleep.

And when the moon shone in the heavens the nightingale flew to the rose tree, and set her breast against the thorn. All night long she sang with her breast against the thorn, and the cold crystal moon leaned down and listened. All night long she sang, and the thorn went deeper and deeper into her breast, and her life-blood ebbed away from her.

She sang first of the birth of love in the heart of a boy and a girl. And on the top-most spray of the rose tree there blossomed a marvellous rose, petal following petal, as song followed song. Pale was it, at first, as the mist that hangs over the river - pale as the feet of the morning, and silver as the wings of the dawn. As the shadow of a rose in a mirror of silver, as the shadow of a rose in a water-pool, so was the rose that blossomed on the topmost spray of the tree.

But the tree cried to the nightingale to press closer against the thorn. "Press closer, little nightingale," cried the tree, "or the day will come before the rose is finished."

So the nightingale pressed closer against the thorn, and louder and louder grew her song, for she sang of the birth of passion in the soul of a man and a maid.

And a delicate flush of pink came into the leaves of the rose, like the flush in the face of the bridegroom when he kisses the lips of the bride. But the thorn had not yet reached her heart, so the rose's heart remained white, for only a nightingale's heart's blood can crimson the heart of a rose.

And the tree cried to the nightingale to press closer against the thorn. "Press closer, little nightingale," cried the tree, "or the day will come before the rose is finished."

So the nightingale pressed closer against the thorn, and the thorn touched her heart, and a fierce pang of pain shot through her. Bitter, bitter was the pain, and wilder and wilder grew her song, for she sang of the love that is perfected by death, of the love that dies not in the tomb.

And the marvellous rose became crimson, like the rose of the eastern sky. Crimson was the girdle of petals, and crimson as a ruby was the heart.

But the nightingale's voice grew fainter, and her little wings began to beat, and a film came over her eyes. Fainter and fainter grew her song, and she felt something choking her in her throat.

Then she gave one last burst of music. The white moon heard it, and she forgot the dawn, and lingered on in the sky. The red rose heard it, and it trembled all over with ecstasy, and opened its petals to the cold morning air. Echo bore it to her purple cavern in the hills, and woke the sleeping shepherds from their dreams. It floated through the reeds of the river, and they carried its message to the sea.

"Look, look!" cried the tree, "the rose is finished now"; but the nightingale made no answer, for she was lying dead in the long grass, with the thorn in her heart.

And at noon the student opened his window and looked out.

"Why, what a wonderful piece of luck!" he cried; "here is a red rose! I have never seen any rose like it in all my life. It is so beautiful that I am sure it has a long Latin name"; and he leaned down and plucked it.

Then he put on his hat, and ran up to the professor's house with the rose in his hand.

The daughter of the professor was sitting in the doorway winding blue silk on a reel, and her little dog was lying at her feet.

"You said that you would dance with me if I brought you a red rose," cried the student. "Here is the reddest rose in all the world. You will wear it tonight next your heart, and as we dance together it will tell you how I love you."

But the girl frowned.

"I am afraid it will not go with my dress," she answered; "and, besides, the chamberlain's nephew has sent me some real jewels, and everybody knows that jewels cost far more than flowers."

"Well, upon my word, you are very ungrateful," said the student angrily; and he threw the rose into the street, where it fell into the gutter, and a cartwheel went over it.

"Ungrateful!" said the girl. "I tell you what, you are very rude; and, after all, who are you? Only a student. Why, I don't believe you have even got silver buckles to your shoes as the chamberlain's nephew has"; and she got up from her chair and went into the house.

"What a silly thing love is," said the student as he walked away. "It is not half as useful as logic, for it does not prove anything, and it is always telling one of things that are not going to happen, and making one believe things that are not true. In fact, it is quite unpractical, and, as in this age to be practical is everything, I shall go back to philosophy and study metaphysics."

So he returned to his room and pulled out a great dusty book, and began to read.

自私的巨人

我要出去把那個可憐的小男孩抱上樹梢，

我還要拆掉那堵牆，

讓我的花園永遠成為孩子們的遊戲天堂。

花園裡有好多美麗的花，

然而孩子們才是最美麗的花朵。

孩子們在每天下午放學之後，都會到巨人的花園裡嬉戲。

花園既大又美，而且有著一片柔軟的嫩綠草坪。草地上到處綻放著像星星般的美麗花朵，而且還種有十二棵桃樹，春天一到，它們就會開出粉紅色及珍珠色的細緻桃花；一到秋天，美麗的花朵就會累累結實。樹枝上，群鳥婉轉曼妙的歌聲總令孩子們停下遊戲，傾心聆聽。「在這裡玩，好開心啊！」孩子們互相訴說著。

有一天，巨人回來了。他到英格蘭西南部去拜訪他的巨人朋友，並在那兒待了七年。七年之後，因為該說的話都說完了（他們的話題滿狹隘的），巨人決定回到自己的地方來。他一回來，便瞧見孩子們在花園裡玩耍。

「你們在這兒幹什麼？」他大吼一聲，孩子們全跑光。

「我的花園是我自己的花園，」巨人說道，「每個人都知道這件事，除了我自己，誰也不許在花園裡玩。」於是，他在花園四周築起一道高牆，還立了一塊告示板，上面寫——

闖入者

必被

起訴

他是一個很自私的巨人。

可憐的孩子們現在無處可玩耍了。他們想在馬路上玩，可是馬路上除了大量的灰塵，還有隨處可見的堅硬石頭，他們不喜歡在馬路上玩耍。他們常常在放學後繞著花園的圍牆漫步，滿心嚮往地談著圍牆內的美麗花園。「我們在那兒玩的時候，多麼開心啊！」孩子們互相訴說著。

春天來了，到處都充滿著春的氣息，花兒綻放，鳥兒歌唱。只有自私巨人的花園裡依然是嚴冬。因為花園裡沒有孩子們的歡聲笑語，鳥兒也就不想在花園裡唱歌，群樹也忘了開花。曾有一朵美麗的花兒從草坪中探出頭來，不過它看到告示板上的文字，很替孩子們感到難過，便把頭縮回土裡，繼續睡覺了。

對於這種情況，唯一感到高興的便是雪和霜。「春天遺忘了這座花園啦！」他們叫道，「我們可以在這兒住上一整年了。」大雪用它厚重的白斗篷覆蓋住草地，寒霜為群樹漆上銀白色調。然後，他們邀請北風入夥，北風很快地來了。他全身包裹著皮裘，整天對著花園猛吹，把煙囪頂管都給吹掉了。「這真是個舒適的據點，」北風說道，「我們得邀冰雹一塊兒來玩。」於是，冰雹也加入陣容。冰雹每天在屋頂上嘎嘎地跳上三個小時，直到弄破了大部分的石板瓦才下來，然後又以最快的速度繞著花園跑；他全身灰色，吐出的氣息就像冰一樣。

「我真不明白，春天為何遲遲不來。」自私的巨人坐在窗前，看著窗外為冰雪封凍的白色世界時，說道，「真希望天氣能夠變一變。」

然而，春天卻一直沒有來，夏天也沒有，而賜予每個花園金黃色果實的秋天也什麼都不給巨人的花園。「巨人太自私了。」秋天說道。於是,巨人的花園裡一直都是冬天,園子裡只有北風、冰雹、寒霜以及在群樹間穿梭飛舞的大雪。

有一天早晨,巨人睡醒但還躺在床上時,聽到一陣可愛的音樂。它是如此地美妙動聽,巨人心想,一定是國王的樂師們打這兒經過。事實上,這只不過是窗口有隻小紅雀在歌唱,巨人卻因太久不曾在花園聽見鳥兒的歌聲,而把它當成天底下最美妙的音樂。然後,巨人頭頂上的冰雹不再嘎吱嘎吱地亂跳,北風也停止了呼嘯,一陣沁人的花香透過窗扉飄向巨人。「我確信春天終於來了。」巨人說道。他跳下床,跑到窗戶前面往外看。

他看到了什麼?

他看到一幅最美的景致。孩子們正從圍牆上的一個小破洞往花園裡爬,而且坐上了群樹的枝幹。他在每棵樹上都看到一位小朋友。群樹對孩子們重返花園感到非常高興,便綻放出美麗的花朵,還在孩子們頭上輕輕地拂動樹枝。鳥兒雀躍地飛舞著,還愉快地唱起歌來。花朵從綠草中露出臉,歡喜地笑著。這真是一幅美好的景象,只不過,花園裡仍有一個角落還是冬天。這個角落位在花園最偏遠處,有個小男孩站在那兒。他的個子太小了,無法爬到樹上去,只好繞著樹走,傷心地哭著。這棵可憐的樹依舊覆蓋著霜雪,北風也繼續在周圍怒吼。「爬上來啊!小朋友。」樹說著,並儘可能地彎下身子。然而,小男孩的個子實在太小了。

巨人一看見窗外的景致,他的心都軟化了。「我是多麼的自私啊!」他說道,「現在,我知道為什麼春天始終不到這兒來的原因了。我要出去把那可憐的小男孩抱上樹梢,我還要拆掉那堵牆,而且要讓我的花園永遠成為孩子們的遊戲天堂。」他對自己過去的所作所為真的感到很後悔。

於是,巨人爬下樓來,輕輕地打開前門,走進花園裡。然而,孩子們一看到他便嚇得四散逃逸,花園又變成了冬天。唯一沒有跑掉的是那個正在哭泣的小男孩，因為他淚眼朦朧，沒有看到巨人朝他走來。於是，巨人躡手躡腳地來到小男孩背後，溫柔地舉起他，將他放上了樹梢。一瞬間，原本被冰雪封凍的大樹立刻綻放出花朵，而且群鳥也飛了過來，高興地唱著歌。小男孩伸出雙臂，緊緊地攀繞住巨人的脖子，親了他一下。其他的孩子看到巨人不再那麼凶惡，也跑了過來，而春天也跟在他們背後回來了。

「小朋友們，現在，這是你們的花園了。」巨人說道，然後他拿起一把大斧頭，拆掉圍牆。

正午時分，到市場去的人們經過巨人的花園時，看到巨人和孩子們一塊兒在他們畢生僅見最美麗的花園中嬉戲。

巨人和孩子們在花園裡玩了一整天，當夜幕低垂時，孩子們都過來和巨人說再見。

「怎麼不見你們那位小夥伴呢？」巨人說道，「就是我抱他上樹梢的那個小男孩啊。」巨人最喜歡這個小男孩，因為，他親了巨人一下。

「不知道，」孩子們回答道，「他已經走了。」

「你們一定要告訴他，請他明天再回來玩。」巨人說道。然而，孩子們卻告訴巨人，他們不知道他住在哪裡，而且他們從未見過他；這些話讓巨人覺得很傷心。

每天下午，孩子們在放學後都來找巨人玩。但是，巨人最愛的那個小男孩卻不再出現。巨人對所有的小孩都非常和藹可親，可是，他仍然非常想念那位小朋友，而且經常提起他。「我多麼想見到他啊！」他總是這樣唸著。

許多年過去了，巨人也變得老邁衰弱。他無法再和孩子們一起玩耍了，於是他坐在一張大搖椅上，看著孩子們嬉戲，也欣賞著美麗的花園。「我有好多美麗的花，」巨人說道，「然而，孩子們卻是最美麗的花朵。」

一個冬天的早晨，巨人一邊穿衣服一邊望向窗外。他現在已經不討厭冬天了，因為他知道冬天是春天睡覺、花兒休息的時候。

　　突然間，他滿心疑惑地揉揉眼睛，一再地往窗外看去。眼前呈現的是令人不敢相信的奇景——花園裡最偏遠的角落，有一棵盛綻著白花的大樹。它的枝幹全是金黃色的，銀色的果實從枝幹間垂掛下來，樹下站著一位小男孩，正是巨人最喜愛的那位。

　　巨人欣喜若狂地奔下樓，衝進花園裡。他很快地越過草坪，來到小男孩身邊。當他距離小男孩夠近的時候，他的臉因憤怒而漲紅，他說道：「是誰這麼大膽，敢傷了你？」因為小男孩雙手的手掌上有兩個釘痕，而且雙腳也有兩個釘痕。

　　「不要這樣！」小男孩答道，「這些釘痕是愛的傷口。」

　　「你是誰？」巨人說道，瞬間，全身掠過一陣奇異的、敬畏的感受，他在小男孩面前跪了下來。

　　小男孩對巨人報以微笑，說道：「你曾經讓我在你的花園裡玩，今天，就和我一起到我的花園去吧，那兒就是天堂。」那天下午，孩子們跑進花園裡來玩時，發現巨人一動也不動地躺臥在那棵大樹下，身上蓋滿了白色的花朵。

The Selfish Giant

Every afternoon, as they were coming from school, the children used to go and play in the giant's garden.

It was a large lovely garden, with soft green grass. Here and there over the grass stood beautiful flowers like stars, and there were twelve peach-trees that in the spring-time broke out into delicate blossoms of pink and pearl, and in the autumn bore rich fruit. The birds sat on the trees and sang so sweetly that the children used to stop their games in order to listen to them. "How happy we are here!" they cried to each other.

One day the giant came back. He had been to visit his friend the Cornish ogre, and had stayed with him for seven years. After the seven years were over he had said all that he had to say, for his conversation was limited, and he determined to return to his own castle. When he arrived he saw the children playing in the garden.

"What are you doing here?" he cried in a very gruff voice, and the children ran away.

"My own garden is my own garden," said the giant; "any one can understand that, and I will allow nobody to play in it but myself." So he built a high wall all round it, and put up a notice-board.

TRESPASSERS

WILL BE

PROSECUTED

He was a very selfish giant.

The poor children had now nowhere to play. They tried to play on the road, but the road was very dusty and full of hard stones, and they did not like it. They used to wander round the high wall when their lessons were over, and talk about the beautiful garden inside. "How happy we were there!" they said to each other.

Then the spring came, and all over the country there were little blossoms and little birds. Only in the garden of the selfish giant it was still winter. The birds did not care to sing in it as there were no children, and the trees forgot to blossom. Once a beautiful flower put its head out from the grass, but when it saw the notice-board it was so sorry for the children that it slipped back into the ground again, and went off to sleep. The only people who were pleased were the snow and the frost. "Spring has forgotten this garden," they cried, "so we will live here all the year round." The snow covered up the grass with her great white cloak, and the Frost painted all the trees silver. Then they invited the north wind to stay with them, and he came. He was wrapped in furs, and he roared all day about the garden, and blew the chimney-pots down. "This is a delightful spot," he said, "we must ask the hail on a visit." So the hail came. Every day for three hours he rattled on the roof of the castle till he broke garden as fast as he could go. He was dressed in grey, and his breath was like ice.

"I cannot understand why the spring is so late in coming," said the selfish giant, as he sat at the window and looked out at his cold white garden; "I hope there will be a change in the weather."

But the spring never came, nor the summer. The autumn gave golden fruit to every garden, but to the giant's garden she gave none. "He is too selfish," she said. So it was always winter there, and the north wind, and the hail, and the frost, and the snow danced about through the trees.

One morning the giant was lying awake in bed when he heard some lovely music. It sounded so sweet to his ears that he thought it must be the king's musicians passing by. It was really only a little linnet singing outside his window, but it was so long since he had heard a bird sing in his garden that it seemed to him to be the most beautiful music in the world. Then the hail stopped dancing over his head, and the north wind ceased roaring, and a delicious perfume came to him through the open casement. "I believe the spring has come at last," said the giant; and he jumped out of bed and looked out.

What did he see?

He saw a most wonderful sight. Through a little hole in the wall the children had crept in, and they were sitting in the branches of the trees. In every tree that he could see there was a little child. And the trees were so glad to have the children back again that they had covered themselves with blossoms, and were waving their arms gently above the children's heads. The birds were flying about and twittering with delight, and the flowers were looking up through the green grass and laughing. It was a lovely scene, only in one corner it was still winter. It was the farthest corner of the garden, and in it was standing a little boy. He was so small that he could not reach up to the branches of the tree, and he was wandering all round it, crying bitterly. The poor tree was still quite covered with frost and snow, and the north wind was blowing and roaring above it. "Climb up! little boy," said the tree, and it bent its branches down as low as it could; but the boy was too tiny.

And the giant's heart melted as he looked out. "How selfish I have been!" he said; "now I know why the spring would not come here. I will put that poor little boy on the top of the tree, and then I will knock down the wall, and my garden shall be the children's playground for ever and ever." He was really very sorry for what he had done.

So he crept downstairs and opened the front door quite softly, and went out into the garden. But when the children saw him they were so frightened that they all ran away, and the garden became winter again. Only the little boy did not run, for his eyes were so full of tears that he did not see the giant coming. And the giant stole up behind him and took him gently in his hand, and put him up into the tree. And the tree broke at once into blossom, and the birds came and sang on it, and the little boy stretched out his two arms and flung them round the giant's neck, and kissed him. And the other children, when they saw that the giant was not wicked any longer, came running back, and with them came the spring. "It is your garden now, little children," said the giant, and he took a great axe and knocked down the wall. And when the people were going to market at twelve o'clock they found the giant playing with the children in the most beautiful garden they had ever seen.

All day long they played, and in the evening they came to the giant to bid him goodbye.

"But where is your little companion?" he said: "the boy I put into the tree." The giant loved him the best because he had kissed him.

"We don't know," answered the children; "he has gone away."

"You must tell him to be sure and come here to-morrow," said the giant. But the children said that they did not know where he lived, and had never seen him before; and the giant felt very sad.

Every afternoon, when school was over, the children came and played with the giant. But the little boy whom the giant loved was never seen again. The giant was very kind to all the children, yet he longed for his first little friend, and often spoke of him. "How I would like to see him!" he used to say.

Years went over, and the giant grew very old and feeble. He could not play about any more, so he sat in a huge armchair, and watched the children at their games, and admired his garden. "I have many beautiful flowers," he said; "but the children are the most beautiful flowers of all."

One winter morning he looked out of his window as he was dressing. He did not hate the winter now, for he knew that it was merely the spring asleep, and that the flowers were resting.

Suddenly he rubbed his eyes in wonder, and looked and looked. It certainly was a marvellous sight. In the farthest corner of the garden was a tree quite covered with lovely white blossoms. Its branches were all golden, and silver fruit hung down from them, and underneath it stood the little boy he had loved.

Downstairs ran the giant in great joy, and out into the garden. He hastened across the grass, and came near to the child. And when he came quite close his face grew red with anger, and he said, "Who <u>hath</u> dared to wound <u>thee?</u>" For on the palms of the child's hands were the prints of two nails, and the prints of two nails were on the little feet. （譯註：hath為have 的第三人稱單數現代式；thee為人稱代名詞，受格，為「你、汝」之意）

"Who hath dared to wound thee?" cried the giant; "tell me, that I may take my big sword and slay him."

"Nay!" answered the child, "but these are the wounds of love." （譯註：Nay意即no）

"Who <u>art thou?</u>" said the giant, and a strange awe fell on him, and he knelt before the little child. （譯註：art為be動詞第二人稱單數現在式；thou為人稱代名詞，主格，所有格為thy或thine，受格為thee。art thou意為are you）

And the child smiled on the giant, and said to him, "You let me play once in your garden, today you shall come with me to my garden, which is Paradise."

And when the children ran in that afternoon, they found the giant lying dead under the tree, all covered with white blossoms.

一個忠實的朋友

嫉妒是最可怕的東西，它會毀了人們的天性，
我絕不能讓漢斯的天性被毀掉。
我是他最好的朋友，我會一直照顧他，
不讓他受到任何試探和引誘。

　　一天早晨，老河鼠將頭探出洞口。他有一雙晶亮的眼睛，灰白粗硬的頰鬚，和一條天然橡膠似的黑長尾巴。池塘上有幾隻正在游泳的小鴨，看起來就像一群顏色鮮黃的金絲雀；白毛紅腳的母鴨正努力地教她的孩子們，如何在水中倒立。

　　「你們若想成為上流社會中的一員，就非得學會倒立不可。」她不斷地告誡孩子們，偶爾還親自示範正確的作法。不過，對於母鴨熱切的教誨，小鴨們卻完全不當一回事。孩子們畢竟太小了，根本不知道躋身上流社會有什麼好處。

　　「真是一群不聽話的孩子！」老河鼠叫道，「溺死活該。」

　　「話不能這麼說，」母鴨答道，「萬事起頭難，況且為人父母本來就該有耐心些。」

　　「啊！我是不懂為人父母者的心態，」老河鼠說道，「我不是一個有家庭的人。事實上啊，我還是一個單身貴族呢！而且，我也不想結婚。愛情是滿好的，不過跟友情一比較啊，那可就遜色多了。說真的，我覺得世界上沒有任何東西可以比誠摯的友情更高貴、更稀罕的了。」

「那麼，你認為一個誠摯的朋友應該作些什麼事呢？」一隻在附近柳樹上歇腳的綠朱雀，聽到了河鼠及母鴨的對話，忍不住開口問道。

「是啊，我正想問呢。」母鴨說著，游到池塘邊上，來一個水中倒立，為孩子們作了個示範。

「真蠢的問題啊！」河鼠叫道，「我當然會要我誠摯的朋友對我誠懇、忠實。」

「那你怎麼回報他呢？」小紅雀說著，一邊繞著池面上的銀波盤旋，抖動自己小小的羽翼。

「我不懂你在說些什麼。」河鼠答道。

「我來舉例說明好了。」小紅雀說道。

「和我有關係嗎？」河鼠問道，「如果是的話，我就聽聽看，因為我最喜歡聽故事了。」

「這個故事和你很相配。」小紅雀答道。他飛下來，棲息在堤防上，開始講述一則〈誠摯友情〉的故事。

「很久以前，」小紅雀開始說道，「有一位誠實的小個子，名叫漢斯。」

「他很有名嗎？」河鼠問道。

「沒有，」小紅雀回答，「我想他是一個沒沒無聞的人，不過他的心地善良，而且有張逗趣、憨厚的小圓臉。他獨自住在一個小農舍裡，每天都在他的花園裡辛勤地工作。他的花園是全村最美的花園，園裡種著美國瞿麥、紫羅蘭、薺屬植物；更有大馬士革薔薇、黃玫瑰、百合花，和金黃、粉紫、純白的香菫；其他還有樓斗菜屬植物、酢漿草、薄荷、野生紫蘇、西洋櫻草、鳶尾花、水仙花、粉紅丁香等各色美麗花卉，各依不同的時節開放，一種花謝了，另一種花便接著開，所以花園裡總是充滿著瑰麗的花朵和沁人的香氣。

「小個子漢斯有許多朋友，而其中最忠實的一位是大個子休伊，他是一家磨坊的主人。其實，富有的休伊對小個子漢斯太過忠實了，忠實到每次拜訪漢斯之後都不會空手而返，不是採了漢斯花園的一大束花就是捧一把薄荷回家；如果碰上水果的生產季節，還會在口袋裡裝滿李子或草莓帶回家。

「『真正的朋友，應該共享一切所有。』休伊總是這麼說，而漢斯則點頭微笑，為自己擁有這麼一位思想高尚的朋友，感到非常驕傲。

「有時候，鄰居對於富有的休伊從不回贈小個子漢斯任何一點東西的作法，覺得很奇怪。而雖然休伊在自己的磨坊裡積貯了一百袋麵粉，擁有六頭乳牛和一大群綿羊，漢斯卻從來不曾打過這些東西的主意。對漢斯來說，只要聽休伊常常講些關於無私、真誠友誼的偉大論調，便已是人生至樂了。

「小個子漢斯每天在花園裡勤勞地工作，春天、夏天和秋天對漢斯而言是幸福愉快的季節。然而，冬天一到，小個子漢斯沒有水果或花卉可以拿到市場上賣，他就得挨餓受凍了，他經常只在晚上吃一點曬乾的梨子和乾硬的果子就上床睡覺。此外，漢斯在冬天也非常寂寞，因為休伊從不曾在冬天來看望他。

「『只要雪花持續飄著，我就沒有去看漢斯的必要。』休伊老是這樣對自己的妻子說，『因為，人一旦陷入困境，就該自己解決問題，訪客不該去打擾他的。這是我對友情最基本的觀念，而且我相信我的觀念是正確的。所以，我會等到春天來臨時再去拜訪漢斯，而且到時候他就可以送我一大袋櫻草花，這樣會讓他很高興的。』

「『你真的很懂得體貼別人，』休伊的妻子坐在舒適的搖椅上烤著暖烘烘的火時，回答道，『實在是太體貼了，聽你講述友情之道真是一大享受。我相信即使是小指頭上戴著金戒指、家住三層樓房的牧師，都無法講出像你這樣動聽的話。』

「『可是，我們不邀請小個子漢斯來我們家嗎？』休伊最小的兒子問道，『如果可憐的漢斯有困難，我會把我的麥片粥分一半給他，還讓他看看我的小白兔。』

「『你這孩子真蠢！』休伊大叫道，『我真不知道送你到學校去幹什麼？你好像什麼事也沒學到。如果小個子漢斯上我們家來，看到我們溫暖的爐火、豐盛的晚餐和那一大桶酒，他可能會嫉妒我們；而嫉妒是最可怕的東西，它會毀了人們的天性，我絕不能讓漢斯的天性被毀掉。我是他最好的朋友，我會一直照顧他，不讓他受到任何試探和引誘。況且，如果漢斯來這兒，他可能會向我賒借一些麵粉，這我可不能答應；麵粉是一回事，友情可就是另一回事了，二者不可混為一談。麵粉和友情是兩個不同的詞彙，所代表的意義也完全不同，這是每個人都看得出來的。』

「『你解釋得真好！』休伊的妻子說道，她為自己倒了一杯溫暖的麥酒，繼續說，『真的，我覺得內心好沉靜，就好像在教堂裡一樣。』

「『會做事的人不少，』休伊答道，『會說話的人卻不多，這代表懂得說話比會做事困難得多，也高級得多。』休伊說著，眼光掠過桌面，瞧著他兒子；他兒子為自己方才的不智言語，羞愧得低下頭來，漲紅了臉，眼淚開始掉進自己的茶杯。畢竟他太年幼了，你得原諒他。」

「故事結束了嗎？」河鼠問道。

「當然還沒，」小紅雀答道，「才剛開始呢！」

「那你可真落伍，」河鼠說道，「現在說故事的行家都是從結尾說起，再回到開頭，然後在故事中段下結論，這是新潮流。這是幾天前我聽一位在池塘邊散步的評論家對一個年輕人說的。那位評論家對此發表了長篇大論，而且我肯定他說的絕對正確，因為那人不但戴了副眼鏡，還有顆禿頭，而且只要年輕人一提出意見，他就答以輕蔑的一聲『呸』！好了好了，繼續說你的故事吧。我很喜歡故事裡的休伊，我自己也具備所有高貴的情操，所以，對於休伊這個人，我有『英雄惜英雄』的感覺。」

「好吧，」小紅雀說道，一會兒以左腳，一會兒以右腳單腳跳來跳去。「冬天一過去，當櫻草花開始綻放出淡黃星形的花瓣，休伊就對他的妻子說，他要去看看小個子漢斯。

「『啊，你心地真好！』休伊的妻子說道，『你總是惦念著他人。回家時別忘了帶一籃花兒回來。』

「於是，休伊用鐵鍊將風車的轉翼綁好，攬起籃子，兀自下山去了。

「『早安，小個子漢斯。』休伊說道。

「『早安。』漢斯歡快地回答。他拄著鏟子站立，臉上帶著大大的微笑。

「『你在冬天裡過得如何？』休伊問道。

「『其實，說真的，』漢斯答道，『你這樣關心我，真是太好心了。只是，冬天真是非常難捱的日子，不過現在春天來了，我很高興，而我的花兒也都欣欣向榮。』

「『在冬天裡，我們常常提到你，漢斯。』休伊說道，『而且擔心你，不曉得你過得好不好？』

「『你們對我真好，』漢斯答道，『我還在擔心你們是否已經忘了我。』

「『漢斯，你這麼說真是嚇我一跳，』休伊說道，『友情是永誌不忘的，這就是友情之美。不過，你大概無法理解這生命中的詩意吧。對了，你的櫻草花開得真漂亮！』

「『這些花的確很美，』漢斯說道，『能夠擁有這麼多美麗的花真是我最大的福氣。我要把這些花拿到市場去賣給市長的女兒，再將賣花所得的錢把我的獨輪手推車買回來。』

「『把你的獨輪手推車買回來？你該不會是把那輛獨輪手推車給賣了吧？真是的，怎麼可以做出這種蠢事！』

「『其實，事情是這樣的，』漢斯說道，『我也是迫不得已。你也知道我冬天裡實在不好過，甚至連買個麵包的錢都沒有。於是，我只好先賣掉禮拜天上教堂時穿的外衣銀鈕扣。然後，我又賣掉我的銀鍊子；再來，又賣掉我的大菸斗；最後，只好把我的獨輪手推車給賣了。不過，我現在就要去把這些東西全部再買回來。』

「『漢斯，』休伊開口道，『我打算把我的獨輪手推車送給你。它目前是需要稍微維修啦！事實上，有一邊壞掉了，而且車輪的幅條也有點問題；雖然如此，我還是會把它送給你的。我知道我這麼做稍嫌大方了些，而且有許多人會覺得我很愚蠢，不過，我和世上的人不一樣。我認為慷慨是友情的本質，況且，我就要有一輛新的獨輪手推車了。聽我的沒錯，你大可稍安勿躁，我會把我的獨輪手推車送給你的。』

「『啊，你真是太慷慨了，』小個子漢斯說著，圓圓的臉上閃現著喜悅的光芒，『我很快就可以把你的獨輪手推車修好，因為我屋裡還有塊厚木板。』

「『有塊厚木板！』休伊大叫：『太好了，它剛好可以用來修理我的穀倉屋頂。因為那裡破了一個大洞，如果我不設法補好它，積貯在穀倉裡的穀物就要受潮發霉了。運氣真好，你正巧提到這件事呢！善有善報真是一點也不假。我給你我的獨輪手推車，你給我你的厚木板。當然啦，獨輪手推車要比厚木板貴重得多，但真正的友情是不會計較這些的。我們快些辦好這事吧，這樣我今天就可以開始修理屋頂了。』

「『當然，當然。』小個子漢斯說著，然後跑進屋裡，拖出了那塊厚木板。

「『這塊厚木板不怎麼大嘛，』休伊瞧著木板，發表評論道，『恐怕我修了屋頂之後，就沒有剩餘的木板可以讓你修獨輪手推車了，不過，這當然不能怪我啊。現在，我既然要給你我的獨輪手推車，我想，你也會回贈我一些花朵。我這兒有個籃子，麻煩你裝滿它。』

「『裝滿？』小個子漢斯說道，心中有些擔憂，因為休伊帶了一個大籃子來，而小個子漢斯心裡明白，如果裝滿這一籃子的花給休伊，就沒有剩下的花可以拿到市場去賣了，況且，他是那麼急切地想買回自己的銀鈕扣。

「『是啊，其實，』休伊答道，『我都已經要把我的獨輪手推車送給你了，向你要一些花，應該不算過份。我也許錯了，不過我仍然認為友情，尤其是真正的友情，是絕對不含自私成份的。』

「『我親愛的朋友，我最好的朋友，』小個子漢斯趕緊解釋道，『你當然可以要我花園裡所有的花，你的寶貴意見無論怎麼說都勝過那幾顆銀鈕扣的價值。』小個子漢斯一邊說著，一邊把花園裡的櫻草花全採下，裝進休伊的大籃裡。

「『再見啦，小個子漢斯。』休伊肩膀上扛著厚木板，手上提著大籃子，走上斜坡時，對小個子漢斯說道。

「『再見。』小個子漢斯答道。他開始愉快地翻土耕種，想著獨輪手推車，心中更是高興。

「第二天，小個子漢斯正準備將忍冬枝藤固定在門廊之時，便聽到休伊大老遠地就叫著他的名字。於是他跳下梯子，跑進花園裡，朝圍牆外頭望。

「休伊正揹了一大袋麵粉走來。

「『親愛的小個子漢斯，』休伊說道，『你幫我把這袋麵粉拿到市場上去賣好嗎？』

「『啊，非常抱歉，』漢斯說道，『我今天真的很忙，因為我得把爬藤植物固定在支架上，又要澆花，還得整理草地。』

「『哦，這樣啊，』休伊說道，『我覺得，我都要把我的獨輪手推車送給你了，你這樣拒絕我，實在太不夠朋友了。』

「『啊，請不要這麼說，』小個子漢斯嚇得叫道，『我絕對不敢有違朋友道義。』說著，便急忙跑進屋裡拿頂帽子戴上，揹起休伊的麵粉蹣跚地走了。

「那一天，天氣很熱，路上又是漫天塵沙，漢斯走不到六哩路就覺得疲累不堪，只好坐下來休息。雖然如此，他還是英勇地繼續前進，最後終於抵達市場。他在市場上待了一會兒，以相當好的價錢將麵粉賣出去後便立刻返家，因為他擔心如果耽擱太久，在路上會遇見盜匪。

「『今天真是累壞人的一天，』小個子漢斯上床時自言自語道，『不過，我很高興我沒有拒絕休伊，因為他是我最要好的朋友，況且他就要把獨輪手推車送給我了。』

「第二天一早，休伊便來向小個子漢斯拿賣麵粉的錢，然而小個子漢斯卻因為前一天的疲勞未解，還躺在床上。

「『依我看，』休伊說道，『你很懶惰。真的，我還以為你會更勤奮工作呢，我就要送你獨輪手推車了哪。怠惰偷懶是很嚴重的罪過，我絕不能坐視我的朋友變成這樣的人。請原諒我的直言，不過，我是拿你當朋友才會說這些話，如果我不拿你當朋友看，我根本不會管你。如果不能直言無諱，那友情又能帶來什麼好處呢？尋常人可以花言巧語，取悅他人或大拍別人馬屁，唯獨真正的朋友總是說些不好聽的實話，不在乎得罪人。說真的，如果是真正的朋友就該這樣做，因為，他知道他做的是一件好事。』

「『非常抱歉，』小個子漢斯說道，揉揉雙眼，摘下睡帽，『我是因為太累了才想在床上多躺一會兒，聽聽小鳥唱歌。你知道嗎，在聽過小鳥的歌聲之後，我工作起來總是特別起勁！』

「『哦，聽到你這麼說，我很高興，』休伊說道，一邊在小個子漢斯的背上拍了一下，『快把衣服穿一穿，到磨坊來，因為我想請你幫我修補穀倉屋頂的破洞。』

「可憐的小個子漢斯很想趕快到花園裡幹活，因為他的花已經兩天沒澆水了，可是他又不想拒絕休伊，因為休伊是他的好朋友。

「『我如果告訴你，我今天很忙，你會不會覺得我不夠朋友？』小個子漢斯不好意思地問道。

「『哦，說真的，』休伊答道，『我覺得我這樣的要求不算過份，畢竟我就要送給你獨輪手推車了哪。不過，當然啦，如果你說聲不，我會立刻離開，自己去修理屋頂的。』

「『啊，我不會這樣的。』小個子漢斯急忙大聲解釋著。他跳下床，穿好衣服，立刻到穀倉去。

「他在那兒工作了一整天，直到日落才休息，而休伊則在日落時來到穀倉，看看小個子漢斯的工作進度。

「『小個子漢斯，屋頂修好了嗎？』休伊輕鬆愉快地問道。

「『都修好了。』小個子漢斯一邊歡快地回答，一邊從梯子上爬下來。

「『啊！』休伊說道，『我說啊，世界上最愉快的事，就是服務他人了。』

「『聽你說話實在是人生一大享受。』小個子漢斯回答道，他坐了下來，抹抹前額，繼續道，『真的是人生一大享受。不過，我這輩子可能永遠無法像你一樣擁有這麼睿智的見解。』

「『哦！會的，會的，』休伊安慰道，『只不過，你得多吃些苦磨練一下。現階段，你只懂得如何實踐友誼；將來有一天，你也能領悟友誼的真諦的。』

「『你真的這樣認為嗎？』小個子漢斯滿懷希望地問道。

「『當然，』休伊答道，『不過，既然你已經把屋頂修好了，你最好回家休息一下，因為，明天我需要你幫忙把羊群趕上山。』

「可憐的小個子漢斯，他對休伊的請求不敢有任何意見。第二天一早，休伊便將他的羊群趕到漢斯家附近，於是小個子漢斯便隨著羊群上山。這麼上山下山，如此一來也就耗去了小個子漢斯一整天的時間；他回到家時已經疲累不堪，坐在椅子上便睡著了，直到第二天天色大亮才醒過來。

「『真想去花園裡工作。』小個子漢斯說完，便立刻到花園裡幹活。

「不過，他再也無法照顧他的花兒了，因為他的朋友休伊老是會來看望他，派給他一些工作或是要他到磨坊幫忙，有時候小個子漢斯心裡很憂愁，因為他擔心那些花兒以為主人已將它們遺忘，可是他又以休伊是自己最要好的朋友為由來自我安慰。而且，小個子漢斯老是這麼安慰自己道：『他就要把他的獨輪手推車送給我了，這可是很慷慨的行為啊！』

「於是，小個子漢斯替休伊做了不少工作，而休伊回報給漢斯的則是頌讚友誼的各種長篇大論。小個子漢斯將休伊的寶貴見解都記在筆記本裡，晚上回家時再拿出來好好研讀一番，因為他是個很用功的學生。

「後來，事情終於發生了。有一天晚上，小個子漢斯正坐在火爐旁烤火，一陣急促的敲門聲響起。那天晚上由於風雨很大，怒吼的風聲在屋子四周徘徊，所以，小個子漢斯起初將敲門聲聽成了風雨的吹襲聲。然而，敲門聲卻接二連三地響起，而且一陣比一陣猛烈、急促。

「『一定是可憐的旅人在敲門。』小個子漢斯自言自語著，急忙跑去開門。

「門口，小個子漢斯看到休伊一手提著燈籠，另一手拄著枴杖出現在門外。

「『親愛的小個子漢斯，』休伊一見到漢斯便哭道，『我遇上大難題了。我兒子從梯子上摔下來，受了傷，我想去請醫生來看看他。可是，醫生住的地方那麼遠，而且今晚的天候又是這樣惡劣，我想，你替我跑一趟會好些。你也知道，我就要把我的獨輪手推車送給你了，你也該做些事情回報我才算公平。』

「『當然，當然。』小個子漢斯急切地答道，『你對我真好，還親自跑這一趟，我這就立刻出發去請醫生。可是，你得把燈籠借給我才行，因為天太黑了，我怕自己會不小心掉到水溝裡去。』

「『很抱歉，』休伊答道，『這是我的新燈籠，如果它有個三長兩短，我的損失可就大了。』

「『啊，沒關係，那我就不要用燈籠好了。』小個子漢斯客氣地答道。他套上厚重的毛皮外套，戴上溫暖的紅色帽子，在脖子上圍了一條圍巾便出發了。

「那天晚上真是可怕！天色黑得幾乎讓小個子漢斯看不到路，而且風大得幾乎讓他站不住。然而，他仍舊勇敢地前進，走了約三個小時的路程後，他來到醫生家門口，敲了敲門。

「『誰啊？』醫生問著，從臥室的窗口探出頭來。

「『醫生，我是小個子漢斯。』

「『有什麼事嗎，小個子漢斯？』

「『磨坊主人休伊的兒子從梯子上摔下來，受了傷，休伊想請你立刻到他家裡去一趟。』

「『好！』醫生答應一聲，立刻吩咐人備妥馬匹。他穿上長靴、帶了燈籠，下樓來，騎上馬立刻向休伊家出發，小個子漢斯則跟在後面，蹣跚地走著。

「然而，天候愈來愈惡劣，風雨也愈來愈大，狂暴的雨勢幾乎讓小個子漢斯迷失了方向，也失去醫生坐騎的蹤跡。最後，小個子漢斯迷了路，在荒野裡繞不出來；這片荒野是危險地帶，因為其中滿佈又大又深的坑洞，小個子漢斯一個不小心，掉進了其中一個坑裡淹死了。第二天，幾個牧羊人發現小個子漢斯的屍體漂浮在一個大水坑上，他們合力將屍體運回漢斯的小屋。

「村裡每一個人都出席了小個子漢斯的葬禮，因為漢斯的人緣很好，而擔任漢斯治喪委員會主席的則是休伊。

「『基於我是他最要好的朋友，』休伊說道，『我得站上最尊貴的位子才算公平。』於是，他走在一長排黑衣人的前頭，並且不時用一條大手帕揩揩雙眼。

「葬禮結束後，一夥人在小酒館裡舒適地坐著，喝著辛辣的酒，吃著甜甜的糕點。鐵匠開口道：『小個子漢斯的死，對每個人來說都是沉重的損失。』」

「『對我而言更是無可比擬的損失。』休伊答道，『我曾經好心的準備把我的獨輪手推車送給他，現在，我真不知道該怎麼處理那輛車。把它放在家裡嫌佔空間，把它賣掉又值不了幾個錢，因為它損壞得太嚴重了。我再也不要隨便送人東西了，太好心也是滿痛苦的。』」

「說完了？」一陣沉默之後，河鼠問道。

「說完了，結局就是這樣。」小紅雀答道。

「那，休伊後來怎麼樣了？」河鼠又問。

「這，我就不知道了。」小紅雀答道，「而且，我也不想知道。」

「由此可知，你沒有同情心。」河鼠說道。

「恐怕，你並沒有聽懂這個故事裡的道德教訓吧。」小紅雀論斷道。

「什麼教訓？」河鼠不甘示弱地問。

「道德教訓。」

「你是說，這個故事帶有道德教訓？」河鼠問。

「沒錯。」小紅雀說。

「哦，說真的，」河鼠非常生氣地說，「我覺得，你早該在說故事之前，就先告訴我這是個道德故事。因為你如果先告訴我，那我絕對不會聽這個故事；事實上，我應該像那位評論家那樣，說一聲『呸！』才對。不過，我現在說也還來得及。」於是，河鼠扯開嗓子，用力地大叫一聲「呸」，然後甩了甩尾巴，鑽回他的洞裡去了。

「你覺得河鼠怎麼樣？」母鴨在水面划了幾分鐘之後問道，接著又說，「他是有許多優點，不過若從我為人母的觀點而言，我對他這個老單身漢倒是滿心同情。」

「我怕是惹惱河鼠了，」小紅雀說，「因為我剛跟他說了一個帶有道德教訓的故事。」

「啊！這麼做是很危險的。」母鴨說道。

而對於她的話，我深表贊同。

The Devoted Friend

One morning the old water-rat put his head out of his hole. He had bright beady eyes and stiff grey whiskers and his tail was like a long bit of black india rubber. The little ducks were swimming about in the pond, looking just like a lot of yellow canaries, and their mother, who was pure white with real red legs, was trying to teach them how to stand on their heads in the water.

"You will never be in the best society unless you can stand on your heads," she kept saying to them; and every now and then she showed them how it was done. But the little ducks paid no attention to her. They were so young that they did not know what an advantage it is to be in society at all.

"What disobedient children!" cried the old water-rat; "they really deserve to be drowned."

"Nothing of the kind," answered the duck, "every one

must make a beginning, and parents cannot be too patient."

"Ah! I know nothing about the feelings of parents," said the water-rat; "I am not a family man. In fact, I have never been married, and I never intend to be. Love is all very well in its way, but friendship is much higher. Indeed, I know of nothing in the world that is either nobler or rarer than a devoted friendship."

"And what, pray, is your idea of the duties of a devoted friend?" asked a green linnet, who was sitting in a willow tree hard by, and had overheard the conversation.

"Yes, that is just what I want to know," said the duck; and she swam away to the end of the pond, and stood upon her head, in order to give her children a good example.

"What a silly question!" cried the water-rat. "I should expect my devoted friend to be devoted to me, of course."

"And what would you do in return?" said the little bird, swinging upon a silver spray, and flapping his tiny wings.

"I don't understand you," answered the water-rat.

"Let me tell you a story on the subject," said the linnet.

"Is the story about me?" asked the water-rat. "If so, I will listen to it, for I am extremely fond of fiction."

"It is applicable to you," answered the linnet; and he flew down, and alighting upon the bank, he told the story of The Devoted Friend.

"Once upon a time," said the linnet, "there was an honest little fellow named Hans."

"Was he very distinguished?" asked the water-rat.

"No," answered the linnet, "I don't think he was distinguished at all, except for his kind heart, and his funny round good-humored face. He lived in a tiny cottage all by himself, and every day he worked in his garden. In all the country-side there was no garden so lovely as his. Sweet william grew there, and gilly-flowers, and shepherds'-purses, and Fair-maids of France. There were damask roses, and yellow roses, lilac crocuses, and gold, purple violets and white. Columbine and ladysmock, marjoram and wild Basil, the cowslip and the Flower-de-luce, the daffodil and the clove-pink bloomed or blossomed in their proper order as the months went by, one flower taking another flower's place, so that there were always beautiful things to look at, and pleasant odors to smell.

"Little Hans had a great many friends, but the most devoted friend of all was big Hugh the miller. Indeed, so devoted was the rich miller to little Hans, that be would never go by his garden without leaning over the wall and plucking a large nosegay, or a handful of sweet herbs, or filling his pockets with plums and cherries if it was the fruit season.

" 'Real friends should have everything in common,' the miller used to say, and little Hans nodded and smiled, and felt very proud of having a friend with such noble ideas.

"Sometimes, indeed, the neighbors thought it strange that the rich miller never gave little Hans anything in return, though he had a hundred sacks of flour stored away in his mill, and six milch cows, and a large flock of woolly sheep; but Hans never troubled his head about these things, and nothing gave him greater pleasure than to listen to all the wonderful things the miller used to say about the unselfishness of true friendship.

"So little Hans worked away in his garden. During the spring, the summer, and the autumn he was very happy, but when the winter came, and he had no fruit or flowers to bring to the market, he suffered a good deal from cold and hunger, and often had to go to bed without any supper but a few dried pears or some hard nuts. In the winter, also, he was extremely lonely, as the miller never came to see him then.

" 'There is no good in my going to see little Hans as long as the snow lasts,' the miller used to say to his wife, 'for when people are in trouble they should be left alone, and not be bothered by visitors. That at least is my idea about friendship, and I am sure I am right. So I shall wait till the spring comes, and then I shall pay him a visit, and he will be able to give me a large basket of primroses and that will make him so happy.'

" 'You are certainly very thoughtful about others,' answered the Wife, as she sat in her comfortable armchair by the big pinewood fire; 'very thoughtful indeed. It is quite a treat to hear you talk about friendship. I am sure the clergyman himself could not say such beautiful things as you do, though he does live in a three-storied house, and wear a gold ring on his little finger.'

" 'But could we not ask little Hans up here?' said the miller's youngest son. 'If poor Hans is in trouble I will give him half my porridge, and show him my white rabbits.'

" 'What a silly boy you are!' cried the miller; 'I really don't know what is the use of sending you to school. You seem not to learn anything. Why, if little Hans came up here, and saw our warm fire, and our good supper, and our great cask of red wine, he might get envious, and envy is a most terrible thing, and would spoil anybody's nature. I certainly will not allow Hans' nature to be spoiled. I am his best friend, and I will always watch over him, and see that he is not led into any temptations. Besides, if Hans came here, he might ask me to let him have some flour on credit, and that I could not do. Flour is one thing, and friendship is another, and they should not be confused. Why, the words are spelt differently, and mean quite different things. Everybody can see that.'

" 'How well you talk!' said the miller's wife, pouring herself out a large glass of warm ale; 'really I feel quite drowsy. It is just like being in church.'

" 'Lots of people act well,' answered the miller; 'but very few people talk well, which shows that talking is much the more difficult thing of the two, and much the finer thing also'; and he looked sternly across the table at his little son, who felt so ashamed of himself that he hung his head down, and grew quite scarlet, and began to cry into his tea. However, he was so young that you must excuse him."

"Is that the end of the story?" asked the water-rat.

"Certainly not," answered the linnet, "that is the beginning."

"Then you are quite behind the age," said the water-rat. "Every good storyteller nowadays starts with the end, and then goes on to the beginning, and concludes with the middle. That is the new method. I heard all about it the other day from a critic who was walking round the pond with a young man. He spoke of the matter at great length, and I am sure he must have been right, for he had blue spectacles and a bald head, and whenever the young man made any remark, he always answered 'Pooh!' But pray go on with your story. I like the miller immensely. I have all kinds of beautiful sentiments myself, so there is a great sympathy between us."

"Well," said the linnet, hopping now on one leg and now on the other, "as soon as the winter was over, and the primroses began to open their pale yellow stars, the miller said to his wife that he would go down and see little Hans.

" 'Why, what a good heart you have!' cried his wife; 'you are always thinking of others. And mind you take the big basket with you for the flowers.'

"So the miller tied the sails of the windmill together with a strong iron chain, and went down the hill with the basket on his arm.

" 'Good morning, little Hans,' said the miller.

" 'Good morning,' said Hans, leaning on his spade, and smiling from ear to ear.

" 'And how have you been all the winter?' said the miller.

" 'Well, really,'cried Hans, 'it is very good of you to ask, very good indeed. I am afraid I had rather a hard time of it, but now the spring has come, and I am quite happy, and all my flowers are doing well.'

" 'We often talked of you during the winter, Hans,' said the miller, 'and wondered how you were getting on.'

" 'That was kind of you,' said Hans; 'I was half afraid you had forgotten me.'

" 'Hans, I am surprised at you,' said the Miller; 'friendship never forgets. That is the wonderful thing about it, but I am afraid you don't understand the poetry of life. How lovely your primroses are looking, by the bye" !

" 'They are certainly very lovely,' said Hans, 'and it is a most lucky thing for me that I have so many. I am going to bring them into the market and sell them to the burgomaster's daughter, and buy back my wheelbarrow with the money.'

" 'Buy back your wheelbarrow? You don't mean to say you have sold it? What a very stupid thing to do!'

" 'Well, the fact is,' said Hans, 'that I was obliged to. You see the winter was a very bad time for me, and I really had no money at all to buy bread with. So I first sold the silver buttons off my Sunday coat, and then I sold my silver chain, and then I sold my big pipe, and at last I sold my wheelbarrow. But I am going to buy them all back again now.'

" 'Hans,' said the miller, 'I will give you my wheelbarrow. It is not in very good repair; indeed, one side is gone, and there is something wrong with the wheel-spokes; but in spite of that I will give it to you. I know it is very generous of me, and a great many people would think me extremely foolish for parting with it, but I am not like the rest of the world. I think that generosity is the essence of friendship, and, besides, I have got a new wheelbarrow for myself. Yes, you may set your mind at ease, I will give you my wheelbarrow.'

" 'Well, really, that is generous of you,' said little Hans, and his funny round face glowed all over with pleasure. 'I can easily put it in repair, as I have a plank of wood in the house.'

" 'A plank of wood!' said the miller; 'why, that is just what I want for the roof of my barn. There is a very large hole in it, and the corn will all get damp if I don't stop it up. How lucky you mentioned it! It is quite remarkable how one good action always breeds another. I have given you my wheelbarrow, and now you are going to give me your plank. Of course, the wheelbarrow is worth far more than the plank, but true, friendship never notices things like that. Pray get it at once, and I will set to work at my barn this very day.'

" 'Certainly,' cried little Hans, and he ran into the shed and dragged the plank out.

" 'It is not a very big plank,' said the miller, looking at it, 'and I am afraid that after I have mended my barn-roof there won't be any left for you to mend the wheelbarrow with; but, of course, that is not my fault. And now, as I have given you my wheelbarrow, I am sure you would like to give me some flowers in return. Here is the basket, and mind you fill it quite full.'

" 'Quite full?' said little Hans, rather sorrowfully, for it was really a very big basket, and he knew that if he filled it he would have no flowers left for the market and he was very anxious to get his silver buttons back.

" 'Well, really,' answered the Miller, 'as I have given you my wheelbarrow, I don't think that it is much to ask you for a few flowers. I may be wrong, but I should have thought that friendship, true friendship, was quite free from selfishness of any kind.'

" 'My dear friend, my best friend,' cried little Hans, 'you are welcome to all the flowers in my garden. I would much sooner have your good opinion than my silver buttons, any day'; and he ran and plucked all his pretty primroses, and filled the miller's basket.

" 'Goodbye, little Hans,' said the miller, as he went up the hill with the plank on his shoulder, and the big basket in his hand.

" 'Good-bye,' said little Hans, and he began to dig away quite merrily, he was so pleased about the wheelbarrow.

"The next day he was nailing up some honeysuckle against the porch, when he heard the miller's voice calling to him from the road. So he jumped off the ladder, and ran down the garden, and looked over the wall.

"There was the miller with a large sack of flour on his back.

" 'Dear little Hans,' said the Miller, 'would you mind carrying this sack of flour for me to market?'

" 'Oh, I am so sorry,' said Hans, 'but I am really very busy today. I have got all my creepers to nail up, and all my flowers to water, and all my grass to roll.'

" 'Well, really,' said the miller, 'I think that, considering that I am going to give you my wheelbarrow, it is rather unfriendly of you to refuse.'

" 'Oh, don't say that,' cried little Hans, 'I wouldn't be unfriendly for the whole world'; and he ran in for his cap, and trudged off with the big sack on his shoulders.

"It was a very hot day, and the road was terribly dusty, and before Hans had reached the sixth milestone he was so tired that he had to sit down and rest. However, he went on bravely, and as last he reached the market. After he had waited there some time, he sold the sack of flour for a very good price, and then he returned home at once, for he was afraid that if he stopped too late he might meet some robbers on the way.

" 'It has certainly been a hard day,' said little Hans to himself as he was going to bed, 'but I am glad I did not refuse the miller, for he is my best friend, and, besides, he is going to give me his wheelbarrow.'

"Early the next morning the miller came down to get the money for his sack of flour, but little Hans was so tired that he was still in bed.

" 'Upon my word,' said the Miller, 'you are very lazy. Really, considering that I am going to give you my wheelbarrow, I think you might work harder. Idleness is a great sin, and I certainly don't like any of my friends to be idle or sluggish. You must not mind my speaking quite plainly to you. Of course I should not dream of doing so if I were not your friend. But what is the good of friendship if one cannot say exactly what one means? Anybody can say charming things and try to please and to flatter, but a true friend always says unpleasant things, and does not mind giving pain. Indeed, if he is a really true friend he prefers it, for he knows that then he is doing good.'

" 'I am very sorry,' said little Hans, rubbing his eyes and pulling off his night-cap, 'but I was so tired that I thought I would lie in bed for a little time, and listen to the birds singing. Do you know that I always work better after hearing the birds sing?'

" 'Well, I am glad of that,' said the miller, clapping little Hans on the back, 'for I want you to come up to the mill as soon as you are dressed, and mend my barn-roof for me.'

"Poor little Hans was very anxious to go and work in his garden, for his flowers had not been watered for two days, but he did not like to refuse the miller, as he was such a good friend to him.

" 'Do you think it would be unfriendly of me if I said I was busy?' he inquired in a shy and timid voice.

" 'Well, really,' answered the miller, 'I do not think it is much to ask of you, considering that I am going to give you my wheelbarrow; but of course if you refuse I will go and do it myself.'

" 'Oh! on no account,' cried little Hans and he jumped out of bed, and dressed himself, and went up to the barn.

"He worked there all day long, till sunset, and at sunset the miller came to see how he was getting on.

" 'Have you mended the hole in the roof yet, little Hans?' cried the miller in a cheery voice.

" 'It is quite mended,'answered little Hans, coming down the ladder.

" 'Ah!' said the Miller, 'there is no work so delightful as the work one does for others.'

" 'It is certainly a great privilege to hear you talk,'answered little Hans, sitting down, and wiping his forehead, 'a very great privilege. But I am afraid I shall never have such beautiful ideas as you have.'

" 'Oh! they will come to you,' said the miller, 'but you must take more pains. At present you have only the practice of friendship; some day you will have the theory also.'

" 'Do you really think I shall?' asked little Hans.

" 'I have no doubt of it,'answered the Miller, 'but now that you have mended the roof, you had better go home and rest, for I want you to drive my sheep to the mountain to-morrow.'

"Poor little Hans was afraid to say anything to this, and early the next morning the miller brought his sheep round to the cottage, and Hans started off with them to the mountain. It took him the whole day to get there and back; and when he returned he was so tired that he went off to sleep in his chair, and did not wake up till it was broad daylight.

" 'What a delightful time I shall have in my garden,' he said, and he went to work at once.

"But somehow he was never able to look after his flowers at all, for his friend the miller was always coming round and sending him off on long errands, or getting him to help at the mill. Little Hans was very much distressed at times, as he was afraid his flowers would think he had forgotten them, but he consoled himself by the reflection that the miller was his best friend. 'Besides,' he used to say, 'he is going to give me his wheelbarrow, and that is an act of pure generosity.'

"So little Hans worked away for the miller, and the miller said all kinds of beautiful things about friendship, which Hans took down in a notebook, and used to read over at night, for he was a very good scholar.

"Now it happened that one evening little Hans was sitting by his fireside when a loud rap came at the door. It was a very wild night, and the wind was blowing and roaring round the house so terribly that at first he thought it was merely the storm. But a second rap came, and then a third, louder than any of the others.

" 'It is some poor traveller,' said little Hans to himself, and he ran to the door.

"There stood the miller with a lantern in one hand and a big stick in the other.

" 'Dear little Hans,' cried the miller, 'I am in great trouble. My little boy has fallen off a ladder and hurt himself, and I am going for the doctor. But he lives so far away, and it is such a bad night, that it has just occurred to me that it would be much better if you went instead of me. You know I am going to give you my wheelbarrow, and so, it is only fair that you should do something for me in return.'

" 'Certainly,' cried little Hans, 'I take it quite as a compliment your coming to me, and I will start off at once. But you must lend me your lantern, as the night is so dark that I am afraid I might fall into the ditch.'

" 'I am very sorry,' answered the miller, 'but it is my new lantern, and it would be a great loss to me if anything happened to it.'

" 'Well, never mind, I will do without it,' cried little Hans, and he took down his great fur coat, and his warm scarlet cap, and tied a muffler round his throat, and started off.

"What a dreadful storm it was! The night was so black that little Hans could hardly see, and the wind was so strong that he could scarcely stand. However, he was very courageous, and after he had been walking about three hours, he arrived at the doctor's house, and knocked at the door.

" 'Who is there?' cried the doctor, putting his head out of his bedroom window.

" 'Little Hans, doctor.'

" 'What do you want, little Hans?'

" 'The miller's son has fallen from a ladder, and has hurt himself, and the miller wants you to come at once.'

" 'All right!' said the doctor; and he ordered his horse, and his big boots, and his lantern, and came downstairs, and rode off in the direction of the miller's house, little Hans trudging behind him.

"But the storm grew worse and worse, and the rain fell in torrents, and little Hans could not see where he was going, or keep up with the horse. At last he lost his way, and wandered off on the moor, which was a very dangerous place, as it was full of deep holes, and there poor little Hans was drowned. His body was found the next day by some goatherds, floating in a great pool of water, and was brought back by them to the cottage.

"Everybody went to little Hans' funeral, as he was so popular, and the miller was the chief mourner.

" 'As I was his best friend,' said the Miller, 'it is only fair that I should have the best place'; so he walked at the head of the procession in a long black cloak, and every now and then he wiped his eyes with a big pocket-handkerchief.

" 'Little Hans is certainly a great loss to every one,' said the blacksmith, when the funeral was over, and they were all seated comfortably in the inn, drinking spiced wine and eating sweet cakes.

" 'A great loss to me at any rate,' answered the miller; 'why, I had as good as given him my wheelbarrow, and now I really don't know what to do with it. It is very much in my way at home, and it is in such bad repair that I could not get anything for it if I sold it. I will certainly take care not to give away anything again. One always suffers for being generous.'"

"Well?" said the water-rat, after a long pause.

"Well, that is the end," said the linnet.

"But what became of the miller?" asked the water-rat.

"Oh! I really don't know," replied the linnet; "and I am sure that I don't care."

"It is quite evident then that you have no sympathy in your nature," said the water-rat.

"I am afraid you don't quite see the moral of the story," remarked the linnet.

"The what?" screamed the water-rat.

"The moral."

"Do you mean to say that the story has a moral?"

"Certainly," said the linnet.

"Well, really," said the water-rat, in a very angry manner, "I think you should have told me that before you began. If you had done so, I certainly would not have listened to you; in fact, I should have said 'Pooh', like the critic. However, I can say it now"; so he shouted out "Pooh" at the top of his voice, gave a whisk with his tail, and went back into his hole.

"And how do you like the water-rat?" asked the duck, who came paddling up some minutes afterwards. "He has a great many good points, but for my own part I have a mother's feelings, and I can never look at a confirmed bachelor without the tears coming into my eyes."

"I am rather afraid that I have annoyed him," answered the linnet. "The fact is, that I told him a story with a moral."

"Ah! that is always a very dangerous thing to do," said the duck.

And I quite agree with her.

驕傲的爆竹

我是一支既不尋常又優秀的爆竹。
我是很有想像力的，
因為我從不以事情的真相為著眼點，
我總是用不同的角度來看事情。

　　國王的兒子即將舉行結婚大典，所以全國都沉浸在普天同慶的氣氛中。他等新娘前來已經足足等了一年，最後，她終於來了。

　　準新娘是俄國公主，她乘坐一架由六隻馴鹿拉的雪橇從芬蘭出發。雪橇的造型有如一隻金色大天鵝，公主就坐在天鵝的雙翼之中。貂皮大衣直披蓋到腳下，她的頭上戴著銀亮的小皇冠，而本人則像她所住的雪白宮殿一樣白皙。當她經過市街，民眾們看到她潔白的肌膚都大為驚豔。「她就像一朵白玫瑰！」市民們叫嚷著，紛紛從陽臺上投送花朵給她。

　　王子正站在他的城堡門口等著迎接她。王子有著夢幻般的紫羅蘭色雙眼，一頭金黃閃耀的頭髮。他一見到公主便單膝跪地，親吻公主的手。

　　「妳的照片已經很美了，」王子喃喃地說著，「然而妳本人卻比照片更加美麗。」公主一聽，雙頰立刻泛上紅霞。

「她剛到時像朵白玫瑰，」一位年輕的書僮對他身旁的人說道，「現在，卻像一朵紅玫瑰。」全宮廷的人都為這件喜事而歡欣不已。

因為在接下來的三天裡，每個人都唱頌著「白玫瑰、紅玫瑰、紅玫瑰、白玫瑰。」而且國王還下令將書僮的薪水調高兩倍；儘管這項命令對不支薪的書僮來說，並沒有什麼好處，但這項命令卻被視為書僮的無上榮耀，而且也適時地在官報上刊載出來。

三天後，舉行隆重的婚禮慶典。在這個令人難忘的結婚典禮上，新郎和新娘手牽著手走在繡有許多小珍珠的紫色絲絨篷幕下。緊接著，是長達五個小時的國宴，王子和王妃坐在大廳最高處，共飲一只水晶杯裡的酒。只有真心相愛的人才能用這只水晶杯喝酒，因為不真誠的人若用這只水晶杯喝酒，杯子就會變成灰色、晦暗、不澄清。

「杯子的色澤證明王子與王妃兩人真心相愛。」上回那位小書僮再度開口道，「這件事明白透徹，就像那只水晶杯一樣！」於是國王第二次宣佈將書僮的薪水調高兩倍。「多麼光榮的賞賜啊！」所有的朝臣齊聲讚道。

宴會之後，接著上場的是大舞會。新郎和新娘兩人相擁起舞，國王還應觀眾要求吹奏長笛。他吹得很差，可是沒有人敢告訴他，因為他是國王。事實上，他只會兩首曲子，但是連他自己都無法肯定，他吹的究竟是哪一首；不過這也沒關係，因為無論他吹的是什麼，每個人都只會高聲叫道：「太好了！太好了！」

慶典的最後一個節目是大型的煙火施放表演，這場壓軸戲特別安排在午夜時分舉行。王妃從小到大都沒看過煙火表演，所以國王特別下令皇家煙火製造商在她婚禮這一天好好地表現表現。

「煙火看起來像什麼？」婚禮前某一天早上，這位來自俄國的公主在露臺上散步，一邊問著王子。

「它們就像北極光一樣，」國王說。他老是喜歡替別人回答問題。「不過，它們比北極光更為自然。我喜愛煙火更甚於喜歡星星，只要妳看過煙火，妳就會明白了，而且它們就像我吹奏出來的笛聲一樣美。妳非得看看煙火不可。」

　　於是，國王命人在皇家花園的盡頭處搭設一座巨大的高臺，待煙火製造商將所有設備擺上定位時，蓄勢待發的煙火們立刻交頭接耳地互訴心聲。

　　「這個世界真是太美了，」一隻小爆竹興奮地叫道，「看看這些黃色的鬱金香。哇！如果它們是爆竹，那它們就是最可愛的爆竹了。我真慶幸自己旅行過，旅行可以擴展視野，還可以去除一個人心中所有的偏見。」

　　「這是皇家花園，不算是全世界。你這枝蠢笨的小爆竹！」一枝大型的羅馬蠟燭說道，「世界是一個廣闊的大地方，你得花上三天的時間才能徹底地逛它一圈。」

　　「你喜愛的地方就是你的世界。」沉思的旋轉煙火開口道；她早期曾和一只舊盒子相偎相依，現在則只剩一顆驕傲且破碎的心；「不過，愛已經不再流行了，因為詩人們扼殺了它。這些詩人對愛情描繪得太多，以致於沒有人要相信他們，不過對我來說，這是意料中的事。真愛既痛苦且沉默，我記得我有一次……算了，現在已經不重要了，浪漫之心誠屬過去式。」

　　「胡說八道！」羅馬蠟燭反擊道，「浪漫之心永遠不死，它如同明月，永久長存。就拿新郎和新娘來說好了，他們深愛著彼此。今天早上，那張泛黃的彈藥紙告訴了我一切有關這對新婚夫婦的消息，它正巧和我待在同一個抽屜裡，而且它知道最新的宮廷消息。」

　　然而旋轉煙火搖搖頭，喃喃道：「浪漫之心死啦，浪漫之心死啦，浪漫之心死啦。」她就是那種，以為某種論調只要不斷重複就會變成真理的人。

　　突然間，一聲尖銳的乾咳聲響起，引得大夥四處張望，尋找聲音的來源。

　　原來，發出聲音的是一枝綁在細長竹枝頂端，高高的、看起來有些驕傲自大的爆竹。他總是在發表評論之前先「咳」一下，藉以引起聽眾的注意。

　　「咳咳！咳咳！」他開口道。每枝爆竹都在聽他說話，除了旋轉煙火，因為她還在搖頭，而且嘴裡仍嘟囔著：「浪漫之心死啦。」

　　「注意秩序！注意秩序！」一枝爆竹大叫道。他深具政治家的氣質，而且在地方選舉上總能占有卓越地位，所以他懂得使用適當的議會用語。

　　「浪漫之心徹底死啦。」旋轉煙火輕聲說道，說完就去睡了。

　　四周一安靜下來，那枝有些驕傲自大的爆竹趕緊咳了第三聲，並且開始說話。他用低沉、高貴的語調說話，彷彿在陳述自己的回憶錄似的，而且目光不時地穿過四周的觀眾，事實上，他的舉止可稱得上合宜而高貴。

　　「國王的兒子何其幸運，」他評論道，「選在我要升空的這一天結婚。說真的，就算是事先安排，也不會有這麼好的結果；不過，作為一名王子總是非常幸運的。」

　　「天啊！」另一枝小爆竹說道，「我的看法和你相反，我們是沾了王子的光才得以在今天升空呢！」

　　「對你來說也許如此，」驕傲的爆竹答道，「我絕對不會懷疑。不過，這樣的說法可就不適用於我了。我是一枝非常傑出的爆竹，擁有優秀的血統。我的母親是她那一輩的爆竹之中最出色的旋轉蠟燭，而且以優雅的舞姿聞名於世。她在廣大的觀眾面前出現時，總共旋轉了十九次才熄滅，而且每一次出場時都在空中爆出七顆粉紅色的星星。她的身高有三英呎半，體內蘊藏最好的火藥。我的父親則和我一樣優秀，我們都具有法國血統。他在升空時飛爬得如此之高，觀眾們還擔心他不再返回地球了。不過，他還是回來了，因為他心地善良；他在一場色彩繽紛的黃金雨中，以最優雅的姿態下降。報紙對他的表演讚譽有加；事實上，官報還稱他為焰火藝術中的代表作。」

「你說的是煙火，煙火。」一枝信號煙火說道，「我知道『煙火』這兩個字，我的殼子上就寫了這兩個字。」

「哦，我說的是焰火。」驕傲的爆竹以嚴肅的語氣答道。信號煙火覺得自尊心受損，立刻欺負一下旁邊的幾枝小爆竹，藉以顯示自己仍是一個重要人物。

「我說，」驕傲的爆竹開口道，「我說——我剛剛說到哪裡？」

「你說到你自己了。」羅馬蠟燭答道。

「對，對！我當然知道，自己是在討論一件大事時被粗魯無禮地打斷了談話。我厭惡粗魯無禮和一切不好的行為舉止，因為我是非常敏感的。全世界再也找不出一個比我更敏感的人了，關於這一點，我非常肯定。」

「什麼是敏感的人？」一枝爆竹向羅馬蠟燭請教道。

「敏感的人就是不看自己的缺點，老愛揭他人瘡疤的人。」羅馬蠟燭低聲地回答。發問的爆竹差點憋不住笑聲。

「喂，你們在笑什麼？」驕傲的爆竹問道：「我可沒笑哦。」

「我是在笑啊，因為我很快樂。」在笑的那枝爆竹說道。

「這個理由很自私。」驕傲的爆竹生氣地說道，「你有什麼權利快樂？你該想想其他人，尤其是該為我想想。我就常常想到我自己，而且我希望大家都能和我一樣，這就是所謂的同理心；這是一種美德，而且我擁有高度的這種美德。試想，如果今天晚上我出了什麼事，將對所有人造成多麼嚴重的不幸！王子和王妃將永遠不再快樂，他們整個婚姻生活將因此被毀；至於國王，更是無法承受這樣的打擊。說真的，每次只要一想到我的重要性，我幾乎就要熱淚盈眶了。」

「如果你想為他人帶來歡樂，」羅馬蠟燭直著脖子喊道，「你最好不要讓淚水弄濕了自己。」

「說得好。」信號煙火附和道，他現在精神振奮多了。「這是常識。」

「常識，真是的！」驕傲的爆竹怒道，「你們忘啦，我可是一枝既不尋常又優秀的爆竹。沒有想像力的人只配擁有常識。但我可是有想像力的，因為我從不以事情的真相為著眼點，我總是用不同的角度來看事情。至於不要弄濕自己的這個說法，足以證明在座的各位絲毫無法欣賞人性的情感面；我真慶幸自己不在乎這樣的說法。對一個人來說，支撐他活下去的唯一力量就是擁有強烈的、優於他人的意識，而我一直在培養這種意識。而在座的各位，則是一點感情也沒有，你們在這兒又笑又樂的，簡直無視於王子和王妃的新婚。」

「啊，不會吧，」一個小小的汽球煙火叫道，「我們怎麼會無視於王子和王妃的新婚呢？這是件愉快的事，當我飛上雲霄之際，我就要將這件事的大小細節全告訴天上的星星。當我向星星們描述新娘的美貌時，你就可以看見他們不斷地在眨眼。」

「啊！多麼平凡的人生觀哪！」驕傲的煙火說道，「不過，這倒是我意料中的事。你什麼也沒有，頭也空空，心也空空。你難道沒有想過，王子和王妃也許會搬到有著大河流過的鄉間居住，也許他們只會生下一個兒子，一個像王子一樣擁有金黃燦爛髮色和紫羅蘭色眼睛的小男孩，而也許有一天這個小男孩會和保母一起散步，也許保母會在高大的老樹下睡一覺，然後也許這個小男孩會掉到河裡溺死。多麼不幸啊！可憐的夫婦，失去了他們的獨生子！太可怕了！我絕對承受不住這樣的打擊。」

「可是他們並沒有失去他們唯一的兒子啊！」羅馬蠟燭叫道，「他們根本沒有發生什麼不幸。」

「我又沒說他們已經出事了，」驕傲的爆竹反駁道，「我只是說有可能會這樣而已。如果他們已經失去了唯一的兒子，那再多的討論也沒有用。我討厭事後諸葛之人，不過，當我想到他們很可能會失去唯一兒子時，我當然會覺得很難過。」

「沒錯！」信號煙火大叫道，「事實上，你是我所見過最令人感到難過的人。」

「你是我所見過最粗魯無禮的人，」驕傲的爆竹不甘示弱地反擊，「你無法明白我跟王子間的友誼。」

「啊，你根本就不認識王子嘛。」羅馬蠟燭咆哮道。

「我又沒說我認識他。」驕傲的爆竹說道，「我若認識他，我就不敢說我是他的朋友了。對一個人來說，認識朋友是非常危險的事。」

「你真的別把自己弄濕，保持乾燥比較好。」汽球煙火說道，「這是很重要的事。」

「毫無疑問，這對你而言是非常重要的。」驕傲的爆竹說道，「但是我卻很想哭。」他說著說著，竟然真的滴下眼淚來了，而且幾乎淹死兩隻正在築巢的小小甲蟲，害他們得趕緊再找個乾燥的地方住。

「他的個性一定很浪漫，」旋轉煙火說道，「因為他會為那種一點也不值得流淚的事而哭。」說罷，她長嘆一聲，想起舊日相偎依的那只盒子。

然而，羅馬蠟燭和信號煙火仍然非常氣憤，他們扯開嗓門一直重複地說著：「胡說八道！胡說八道！」他們是非常實際的人，只要是他們反對的事，便一律以「胡說八道」稱之。

此時，月亮高掛夜空有如一只銀盤，星星開始閃爍，宮廷裡也傳出了悠揚的樂聲。

王子和王妃兩人在舞會中開舞，他們的舞姿曼妙優雅，連百合花都忍不住探頭到窗邊偷看，豔紅的罌粟花也隨著音樂點頭打起了拍子。

時鐘敲了十響，然後十一響、十二響，當午夜最後一道鐘聲響起時，每個人都跑到陽臺上，國王接著傳喚皇家煙火隊。

　　「開始施放煙火。」國王說。於是皇家煙火隊的隊長深深鞠了個躬，大踏步地走向花園盡頭。他帶了六位助手，每位助手都拿著長長的火炬。

　　這是個壯麗盛大的煙火表演。

　　「颼颼！颼颼！」旋轉煙火出發了，他不停地旋轉著。「轟！轟！」羅馬蠟燭也露了一手。然後小爆竹們滿地飛舞著，信號煙火則將大地染成一片緋紅。「再見啦。」汽球煙火飛入高空，他在撒下許多藍色小火花時如此叫道。「砰！砰！」興奮不已的鞭炮們熱烈地回應著。除了那枝驕傲的爆竹，大夥的表演都很成功。他因為讓淚水濕濕了身體，根本就點不著。他全身上下最貴重的東西就是火藥粉，而現在火藥粉讓淚水浸濕了，一點用也沒有。那些被他冷嘲熱諷、不屑一顧的窮酸親友們，一個個如火樹銀花般飛入天際。「萬歲！萬歲！」整個宮廷的人都高興地大叫，就連美麗的王妃也愉快地笑著。

　　「我猜，他們要留著我，待到某些大場合再用。」驕傲的爆竹說道，「一定是這樣沒錯。」他的臉上出現了一種前所未見的高傲神情。

　　第二天，工人來到花園打掃。「這一定是國王派出來的大臣，」驕傲的爆竹說道，「我得以合宜的威嚴迎接他們才是。」於是他鼻子朝天，眉頭緊鎖，一副正在思量重要事情的模樣。然而，工人們卻無視於他的存在，自顧自地走開。突然，有個工人發現了他。

　　「呦呴！」工人大叫，「這枝爆竹真爛！」隨即將他拋到牆外的水溝裡。

　　「爛爆竹？爛爆竹？」他在空中翻滾時說道，「不可能！那個人一定是說棒爆竹。『爛』和『棒』聽起來很像，說真的，有時候它們簡直就是一樣啊。」說完，他便跌進爛泥巴堆裡。

「這兒真讓人感到不舒服，」他評判道，「但是毫無疑問，這是最新流行的海水浴場，他們是送我到這兒來療養的。我的精神的確感到非常緊張，是我要求休息一陣子的。」

有隻雙眼閃亮、身披斑點綠外套的小青蛙跳到他身邊來。「我知道！你是新來的。」青蛙說道，「哇！沒有比爛泥巴地更舒服的地方了。給我一個下雨天和一條水溝，我就會很快樂。你想，今天下午會下雨嗎？我希望如此，只不過天空湛藍而且萬里無雲，真可惜！」

「咳咳！咳咳！」驕傲的爆竹開口道，他又開始咳了。

「你的聲音真好聽！」青蛙讚美道，「聽起來好像蛙鳴，不可否認，蛙鳴是世界上最動人的音樂。今天晚上你就可以聽見我們合唱團的歌聲，我們會坐在農舍旁的舊鴨池邊，一等月亮升起，就開始唱。我們的歌聲是如此美妙，以致於每個人躺在床上寧願不睡覺也要聆聽我們唱歌。事實上，就在昨天，我聽到農夫的妻子對她母親說，由於我們這些青蛙的緣故，令她一夜未能闔眼。發覺自己這麼受歡迎，真是人生最快樂的事。」

「咳咳！咳咳！」驕傲的爆竹生氣了。他對於自己未能插上話，覺得很不服氣。

「哇，真好聽的聲音。」青蛙繼續道，「我希望你能到鴨池來一趟。我要去找我女兒了。我有六個美麗大方的女兒，我好擔心她們會碰上梭子魚。他可是個厲害的怪物，我怕他會把我的女兒們當成早餐吃掉。好啦，再見啦！和你聊天真愉快，我相信你一定也有同感。」

「聊天，真虧你說得出口！」驕傲的爆竹總算有機會說話了，「全部都是你一個人在講，這根本不能算是聊天。」

「總得有人當聽眾啊，」青蛙答道，「而且我喜歡從頭講到尾，這樣不但省時還可以避免爭執。」

「可是我喜歡爭執。」驕傲的爆竹說道。

「不會吧，」青蛙自信滿滿地說道，「爭執是非常粗俗的行為，因為上流社會的人總是意見一致的。再次向你道聲再見，我看到我女兒了。」青蛙說完，便游走了。

「你真是個惱人的傢伙，」驕傲的爆竹叫道，「而且教養很差。我討厭老是談論自己、而不給對方機會讓人談談自己的人，對，就是你這樣的人。這就是我所謂的自私，而自私是最可憎的事，尤其是對我這種天性淳厚、深富同情心的人來說，更是無法忍受。事實上，你該學學我，我是最佳示範。既然你有這個機會，就好好利用一下，我可是馬上就要回宮廷裡去的，我是宮廷裡備受歡迎的人物。事實上，王子和王妃昨天才在我的祝福之下舉行了婚禮。當然啦，你是不可能知道這些事情的，因為你是井底之蛙嘛！」

「多說無益啦，」一隻停在高大褐色蘆葦上的蜻蜓開口道，「一點用也沒有啦，因為青蛙已經走遠了。」

「哦，這倒是他的損失。」驕傲的爆竹說道，「不過，我不會因為他不聽我說話就閉口不言。我喜歡聽我自己發表言論，這是我人生中的一大樂事。我常常發表長篇大論給自己聽，而且我是如此聰明，以致於有時候我也無法了解自己在說些什麼。」

「那麼，我想，你最適合發表哲學方面的演說。」蜻蜓說道，然後展開可愛如薄紗的翅翼飛上了青空。

「怎麼飛走了呢？真蠢！」驕傲的爆竹說道，「我肯定他不是常有機會，能聽到這類擴展視野的言談。不管啦，我是不會在意的。有朝一日終會有伯樂識得我這匹千里馬。」他說著，一邊又在泥堆裡陷得更深了點。

過了一會兒，一隻大白鴨走近他身旁。這隻大白鴨有一雙黃色的腳，腳趾間有蹼，走起路來婀娜多姿的樣子，讓她成了公認的萬人迷。

「呱，呱，呱，」大白鴨開口道，「你長得真古怪！請問你是生來如此，還是遭逢意外的結果？」

「妳真是個鄉巴佬，」驕傲的爆竹說道，「不然的話，妳早該知道我是誰了。不管怎麼說，我原諒妳的愚昧無知就是了。老是要求別人和自己一樣優秀是不公平的。妳若聽到我可以飛上雲霄，再像一陣黃金雨般返回地面，一定會嚇一大跳。」

「我倒是沒想那麼多。」大白鴨說道，「因為我不知道你所說的事對誰有好處。聽著，你若能像牛一樣犁田，或像馬一樣拉車，或像牧羊犬一樣看顧羊群，倒還有些用處。」

「我的天哪！」驕傲的爆竹鄙夷地大叫，「我看妳肯定是從下流社會來的。像我這種身份地位的人從來都不需要具備實用價值，但我們的成就卻遠超乎所謂的實用價值。我個人對於任何一種行業都沒什麼好感，尤其是妳剛剛推崇的那些行業。事實上，我一直認為粗活是無所事事之人的慰藉。」

「好，好，」大白鴨答道。她愛好和平，從不跟人起爭執，「每個人的品味不同。我想，你要在這兒住下了。」

「哦！不會的。」驕傲的爆竹趕緊解釋，「我只是個訪客，一個優秀的訪客。事實上，我覺得這地方很沉悶，既不是熱鬧的市區，也不是與世隔絕的化外之地。說真的，這兒算是個鄉下地方。我可能要回宮廷去了，因為我知道我註定要為這世界帶來光彩。」

「我曾經有過成為公眾人物的念頭，」大白鴨道，「畢竟需要改革的事這麼多。說真的，以前我曾擔任過一次會議的主席，會中決議譴責我們所厭惡的一切事情。然而，這些決議似乎沒有什麼效果。現在我專心在家務上，致力於照顧家人。」

「我是註定要成為公眾人物的。」驕傲的爆竹說道，「我的親戚們也一樣，而且他們之中即使是身分最卑微的，也是如此。只要我們一出現，必定掀起高潮。我還沒有完全顯露出自己的本領，不過一旦我現身，必定會令人嘆為觀止。至於專心於家務嘛，這可是會讓人快速老化，使人對大事分心的。」

「啊！人生的大事，可真是重要呢！」大白鴨說道，「這倒是提醒了我，肚子好餓啊。」她說著，往下游走去了，嘴裡一邊叫著：「呱，呱，呱。」

「回來！回來啊！」驕傲的爆竹尖叫道，「我有很多話要告訴妳！」可是大白鴨並不理睬他。

「她走了也好。」驕傲的爆竹自言自語，「她存著一副絕對的中產階級心態。」他又往泥巴堆更深陷了一點，開始思索起「天才的孤寂」這個課題。突然間，兩個身著白色工作服的小男孩跑到溝堤來，手中拿著水壺和一些柴薪。

「這一定是國王派出的代表團。」驕傲的爆竹說著，盡力裝出一副高貴的模樣。

「喂！」其中一個小男孩高叫道，「看看這枝老舊的爆竹！不曉得它怎麼會出現在這裡。」他將驕傲的爆竹從溝裡拿出來。

「老舊的爆竹！」驕傲的爆竹尋思道，「不可能！他一定是說閃耀的爆竹，閃耀二字倒是很不錯的恭維。他一定把我當成了宮廷裡顯貴的人物！」

「我們把它丟進火裡去！」另一個小男孩說道，「這樣也許能助我們一臂之力，把壺裡的水燒開。」

於是他們一起將帶來的柴薪堆起，再將驕傲的爆竹放在最頂端，然後點起火來。

「我們可以去睡一覺，」兩個小男孩說道，「等我們睡醒，壺裡的水也就燒開了。」他們便在草地上躺了下來，閉上眼睛。

驕傲的爆竹因為身上太潮濕，所以花了一段時間才開始燃燒。最後，他終於著火了。

「現在，我要升空啦！」他大叫道，盡力做出英挺昂揚的姿態。「我知道，我會飛得比星星還高、比月亮還高、比太陽還高。事實上，我會如此之高，以致於……。」

「嘶！嘶！嘶嘶！」他直飛天際。

「好極了！」他高興地大叫道，「我將永遠像這樣翱翔，我是多麼成功的爆竹啊！」

然而卻沒有任何人看到他。之後，他開始覺得渾身打顫。

「現在我要爆炸了，」他叫道，「我要讓全世界燃燒起來，還要發出讓所有人在一整年之內都無法將話題離開我的聲響。」驕傲的爆竹的確爆炸了。「砰！砰！砰！」火藥粉發揮效力了，此乃無庸置疑的事。

然而，卻沒有人聽到他發出的聲響，就連那兩個小男孩也一樣，因為他們正睡得香甜，並且還發出鼾聲呢！

燃燒過後的爆竹只剩下一段細長的竹枝，而竹枝返回地面時，正好落在沿著水溝散步的一隻鵝的背後。

「天哪！」鵝兒驚叫道，「老天要下起竹枝雨來了。」說罷，趕緊衝進水裡。

「我就知道，我會引起大騷動的。」驕傲的爆竹用盡最後一口氣如此說道。

The Remarkable Rocket

The king's son was going to be married, so there were general rejoicings. He had waited a whole year for his bride, and at last she had arrived. She was a Russian princess, and had driven all the way from Finland in a sledge drawn by six reindeer. The sledge was shaped like a great golden swan, and between the swan's wings lay the little princess herself. Her long ermine cloak reached right down to her feet, on her head was a tiny cap of silver tissue, and she was as pale as the Snow Palace in which she had always lived. So pale was she that as she drove through the streets all the people wondered. "She is like a white rose!" they cried, and they threw down flowers on her from the balconies.

At the gate of the castle the prince was waiting to receive her. He had dreamy violet eyes, and his hair was like fine gold. When he saw her he sank upon one knee, and kissed her hand.

"Your picture was beautiful," he murmured, "but you

are more beautiful than your picture"; and the little princess blushed.

"She was like a white rose before," said a young page to his neighbor, "but she is like a red rose now"; and the whole court was delighted.

For the next three days everybody went about saying, "White rose, red rose, red rose, white rose"; and the king gave orders that the page's salary was to be doubled. As he received no salary at all this was not of much use to him, but it was considered a great honor, and was duly published in the Court Gazette.

When the three days were over the marriage was celebrated. It was a magnificent ceremony, and the bride and bridegroom walked hand in hand under a canopy of purple velvet embroidered with little pearls. Then there was a state banquet, which lasted for five hours. The prince and princess sat at the top of the great hall and drank out of a cup of clear crystal. Only true lovers could drink out of this cup, for if false lips touched it, it grew grey and dull and cloudy.

"It's quite clear that they love each other," said the little Page, "as clear as crystal!" and the king doubled his salary a second time. "What an honor!" cried all the courtiers.

After the banquet there was to be a ball. The bride and bridegroom were to dance the rose-dance together, and the king had promised to play the flute. He played very badly, but no one had ever dared to tell him so, because he was the king. Indeed, he knew only two airs, and was never quite certain which one he was playing; but it made no matter, for, whatever he did, everybody cried out, "Charming! charming!"

The last item on the program was a grand display of fireworks, to be let off exactly at midnight. The little princess had never seen a firework in her life, so the king had given orders that the royal pyrotechnist should be in attendance on the day of her marriage.

"What are fireworks like?" she had asked the prince, one morning, as she was walking on the terrace.

"They are like the aurora borealis," said the king, who always answered questions that were addressed to other people, "only much more natural. I prefer them to stars myself, as you always know when they are going to appear, and they are as delightful as my own flute-playing. You must certainly see them."

So at the end of the king's garden a great stand had been set up, and as soon as the royal pyrotechnist had put everything in its proper place, the fireworks began to talk to each other.

"The world is certainly very beautiful," cried a little squib. "Just look at those yellow tulips. Why! if they were real crackers they could not be lovelier. I am very glad I have travelled. Travel improves the mind wonderfully, and does away with all one's prejudices."

"The king's garden is not the world, you foolish squib," said a big roman candle; "the world is an enormous place, and it would take you three days to see it thoroughly."

"Any place you love is the world to you," exclaimed a pensive catherine wheel, who had been attached to an old deal box in early life, and prided herself on her broken heart; "but love is not fashionable any more, the poets have killed it. They wrote so much about it that nobody believed them, and I am not surprised. True love suffers, and is silent. I remember myself once - But it is no matter now. Romance is a thing of the past."

"Nonsense!" said the roman candle, "Romance never dies. It is like the moon, and lives for ever. The bride and bridegroom, for instance, love each other very dearly. I heard all about them this morning from a brown-paper cartridge, who happened to be staying in the same drawer as myself, and knew the latest court news."

But the catherine wheel shook her head. "Romance is dead, romance is dead, romance is dead," she murmured. She was one of those people who think that, if you say the same thing over and over a great many times, it becomes true in the end.

Suddenly, a sharp, dry cough was heard, and they all looked round.

It came from a tall, supercilious-looking rocket, who was tied to the end of a long stick. He always coughed before he made any observation, so as to attract attention.

"Ahem! ahem!" he said, and everybody listened except the poor catherine wheel, who was still shaking her head, and murmuring, "Romance is dead."

"Order! order!" cried out a cracker. He was something of a politician, and had always taken a prominent part in the local elections, so he knew the proper Parliamentary expressions to use.

"Quite dead," whispered the catherine wheel, and she went off to sleep.

As soon as there was perfect silence, the rocket coughed a third time and began. He spoke with a very slow, distinct voice, as if he was dictating his memoirs, and always looked over the shoulder of the person to whom he was talking. In fact, he had a most distinguished manner.

"How fortunate it is for the king's son," he remarked, "that he is to be married on the very day on which I am to be let off. Really, if it had been arranged beforehand, it could not have turned out better for him; but, princes are always lucky."

"Dear me!" said the little squib, "I thought it was quite

the other way, and that we were to be let off in the prince's honor."

"It may be so with you," he answered; "indeed, I have no doubt that it is, but with me it is different. I am a very remarkable rocket, and come of remarkable parents. My mother was the most celebrated catherine wheel of her day, and was renowned for her graceful dancing. When she made her great public appearance she spun round nineteen times before she went out, and each time that she did so she threw into the air seven pink stars. She was three feet and a half in diameter, and made of the very best gunpowder. My father was a rocket like myself, and of French extraction. He flew so high that the people were afraid that he would never come down again. He did, though, for he was of a kindly disposition, and he made a most brilliant descent in a shower of golden rain. The newspapers wrote about his performance in very flattering terms. Indeed, the Court Gazette called him a triumph of pylotechnic art."

"Pyrotechnic, pyrotechnic, you mean," said a bengal light; "I know it is pyrotechnic, for I saw it written on my own canister."

"Well, I said pylotechnic," answered the rocket, in a severe tone of voice, and the bengal light felt so crushed that he began at once to bully the little squibs, in order to show that he was still a person of some importance.

"I was saying," continued the rocket, "I was saying - What was I saying?"

"You were talking about yourself," replied the roman candle.

"Of course; I knew I was discussing some interesting subject when I was so rudely interrupted. I hate rudeness and bad manners of every kind, for I am extremely sensitive. No one in the whole world is so sensitive as I am, I am quite sure of that."

"What is a sensitive person?" said the cracker to the roman candle.

"A person who, because he has corns himself, always treads on other people's toes," answered the roman candle in a low whisper; and the cracker nearly exploded with laughter.

"Pray, what are you laughing at?" inquired the rocket; "I am not laughing."

"I am laughing because I am happy," replied the cracker.

"That is a very selfish reason," said the rocket angrily. "What right have you to be happy? You should be thinking about others. In fact, you should be thinking about me. I am always thinking about myself, and I expect everybody else to do the same. That is what is called sympathy. It is a beautiful virtue, and I possess it in a high degree. Suppose, for instance, anything happened to me to-night, what a misfortune that would be for every one! The prince and princess would never be happy again, their whole married life would be spoiled; and as for the king, I know he would not get over it. Really, when I begin to reflect on the importance of my position, I am almost moved to tears."

"If you want to give pleasure to others," cried the roman candle, "you had better keep yourself dry."

"Certainly," exclaimed the bengal light, who was now in better spirits; "that is only common sense."

"Common sense, indeed!" said the rocket indignantly; "you forget that I am very uncommon, and very remarkable. Why, anybody can have common sense, provided that they have no imagination. But I have imagination, for I never think of things as they really are; I always think of them as being quite different. As for keeping myself dry, there is evidently

9
5

驕傲的爆竹　The Remarkable Rocket

no one here who can at all appreciate an emotional nature. Fortunately for myself, I don't care. The only thing that sustains one through life is the consciousness of the immense inferiority of everybody else, and this is a feeling that I have always cultivated. But none of you have any hearts. Here you are laughing and making merry just as if the prince and princess had not just been married."

"Well, really," exclaimed a small fire-balloon, "why not? It is a most joyful occasion, and when I soar up into the air I intend to tell the stars all about it. You will see them twinkle when I talk to them about the pretty bride."

"Ah! what a trivial view of life!" said the rocket; "but it is only what I expected. There is nothing in you; you are hollow and empty. Why, perhaps the prince and princess may go to live in a country where there is a deep river, and perhaps they may have one only son, a little fair-haired boy with violet eyes like the prince himself; and perhaps some day he may go out to walk with his nurse; and perhaps the nurse may go to sleep under a great elder-tree; and perhaps the little boy may fall into the deep river and be drowned. What a terrible misfortune! Poor people, to lose their only son! It is really too dreadful! I shall never get over it."

"But they have not lost their only son," said the roman candle; "no misfortune has happened to them at all."

"I never said that they had," replied the rocket; "I said that they might. If they had lost their only son there would be no use in saying anything more about the matter. I hate people who cry over spilt milk. But when I think that they might lose their only son, I certainly am very much affected."

"You certainly are!" cried the bengal light. "In fact, you are the most affected person I ever met."

"You are the rudest person I ever met," said the rocket, "and you cannot understand my friendship for the prince."

"Why, you don't even know him," growled the roman candle.

"I never said I knew him," answered the rocket. "I dare say that if I knew him I should not be his friend at all. It is a very dangerous thing to know one's friends."

"You had really better keep yourself dry," said the fire-balloon. "That is the important thing."

"Very important for you, I have no doubt," answered the rocket, "but I shall weep if I choose"; and he actually burst into real tears, which flowed down his stick like rain-drops, and nearly drowned two little beetles, who were just thinking of setting up house together, and were looking for a nice dry spot to live in.

"He must have a truly romantic nature," said the catherine wheel, "for he weeps when there is nothing at all to weep about"; and she heaved a deep sigh, and thought about the deal box.

But the roman candle and the bengal light were quite indignant, and kept saying, "Humbug! humbug!" at the top of their voices. They were extremely practical, and whenever they objected to anything they called it humbug.

Then the moon rose like a wonderful silver shield; and the stars began to shine, and a sound of music came from the palace.

The prince and princess were leading the dance. They danced so beautifully that the tall white lilies peeped in at the window and watched them, and the great red poppies nodded their heads and beat time.

Then ten o'clock struck, and then eleven, and then twelve, and at the last stroke of midnight every one came out on the terrace, and the king sent for the royal pyrotechnist.

"Let the fireworks begin," said the king; and the royal pyrotechnist made a low bow, and marched down to the end of the garden. He had six attendants with him, each of whom carried a lighted torch at the end of a long pole.

It was certainly a magnificent display.

Whizz! Whizz! went the catherine wheel, as she spun round and round. Boom! Boom! went the roman candle. Then the squibs danced all over the place, and the Bengal lights made everything look scarlet. "Good-bye," cried the fire-balloon, as he soared away, dropping tiny blue sparks. Bang! Bang! answered the crackers, who were enjoying themselves immensely. Every one was a great success except the remarkable rocket. He was so damp with crying that he could not go off at all. The best thing in him was the gunpowder, and that was so wet with tears that it was of no use. All his poor relations, to whom he would never speak, except with a sneer, shot up into the sky like wonderful golden flowers with blossoms of fire. Huzza! Huzza! cried the court; and the little princess laughed with pleasure.

"I suppose they are reserving me for some grand occasion," said the Rocket; "no doubt that is what it means," and he looked more supercilious than ever.

The next day the workmen came to put everything tidy. "This is evidently a deputation," said the rocket; "I will receive them with becoming dignity" so he put his nose in the air, and began to frown severely as if he were thinking about some very important subject. But they took no notice of him at all till they were just going away. Then one of them caught sight of him. "Hallo!" he cried, "what a bad rocket!" and he threw him over the wall into the ditch.

"Bad rocket? Bad rocket?" he said, as he whirled through the air; "impossible! Grand rocket, that is what the man said. Bad and grand sound very much the same, indeed they often are the same" ; and he fell into the mud.

"It is not comfortable here," he remarked, "but no doubt it is some fashionable watering-place, and they have sent me away to recruit my health. My nerves are certainly very much shattered, and I require rest."

Then a little frog, with bright jewelled eyes, and a green mottled coat, swam up to him.

"A new arrival, I see!" said the frog. "Well, after all there is nothing like mud. Give me rainy weather and a ditch, and I am quite happy. Do you think it will be a wet afternoon? I am sure I hope so, but the sky is quite blue and cloudless. What a pity!"

"Ahem! ahem!" said the rocket, and he began to cough.

"What a delightful voice you have!" cried the frog. "Really it is quite like a croak, and croaking is of course the most musical sound in the world. You will hear our glee-club this evening. We sit in the old duck pond close by the farmer's house, and as soon as the moon rises we begin. It is so entrancing that everybody lies awake to listen to us. In fact, it was only yesterday that I heard the farmer's wife say to her mother that she could not get a wink of sleep at night on account of us. It is most gratifying to find oneself so popular."

"Ahem! ahem!" said the rocket angrily. He was very much annoyed that he could not get a word in.

"A delightful voice, certainly," continued the frog; "I hope you will come over to the duck-pond. I am off to look for my daughters. I have six beautiful daughters, and I am so afraid the pike may meet them. He is a perfect monster, and would have no hesitation in breakfasting off them. Well, good-bye: I have enjoyed our conversation very much, I assure you."

"Conversation, indeed!" said the rocket. "You have talked the whole time yourself. That is not conversation."

9 9

騎傲的爆竹　The Remarkable Rocket

"Somebody must listen," answered the frog, "and I like to do all the talking myself. It saves time, and prevents arguments."

"But I like arguments," said the rocket.

"I hope not," said the frog complacently. "Arguments are extremely vulgar, for everybody in good society holds exactly the same opinions. Good-bye a second time; I see my daughters in the distance and the little frog swam away.

"You are a very irritating person," said the rocket, "and very ill-bred. I hate people who talk about themselves, as you do, when one wants to talk about oneself, as I do. It is what I call selfishness, and selfishness is a most detestable thing, especially to any one of my temperament, for I am well known for my sympathetic nature. In fact, you should take example by me; you could not possibly have a better model. Now that you have the chance you had better avail yourself of it, for I am going back to court almost immediately. I am a great favorite at court; in fact, the prince and princess were married yesterday in my honor. Of course you know nothing of these matters, for you are a provincial."

"There is no good talking to him," said a dragon-fly, who was sitting on the top of a large brown bulrush; "no good at all, for he has gone away."

"Well, that is his loss, not mine," answered the rocket. "I am not going to stop talking to him merely because he pays no attention. I like hearing myself talk. It is one of my greatest pleasures. I often have long conversations all by myself, and I am so clever that sometimes I don't understand a single word of what I am saying."

"Then you should certainly lecture on philosophy," said the dragon- fly; and he spread a pair of lovely gauze wings and soared away into the sky.

"How very silly of him not to stay here!" said the rocket. "I am sure that he has not often got such a chance of improving his mind. However, I don't care a bit. Genius like mine is sure to be appreciated some day"; and he sank down a little deeper into the mud.

After some time a large white duck swam up to him. She had yellow legs, and webbed feet, and was considered a great beauty on account of her waddle.

"Quack, quack, quack," she said. "What a curious shape you are! May I ask were you born like that, or is it the result of an accident?"

"It is quite evident that you have always lived in the country," answered the rocket, "otherwise you would know who I am. However, I excuse your ignorance. It would be unfair to expect other people to be as remarkable as oneself. You will no doubt be surprised to hear that I can fly up into the sky, and come down in a shower of golden rain."

"I don't think much of that," said the duck, "as I cannot see what use it is to any one. Now, if you could plough the fields like the ox, or draw a cart like the horse, or look after the sheep like the collie-dog, that would be something."

"My good creature," cried the rocket in a very haughty tone of voice, "I see that you belong to the lower orders. A person of my position is never useful. We have certain accomplishments, and that is more than sufficient. I have no sympathy myself with industry of any kind, least of all with such industries as you seem to recommend. Indeed, I have always been of opinion that hard work is simply the refuge of people who have nothing whatever to do."

"Well, well," said the duck, who was of a very peaceable disposition, and never quarrelled with any one, "everybody has different tastes. I hope, at any rate, that you are going to take up your residence here."

"Oh! dear no," cried the rocket. "I am merely a visitor, a distinguished visitor. The fact is that I find this place rather tedious. There is neither society here, nor solitude. In fact, it is essentially suburban. I shall probably go back to court, for I know that I am destined to make a sensation in the world."

"I had thoughts of entering public life once myself," remarked the duck; "there are so many things that need reforming. Indeed, I took the chair at a meeting some time ago, and we passed resolutions condemning everything that we did not like. However, they did not seem to have much effect. Now I go in for domesticity, and look after my family."

"I am made for public life," said the rocket, "and so are all my relations, even the humblest of them. Whenever we appear we excite great attention. I have not actually appeared myself, but when I do so it will be a magnificent sight. As for domesticity, it ages one rapidly, and distracts one's mind from higher things."

"Ah! the higher things of life, how fine they are!" said the duck; "and that reminds me how hungry I feel" : and she swam away down the stream, saying, "Quack, quack, quack."

"Come back! come back!" screamed the rocket, "I have a great deal to say to you" ; but the duck paid no attention to him. "I am glad that she has gone," he said to himself, "she has a decidedly middle-class mind" ; and he sank a little deeper still into the mud, and began to think about the loneliness of genius, when suddenly two little boys in white smocks came running down the bank, with a kettle and some faggots.

"This must be the deputation," said the rocket, and he tried to look very dignified.

"Hallo!" cried one of the boys, "look at this old stick! I wonder how it came here" ; and he picked the rocket out of the ditch.

"Old stick!" said the rocket, "impossible! gold stick, that is what he said. gold stick is very complimentary. In fact, he mistakes me for one of the court dignitaries!"

"Let us put it into the fire!" said the other boy, "it will help to boil the kettle."

So they piled the faggots together, and put the rocket on top, and lit the fire.

"This is magnificent," cried the rocket, "they are going to let me off in broad day-light, so that every one can see me."

"We will go to sleep now," they said, "and when we wake up the kettle will be boiled" ; and they lay down on the grass, and shut their eyes.

The rocket was very damp, so he took a long time to burn. At last, however, the fire caught him.

"Now I am going off!" he cried, and he made himself very stiff and straight. "I know I shall go much higher than the stars, much higher than the moon, much higher than the sun. In fact, I shall go so high that - "

Fizz! Fizz! Fizz! and he went straight up into the air.

"Delightful!" he cried, "I shall go on like this for ever. What a success I am!"

But nobody saw him.

Then he began to feel a curious tingling sensation all over him.

"Now I am going to explode," he cried. "I shall set the whole world on fire, and make such a noise that nobody will talk about anything else for a whole year." And he certainly did explode. Bang! Bang! Bang! went the gunpowder. There was no doubt about it.

But nobody heard him, not even the two little boys, for they were sound asleep.

Then all that was left of him was the stick, and this fell down on the back of a goose who was taking a walk by the side of the ditch.

"Good heavens!" cried the goose. "It is going to rain sticks" ; and she rushed into the water.

"I knew I should create a great sensation," gasped the rocket, and he went out.

年輕的國王

貧窮爬過暗無天日的巷道，飢餓地看著我們，

清晨，悲慘將我們搖醒，夜裡陪著我們的是恥辱。

然而，這些事與你何干？

你又不屬於我們這一群。

你的臉看起來太幸福了。

這是加冕典禮的前一夜，即將登基的年輕國王正獨自一人坐在他的寢宮裡。他的朝臣們全按照白天的禮節俯首觸地鞠躬告退，退到皇宮大廳裡，去上「宮廷禮儀學」教授的最後幾堂課。那些大臣裡有些人仍保有非常自然的儀態，然而，身為朝廷大臣卻還這麼自然，我不得不說，此乃非常不得體的行為。

那少年（因為他只不過是一個十六歲的男孩）對朝臣們的離開鬆了口氣，他往後仰躺，跌進了裝飾華麗的長椅，靠在柔軟舒適的靠墊上。他就這麼躺在那兒，眼睛睜得大大的，嘴巴張開著，活像森林裡的牧神，也像林子裡剛被獵人陷阱逮到的幼獸。

事實上，他的確是由一群尋覓者在「踏破鐵鞋無覓處，得來全不費工夫」的機緣裡遇上的。那時他赤著身子，手裡握了根笛子，替一位窮牧羊人照顧羊群。他由這位牧羊人撫養長大，也一直以為自己是牧羊人的兒子。

國王的獨生女和一名階級卑下的男子祕密結婚，生下了一個男孩。有人說這陌生男子以神乎其技的笛聲擄獲公主的心；也有人說這個陌生男子是一位來自他國的藝術家，因為公主對他展現過分的好感，使得他在完成大教堂的工作前就神祕地失蹤了。公主和陌生男子所生的孩子，在出生一週後就被人趁公主熟睡之際偷抱走。這孩子被送往一戶鄉下牧羊人家中，他們沒有子女，住在離城裡很遠的林間深處，光是騎馬也得花上一天以上的時間才能到達。公主醒來之後不及一小時便與世長辭，御醫說她是憂傷成疾致死，其他人則說她是服毒而死。國王的心腹則已將公主之子快馬送至牧羊人家中。公主下葬在城門後方一處荒涼的墓地中，據說，公主是和一位長著外國輪廓、俊美非凡的男子葬在一起，這名男子雙手被反綁，胸前仍留有刀刺的斑斑血跡。

　　以上就是人們交頭接耳流傳開來的故事。後來，病入膏肓的國王不知是後悔當年鑄下的大錯，或者只是單純地不想讓王位旁落，於是下令帶回當年被送走的孩子，並且宣佈立他為王位繼承人。

　　男孩似乎一入籍皇家就對那些貴重的華美之物有著異乎尋常的喜愛。服侍他的僕從常對人訴說，他見到為自己準備的精緻衣裳和名貴珠寶時是多麼地讚嘆，而且以樂得近乎瘋狂的姿態脫下原本粗糙的皮製上衣和羊皮斗篷。他有時會很懷念過去自由自在的林間生活，也總是對每天冗長而沉悶的宮廷會議感到不耐煩，然而身為這座華美的宮殿（人們稱之為「歡樂宮」）的主人，對他而言卻是新鮮有趣的愉快經驗。只要能逃離會議室或謁見室，他就會跑下以青銅鍍金獅子徽為標誌、以明亮斑岩為材質的壯麗階梯，尋訪每一個房間，拜訪每一條長廊，就像想以止痛劑緩解痛楚的人那樣，如此尋求美的撫慰也能讓人從病中康復。

　　在這些對男孩來說有如發現之旅的過程中（事實上也是他真正的寶地旅行），有時候會由穿著華美、身形苗條、金髮的宮廷書僮們陪同；然而有更多時候卻是他獨自一人，體驗心中的靈光乍現。

這幾乎是參透玄機的一種學習方式，因為藝術的奧祕只可祕密地習得，而美，如同智慧，只接受孤單的崇拜者。

　　這段時期裡，有關男孩的許多奇怪傳聞開始不脛而走。有人說，一位胖市長代表市民前來向他獻上祝賀詞時，看到他跪在一幅剛從威尼斯送來、描述對新神祇之崇拜的畫像前，真誠地讚嘆著。還有一次，他失蹤了好幾個小時。後來，大家好不容易才在皇宮北邊角樓群中的一個小房間發現他。當時，他神情恍惚，目不轉睛地看著一尊以寶玉雕刻而成的希臘神話中的美男子阿多尼斯。傳聞還說，他曾將溫熱的雙唇貼在一尊從河裡打撈上來、歷史悠久的奴隸雕像前額。甚至他還曾經花上一整晚觀看映著月光的英俊牧童，那位希臘神話中的安狄米倫銀製肖像。

　　對男孩而言，一切稀有、珍貴的物品都有著非比尋常的魅力，為了滿足擁有稀世真品的慾望，他派出了許多商人，或到北海向辛苦的漁夫們蒐購琥珀，或到埃及尋找只在國王的墓穴才有、傳說中神祕的綠松石，或到波斯購買絲製的地毯和彩繪的陶器，或到印度採買輕紗和彩色的象牙、月長石、翡翠手鐲、白檀木、藍色琺瑯，以及用上好羊毛製成的圍巾。

　　然而，最讓他魂牽夢縈的則是那件在加冕典禮上要穿的外袍，那是件由金線織成的袍子；此外，他在那個大日子裡要穿戴的行頭，還有鑲嵌著紅寶石的皇冠，以及飾有成排珍珠的王杖。事實上，今晚的他坐在昂貴奢華的長椅上，眼睛注視著壁爐裡熊熊燃燒的大塊松木，腦子裡想的就是這些事物。這些行頭是由最著名的藝術家所設計，而且早在幾個月前就已向他提出報告，他也下令技師們日夜趕工完成工作，此外，蒐購上好珠寶的行動也在全世界展開。年輕的王位繼承人想像著，自己披上國王專屬的華貴外袍，站在教堂裡的大祭壇前；他的臉上更盪漾著孩子似的笑容，深邃的雙眸閃耀著明亮的光彩。

　　過了一會兒，他從長椅上站起來，斜倚著雕刻精美的煙囪遮檐，環視微暗的寢宮。四周牆上掛著精緻美絕的掛毯，牆角處則是一座鑲嵌有瑪瑙和琉璃的大櫥櫃，窗前擺放著一個純金精鑲的小玻璃櫥，裡面陳列著幾只精緻的威尼斯式高腳杯，還有一只用黑紋鎬瑪瑙製成的咖啡杯。絲質床單上繡有蒼白的罌粟花，彷彿脫胎自疲憊已極的睡神手中，懸於睡床上空的絲絨蓋篷則由高大的象牙支撐著，其上還延伸出一大叢鴕鳥的羽毛，看起來彷彿從格子狀的天花板上冒出幾朵銀白海浪。有尊青銅製作、笑開來的納希瑟斯（譯註：希臘神話中的美少年），正將一面擦拭得發亮的鏡子高舉於頭頂。寫字檯上擺著一只紫水晶製成的淺平底的碗。

遠眺窗外，大教堂的巨大圓頂清晰可見，在朦朧的月影下，它彷若一顆罩在影子般大屋子上空的泡泡，而睏倦的衛兵正在河畔的陽臺上來回逡巡。遠處的果樹園裡，一隻夜鶯正在引吭高歌。一陣醉人的茉莉花香透過開著的窗戶飄了進來。男孩將額前的棕色鬈髮向後拂去，拿起一把絃樂器，隨手撥弄著。然而，他沉重的眼皮幾乎闔起，心頭浮上一股異樣的沉鬱感，可是不久之前他還對這些奇特而神祕的華美物件如此地狂熱喜愛啊。

當鐘樓傳來午夜時分的鐘聲時，他拉了拉鈴，侍從們立刻進來，按照禮節為他脫去衣飾，並在他雙手澆上玫瑰花水，在枕頭上撒下鮮花。侍從們離開一會兒之後，他便進入了夢鄉。

睡著之後，他做了一個夢。

他猜自己所在位置是一座低而長的閣樓，四周充滿織布機吵雜的聲響。慘淡的日光從鐵窗外透進來，將面容憔悴枯槁、佝僂著身子工作的織工們映在他眼前。面色慘白、滿臉病容的孩子們蹲伏在一個大橫木旁，當紡織機上的梭推過來時，他們將厚重的壓條抬起；當紡梭停下來時，他們放下已抬起的壓條，將線壓在一塊兒。這些孩子的臉上顯出因飢餓而產生的痛苦，脆弱的小手不住地抖動著；另外有一些憔悴的婦人坐在桌旁做針線活。四周充滿一股令人作嘔的味道，空氣污濁而沉重，牆壁潮濕得可以滴出水來。

這位即將登基的年輕國王走到一位織工身旁，站在那兒，目不轉睛地看著。

織工怒目回視他，說道：「你為什麼這樣看我？你是我們主人派來監視我們的間諜吧？」

「你們的主人是誰？」年輕的國王問道。

「我們的主人！」織工大叫，聲音充滿痛苦。「他跟我一樣是人，只不過他穿著綾羅綢緞，而我穿破衣。我因飢餓而消瘦，他卻不會因為吃得過多而感到丁點不適。」

「這裡是自由樂土，」年輕的國王說道，「沒有人能當你是奴隸。」

「在戰爭中，」織工答道，「強者役使弱者為奴，在太平時期，富人役使窮人為奴。我們必須工作才能維持生計，而他們又以苛刻的工資折磨我們。窮人整天勞苦，所得的一切卻成為富人累積在保險櫃中的黃金，而我們的子弟早在長大成人以前就已凋萎，我們所摯愛的孩子面容也變得僵硬可怕。我們榨葡萄釀酒，卻由別人品嚐其美味；我們播撒麥種，卻由別人收割。我們身上套著枷鎖，卻沒有人能看見；我們是奴隸，別人卻說我們是自由的。」

「每個人都一樣嗎？」年輕的國王問道。

「每個人都一樣。」織工答道，「年少的、年長的、女人、男人、小孩、老人全都一樣。商人苛刻虐待我們，而我們除了照他們的命令行事之外，別無選擇。牧師走過我們身邊也只能禱告，沒有人關心我們。貧窮爬過暗無天日的巷道，飢餓地看著我們，尾隨其後的則是腫脹著臉的犯罪率。清晨，悲慘將我們搖醒，夜裡陪著我們的是恥辱。然而，這些事與你何干？你又不屬於我們這一群。你的臉看起來太幸福了。」織工眉頭緊鎖地別過臉去，繼續拿起織布機上的紡梭，來回穿動。年輕的國王瞧見，織布機上的布匹是用金線織的。

他打了一個寒顫，問織工道：「你正在織的這一件袍子是做什麼用的？」

「這是國王在加冕典禮上要穿的袍子，」織工道，「跟你有什麼關係嗎？」

年輕的國王一聽慘叫一聲，醒了過來，驚惶地看看四周！他仍在自己的寢宮裡。他望向窗外，看見微暗的空中掛著一輪蜂蜜色的明月。

於是他再度進入夢鄉，這是他第二個夢境。

他猜自己正躺在一艘由一百個奴隸所划動的大船甲板上，他身旁的地毯上坐著這艘大船的船長。船長的皮膚像黑檀木般黝黑，頭上戴著鮮紅色的絲質頭巾，厚實的耳垂上掛了一副大銀耳環，手中拿著象牙做成的天秤。

奴隸們身上除了破爛不堪的纏腰布，幾近全裸，而且一個接一個全被鐵鍊鍊住。酷熱的豔陽火辣地烤著他們，船上的黑人不住地跑來跑去，不時用鞭子抽打他們。奴隸們伸出瘦骨嶙峋的手臂，推著沉重的槳，向前划去。槳葉激盪出鹹鹹的水花。

最後，他們來到一個小港灣，開始測量水深。岸上吹來一陣微風，令甲板和大三角帆都罩上一層細細的紅土。三個阿拉伯人騎著野驢過來，朝他們投擲手裡的矛。船長見狀，拿起一把彩色的弓，飛射出一箭，正中其中一人的咽喉。中箭的那人重重摔在地上，他的同伴快快離開。一個蒙著黃色面紗的婦女坐在漸行漸遠的一匹駱駝上，不時地回頭看看倒在地上的死屍。

大船一下好錨，收好帆，黑人就進到船艙搬出一副用鉛塊加重的長繩梯。船長拋下繩梯，將一端緊緊於船上的兩個鐵支柱。然後，黑人從奴隸群中抓了一個年紀最小的奴隸來，撤掉他的腳鐐，在他的鼻孔和耳中塞上蠟，還在他的腰上綁了一塊大石頭。小奴隸虛弱地攀下繩梯，消失在海面；他潛入海中的那處水面仍冒出一些泡泡，其他幾個奴隸則在船上緊張地偷看著。一位魔法師坐在船首，正單調地敲擊著鼓。

過了一會兒，方才潛入水中的小奴隸浮出水面，急喘不已地攀住繩梯，右手握著一顆珍珠。黑人一把搶過奴隸手中的珍珠，然後又將他推回海中。奴隸們全都趴在槳柄上睡著了。

小奴隸一次又一次地浮出水面，每次都交上來一顆美麗的珍珠。船長秤著這些珍珠的重量，然後將它們裝進一只小小的綠色皮袋裡。

年輕的國王想說話，舌頭卻像黏住了上顎似的，而且嘴唇也沒辦法動。黑人們彼此喋喋不休地私語著，而且開始為一串耀眼的念珠爭吵。兩隻蒼鷺繞著船，一圈又一圈地飛翔。

之後，小奴隸最後一次浮上水面，也帶上來最美的一顆珍珠，它的形狀如一輪滿月，顏色潔白更甚晨星。然而，小奴隸的臉卻蒼白得可怕，他在甲板上一躺下，鮮血立刻從他的鼻孔和耳中噴出。他掙扎著顫動了一會兒，便再也不省人事了。黑人聳聳肩，將死去的小奴隸拋出船外。

船長笑著接過這顆珍珠。他一看到它，便將之貼在額頭，彎腰說道：「就是這顆珍珠了，國王的王杖就是它的歸處。」說罷，船長向黑人打了個手勢，要他們起錨開航。

年輕的國王一聽到船長的話，慘叫一聲，醒了過來。他看看窗外，破曉的纖纖十指正抓著光亮快要褪盡的繁星。

於是他再度入睡，並且造訪另一個夢境。

他猜自己正走在一座光線微暗的森林中，裡頭長著奇怪的水果和美麗的有毒花卉。在他經過的路上有毒蛇對他嘶嘶吐信，還有聰明伶俐的鸚鵡尖聲叫著在樹上飛來飛去，巨大的烏龜在熱泥巴堆裡打盹，樹上滿是無尾猿和孔雀。

他一直走著，終於來到森林的邊緣。在那兒，他看到數不清的一大群人在乾涸的河床上辛勤地工作著，而且像螞蟻似的聚在一起。有些在地上挖出深坑，然後走進坑裡；有些則用大斧劈開岩石；而其他人則在沙堆裡匍匐搜索，他們將仙人掌連根拔起，踩碎其上的鮮紅色花朵。那些人個個匆忙，彼此招呼著前進，沒有一個人是閒散的。

「死亡」和「貪婪」從黑暗的洞穴裡注視著他們，死亡說道：「我累了，把三分之一的人給我，讓我走吧。」

貪婪卻搖搖頭，答道：「他們是我的僕役。」

死亡繼續問道：「妳手裡拿著的是什麼東西？」

「我有三顆穀粒，」她答道，「你問這個幹什麼？」

「給我一顆，」死亡央求道，「我要把它種在我的園子裡，給我一顆就好，我拿了就走。」

「我什麼也不給你。」貪婪說著，把手藏進大衣的夾層中。

死亡笑了，取出一個杯子，探進水池中，舀出瘧疾。瘧疾行過那一群人，令三分之一的人喪生。尾隨瘧疾而至的是一陣寒霧，以及隨行其側的水蛇。

當貪婪看到人群中的三分之一已經死亡時，她捶胸痛哭。她捶打著自己貧瘠的胸膛，大哭道：「你殺了我三分之一的僕役，快給我滾開。韃靼山區已經爆發戰事，兩邊的國王都在呼喚你。阿富汗人宰了黑公牛，部隊正向戰場開拔。他們全副武裝地上陣了。對你而言，我的小村根本不值得一顧，你還留在這兒幹什麼？快滾吧，不要再回來了。」

「才不咧，」死亡答道，「除非妳給我一顆妳手上的穀粒，否則我絕不離開。」

但是貪婪緊握拳頭，咬牙切齒，從牙縫迸出一句話：「我什麼也不會給你。」

死亡笑道，取了一只杯子和石塊，扔進森林裡，於是野生的毒胡蘿蔔叢中冒出身著火焰外袍的熱病。熱病走過人群，伸手觸碰人們，凡被熱病碰過的人霎時全都倒地不起。就連熱病踩過的草地也枯萎了。

貪婪不住地顫慄著，將灰燼撒在頭上，大叫道：「你好殘忍，你好殘忍。印度的城市正在鬧飢荒；撒馬爾罕正為乾旱所苦；埃及的城市不僅鬧飢荒，更有大批蝗蟲從沙漠地帶前來拜訪。尼羅河不幫忙農田耕作，祭司詛咒了埃及掌管生命和死亡的神祇。到那些需要你的人那兒去吧，不要再碰我的僕役了。」

「才不咧，」死亡答道，「除非妳給我一顆妳手上的穀粒，否則我絕不離開。」

「我什麼也不會給你。」貪婪說道。

死亡再次笑笑，吹了個口哨，一個女人從空中應聲而出。她的額頭上寫著瘟疫，身旁聚集著一群瘦瘦的禿鷹。她一伸展雙臂，整座村子盡在她的籠罩之下，再沒有一個活著的人。

貪婪慘叫著逃進森林，死亡則躍上他的紅色坐騎，疾馳而去，速度比風還快。

村莊遠處的泥地外，則有長著鱗片的可怕生物、大蜥蜴，以及在沙中來回逡巡、鼻孔噴著煙的猛獸。

年輕的國王哭了，他問道：「他們是什麼人？在尋找什麼呢？」

「他們在尋找要鑲嵌在國王皇冠上的寶石。」站在他身邊的一個人答道。

年輕的國王轉過身，看見一位衣著打扮像是朝聖者的人，手裡握著一面銀製的鏡子。

年輕的國王蒼白著臉問道：「哪一位國王？」

像朝聖者的人回答道：「看著鏡子，你就可以知道答案了。」

年輕的國王依言而行，卻在鏡中看見自己……

他大叫一聲，醒了過來，明亮的日光瀉進屋裡，花園裡一片粲然，群鳥也快樂地歌唱。

內廷大臣和宮內其他重臣們依序進來向他鞠躬行禮，服侍他的書僮將金線織成的皇袍、耀眼光燦的皇冠和威儀閃亮的王杖擺在他面前。

年輕的國王看著這些寶貝，它們的確精緻而美麗，堪稱他所見過最美的東西。然而，他卻想起夢中所見情景，於是他告訴大臣們：「把這些東西拿走，我不想穿戴這些東西。」

朝臣們大吃一驚，不過有些人則笑了出來，因為他們覺得年輕的國王不過是開開玩笑罷了。

但是，年輕的國王卻語氣堅定地重申，還說道：「把這些東西拿走，不要讓我再看到它們。雖然今天是我的加冕典禮，不過，我是不會穿戴它們的。因為這件為我準備的皇袍是由痛苦慘白的手用憂傷的織布機織成的；寶石的中心處沾染著血跡，而珍珠裡頭飽含死亡。」年輕的國王將他的三個夢境告訴大家。

朝臣們聽完之後，彼此對看著，輕聲說道：「他一定是瘋了！夢不過就是夢而已，正常人不該為這種事費心的。對於那些為我們辛勤勞苦的人，我們還能怎麼樣呢？人們為了生活而付出代價，不是理所當然的嗎？」

內廷大臣對年輕的國王勸道：「陛下，我懇求你將這些晦澀的想法置之於腦後，穿上這華美的皇袍，戴上皇冠。如果你不穿上國王該穿的服飾，那麼人們怎麼知道你就是國王陛下呢？」

年輕的國王看著他，問道：「真的是這樣嗎？如果我沒有穿上國王該穿的服飾，人們就不知道我是一國之君嗎？」

「是的，國王陛下。」內廷大臣大聲地回答。

「我想，這世界上的確有許多看起來很像國王的人，」年輕的國王說道，「不過，也許正像你所說的，他們都沒有穿戴國王的服飾，所以人們認不出他們來。即使如此，我也不想穿上這件皇袍，戴上這頂皇冠。我怎麼來到皇宮裡，就要怎麼走出皇宮去。」

於是，他下令所有的人都離開，只留下一個小他一歲的書僮陪伴他。年輕的國王自己用潔淨的水梳洗，然後，他打開一座巨型的彩色櫥櫃，取出他過往在山坡上為牧羊人看管羊群時，所穿的皮製衣服和粗糙的羊皮斗篷。穿戴整齊之後，手裡還握著一根簡陋的牧羊人手杖。

書僮看著他，驚訝得瞪大一雙湛藍大眼，微笑道：「國王陛下，我看見你的皇袍和王杖了，可是你沒戴皇冠哪？」

年輕的國王隨手摘下陽臺上蔓生進來的野薔薇花枝，將它彎曲成圓，然後戴在自己頭上。

「這就是我的皇冠。」年輕的國王說道。

他就以這樣的裝扮走出了寢宮，走進王公貴族們正等待著他的大廳。

他們一看到他的樣子便笑得人仰馬翻，有些貴族對他大叫道：「國王陛下，人們期待一見的是他們的國王，你卻帶了個乞丐來。」另外有些人則生氣評道：「他使我們國家蒙羞，根本不配當我們的主人。」對於這一切批評，年輕的國王始終不發一語，他走過他們面前，走下明亮的斑岩階梯，走出青銅大門，跨上馬背，直向大教堂前進，小書僮則跟在他身邊跑著。

街上的人們看到他笑道：「國王身邊的小丑來囉。」他們嘲諷著年輕的國王。

於是他拉住馬，說道：「我不是小丑，我是你們的國王。」而且他將自己的三個夢境告訴他們。

人群裡走出一個人，譏諷地說道：「先生，你大概不知道，窮人得倚靠奢華的富人而生存吧？你們的浮華餵養了我們，你們的罪惡賜給我們食物。為苛刻的主人工作是一種痛苦，但是找不到主人，沒有工作卻更痛苦。你以為天上會掉下食物來嗎？你對這一切有解決的對策嗎？你可以對買方說『你該給這些錢』，然後對賣方說『你該以這個價錢賣出』嗎？我想不行吧。所以，回你的皇宮去，披上你那高貴華美的衣飾吧。對於我們和我們所受的痛苦，你又能怎麼樣呢？」

「富人和窮人不是兄弟嗎？」年輕的國王問道。

「是啊，」那人回答道，「我們富人哥哥的名字就叫該隱。」

（譯註：該隱在《聖經中》被記載，謀殺了其弟亞伯。）

年輕的國王雙眼飽含淚水，他在眾人的議論聲中繼續策馬前進，而身旁的書僮覺得愈來愈害怕，便離開了他。

年輕的國王來到教堂門口，守衛的士兵卻用戟擋住門口，說道：「你來這兒幹什麼？除了國王之外，誰也不准進這個門。」

年輕的國王氣紅了臉，他告訴守衛：「我就是國王。」然後一把推開他們架在門口的戟，走進大教堂。

老主教看見身穿牧羊人衣服的年輕國王走進來，滿臉疑惑地從座位上走下來迎接他，對他說道：「孩子，這是國王的裝扮嗎？我該用什麼樣的皇冠來為你加冕？我該將什麼樣的王杖交到你手中？對你而言，這該是喜悅的一天，而不是自取羞辱的一天。」

「喜悅，該穿上憂傷所織成的衣服嗎？」年輕的國王說道。然後他告訴老主教他的三個夢境。

老主教一聽完，眉頭深鎖，說道：「孩子，我年紀大了，所剩的時日不多，我知道在這廣大的世界上存在著許多罪惡。粗暴的搶匪從山裡下來，劫走小孩，然後將他們賣給摩爾人。獅子躺在地上靜候前來的旅行商隊，然後縱身撲向駱駝。野豬將村莊裡的穀物連根刨起，狐狸嚙咬山坡上的葡萄藤。海盜盤據著海岸，放火燒了漁人的船，拿走他們捕魚的工具。鹹濕的沼澤地住有痲瘋病患者，他們住在蘆葦編成的屋子裡，沒有人願意靠近他們。乞丐在城裡四處流浪，和野狗一同分享食物。

「你能阻止這些事情發生嗎？你會讓痲瘋病患睡你的床，讓乞丐和你同桌吃飯嗎？獅子會聽你的命令，野豬會服從你嗎？上帝的作為自有上帝的旨意，不是嗎？所以，我不贊同你的作法。快回皇宮去，讓你的臉龐充滿喜悅，換上和國王的身分相稱的服飾，我會用黃金打造的皇冠為你加冕，將珍珠飾成的王杖交到你手上。至於你的夢境，忘了吧。對個人而言，人間的負擔大得無法承受，而人世間的苦難也重得無法負荷。」

「你在這座屋子裡說這樣的話？」年輕的國王說道，大踏步走過老主教身邊，登上祭壇的階梯，站在耶穌像前。

他站在耶穌像前，左手和右手上各拿了黃金打造成的精緻容器——高腳杯裡裝盛著黃酒，小瓶子裡裝盛著聖油。

他跪了下來，蠟燭在鑲嵌著寶石的神龕上燦爛地燃燒著，馨香的煙繞成淡藍色圈狀，冉冉地朝屋頂飄去。他低下頭來祈禱，穿著筆挺袍服的教士們悄悄地離開祭壇。

突然間，外面街道傳來一陣狂亂的喧囂，貴族們戴著頭盔，手裡拿著出鞘的寶劍和閃亮的盾牌，衝了進來。

「那個作夢的傢伙在哪裡？」他們大叫道，「那個穿得像乞丐的國王在哪裡？那個為我們國家帶來恥辱的男孩在哪裡？我們一定得殺了他，他根本不夠資格統治我們。」

年輕的國王再度低頭祈禱，他祈禱完畢後站起來，轉過身去，悲傷地看著他們。

看哪！日光從彩色的窗戶透進來，傾瀉在他身上，陽光圍繞著他，織成一件皇袍，比那件為了他加冕典禮所織的袍服還要華美。死去的植物開出了花朵，盛綻的百合花比珍珠還要潔白；枯萎的玫瑰花叢也綻放出比紅寶石還要豔紅的紅玫瑰。百合花的花朵，潔白勝珍珠，花梗也閃耀著銀光；紅玫瑰的花朵，豔紅賽過紅寶石，葉片有如金箔。

他站在那兒，身著國王的服飾，而鑲嵌著寶石的神龕大門打開了，從色彩繽紛的水晶聖體匣上射出一道不尋常的神祕光芒。他站在那兒，身著國王的服飾，上帝的榮光充滿整座教堂，光芒於壁龕上流淌著，令其上的聖者塑像有如正在行進。他穿著國王專屬的精緻衣裳站在眾人面前，風琴奏出響亮的樂曲，喇叭手開始吹奏喇叭，唱詩歌的男孩們也開始獻唱。

人們心存敬畏地跪了下來，貴族們將劍收回鞘中，宣誓對他效忠，而老主教則蒼白著臉，雙手發顫——「比我更偉大的那一位已經為你加冕了。」他大叫道，在年輕的國王面前跪下。

年輕的國王走下高築的祭壇，在人群的簇擁中走上歸途。不過卻沒有人敢直視他的臉，因為他看起來就像個天使。

The Young King

It was the night before the day fixed for his coronation, and the young King was sitting alone in his beautiful chamber. His courtiers had all taken their leave of him, bowing their heads to the ground, according to the ceremonious usage of the day, and had retired to the Great Hall of the Palace, to receive a few last lessons from the Professor of Etiquette; there being some of them who had still quite natural manners, which in a courtier is, I need hardly say, a very grave offence.

The lad - for he was only a lad, being but sixteen years of age - was not sorry at their departure, and had flung himself back with a deep sigh of relief on the soft cushions of his embroidered couch, lying there, wild-eyed and open-mouthed, like a brown woodland Faun, or some young animal of the forest newly snared by the hunters.

And, indeed, it was the hunters who had found him, coming upon him almost by chance as, bare-limbed and pipe in hand, he was following the flock of the poor goatherd who had brought him up, and whose son he had always fancied himself to be. The child of the old King's only daughter by a secret marriage with one much beneath her in station - a stranger, some said, who, by the wonderful magic of his lute-playing, had made the young Princess love him; while others spoke of an artist from Rimini, to whom the Princess had shown much, perhaps too much honor, and who had suddenly disappeared from the city, leaving his work in the Cathedral unfinished - he had been, when but a week old, stolen away from his mother's side, as she slept, and given into the charge of a common peasant and his wife, who were without children of their own, and lived in a remote part of the forest, more than a day's ride from the town. Grief, or the plague, as the court physician stated, or, as some suggested, a swift Italian poison administered in a cup of spiced wine, slew, within an hour of her wakening, the white girl who had given him birth, and as the trusty messenger who bare the child across his saddle-bow, stooped from his weary horse and knocked at the rude door of the goatherd's hut, the body of the Princess was being lowered into an open grave that had been dug in a deserted churchyard, beyond the city gates, a grave where, it was said, that another body was also lying, that of a young man of marvellous and foreign beauty, whose hands were tied behind him with a knotted cord, and whose breast was stabbed with many red wounds.

Such, at least, was the story that men whispered to each other. Certain it was that the old King, when on his death-bed, whether moved by remorse for his great sin, or merely desiring that the kingdom should not pass away from his line, had had the lad sent for, and, in the presence of the Council, had acknowledged him as his heir.

And it seems that from the very first moment of his recognition he had shown signs of that strange passion for beauty that was destined to have so great an influence over his life. Those who accompanied him to the suite of rooms set apart for his service, often spoke of the cry of pleasure that broke from his lips when he saw the delicate raiment and rich jewels that had been prepared for him, and of the almost fierce joy with which he flung aside his rough leathern tunic and coarse sheepskin cloak. He missed, indeed, at times the fine freedom of his forest life, and was always apt to chafe at the tedious Court ceremonies that occupied so much of each day, but the wonderful palace - Joyeuse, as they called it - of which he now found himself lord, seemed to him to be a new world fresh-fashioned for his delight; and as soon as he could escape from the council-board or audience-chamber, he would run down the great staircase, with its lions of gilt bronze and its steps of bright porphyry, and wander from room to room, and from corridor to corridor, like one who was seeking to find in beauty an anodyne from pain, a sort of restoration from sickness.

Upon these journeys of discovery, as he would call them - and, indeed, they were to him real voyages through a marvellous land, he would sometimes be accompanied by the slim, fair-haired Court pages, with their floating mantles, and gay fluttering ribands; but more often he would be alone, feeling through a certain quick instinct, which was almost a divination, that the secrets of art are best learned in secret, and that Beauty, like Wisdom, loves the lonely worshipper.

Many curious stories were related about him at this period. It was said that a stout Burgomaster, who had come to deliver a florid oratorical address on behalf of the citizens of the town, had caught sight of him kneeling in real adoration before a great picture that had just been brought from Venice, and that seemed to herald the worship of some new gods. On another occasion he had been missed for several hours, and after a lengthened search had been discovered in a little chamber in one of the northern turrets of the palace gazing, as one in a trance, at a Greek gem carved with the figure of Adonis. He had been seen, so the tale ran, pressing his warm lips to the marble brow of an antique statue that had been discovered in the bed of the river on the occasion of the building of the stone bridge, and was inscribed with the name of the Bithynian slave of Hadrian. He had passed a whole night in noting the effect of the moonlight on a silver image of Endymion.

All rare and costly materials had certainly a great fascination for him, and in his eagerness to procure them he had sent away many merchants, some to traffic for amber with the rough fisher-folk of the north seas, some to Egypt to look for that curious green turquoise which is found only in the tombs of kings, and is said to possess magical properties, some to Persia for silken carpets and painted pottery, and others to India to buy gauze and stained ivory, moonstones and bracelets of jade, sandalwood and blue enamel and shawls of fine wool.

But what had occupied him most was the robe he was to wear at his coronation, the robe of tissued gold, and the ruby-studded crown, and the sceptre with its rows and rings of pearls. Indeed, it was of this that he was thinking to-night, as he lay back on his luxurious couch, watching the great pinewood log that was burning itself out on the open hearth. The designs, which were from the hands of the most famous artists of the time, had been submitted to him many months before, and he had given orders that the artificers were to toil night and day to carry them out, and that the whole world was to be searched for jewels that would be worthy of their work. He saw himself in fancy standing at the high altar of the cathedral in the fair raiment of a King, and a smile played and lingered about his boyish lips, and lit up with a bright luster his dark woodland eyes.

After some time he rose from his seat, and leaning against the carved penthouse of the chimney, looked round at the dimly-lit room. The walls were hung with rich tapestries representing the Triumph of Beauty. A large press, inlaid with agate and lapis-lazuli, filled one corner, and facing the window stood a curiously wrought cabinet with lacquer panels of powdered and mosaiced gold, on which were placed some delicate goblets of Venetian glass, and a cup of dark-veined onyx. Pale poppies were broidered on the silk coverlet of the bed, as though they had fallen from the tired hands of sleep, and tall reeds of fluted ivory bare up the velvet canopy, from which great tufts of ostrich plumes sprang, like white foam, to the pallid silver of the fretted ceiling. A laughing Narcissus in green bronze held a polished mirror above its head. On the table stood a flat bowl of amethyst.

Outside he could see the huge dome of the cathedral, looming like a bubble over the shadowy houses, and the weary sentinels pacing up and down on the misty terrace by the river. Far away, in an orchard, a nightingale was singing. A faint perfume of jasmine came through the open window. He brushed his brown curls back from his forehead, and taking up a lute, let his fingers stray across the cords. His heavy eyelids drooped, and a strange languor came over him. Never before had he felt so keenly, or with such exquisite joy, the magic and the mystery of beautiful things.

When midnight sounded from the clock-tower he touched a bell, and his pages entered and disrobed him with much ceremony, pouring rose-water over his hands, and strewing flowers on his pillow. A few moments after that they had left the room, he fell asleep.

And as he slept he dreamed a dream, and this was his dream. He thought that he was standing in a long, low attic, amidst the whirr and clatter of many looms. The meager daylight peered in through the grated windows, and showed him the gaunt figures of the weavers bending over their cases. Pale, sickly-looking children were crouched on the huge cross-beams. As the shuttles dashed through the warp they lifted up the heavy battens, and when the shuttles stopped they let the battens fall and pressed the threads together. Their faces were pinched with famine, and their thin hands shook and trembled. Some haggard women were seated at a table sewing. A horrible odor filled the place. The air was foul and heavy, and the walls dripped and streamed with damp.

The young King went over to one of the weavers, and stood by him and watched him.

And the weaver looked at him angrily, and said, "Why art thou watching me? Art thou a spy set on us by our master?"

"Who is thy master?" asked the young King.

"Our master!" cried the weaver, bitterly. "He is a man like myself. Indeed, "there is but this difference between us that he wears fine clothes while I go in rags, and that while I am weak from hunger he suffers not a little from overfeeding."

"The land is free," said the young King, "and thou art no man's slave."

"In war," answered the weaver, "the strong make slaves of the weak, and in peace the rich make slaves of the poor. We must work to live, and they give us such mean wages that we die. We toil for them all day long, and they heap up gold in their coffers, and our children fade away before their time, and the faces of those we love become hard and evil. We tread out the grapes, and another drinks the wine. We sow the corn, and our own board is empty. We have chains, though no eye beholds them; and are slaves, though men call us free."

"Is it so with all?" he asked.

"It is so with all," answered the weaver, "with the young as well as with the old, with the women as well as with the men, with the little children as well as with those who are stricken in years. The merchants grind us down, and we must needs do their bidding. The priest rides by and tells his beads, and no man has care of us. Through our sunless lanes creeps Poverty with her hungry eyes, and Sin with his sodden face follows close behind her. Misery wakes us in the morning, and Shame sits with us at night. But what are these things to thee? Thou art not one of us. Thy face is too happy." And he turned away scowling, and threw the shuttle across the loom, and the young King saw that it was threaded with a thread of gold.

And a great terror seized upon him, and he said to the

weaver, "What robe is this that thou art weaving?"

"It is the robe for the coronation of the young King," he answered; "what is that to thee?"

And the young King gave a loud cry and woke, and lo! he was in his own chamber, and through the window he saw the great honey-colored moon hanging in the dusky air.

And he fell asleep again and dreamed, and this was his dream.

He thought that he was lying on the deck of a huge galley that was being rowed by a hundred slaves. On a carpet by his side the master of the galley was seated. He was black as ebony, and his turban was of crimson silk. Great earrings of silver dragged down the thick lobes of his ears, and in his hands he had a pair of ivory scales.

The slaves were naked, but for a ragged loincloth, and each man was chained to his neighbor. The hot sun "beat brightly upon them, and the negroes ran up and down the gangway and lashed them with whips of hide. They stretched out their lean arms and pulled the heavy oars through the water. The salt spray flew from the blades.

At last they reached a little bay, and began to take soundings. A light wind blew from the shore, and covered the deck and the great lateen sail with a fine red dust. Three Arabs mounted on wild asses rode out and threw spears at them. The master of the galley took a painted bow in his hand and shot one of them in the throat. He fell heavily into the surf, and his companions galloped away. A woman wrapped in a yellow veil followed slowly on a camel, looking back now and then at the dead body.

As soon as they had cast anchor and hauled down the sail, the negroes went into the hold and brought up a long rope-ladder, heavily weighted with lead. The master of the galley threw it over the side, making the ends fast to two iron stanchions. Then the negroes seized the youngest of the slaves, and knocked his gyves oil, and filled his nostrils and his ears with wax, and tied a big stone round his waist. He crept wearily down the ladder, and disappeared into the sea. A few bubbles rose where he sank. Some of the other slaves peered curiously over the side. At the prow of the galley sat a shark-charmer, beating monotonously upon a drum.

After some time the diver rose up out of the water, and clung panting to the ladder with a pearl in his right hand. The negroes seized it from him, and thrust him back. The slaves fell asleep over their oars.

Again and again he came up, and each time that he did so he brought with him a beautiful pearl. The master of the galley weighed them, and put them into a little bag of green leather.

The young King tried to speak, but his tongue seemed to cleave to the roof of his mouth, and his lips refused to move. The negroes chattered to each other, and began to quarrel over a string of bright beads. Two cranes flew round and round the vessel.

Then the diver came up for the last time, and the pearl that he brought with him was fairer than all the pearls of Ormuz, for it was shaped like the full moon, and whiter than the morning star. But his face was strangely pale, and as he fell upon the deck the blood gushed from his ears and nostrils. He quivered for a little, and then he was still. The negroes shrugged their shoulders, and threw the body overboard.

And the master of the galley laughed, and, reaching out, he took the pearl, and when he saw it he pressed it to his forehead and bowed. "It shall be," he said, "for the sceptre of the young King," and he made a sign to the negroes to draw up the anchor.

And when the young King heard this he gave a great cry,

and woke, and through the window he saw the long grey fingers of the dawn clutching at the fading stars.

And he fell asleep again, and dreamed, and this was his dream.

He thought that he was wandering through a dim wood, hung with strange fruits and with beautiful poisonous flowers. The adders hissed at him as he went by, and the bright parrots flew screaming from branch to branch. Huge tortoises lay asleep upon the hot mud. The trees were full of apes and peacocks.

On and on he went, till he reached the outskirts of the wood, and there he saw an immense multitude of men toiling in the bed of a dried-up river. They swarmed up the crag like ants. They dug deep pits in the ground and went down into them. Some of them cleft the rocks with great axes; others grabbled in the sand. They tore up the cactus by its roots, and trampled on the scarlet blossoms. They hurried about, calling to each other, and no man was idle.

From the darkness of a cavern Death and Avarice watched them, and Death said, "I am weary; give me a third of them and let me go."

But Avarice shook her head. "They are my servants," she answered.

And Death said to her, "What hast thou in thy hand?"

"I have three grains of corn," she answered; "what is that to thee?"

"Give me one of them," cried Death, "to plant in my garden; only one of them, and I will go away."

"I will not give thee anything," said Avarice, and she hid her hand in the fold of her raiment.

And Death laughed, and took a cup, and dipped it into a pool of water, and out of the cup rose Ague. She passed through the great multitude, and a third of them lay dead. A cold mist followed her, and the water-snakes ran by her side.

And when Avarice saw that a third of the multitude was dead she beat her breast and wept. She beat her barren bosom and cried aloud. "Thou hast slain a third of my servants," she cried, "get thee gone. There is war in the mountains of Tartary, and the kings of each side are calling to thee. The Afghans have slain the black ox, and are marching to battle. They have beaten upon their shields with their spears, and have put on their helmets of iron. What is my valley to thee, that thou should'st tarry in it? Get thee gone, and come here no more.

"Nay," answered Death, "but till thou hast given me a grain of corn I will not go."

But Avarice shut her hand, and clenched her teeth. "I will not give thee anything,'she muttered.

And Death laughed, and took up a black stone, and threw it into the forest, and out of a thicket of wild hemlock came Fever in a robe of flame. She passed through the multitude, and touched them, and each man that she touched died. The grass withered beneath her feet as she walked.

And Avarice shuddered, and put ashes on her head. "Thou art cruel," she cried; "thou art cruel. There is famine in the walled cities of India, and the cisterns of Samarcand have run dry. There is famine in the walled cities of Egypt, and the locusts have come up from the desert. The Nile has not overflowed its banks, and the priests have cursed Isis and Osiris. Get thee gone to those who need thee, and leave me my servants."

"Nay," answered Death, "but till thou hast given me a grain of corn I will not go."

"I will not give thee anything," said Avarice.

And Death laughed again, and he whistled through his fingers, and a woman came flying through the air. Plague was written upon her forehead, and a crowd of lean vultures wheeled round her. She covered the valley with her wings, and no man was left alive.

And Avarice fled shrieking through the forest, and Death leaped upon his red horse and galloped away, and his galloping was faster than the wind.

And out of the slime at the bottom of the valley crept dragons and horrible things with scales, and the jackals came trotting along the sand, sniffing up the air with their nostrils.

And the young King wept, and said: "Who were these men and for what were they seeking?"

"For rubies for a king's crown," answered one who stood behind him.

And the young King started, and, turning round, he saw a man habited as a pilgrim and holding in his hand a mirror of silver.

And he grew pale, and said: "For what king?"

And the pilgrim answered: "Look in this mirror, and thou shalt see him."

And he looked in the mirror, and, seeing his own face, he gave a great cry and woke, and the bright sunlight was streaming into the room, and from the trees of the garden and pleasance the birds were singing.

And the Chamberlain and the high officers of State came in and made obeisance to him, and the pages brought him the robe of tissued gold, and set the crown and the sceptre before him.

And the young King looked at them, and they were beautiful.

More beautiful were they than aught that he had ever seen. But he remembered his dreams, and he said to his lords: "Take these things away, for I will not wear them."

And the courtiers were amazed, and some of them laughed, for they thought that he was jesting.

But he spake sternly to them again, and said: "Take these things away, and hide them from me. Though it be the day of my coronation, I will not wear them. For on the loom of Sorrow, and by the white hands of Pain, has this my robe been woven. There is Blood in the heart of the ruby, and Death in the heart of the pearl." And he told them his three dreams.

And when the courtiers heard them they looked at each other and whispered, saying: "Surely he is mad; for what is a dream but a dream, and a vision but a vision? They are not real things that one should heed them. And what have we to do with the lives of those who toil for us? Shall a man not eat bread till he has seen the sower, nor drink wine till he has talked with the vinedresser?"

And the Chamberlain spake to the young King, and said, "My lord, I pray thee set aside these black thoughts of thine, and put on this fair robe, and set this crown upon thy head. For how shall the people know that thou art a king, if thou hast not a king's raiment?"

And the young King looked at him. "Is it so, indeed?" he questioned. "Will they not know me for a king if I have not a king's raiment?"

"They will not know thee, my lord," cried the Chamberlain.

"I had thought that there had been men who were kinglike," he answered, "but it may be as thou sayest. And yet I will not wear this robe, nor will I be crowned with this crown, but even as I came to the palace so will I go forth from it."

And he bade them all leave him, save one page whom he kept as his companion, a lad a year younger than himself. Him he kept for his service, and when he had bathed himself in clear water, he opened a great painted chest, and from it he took the leathern tunic and rough sheepskin cloak that he had worn when he had watched on the hillside the shaggy goats of the goatherd. These he put on, and in his hand he took his rude shepherd's staff.

And the little page opened his big blue eyes in wonder, and said smiling to him, "My lord, I see thy robe and thy sceptre, but where is thy crown?"

And the young King plucked a spray of wild briar that was climbing over the balcony, and bent it, and made a circlet of it, and set it on his own head.

"This shall be my crown," he answered.

And thus attired he passed out of his chamber into the Great Hall, where the nobles were waiting for him.

And the nobles made merry, and some of them cried out to him, "My lord, the people wait for their king, and thou showest them a beggar," and others were wroth and said, "He brings shame upon our state, and is unworthy to be our master." But he answered them not a word, but passed on, and went down the bright porphyry staircase, and out through the gates of bronze, and mounted upon his horse, and rode towards the cathedral, the little page running beside him.

And the people laughed and said, "It is the King's fool who is riding by," and they mocked him.

And he drew rein and said, "Nay, but I am the King." And he told them his three dreams.

And a man came out of the crowd and spake bitterly to him, and said, "Sir, knowest thou not that out of the luxury of the rich cometh the life of the poor? By your pomp we are nurtured, and your vices give us bread. To toil for a hard master is bitter, but to have no master to toil for is more bitter still. Thinkest thou that the ravens will feed us? And what cure hast thou for these things? Wilt thou say to the buyer, "Thou shalt buy for so much," and to the seller, "Thou shalt sell at this price?" I trow not. Therefore go back to thy Palace and put on thy purple and fine linen. What hast thou to do with us, and what we suffer?"

"Are not the rich and the poor brothers?" asked the young King.

"Aye," answered the man, "and the name of the rich brother is Cain."

And the young King's eyes filled with tears, and he rode on through the murmurs of the people, and the little page grew afraid and left him.

And when he reached the great portal of the cathedral, the soldiers thrust their halberts out and said, "What dost thou seek here? None enters by this door but the King."

And his face flushed with anger, and he said to them, "I am the King," and waved their halberts aside and passed in.

And when the old Bishop saw him coming in his goatherd's dress, he rose up in wonder from his throne, and went to meet him, and said to him, "My son, is this a king's apparel? And with what crown shall I crown thee, and what sceptre shall I place in thy hand? Surely this should be to thee a day of joy, and not a day of abasement."

"Shall Joy wear what Grief has fashioned?" said the young King. And he told him his three dreams.

And when the Bishop had heard them he knit his brows, and said, "My son, I am an old man, and in the winter of my days, and I know that many evil things are done in the wide world. The fierce robbers come down from the mountains, and carry off the little children, and sell them to the Moors. The lions lie in wait for the caravans, and leap upon the camels. The wild boar roots up the corn in the valley, and the foxes gnaw the vines upon the hill. The pirates lay waste the sea-coast and burn the ships of the fishermen, and take their nets from them. In the salt-marshes live the lepers; they have houses of wattled reeds, and none may come nigh them. The beggars wander through the cities, and eat their food with the dogs. Canst thou make these things not to be? Wilt thou take the leper for thy bedfellow, and set the beggar at thy board? Shall the lion do thy bidding, and the wild boar obey thee? Is not He who made misery wiser than thou art? Wherefore I praise thee not for this that thou hast done, but I bid thee ride back to the Palace and make thy face glad, and put on the raiment that beseemeth a king, and with the crown of gold I will crown thee, and the sceptre of pearl will I place in thy hand. And as for thy dreams, think no more of them. The burden of this world is too great for one man to bear, and the world's sorrow too heavy for one heart to suffer."

"Sayest thou that in this house?" said the young King, and he strode past the Bishop, and climbed up the steps of the altar, and stood before the image of Christ.

He stood before the image of Christ, and on his right hand and on his left were the marvellous vessels of gold, the chalice with the yellow wine, and the vial with the holy oil. He knelt before the image of Christ, and the great candles burned brightly by the jewelled shrine, and the smoke of the incense curled in thin blue wreaths through the dome. He bowed his head in prayer, and the priests in their stiff copes crept away from the altar.

And suddenly a wild tumult came from the street outside, and in entered the nobles with drawn swords and nodding plumes, and shields of polished steel. "Where is this dreamer of dreams?" they cried. "Where is this King, who is apparelled like a beggar - this boy who brings shame upon our state? Surely we will slay him, for he is unworthy to rule over us."

And the young King bowed his head again, and prayed, and when he had finished his prayer he rose up, and turning round he looked at them sadly.

And lo! through the painted windows came the sunlight streaming upon him, and the sunbeams wove round him a tissued robe that was fairer than the robe that had been fashioned for his pleasure. The dead staff blossomed, and bare lilies that were whiter than pearls. The dry thorn blossomed, and bare roses that were redder than rubies. Whiter than fine pearls were the lilies, and their stems were of bright silver. Redder than male rubies were the roses, and their leaves were of beaten gold.

He stood there in the raiment of a king, and the gates of the jewelled shrine flew open, and from the crystal of the many-rayed monstrance shone a marvellous and mystical light. He stood there in a king's raiment, and the Glory of God filled the place, and the saints in their carven niches seemed to move. In the fair raiment of a king he stood before them, and the organ pealed out its music, and the trumpeters blew upon their trumpets, and the singing boys sang.

And the people fell upon their knees in awe, and the nobles sheathed their swords and did homage, and the Bishop's face grew pale, and his hands trembled. "A greater than I hath crowned thee," he cried, and he knelt before him.

And the young King came down from the high altar, and passed home through the midst of the people. But no man dared look upon his face, for it was like the face of an angel.

公主的生日

原來這個全身沒有一處地方對勁，
駝背彎腳，既奇怪又醜陋的人就是他自己。
原來他就是怪物，逗得所有小朋友大笑的就是他的長相。
他錯了，他以為小公主愛他，原來她也跟其他人一樣，
嘲笑他的醜陋，把他那扭曲變形的四肢當作笑柄。

　　那天是公主十二歲的生日，皇宮的花園裡充滿了燦爛的陽光。
雖然她是一位身分高貴的西班牙公主，不過，卻也和貧窮的孩子一
樣，一年只能過一次生日，所以，對整個國家來說，讓她過個愉快
的生日自然是非常重要的事了。

　　事實上，公主真的過了一個非常愉快的生日。長著條紋的瘦長
鬱金香伸長了莖，直挺挺地站立著，好像一排排整齊的士兵，它們
挑釁地看著對面草地上的玫瑰，說：「現在我們可和你們一樣耀眼
了。」紫色的蝴蝶揮舞著灑了金粉的薄翼，造訪每一朵花，小蜥蜴
從牆角的隙縫爬了出來，躺在明亮的陽光下作日光浴；石榴因熱氣
蒸騰而從中裂開，露出了淌著血的紅心。就連掛在微暗拱廊和破舊
籬笆上的那一大簇顏色蒼白的黃檸檬，也因亮燦燦的陽光而加添了
不少豐富色彩。木蘭花綻放出像球一樣的花朵，它的花瓣有如層層
疊疊的象牙薄片。空氣中滿是濃郁的花香。

小公主和她的玩伴們在露臺上跑上跑下，還玩起了捉迷藏遊戲，在大石壺和長著青苔的舊雕像附近躲來躲去。平常，小公主只能和她同樣尊貴的人一起玩耍，所以她往往只能一個人玩。然而，她的生日是個不尋常的日子，國王特別下令准許小公主邀請她想與之一齊同樂的小朋友來。

　　這些身形纖細的西班牙小朋友出場真可說是威風凜凜，男孩們戴著飾有長羽毛的帽子，披著迎風飛揚的披風；女孩們一手握著錦緞禮服的長裙襬，另一手則拿著銀黑兩色的大扇子遮擋炫目的陽光。但是，這群孩子中最高雅的還是小公主，她的穿著也最為華麗，相當符合時下流行的累贅風尚——她的外袍是用灰色的緞子做成，裙子和膨膨的袖子都層層地繡上銀線，漿挺的束腹上更鑲嵌著一排排上好的珍珠。她一走動，小鞋上的兩朵大薔薇花結便爭相探出頭來看看外面的花花世界。她手裡拿著粉紅色和珍珠色相間的美麗薄扇，她的金黃髮絲被整理得像閃耀交疊的金色光環，直挺挺環繞著她蒼白的小臉，而她的小臉則彷若一朵美麗的白玫瑰。

　　沉鬱憂傷的國王正站在皇宮的窗戶旁，看著公主和她的朋友們。站在國王身後的是國王所討厭的人，他的弟弟亞拉岡·裴多閣下；坐在國王身旁的則是常聽國王告解的神父，格拉那達的宗教裁判所所長。今天的國王比往常還要憂鬱，因為當他看著小公主以稚嫩的莊嚴神態向集會的朝臣們打招呼，或用扇子遮嘴對常常陪伴在她身邊、冷漠的艾爾伯魁克女伯爵微笑時，他就會想起他的年輕皇后，也就是公主的母親。對國王而言，一切往事歷歷如昨。

　　皇后來自光華四射的法國，卻在灰濛濛的西班牙宮廷中凋萎；在小公主出生六個月後，皇后便與世長辭。在這兒，她曾看過兩次果樹園裡綻放杏花，於第二年摘下無花果樹上的果實，那顆果樹生長在中庭中央，中庭現已綠草連綿，果樹也已老而多節。國王對皇后的愛深得無法將她下葬。皇后的身軀是由一位摩爾醫生施以防腐，而這位因使用魔術被宗教法庭判處死刑的異端醫生，也因此撿回一條命。皇后的屍體至今仍躺在皇宮的黑色大理石教堂中，在那鋪著地毯的棺架上，一切都和十二年前那個起風的三月天，教士們將她抬進教堂時一樣。國王每個月都要披上黑披風，帶著加了一層布罩的燈籠去看她一次，跪在她身旁，悲傷地叫著：「我的愛人！我的愛人！」有時候，他甚至會痛苦狂亂地緊抓皇后那戴著珠寶的慘白雙手，試圖以撒落在皇后冰冷粉頰上的癡狂熱吻喚醒她。

今天，他彷彿再次見到活生生的皇后，就像他在楓丹白露宮初見她時一樣，那時他才十五歲，皇后比他更小些。在法國國王和全宮廷的大臣面前，他們兩人於羅馬教廷大使的主持下正式訂婚，之後，他便帶著一小撮金色鬈髮，和臨上馬車之際飛落在他手上的兩片童稚唇印，回到了家鄉。後來，婚禮很快地在兩國邊境上的一個城市舉行，進西班牙國門的禮俗則依照傳統，在拉阿多加教堂舉行盛大彌撒，而且這次的彌撒中還依宗教判決，將大約三百名的異教徒送上火刑架，在這批人當中有許多英國人。

國王深愛皇后，而且愛得近乎瘋狂，許多臣民都這麼說，即使在西班牙與英國為了爭奪海外殖民地而大打出手之際，國王也不讓皇后離開他的視線，因為只要一瞧見皇后，國王似乎就能忘了那煩悶擾人的國事。但是，這份情狂引發的盲目以及影響，讓國王忽略了他的本意是要取悅皇后，可是在那時卻反而加重皇后病情的負擔。皇后過世時，他有一段時間就像瘋子一樣，也曾想過要將王位讓給自己弟弟，然後到格瑞那達的修道院了此殘生。然而，他又怕從此得將小公主交給自己那殘忍且惡名昭彰的弟弟撫養，最後終於打消了遜位的念頭。而且不少人傳論著國王的弟弟和皇后的死有關，因為皇后生前到亞拉岡的城堡探訪國王的弟弟時，曾收到他送的一雙浸過毒藥的手套。

國王為皇后的死，下詔全國百姓須公開服喪三年，而且服喪期滿後，國王仍不准大臣們提起要他再婚的事，就連羅馬帝國的皇帝親自作媒，要將自己的姪女（可愛的波希米亞公主）嫁給他，也遭到拒絕。他吩咐前來的大使回去告訴羅馬帝國的皇帝——西班牙國王已經和憂傷結婚了，他愛貧乏的憂傷更甚於愛世間的美人。國王此舉的結果，也導致了尼德蘭地區幾個富庶的省分，在羅馬帝國皇帝的教唆下，由一些宗教改革派狂熱領袖發動了叛變。

　　而今天，當國王看著在露臺上嬉戲的公主時，他那曾經以狂喜為始、卻以皇后突然辭世的悲怨作結的婚姻生活，似乎一幕幕重現眼前。小公主承襲了死去皇后所有迷人的儀態，一樣任性的甩頭模樣，一樣驕傲且線條優美的唇型，一樣美麗嬌柔的笑臉，這些都在她不時望向國王所在的窗口，或伸出手來讓那些高貴的西班牙紳士行吻手禮的時候，一一展現了她獨特吸引人的特質。然而，小朋友們激越的笑聲摩擦著他的耳膜，燦爛、毫無同情心的陽光嘲諷著他的憂傷，一股異樣的辛辣味刺激著他的鼻子，那好像是為屍體實施防腐術所使用的藥品，彷彿有東西腐爛掉了。或者，這只是幻覺，畢竟這是個空氣清新的早晨。他把臉埋在雙手中，而當小公主再度望向窗口時，窗簾已經拉上，國王已經離開了。

　　小公主失望地皺起眉頭，聳聳肩。父王理當在她生日這天陪伴在她身邊。那些愚蠢的國家大事有什麼了不起！或者，父王又到那座長年點著蠟燭、且不准她進去的幽暗小教堂裡去了？父王真夠笨的，今天天氣這麼好，而且每個人都這麼快樂，他為什麼還要獨自憂傷！而且，號角已經吹響，他將會錯過一場模擬鬥牛賽，更別提木偶劇和其他一些精采的表演了。她的叔叔和宗教裁判所所長都比父王感性多了，他們兩個走到露臺上來，還讚美了她一番。於是公主甩甩她那美麗的頭髮，拉起叔叔的手慢慢步下臺階，一起走向位於花園一側、用紫色絲綢搭建起來的大帳棚，其他的小朋友則依嚴格的禮儀，按尊卑順序跟在他們身後；無疑地，名字最長的小朋友走在最前面。

　　擁有貴族血統的男孩們打扮成耀眼的鬥牛士，排著隊來見公主。十四歲的俊美少年，也就是泰爾努維亞伯爵，他以西班牙紳士的優雅風範摘下帽子，莊重地引領公主來到看臺上一張特別設置、以金箔和象牙製成的小椅子。公主坐定之後，其他小朋友便在附近坐了下來，不住地搖動手中的大扇子，和鄰座的人竊竊私語。而公主的叔叔和宗教裁判所所長則笑著站在入口處；就連長相刻薄、身材細瘦、穿著黃色襞襟的女伯爵也不像往常那麼壞脾氣，她皺皺的臉上彷彿浮出一個冷笑似的，沒有血色的嘴唇微微彎曲著。

小公主覺得這一場模擬鬥牛賽真是好看極了，比真正的鬥牛賽還好看；之前，帕馬公爵來拜訪國王時，國王曾經帶小公主去看了一場真正的鬥牛賽。在今天的模擬鬥牛賽中，有些男孩騎在裝飾華麗的木馬上，揮舞著綁有美麗絲帶的長槍；其他男孩則走在牛前揮動他們的紅色披風，當他們刺到牛的時候便輕巧地躍過柵欄；至於牛隻嘛，雖然是用柳條編成的，倒也頗像真的牛，不過，它有時只用後腳就可繞著舞臺轉，這門功夫倒是真正的牛無法作到的。假牛在這場鬥牛賽中的表現精采萬分，看得小朋友們全站到椅子上，揮舞著蕾絲手帕，學著大人們的神態，大聲喊著：「好啊！好啊！」最後，在延長賽之後，在刺傷了幾匹木馬、摔下幾位騎士之後，年輕的泰爾努維亞伯爵制伏了這頭牛，並在公主的命令下對這頭牛刺下致命的一擊。他拿著木劍用力一劃，牛頭立刻掉了下來，然而他這一劃卻令法國大使的兒子收住了笑臉。

僕人在讚美和喝采聲中清理舞臺，兩位穿著黃、黑制服的摩爾書僮隆重地將倒在地上的木馬抬出場去。短暫的中場休息之後，接著上場的是一位法國體操名家，他於拉緊的繩索上展現舞姿。然後是義大利的木偶劇團在特別搭建的小劇院中，表演半古典的悲劇故事；木偶們演得如此感人，動作又栩栩如生，以致於小公主在落幕時都忍不住熱淚盈眶。事實上，好幾個小朋友都看得哭出聲來，還得用糖果來哄才能止住哭泣。就連宗教裁判所所長也感動不已，他忍不住告訴公主的叔叔，這些用木頭和彩蠟做成、受一堆線操縱只能機械化活動的人物竟然如此不幸，遭逢如此悲慘的命運，真是叫他無法忍受。

接著下來表演的是一位非洲的魔術師，他將一個罩上紅布的淺平大籃子放在看臺中央，從頭巾裡抽出一根古怪的牧笛，接著便吹奏起來。不一會兒，蓋在籃子上的紅布開始移動，愈來愈尖銳的笛聲，引得一條綠色和一條金色的蛇探出牠們奇異的楔形蛇頭來，然後身形緩緩上升，隨著音樂前後擺曳生姿，就像水草在水中擺動一樣。牠們那有著斑點的頭和不時向前吐出的舌頭，著實讓小朋友們嚇了一跳。不過，接下來的表演就讓小朋友們開心多了，魔術師從沙堆裡變出一棵橘子樹，還讓它開出美麗的白色花朵，結出成串真正的果實。當他拿起拉斯托斯侯爵小女兒的扇子，把它變成一隻繞著帳棚飛翔唱歌的青鳥時，小朋友們驚喜得簡直要飛上天了。

之後是由教堂的舞蹈班男孩所表演的莊嚴小步舞曲，非常精湛美妙。每年五月份，這個節目都會在聖母瑪利亞崇高的祭壇前演出，然而，小公主卻從不曾觀看過——事實上，自從一位瘋狂的神父（據許多人說，他是受了英國女王伊莉莎白一世之賄賂），試圖拿有毒的聖餐麵包給阿斯翠斯王子吃之後，西班牙皇室的成員便再也沒有踏進薩爾哥薩大教堂一步。所以，公主便僅耳聞「聖母瑪利亞之舞」，直到今日才得以親見，這真是優雅的舞蹈啊。跳舞的男孩們穿著舊式的白絲綢宮廷服裝，頭上戴著奇特的三角帽，上頭綴繡著銀邊，還插著一根長長的鴕鳥羽毛。當他們在陽光下移動時，身上的制服便發出令人目眩的白光，他們黝黑的臉龐和既黑且長的頭髮更是引人側目。每個人都被他們威儀凜凜的表現所吸引，他們流利地跳著複雜的舞步，慢舞時卻又是如此的細緻優雅，鞠躬的姿態又是如此高貴。而當表演結束時，他們則將飾有長羽毛的帽子拋給公主，公主謙遜地接受他們的敬意，並發下誓言要送一支大蠟燭到聖母瑪利亞的神龕上，以回報祂賞賜給自己的歡樂。

一支英俊的埃及人隊伍（當時對吉普賽人的稱呼）接著走上舞臺，圍成一個圓圈，翹著二郎腿坐著，開始輕柔地撥弄著手中的樂器，依著旋律扭動身體，以近乎夢幻的低聲嗡嗡吟唱著。當他們瞥見公主的叔叔時，臉色立刻陰鬱下來，其中有些人甚至露出了驚惶的表情，因為幾個星期前，公主的叔叔才以他們耍巫術為由，在市集上吊死兩個他們的族人。不過，小公主倒是很得他們喜歡，當她往後躺進椅子裡，用湛藍的大眼睛從扇子後面偷看他們時，模樣真是可愛極了，他們肯定這個可愛的女孩絕不會對任何人殘暴不仁。於是他們溫柔和緩地彈奏著，以長而尖的指甲撫觸絲弦，他們開始點起頭來，好像正打著瞌睡。

突然間，場中爆出一聲尖叫，所有小朋友都嚇了一跳，公主的叔叔立刻伸手按上他那瑪瑙製的短劍劍柄。表演的人全都跳了起來，瘋狂似的聚在一起，圍繞著舞臺行走，用手擊打著鼓，並且用他們奇怪的喉音唱出狂野的戀歌。然後在另一個信號之下，他們全撲倒在地，躺在舞臺上動也不動，只有沉悶而奇怪的樂器彈奏聲，在寂靜的空間中迴響。當重複過幾次這樣的場面之後，他們消失了一會兒，再次出現時，帶回了一隻鎖上鎖鏈的毛茸茸棕色熊，和幾隻掛在人類肩膀上的北非無尾猿猴。那隻熊以無比認真的姿態表演倒立，而那幾隻乾瘦的猿猴則在兩個吉普賽男孩（似乎是牠們的小主人）帶領下，耍了許多有趣的花招，不但舞劍玩槍，還像國王的禁衛隊似的，以訓練有素的整齊步伐行進。這些吉普賽人表演得很成功。

不過，就整個上午的表演來說，最精采的一個節目非小矮人的舞蹈莫屬。當小矮人用他那雙彎彎曲曲的腳跌跌撞撞地走上舞臺，還搖晃著他那似乎長錯位置的大頭時，小朋友們立刻爆出震耳欲聾的笑聲，就連公主也笑得非常誇張，公主身旁的女伯爵不得不提醒她：「在西班牙歷史上，的確曾出現國王的女兒在同等地位的人面前哭泣的例子。不過，在出身比她低的人面前這麼高興地笑，對一位擁有皇家尊貴血統的公主來說，卻是絕無僅有的事。」然而，小矮人實在深具擋不住的魅力，即使對酷愛醜怪事物聞名的西班牙宮廷而言，也從沒有人看過這麼吸引人的小怪物。

這次的表演也是小矮人的處女秀。他在兩天前才被人發現，當時的他正在森林裡狂奔，兩位到森林裡去打獵的貴族發現了他，便將他帶回宮廷裡，送給小公主做為禮物。小矮人的父親是個貧窮的燒炭工人，也樂得將這個長得奇醜無比又沒有什麼用處的孩子送走。也許，這個小矮人最令人覺得不可思議的地方，就是他根本不知道自己的外表長得多麼的醜怪。事實上，他似乎是一個很快樂、很樂觀、很積極的人。當小朋友們大笑時，小矮人也跟著大笑，而且笑得和他們每個人一樣開心。每一支舞結束後，他對每個人深深鞠躬，態度自然地微笑、點頭，彷彿自己真的是觀眾群中的一份子，然而從某些幽默的角度來看，這種自然毫不做作的舉止，竟是他招致別人無情嘲諷的主要原因。對小矮人來說，他則完全讓公主給迷住了。他無法將視線從公主身上移開，他覺得自己像是為公主一人而舞似的。

小矮人的舞蹈表演結束時，公主想起，有一次，教宗為了治療國王的憂傷，從自己的教堂選派了一位男高音為國王進行御前獻唱，希望男高音優美的嗓音能治癒國王的傷心。在那次的演唱會結束時，宮廷裡許多高貴的仕女們，都將手中的花束拋給那位著名的義大利男高音卡佛瑞里，於是公主也從鬢髮上摘下一朵漂亮的白玫瑰，半開玩笑、半要氣氣身旁的女伯爵似的，漾著最甜美的笑容，將手中的花拋給舞臺上的小矮人。小矮人虔敬地收下這朵花，以他粗糙難看的嘴唇親吻這美麗的花朵，還將手按在自己的心上，單膝跪地，回給公主一個咧開大嘴的笑容，他小小的眼睛裡閃爍著喜悅的光芒。

小矮人這樣的舉動讓公主在他退出舞臺之後，依然大笑不已，她要求叔叔下令讓小矮人的舞蹈立刻重來一次。然而，女伯爵卻以陽光太強為由，建議公主應該立刻回到皇宮，不該再有任何延誤。皇宮裡已經為公主準備好精緻的午餐，包括一個真正的生日蛋糕，上面以彩色糖漿寫著公主名字的縮寫，而且上頭還有一面迎風飛舞的銀色小旗子。於是公主順從地以高貴的姿態站了起來，並且下令要小矮人於她午睡結束之後，再為她跳一支舞，公主也向泰爾努維亞伯爵致意，對他的熱心帶領表示謝意。接著她便起駕回宮，小朋友們則依照先前進場時的順序，跟在公主身後走著。

當小矮人聽到他將要在公主面前再次獻舞，而且還是公主親自下達的命令時，不禁高興地衝進花園，以忘我的狂喜親吻那朵白玫瑰，而且以最笨拙、最粗俗的姿態跳著最快樂的舞。

花園裡的花兒們對於小矮人膽敢闖入它們美麗的家園，感到氣憤不已，而當它們看到小矮人在走道上將手高舉過頭，古裡古怪地跳來跳去時，便再也無法控制住脾氣了。

「他實在醜得不能在任何有花朵的地方玩耍。」鬱金香為之氣結地大叫道。

「他真該去喝罌粟花汁，然後好好地睡上一千年。」大紅百合說道，它們現在已經又熱又氣了。

「他真是個完美的怪物！」仙人掌尖叫道，「他不但渾身扭曲變形，又矮矮胖胖的，他的頭和他的腳完全不成比例。他真是讓我全身上下都有如針刺般不舒服，如果他走近我，我一定要用全身的刺去刺他。」

「他真的拿到我最美的一朵花了！」白玫瑰叢驚叫道，「今天早上我親自將那朵花送給公主作為生日禮物，他從公主那兒偷了花啦。」於是白玫瑰叢扯開嗓子，高叫道，「小偷，小偷，小偷！」

就連平常較為沒沒無聞、有著一堆窮親戚的天竺葵，在看到小矮人之後也嫌惡地捲起身子來；紫羅蘭則溫順地評論道，小矮人是長得醜陋不堪，不過這也是沒有辦法的事啊。然後大家七嘴八舌地下著結論，它們認為長得醜是小矮人最大的缺點，而且他也不必因為長得無可救藥就這麼樂啊！事實上，有些紫羅蘭還認為小矮人是在賣弄自己的醜怪，如果他因為自己長得這麼醜而表現出一點傷心，至少也要顯得有些淒慘，它們還會覺得好受些，可是他偏偏把自己蠢笨的行為都表現出來，還樂得蹦蹦跳跳的。

那副曾經為羅馬帝國皇帝查理五世報時、優秀獨立的老日晷，對於小矮人的出現也嚇了一大跳，差點忘了得循著地球運轉將細長的分針往前推兩格。它忍不住告訴在欄杆上作日光浴的白孔雀，大家都知道國王的子孫都是國王，而燒炭工人的子孫都是燒炭工人，這是假不了的事實；白孔雀完全同意他的說法，事實上，白孔雀甚至還尖叫道：「那當然，那當然。」由於白孔雀的聲音又尖又亮，使得兩隻在噴水池底部的金魚探出頭來，詢問噴水池上的巨型海神雕像，究竟發生了什麼事？

還好鳥兒們很喜歡小矮人。牠們以前就在森林裡看過他像隻猿猴似的，在翻飛的樹葉上跳舞，他有時還會蜷縮在老橡樹那中空的樹幹裡，和松鼠們分享堅果。牠們根本就不在意他醜陋的外表。甚至連夜晚在橘子園裡唱著美麗歌謠的夜鶯（有時，連月亮都忍不住低垂身子佇足聆聽她的歌聲），對於小矮人的外表也沒有什麼不好的批評；何況，小矮人對於森林裡的朋友向來很親切，特別是在嚴寒的冬季裡，當樹上沒有果實，地面也硬得像鐵一樣，狼群開始進城找食物的時候，小矮人也從未忘記他的朋友。他總是從自己少許的黑麵包中再分出麵包屑來給朋友，無論他的早餐如何貧乏，他也總是和朋友一起分享。

於是，鳥兒們繞著小矮人飛翔，在飛過小矮人身邊時便用牠們的翅膀摸摸小矮人的臉頰，還不時和他聊聊天。小矮人實在太高興了，忍不住把那朵白玫瑰花拿給牠們看，還告訴牠們，這花是公主親自送給他的，因為公主愛他。

鳥兒們聽不懂小矮人的話，不過也無所謂啦，因為他們總是把頭偏向一旁，露出一副聰明的樣子，彷彿完全了解似的，而且擺擺姿態總是比較容易。

蜥蜴們也很喜歡小矮人。當他跑跳得累了，躺在草地上休息的時候，蜥蜴們便過來陪他玩。牠們想盡辦法要取悅小矮人。「世界上再沒有比蜥蜴更漂亮的動物了，」牠們高叫道，「這麼說雖然有些妄想，而且一聽就知道是開玩笑，但是蜥蜴終究也醜不到哪裡去。倘若你真覺得小矮人醜，就閉起眼睛，不看他吧。」蜥蜴天生是當哲學家的料，常常一塊兒坐在一起展開數小時的沉思，每當無事可做或下雨天無法外出時，牠們就開始沉思了。

然而，花兒們對蜥蜴和鳥兒的行為卻惱怒已極。「這只能表示，」花兒們說道，「爬來爬去和飛來飛去的傢伙，是多麼的粗俗罷了，擁有良好教養的人總有個固定的居處，就像我們一樣。從來沒有人會看到我們在走道上跑跳，或在草地上狂奔追逐蜻蜓。當我們想換個環境時，我們就告訴園丁，他就會將我們移到另一個花床上，這就是所謂的尊嚴。可是蜥蜴和鳥兒都是靜不下來的啊！事實上，鳥兒甚至沒有永久住址，讓牠們享受與吉普賽人同等的待遇就可以了。」花兒們說，並且高傲地仰起臉，一副不可一世的樣子。後來，它們看到小矮人從草地上爬起來，穿過露臺走到皇宮去，實在開心極了。

「他真該一輩子都被關在屋裡才是。」花兒說道，「看看他的駝背，還有那彎曲的腳。」花兒又開始對小矮人冷嘲熱諷了。

然而，對於這一切，小矮人毫不知情。他非常喜愛蜥蜴和鳥兒，也覺得花兒是全世界最美麗的東西，不過，當然還是比不上公主的美啦！因為公主把那朵美麗的白玫瑰花送給了他，而且公主愛他，這就足以分別花兒的美和公主的美有多大的不同了。小矮人多麼希望自己能和公主一起回去！他想公主會讓他坐在她的右手邊，對著他微笑，而他將永不離開她。他要和公主成為玩伴，把所有好玩的把戲全都教給公主；儘管他從來沒有過過宮廷生活，但他也知道不少有趣好玩的事呢。

他會用燈心草編成小草籠，讓蟋蟀住在裡面唱歌，也會將長長的竹子裁製成牧神喜歡的牧笛。他可以辨認出各種鳥類的叫聲，可以將鷗掠鳥從樹上呼喚下來，也可以從沼地喚來蒼鷺。他認得每一種動物的腳印，可以靠著兔子細微的腳印找到牠們的藏身處，也可以憑著樹葉被踩壞的情況找到野豬。他懂得風的每一種舞步，風穿著紅色大衣和秋天狂舞；腳蹬藍色涼鞋輕輕在穀物上翻飛；冬季時和片片雪花翩翩起舞；在春季更和果樹園裡盛綻的花朵共舞。他知道何處是野鴿子的家，有一次一名捕鳥人設陷阱抓走了一對成鳥，小矮人便接下餵養幼鳥的任務，親自將幼鳥們拉拔長大，還在榆樹殘株的裂縫處造了一座小鳥屋。這些鳥都很溫馴，小矮人會在每天早晨餵牠們吃早餐，公主會喜歡牠們的。還有在羊齒植物叢裡奔跑的兔子們；有著黑色嘴巴、銀灰羽毛的松鴉；可以將自己捲成一顆刺球似的豪豬；以及那走起路來慢條斯理、搖頭晃腦，愛吃嫩葉的烏龜。

沒錯，公主真該來森林裡和他一塊兒玩耍的。他會將自己的小床讓給她，然後在窗外守著她直到天亮，以確保長著角的野牛無法傷害她，也不讓可怕的狼群逼近小屋。等到天一亮，他要輕輕敲著窗戶喚醒她，然後他們兩人就可以一塊兒出去，在森林裡跳一整天的舞。在森林裡絕對嗅不到一絲寂寞的氣味。有時候，主教也會騎著白驢從森林裡經過，還在驢上看著彩色的書。有時候，獵鷹的人會戴著無邊綠絲絨帽，穿著黃褐色的鹿皮製短上衣，手腕上架著蒙上頭罩的鷹行經而過。在葡萄收成的季節，踩榨葡萄的人會來到，雙手雙腳都沾染了葡萄汁的顏色，用光滑的長春藤編織成花環，帶走滿滿的酒袋。夜晚，燒炭工人圍著大火爐坐，看著乾柴在火中慢慢燒成木炭，然後用餘下的灰燼炒栗子，此時盜賊就會從山洞裡出來和他們同樂。有一次，他也曾看見一支壯麗的隊伍沿著灰塵漫天的長路蜿蜒而行。走在前面的僧侶們愉快地唱著歌，擎著色彩鮮亮的旗幟和黃金作成的十字架；再來是穿著銀鎧甲、手執火繩槍和長矛的士兵，三位赤著腳的人走在他們中間，穿著奇怪的黃色衣服，衣服上畫滿了美麗的圖案，手中還捧著燃亮的蠟燭。當然啦，除了

這些，森林裡還有很多可看的東西，如果公主累了，他可以為公主
找一處長滿青苔的柔軟河堤休息，或者他可以抱著公主走，因為他
很強壯──儘管他知道自己長得並不高。他會用紅色的漿果為公主
串一條項鍊，他想，那些紅色的漿果就和公主妝點在她衣服上的白
色漿果一樣美麗；而且如果公主對漿果項鍊生膩了，她大可以把它
給扔了，他會再找其他東西來給她的。他還會找來橡子的花萼，露
珠未乾的白頭翁花，和閃亮的小螢火蟲，來裝飾公主她那金黃燦爛
的頭髮。

可是，公主人呢？他問問白玫瑰花，它卻什麼話都沒有說。
整座皇宮似乎都睡著了，窗戶也沒有關上，只是放下厚重的窗簾遮
擋陽光而已。他四處走動，看看可不可以找到通向宮殿的入口，後
來，他終於看到一扇隱蔽的小門是開著的。他溜進小門，立刻發覺
自己置身於一個極為華麗的大廳裡，他覺得這個大廳比森林可怕，
因為這裡到處都貼金飾銀的，而且地板也是用大塊的彩色石頭做
的，還拼成幾何圖形呢。可是小公主不在大廳裡，這兒只有一些美
麗的雕像，它們從寶石做的雕像架上俯視著他，眼神悲傷空洞，笑
容則很奇怪。

大廳的盡頭懸掛著一幅繡得美輪美奐的黑絲絨布帘，其上灑佈
著精心繡成的太陽和星星，這是國王最喜歡的圖案，也是用國王最
喜歡的顏色繡成的。也許，公主就躲在布帘後面吧！小矮人想冒險
一試。

於是他偷偷地走過去掀開布帘。公主不在那兒，布帘之後不
過是另一間房間，他看看房間，心想這裡的確比剛剛那個房間漂亮
些。四面牆上都掛著不同圖案的綠色花毯，這是一幅描述打獵情形
的手工織花毯，由荷蘭的幾位藝術家花了七年時間才完成。這兒曾
經是人稱「瘋子唐璜」的寢室，這位瘋子國王非常沉迷於狩獵。在
他精神錯亂的時候，他常騎上因受驚嚇而揚起前蹄、只用後腳站立
的高大馬匹，然後拖走巨型獵犬爭逐的獵物，吹響獵號，還想用短

劍去刺行動迅捷的鹿。現在這個房間已被當成會議室，正中央的桌子上放著部會首長們的公事包，上面印著代表西班牙皇室的金色鬱金香以及哈布斯堡家族的標幟。

小矮人滿心驚異地看看四周，不太敢繼續前進。他看著花毯上的場景，那異樣沉靜的騎士如此輕盈地奔馳過長長的草地，卻沒有發出任何聲響，他覺得這些騎士就像燒炭工人所說的恐怖幽靈——坎伯瑞克斯一樣，他們只在晚上才出來狩獵，如果他們遇上人類的話，就叫人向後轉，然後在後面騎著馬追他。但是，一想到美麗的小公主，他便又重新拾起勇氣。他想單獨見見公主，並且告訴她，他也愛她。也許，她會在後面的房間裡。

他跑過柔軟的摩爾地毯，打開門。沒有！她也不在這兒，這是間空房間。

原本這房間是用來接待外國大使的，只不過，近來國王已不常在這兒接見賓客了。多年以前，國王曾經在這兒接見英國使節，他們乃為英國女王的婚事而來；之後，歐洲天主教教廷的一位重要人物和羅馬帝國皇帝的長子，也曾經到過這個房間。四周的壁飾是加了金箔的紋路、細緻而有光澤的上等的哥多華皮革，黑白相間的天花板懸吊著鍍上金箔的巨型枝狀吊燈，上面排列著三百枝蠟燭。以小粒珍珠繡上獅子和卡斯提爾高塔的金黃色天篷下，就是皇座所在，皇座上罩著一塊厚實的黑色絲絨蓋套，上面鑲嵌著銀製鬱金香，縫邊還細細地繡上銀線和珍珠。皇座的第二級階梯上放著公主的墊凳，墊凳之上擺著用銀線織布靠墊。在皇座底下，天篷之外，則擺放著教皇的座椅；在任何公開典禮儀式中，教皇是唯一一位有資格在國王面前擁有座位的人，而他那飾著紅色穗子的主教帽子就放在前面的紫色小桌上。而面對皇座的那面牆上，掛著一幅真人大小的查理五世畫像，畫中的他穿著獵裝，身旁還跟著一隻高大的猛犬；另一面牆的中央則掛了一幅菲力浦二世接受荷蘭人宣誓效忠的圖。兩扇窗戶之間有一個鑲嵌著象牙的黑檀木櫥櫃，上面還刻畫著荷賓的「死神之舞」舞步——有人說，這是享有盛名的荷賓親自刻上去的。

然而，對於這些貴重物品，小矮人根本不屑一顧。即使拿縫飾在天篷上的所有珍珠，來換他手中的白玫瑰花，他也不換，就算拿皇位來換他手中的一片花瓣，他也不會答應。他只想在公主回到大帳棚裡看表演之前見她一面，並邀請她在他表演完畢後和他一起離去。皇宮裡的空氣又濁又重，森林裡卻有輕拂的微風和溫煦的陽光。森林裡也有許多花兒，也許不如皇宮花園裡的花兒豔麗，但卻清香許多；早春時，盛綻在冰冷山谷中的風信子，有如湧動的紫色波浪隨風浮動著；小山上則是一片翠綠；成串的黃色櫻草花環繞在橡樹粗糙的根節上，迎風招展；還有明淨的白屈菜，藍色的威靈仙，和粉彩的紫丁香。是的，如果小矮人能找到公主，公主一定會答應和他一起離開！她會和他一起到美麗的森林裡去，而且只要小公主高興，小矮人願意為她跳一整天的舞。一想到這兒，小矮人不禁連眼角都盪出笑意，他走進了另一個房間裡。

小矮人現在看到的這間房間，是皇宮裡最閃亮、最美麗的房間。牆上掛著粉紫色的緞子，上面用銀線繡著可愛的花鳥，家具是純銀打造的，還結飾著鮮麗的花環和擺盪搖曳的愛神塑像；兩座大壁爐前面還放著繡上了孔雀和鸚鵡的大屏風，鑲瑪瑙綠的地板彷彿延伸至遙不可及的遠方。小矮人這回可有伴了，站在門口陰影處的小矮人看到房間遙遠的盡頭處竟有個人在看他。他心跳加快，忍不住高興地叫了一聲，隨即向陽光明亮處跑去。當他跑向前去時，那個人也跑了過來，小矮人現在可以清楚地看到他了。

公主！哦，不是，這是一個怪物，一個他生平僅見最醜陋的怪物。他根本不像一般人，他全身的部位似乎全長錯地方了，背駝駝的，四肢扭曲變形，突兀的大頭上頂著一堆焦黑的頭髮。小矮人皺了皺眉，那人也跟著皺了皺眉。他大笑，那人也大笑，還搖晃著手臂，就和小矮人的動作一樣。小矮人嘲諷地對那人鞠躬，那人也照樣鄙夷地回他一鞠躬。小矮人跑近他，那人也以同樣的步伐跑向小矮人，而且小矮人一停下來，那人便也跟著停下來。小矮人裝模作樣地大叫，伸出手來向前跑去，卻碰到那人的手，而那人的頭也碰著了小矮人的頭，可是那人卻平滑冰涼的像冰一樣。小矮人開始覺得害怕了，他將手臂交叉，那人立刻作出和小矮人相同的姿勢。小矮人使勁地向前推，但是那平滑堅實的東西卻動也不動。現在，那個怪物的臉正貼在小矮人的臉上，看起來也同樣一臉驚懼。小矮人將蓋到眼睛的頭髮撥開，那人也模仿他的動作。小矮人忍不住揍他，那人便也以牙還牙。小矮人討厭那個人，那個人便也擺了一張臭臉回敬他。小矮人往後退去，那人便也離開他幾步。

那個東西到底是什麼？小矮人沉思片刻，然後環視整個房間。在這面用晶亮的水所做成的隱形牆上，竟可以看到和房裡擺設一模一樣的東西，真是奇怪。沒錯，房間裡有一幅畫，那兒也有一幅畫，房間有一套沙發，那兒也有一套沙發。門邊壁龕上有一座沉睡的雕像，那兒也出現一座打盹的雙胞胎雕像；而站在陽光下的銀製維納斯，也朝著和她一般美麗的維納斯招手。

這是回音嗎？小矮人曾在山谷裡和回音說話，無論他說什麼，回音總是將他的話逐字奉還。難道回音能像模仿聲音這樣，模仿你所見到的東西嗎？回音可以仿製真實的世界嗎？影子能夠擁有色彩、生命和自己的行動嗎？它能夠……？

他從懷裡拿出那朵漂亮的白玫瑰花，轉過身，親吻花兒。那怪物竟然也有一朵玫瑰花，和他的一模一樣！那怪物也像小矮人一樣親吻那朵玫瑰花，而且也驚懼地將花緊貼在胸口上。

當小矮人明白這到底是怎麼一回事時，他絕望地慘叫一聲，哭倒在地上。原來，這個全身沒有一處地方對勁，駝背彎腳，既奇怪又醜陋的人就是他自己。原來他就是怪物，逗得所有小朋友大笑的就是他的長相，而他一直認為愛著他的小公主，原來也跟其他人一樣嘲笑他的醜陋，把他那扭曲變形的四肢當作笑柄。為什麼他們不

讓他留在沒有鏡子的森林裡？那樣，他就不會知道自己長得有多惹
人嫌了。為什麼他的父親不殺了他，反倒將他賣人以羞辱他？小矮
人的雙頰氾濫著奔流的熱淚，手中的玫瑰花也已被撕成片片。鏡中
那個模樣可怕的怪物也模仿他的動作，將片片花瓣撒向空中。鏡中
人倒臥在地，小矮人看著他，他也以飽受痛苦的表情回看小矮人。
小矮人害怕再見到那個怪物，他用手遮住雙眼爬走。他像一隻受傷
的動物，爬進陰暗的角落，躲在那兒哭泣。

這時候，小公主和她的同伴們從敞開著的大窗戶那邊走進來，
當他們看到醜怪的小矮人躺在地板上，用他那彎曲的手臂以最奇
特、最誇張的姿態捶擊著地板時，他們高興得大笑不已，還團團圍
在他身邊，看著他。

「他跳的舞好好笑，」小公主說道，「可是，他的舉止更好
笑。說真的，他的表演幾乎和木偶們一樣精采，不過，當然啦，比
不上木偶那麼自然就是了。」說完，搖搖手中的大扇子，還誇了小
矮人幾句。

然而，小矮人卻沒有抬起頭來，他的啜泣聲也愈來愈微弱。突
然間，他急迫地喘了個大氣，痙攣地翻向側面，之後，他便躺回原
來的姿勢，一動也不動。

「你這樣可是要判死刑哦，」小公主等了一會兒，不耐地說
道，「你現在得先起來為我跳舞。」

「起來跳舞，」所有的小朋友齊聲喊道，「你必須起來跳舞，
因為你像北非無尾猿猴一樣敏捷，而且比牠們還要滑稽。」

然而，小矮人仍然不說一句話。

小公主氣得踩腳，派人找來她的叔叔。那時，公主的叔叔正和
內廷大臣一起站在露臺上，讀著從墨西哥傳來的緊急文件，那兒新
近成立了宗教法庭。小公主大聲地哭訴著：「我那逗笑的小矮人鬧
彆扭，不聽話，你得叫他起來為我跳舞。」

公主的叔叔和內廷大臣相視而笑，一起走了過來，公主的叔叔

蹲下身，用他那刺繡精美的手套打了小矮人幾個耳光。「你必須起來跳舞，小怪物，」他說道，「你非跳不可。統治西班牙和印度之王的女兒，要你娛樂她。」

然而，小矮人還是靜靜地躺在地上，一動也不動。

「叫執鞭刑的人過來。」公主的叔叔嫌惡地說著，一邊走向露臺。不過，內廷大臣卻一臉認真的樣子，他在小矮人身旁蹲了下來，將手放在小矮人的胸口上。一會兒之後，他聳聳肩地站了起來，對公主深深地鞠了個躬，說道：

「美麗的公主殿下，您逗笑的小矮人再也無法跳舞了。真可惜，他長得這麼醜，極可能會逗國王開心的。」

「為什麼他不能再跳舞了呢？」小公主笑問道。

「因為他的心已經破碎了。」內廷大臣答道。

小公主皺皺眉頭，她那嬌美如玫瑰花瓣的雙唇，抿出一了道鄙夷的線條。「以後，讓沒有心的人來陪我玩吧。」她大聲說著，然後跑進花園。

The Birthday
of the Infanta

It was the birthday of the Infanta. She was just twelve years of age, and the sun was shining brightly in the gardens of the palace.

Although she was a real Princess and the Infanta of Spain, she had only one birthday every year, just like the children of quite poor people, so it was naturally a matter of great importance to the whole country that she should have a really fine day for the occasion. And a really fine day it certainly was. The tall striped tulips stood straight up upon their stalks, like long rows of soldiers, and looked defiantly across the grass at the roses, and said: We are quite as splendid as you are now. The purple butterflies fluttered about with gold dust on their wings, visiting each flower in turn; the little lizards crept out of the crevices of the wall, and lay basking in the white glare; and the pomegranates split and cracked with the heat, and showed their bleeding red hearts. Even the pale yellow lemons, that hung in such profusion from the mouldering trellis and along the dim arcades, seemed to have caught a richer color from the wonderful sunlight, and the magnolia trees opened their great globe-like blossoms of folded ivory, and filled the air with a sweet heavy perfume.

The little Princess herself walked up and down the terrace with her companions, and played at hide and seek round the stone vases and the old moss-grown statues. On ordinary days she was only allowed to play with children of her own rank, so she had always to play alone, but her birthday was an exception, and the King had given orders that she was to invite any of her young friends whom she liked to come and amuse themselves with her. There was a stately grace about these slim Spanish children as they glided about, the boys with their large-plumed hats and short fluttering cloaks, the girls holding up the trains of their long brocaded gowns, and shielding the sun from their eyes with huge fans of black and silver. But the Infanta was the most graceful of all, and the most tastefully attired, after the somewhat cumbrous fashion of the day. Her robe was of grey satin, the skirt and the wide puffed sleeves heavily embroidered with silver, and the stiff corset studded with rows of fine pearls. Two tiny slippers with big pink rosettes peeped out beneath her dress as she walked. Pink and pearl was her great gauze fan, and in her hair, which like an aureole of faded gold stood out stiffly round her pale little face, she had a beautiful white rose.

From a window in the palace the sad melancholy King watched them. Behind him stood his brother, Don Pedro of Aragon, whom he hated, and his confessor, the Grand Inquisitor of Granada, sat by his side. Sadder even than usual was the King, for as he looked at the Infanta bowing with childish gravity to the assembling courtiers, or laughing behind her fan at the grim Duchess of Albuquerque who always accompanied her, he thought of the young Queen, her mother, who but a short time before - so it seemed to him - had come from the gay country of France, and had withered away in the somber splendor of the Spanish court, dying just six months after the birth of her child, and before she had seen the almonds blossom twice in the orchard, or plucked the second year's fruit from the old gnarled fig-tree that stood in the centre of the now grass-grown courtyard. So great had been his love for her that he had not suffered even the grave to hide her from him. She had been embalmed by a Moorish physician, who in return for this service had been granted his life, which for heresy and suspicion of magical practices had been already forfeited, men said, to the Holy Office, and her body was still lying on its tapestried bier in the black marble chapel of the Palace, just as the monks had borne her in on that windy March day nearly twelve years before. Once every month the King, wrapped in a dark cloak and with a muffled lantern in his hand, went in and knelt by her side, calling out, "Mi reina! Mi reina!" and sometimes breaking through the formal etiquette that in Spain governs every separate action of life, and sets limits even to the sorrow of a King, he would clutch at the pale jewelled hands in a wild agony of grief, and try to wake by his mad kisses the cold painted face.

To-day he seemed to see her again, as he had seen her first at the Castle of Fontainebleau, when he was but fifteen years of age, and she still younger. They had been formally betrothed on that occasion by the Papal Nuncio in the presence of the French King and all the Court, and he had returned to the Escurial bearing with him a little ringlet of yellow hair, and the memory of two childish lips bending down to kiss his hand as he stepped into his carriage. Later on had followed the marriage, hastily performed at Burgos, a small town on the frontier between the two countries, and the grand public entry into Madrid with the customary celebration of high mass at the Church of La Atocha, and a more than usually solemn auto-da-fe, in which nearly three hundred heretics, amongst whom were many Englishmen, had been delivered over to the secular arm to be burned.

Certainly he had loved her madly, and to the ruin, many thought, of his country, then at war with England for the possession of the empire of the New World. He had hardly ever permitted her to be out of his sight: for her, he had forgotten, or seemed to have forgotten, all grave affairs of State; and, with that terrible blindness that passion brings upon its servants, he had failed to notice that the elaborate ceremonies by which he sought to please her did but aggravate the strange malady from which she suffered. When she died he was, for a time, like one bereft of reason. Indeed, there is no doubt but that he would have formally abdicated and retired to the great Trappist monastery at Granada, of which he was already titular Prior, had he not been afraid to leave the little Infanta at the mercy of his brother, whose cruelty, even in Spain, was notorious, and who was suspected by many of having caused the Queen's death by means of a pair of poisoned gloves that he had presented to her on the occasion of her visiting his castle in Aragon. Even after the expiration of the three years of public mourning that he had ordained throughout his whole dominions by royal edict, he would never suffer his ministers to speak about any new alliance, and when the Emperor himself sent to him, and offered him the hand of the lovely Archduchess of Bohemia, his niece, in marriage, he bade the ambassadors tell their master that the King of Spain was already wedded to Sorrow, and that though she was but a barren bride he loved her better than Beauty; an answer that cost his crown the rich provinces of the Netherlands, which soon after, at the Emperor's instigation, revolted against him under the leadership of some fanatics of the Reformed Church.

His whole married life, with its fierce, fiery-colored joys and the terrible agony of its sudden ending, seemed to come back to him to-day as he watched the Infanta playing on the terrace. She had all the Queen's pretty petulance of manner, the same wilful way of tossing her head, the same proud curved beautiful mouth, the same wonderful smile - vrai sourire de France indeed - as she glanced up now and then at the window, or stretched out her little hand for the stately Spanish gentlemen to kiss. But the shrill laughter of the children grated on his ears, and the bright pitiless sunlight mocked his sorrow, and a dull odor of strange spices, spices such as embalmers use, seemed to taint - or was it fancy? - the clear morning air. He buried his face in his hands, and when the Infanta looked up again the curtains had been drawn, and the King had retired.

She made a little moue of disappointment, and shrugged her shoulders. Surely he might have stayed with her on her birthday. What did the stupid State-affairs matter? Or had he gone to that gloomy chapel, where the candles were always burning, and where she was never allowed to enter? How silly of him, when the sun was shining so brightly, and everybody was so happy! Besides, he would miss the sham bull-fight for which the trumpet was already sounding, to say nothing of the puppet show and the other wonderful things. Her uncle and the Grand Inquisitor were much more sensible. They had come out on the terrace, and paid her nice compliments. So she tossed her pretty head, and taking Don Pedro by the hand, she walked slowly down the steps towards a long pavilion of purple silk that had been erected at the end of the garden, the other children following in strict order of precedence, those who had the longest names going first.

A procession of noble boys, fantastically dressed as toreadors, came out to meet her, and the young Count of Tierra-Nueva, a wonderfully handsome lad of about fourteen years of age, uncovering his head with all the grace of a born hidalgo and grandee of Spain, led her solemnly in to a little gilt and ivory chair that was placed on a raised dais above the arena. The children grouped themselves all round, fluttering their big fans and whispering to each other, and Don Pedro and the Grand Inquisitor stood laughing at the entrance. Even the Duchess - the Camerera-Mayor as she was called - a thin, hard-featured woman with a yellow ruff did not look quite so bad-tempered as usual, and something like a chill smile flitted across her wrinkled face and twitched her thin bloodless lips.

It certainly was a marvellous bullfight, and much nicer, the Infanta thought, than the real bull-fight that she had been brought to see at Seville, on the occasion of the visit of the Duke of Parma to her father. Some of the boys pranced about on richly-caparisoned hobby-horses brandishing long javelins with gay streamers of bright ribands attached to them; others went on foot waving their scarlet cloaks before the bull, and vaulting lightly over the barrier when he charged them; and as for the bull himself he was just like a live bull, though he was only made of wicker-work and stretched hide, and sometimes insisted on running round the arena on his hind legs, which no live bull ever dreams of doing. He made a splendid fight of it too, and the children got so excited that they stood up upon the benches, and waved their lace handkerchiefs and cried out: Bravo toro! Bravo toro! just as sensibly as if they had been grown-up people. At last, however, after a prolonged combat, during which several of the hobby-horses were gored through and through, and their riders dismounted, the young Count of Tierra-Nueva brought the bull to his knees, and having obtained permission from the Infanta to give the coup de grace, he plunged his wooden sword into the neck of the animal with such violence that the head came right off and disclosed the laughing face of little Monsieur de Lorraine, the son of the French Ambassador at Madrid.

The arena was then cleared amidst much applause, and the dead hobby-horses dragged solemnly away by two Moorish pages in yellow and black liveries, and after a short interlude, during which a French posture-master performed upon the tight rope, some Italian puppets appeared in the semi-classical tragedy of Sophonisba on the stage of a small theatre that had been built up for the purpose. They acted so well, and their gestures were so extremely natural, that at the close of the play the eyes of the Infanta were quite dim with tears. Indeed some of the children really cried, and had to be comforted with sweetmeats, and the Grand Inquisitor himself was so affected that he could not help saying to Don Pedro that it seemed to him intolerable that things made simply out of wood and colored wax, and worked mechanically by wires, should be so unhappy and meet with such terrible misfortunes. An African juggler followed, who brought in a large flat basket covered with a red cloth, and having placed it in the centre of the arena, he took from his turban a curious reed pipe, and blew through it. In a few moments the cloth began to move, and as the pipe grew shriller and shriller two green and gold snakes put out their strange wedge-shaped heads and rose slowly up, swaying to and fro with the music as a plant sways in the water.

The children, however, were rather frightened at their spotted hoods and quick darting tongues, and were much more pleased when the juggler made a tiny orange-tree grow out of the sand and bear pretty white blossoms and clusters of real fruit; and when he took the fan of the little daughter of the Marquess de Las-Torres, and changed it into a blue bird that flew all round the pavilion and sang, their delight and amazement knew no bounds. The solemn minuet, too, performed by the dancing boys from the church of Nuestra Senora Del Pilar, was charming. The Infanta had never before seen this wonderful ceremony which takes place every year at May-time in front of the high altar of the Virgin, and in her honor; and indeed none of the royal family of Spain had entered the great cathedral of Saragossa since a mad priest, supposed by many to have been in the pay of Elizabeth of England, had tried to administer a poisoned wafer to the Prince of the Asturias. So she had known only by hearsay of "Our Lady's Dance," as it was called, and it certainly was a beautiful sight. The boys wore old-fashioned court dresses of white velvet, and their curious three-cornered hats were fringed with silver and surmounted with huge plumes of ostrich feathers, the dazzling whiteness of their costumes, as they moved about in the sunlight, being still more accentuated by their swarthy faces and long black hair. Everybody was fascinated by the grave dignity with which they moved through the intricate figures of the dance, and by the elaborate grace of their slow gestures, and stately bows, and when they had finished their performance and doffed their great plumed hats to the Infanta, she acknowledged their reverence with much courtesy, and made a vow that she would send a large wax candle to the shrine of Our Lady of Pilar in return for the pleasure that she had given her.

A troop of handsome Egyptians - as the gypsies were termed in those days - then advanced into the arena, and sitting down cross-legs, in a circle, began to play softly upon their zithers, moving their bodies to the tune, and humming, almost below their breath, a low dreamy air. When they caught sight of Don Pedro they scowled at him, and some of them looked terrified, for only a few weeks before he had had two of their tribe hanged for sorcery in the marketplace at Seville, but the pretty Infanta charmed them as she leaned back peeping over her fan with her great blue eyes, and they felt sure that one so lovely as she was could never be cruel to anybody. So they played on very gently and just touching the cords of the zithers with their long pointed nails, and their heads began to nod as though they were falling asleep. Suddenly, with a cry so shrill that all the children were startled and Don Pedro's hand clutched at the agate pommel of his dagger, they leapt to their feet and whirled madly round the enclosure beating their tambourines, and chanting some wild love-song in their strange guttural language. Then at another signal they all flung themselves again to the ground and lay there quite still, the dull strumming of the zithers being the only sound that broke the silence. After that they had done this several times, they disappeared for a moment and came back leading a brown shaggy bear by a chain, and carrying on their shoulders some little Barbary apes. The bear stood upon his head with the utmost gravity, and the wizened apes played all kinds of amusing tricks with two gipsy boys who seemed to be their masters, and fought with tiny swords, and tired off guns, and went through a regular soldier's drill just like the King's own bodyguard. In fact the gypsies were a great success.

But the funniest part of the whole morning's entertainment, was undoubtedly the dancing of the little Dwarf. When he stumbled into the arena, waddling on his crooked legs and Wagging his huge misshapen head from side to side, the children went off into a loud shout of delight, and the Infanta herself laughed so much that the Camerera was obliged to remind her that although there were many precedents in Spain for a King's daughter weeping before her equals, there were none for a Princess of the blood royal making so merry before those who were her inferiors in birth. The Dwarf however, was really quite irresistible, and even at the Spanish Court, always noted for its cultivated passion for the horrible, so fantastic a little monster had never been seen. It was his first appearance, too. He had been discovered only the day before, running wild through the forest, by two of the nobles who happened to have been hunting in a remote part of the great cork-wood that surrounded the town, and had been carried off by them to the Palace as a surprise for the Infanta, his father, who was a poor charcoal-burner, being but too well pleased to get rid of so ugly and useless a child. Perhaps the most amusing thing about him was his complete unconsciousness of his own grotesque appearance. Indeed he seemed quite happy and full of the highest spirits. When the children laughed, he laughed as freely and as joyously as any of them, and at the close of each dance he made them each the funniest of bows, smiling and nodding at them just as if he was really one of themselves, and not a little misshapen thing that Nature, in some humorous mood, had fashioned for others to mock at. As for the Infanta, she absolutely fascinated him. He could not keep his eyes off her, and seemed to dance for her alone, and when at the close of the performance, remembering how she had seen the great ladies of the Court throw bouquets to Caffarelli the famous Italian treble, whom the Pope had sent from his own chapel to Madrid that he might cure the King's melancholy by the sweetness of his voice, she took out of her hair the beautiful white rose, and partly for a jest and partly to tease the Camerera, threw it to him across the arena with her sweetest smile, he took the whole matter quite seriously, and pressing the flower to his rough coarse lips he put his hand upon his heart, and sank on one knee before her, grinning from ear to ear, and with his little bright eyes sparkling with pleasure.

This so upset the gravity of the Infanta that she kept on laughing long after the little Dwarf had run out of the arena, and expressed a desire to her uncle that the dance should be immediately repeated. The Camerera, however, on the plea that the sun was too hot, decided that it would be better that her Highness should return without delay to the Palace, where a wonderful feast had been already prepared for her, including a real birthday cake with her own initials worked all over it in painted sugar and a lovely silver flag waving from the top. The Infanta accordingly rose up with much dignity, and having given orders that the little dwarf was to dance again for her after the hour of siesta, and conveyed her thanks to the young Count of

Tierra-Nueva for his charming reception, she went back to her apartments, the children following in the same order in which they had entered.

Now when the little Dwarf heard that he was to dance a second time before the Infanta, and by her own express command, he was so proud that he ran out into the garden, kissing the white rose in an absurd ecstasy of pleasure, and making the most uncouth and clumsy gestures of delight.

The Flowers were quite indignant at his daring to intrude into their beautiful home, and when they saw him capering up and down the walks, and waving his arms above his head in such a ridiculous manner, they could not restrain their feelings any longer.

"He is really far too ugly to be allowed to play in any place where we are," cried the Tulips.

"He should drink poppy-juice, and go to sleep for a thousand years," said the great scarlet Lilies, and they grew quite hot and angry.

"He is a perfect horror!" screamed the Cactus. "Why, he is twisted and stumpy, and his head is completely out of proportion with his legs. Really he makes me feel prickly all over, and if he comes near me I will sting him with my thorns."

"And he has actually got one of my best blooms," exclaimed the White Rose-Tree. "I gave it to the Infanta this morning myself as a birthday present, and he has stolen it from her." And she called out: "Thief thief thief!" at the top of her voice.

Even the red Geraniums, who did not usually give themselves airs, and were known to have a great many poor relations themselves, curled up in disgust when they saw him, and when the Violets meekly remarked that though he was certainly extremely plain, still he could not help it, they retorted with a good deal of justice that that was his chief defect, and that there was no reason why one should admire a person because he was incurable; and, indeed, some of the Violets themselves felt that the ugliness of the little Dwarf was almost ostentatious, and that he would have shown much better taste if he had looked sad, or at least pensive, instead of jumping about merrily, and throwing himself into such grotesque and silly attitudes.

As for the old Sundial, who was an extremely remarkable individual, and had once told the time of day to no less a person than the Emperor Charles V himself, he was so taken aback by the little Dwarf's appearance, that he almost forgot to mark two whole minutes with his long shadowy finger, and could not help saying to the great milk-white Peacock, who was sunning herself on the balustrade, that everyone knew that the children of Kings were Kings, and that the children of charcoal-burners were charcoal-burners, and that it was absurd to pretend that it wasn't so; a statement with which the Peacock entirely agreed, and indeed screamed out, "Certainly, certainly," in such a loud, harsh voice, that the gold-fish who lived in the basin of the cool splashing fountain put their heads out of the water, and asked the huge stone Tritons what on earth was the matter.

But somehow the Birds liked him. They had seen him often in the forest, dancing about like an elf after the eddying leaves, or crouched up in the hollow of some old oak-tree, sharing his nuts with the squirrels. They did not mind his being ugly, a bit. Why, even the nightingale herself, who sang so sweetly in the orange groves at night that sometimes the Moon leaned down to listen, was not much to look at after all; and, besides, he had been kind to them, and during that terribly bitter winter, when there were no berries on the trees, and the ground was as hard as iron, and the wolves had come down to the very gates of the city to look for food, he had never once forgotten them, but had always given them crumbs out of his little hunch of black bread, and divided with them whatever poor breakfast he had.

So they flew round and round him, just touching his cheek with their wings as they passed, and chattered to each other, and the little Dwarf was so pleased that he could not help showing them the beautiful white rose, and telling them that the Infanta herself had given it to him because she loved him.

They did not understand a single word of what he was saying, but that made no matter, for they put their heads on one side, and looked wise, which is quite as good as understanding a thing, and very much easier.

The Lizards also took an immense fancy to him, and when he grew tired of running about and flung himself down on the grass to rest, they played and romped all over him, and tried to amuse him in the best way they could. "Every one cannot be as beautiful as a lizard," they cried; "that would be too much to expect. And, though it sounds absurd to say so, he is really not so ugly after all, provided, of course, that one shuts one's eyes, and does not look at him." The Lizards were extremely philosophical by nature, and often sat thinking for hours and hours together, when there was nothing else to do, or when the weather was too rainy for them to go out.

The Flowers, however, were excessively annoyed at their behavior, and at the behavior of the birds. "It only shows, they said, "what a vulgarising effect this incessant rushing and flying about has. Well-bred people always stay exactly in the same place, as we do. No one ever saw us hopping up and down the walks, or galloping madly through the grass after dragon-flies. When we do want change of air, we send for the gardener, and he carries us to another bed. This is dignified, and as it should be. But birds and lizards have no sense of repose, and indeed birds have not even a permanent address. They are mere vagrants like the gypsies, and should be treated in exactly the same manner." So they put their noses in the air, and looked very haughty, and were quite delighted when after some time they saw the little Dwarf scramble up from the grass, and make his way across the terrace to the palace.

"He should certainly be kept indoors for the rest of his natural life," they said. "Look at his hunched back, and his crooked legs," and they began to titter.

But the little Dwarf knew nothing of all this. He liked the birds and the lizards immensely, and thought that the flowers were the most marvellous things in the whole world, except of course the Infanta, but then she had given him the beautiful white rose, and she loved him, and that made a great difference. How he wished that he had gone back with her! She would have put him on her right hand, and smiled at him, and he would have never left her side, but would have made her his playmate, and taught her all kinds of delightful tricks. For though he had never been in a palace before, he knew a great many wonderful things. He could make little cages out of rushes for the grasshoppers to sing in, and fashion the long-jointed bamboo into the pipe that Pan loves to hear. He knew the cry of every bird, and could call the starlings from the tree-top, or the heron from the mere. He knew the trail of every animal, and could track the hare by its delicate footprints, and the boar by the trampled leaves. All the wind-dances he knew, the mad dance in red raiment with the autumn, the light dance in blue sandals over the corn, the dance with white snow-wreaths in winter, and the blossom-dance through the orchards in spring. He knew where the wood-pigeons built their nests, and once when a fowler had snared the parent birds, he had brought up the young ones himself, and had built a little dovecote for them in the cleft of a pollard elm. They were quite tame, and used to feed out of his hands every morning. She would like them, and the rabbits that scurried about in the long fern, and the jays with their steely feathers and black bills, and the hedgehogs that could curl themselves up into prickly balls, and the great wise tortoises that crawled slowly about, shaking their heads and nibbling at the young leaves. Yes, she must certainly come to the forest and play with him. He would give her his own little bed, and would watch outside the window till dawn, to see that the wild horned cattle did not harm her, nor the gaunt wolves creep too near the hut. And at dawn he would tap at the shutters and wake her, and they would go out and dance together all the day long. It was really not a bit lonely in the forest. Sometimes a Bishop rode through on his white mule, reading out of a painted book. Sometimes in their green velvet caps, and their jerkins of tanned deerskin, the falconers passed by, with hooded hawks on their wrists. At vintage time came the grape-treaders, with purple hands and feet, wreathed with glossy ivy and carrying dripping skins of wine; and the charcoal-burners sat round their huge braziers at night, watching the dry logs charring slowly in the fire, and roasting chestnuts in the ashes, and the robbers came out of their caves and made merry with them. Once, too, he had seen a beautiful procession winding up the long dusty road to Toledo. The monks went in front singing sweetly, and carrying bright banners and crosses of gold, and then, in silver armour, with matchlocks and pikes, came the soldiers, and in their midst walked three barefooted men, in strange yellow dresses painted all over with wonderful figures, and carrying lighted candles in their hands. Certainly there was a great deal to look at in the forest, and when she was tired he would find a soft bank of moss for her, or carry her in his arms, for he was very strong, though he knew that he was not tall. He would make her a necklace of red bryony berries, that would be quite as pretty as the white berries that she wore on her dress, and when she was tired of them, she could throw them away, and he would find her others. He would bring her acorn-cups and dew-drenched anemones, and tiny glow-worms to be stars in the pale gold of her hair.

But where was she? He asked the white rose, and it made him no answer.

The whole palace seemed asleep, and even where the shutters had not been closed, heavy curtains had been drawn across the windows to keep out the glare. He wandered all round looking for some place through which he might gain an entrance, and at last he caught sight of a little private door that was lying open. He slipped through, and found himself in a splendid hall, far more splendid, he feared, than the forest, there was so much more gilding everywhere, and even the floor was made of great colored stones, fitted together into a sort of geometrical pattern. But the little Infanta was not there, only some wonderful white statues that looked down on him from their jasper pedestals, with sad blank eyes and strangely smiling lips.

At the end of the hall hung a richly embroidered curtain of black velvet, powdered with suns and stars, the King's favorite devices, and broidered on the color he loved best. Perhaps she was hiding behind that? He would try at any rate.

So he stole quietly across, and drew it aside. No; there was only another room, though a prettier room, he thought, than the one he had just left. The walls were hung with a many-figured green arras of needle-wrought tapestry representing a hunt, the work of some Flemish artists who had spent more than seven years in its composition. It had once been the chamber of Jean le Fou, as he was called, that mad King who was so enamored of the chase, that he had often tried in his delirium to mount the huge rearing horses, and to drag down the stag on which the great hounds were leaping, sounding his hunting horn, and stabbing with his dagger at the pale flying deer. It was now used as the council-room, and on the centre table were lying the red portfolios of the ministers, stamped with the gold tulips of Spain, and with the arms and emblems of the house of Hapsburg.

The little Dwarf looked in wonder all round him, and was half-afraid to go on. The strange silent horsemen that galloped so swiftly through the long glades without making any noise, seemed to him like those terrible phantoms of whom he had heard the charcoal-burners speaking - the Comprachos, who hunt only at night, and if they meet a man, turn him into a hind, and chase him. But he thought of the pretty Infanta, and took courage. He wanted to find her alone, and to tell her that he too loved her. Perhaps she was in the room beyond.

He ran across the soft Moorish carpets, and opened the door. No! She was not here either. The room was quite empty.

It was a throne-room, used for the reception of foreign ambassadors, when the King, which of late had riot been often, consented to give them a personal audience; the same room in which, many years before, envoys had appeared from England to make arrangements for the marriage of their Queen, then one of the Catholic sovereigns of Europe, with the Emperor's eldest son. The hangings were of gilt Cordovan leather, and a heavy gilt chandelier with branches for three hundred wax lights hung down from the black and white ceiling. Underneath a great canopy of gold cloth, on which the lions and towers of Castile were broidered in seed pearls, stood the throne itself covered with a rich pall of black velvet studded with silver tulips and elaborately fringed with silver and pearls. On the second step of the throne was placed the kneeling-stool of the Infanta, with its cushion of cloth of silver tissue, and below that again, and beyond the limit of the canopy, stood the chair for the Papal Nuncio, who alone had the right to be seated in the King's presence on the occasion of any public ceremonial, and whose Cardinal's hat, with its tangled scarlet tassels, lay on a purple tabouret in front. On the wall, facing the throne, hung a life-sized portrait of Charles V in hunting dress, with a great mastiff by his side, and a picture of Philip II receiving the homage of the Netherlands occupied the centre of the other wall. Between the windows stood a black ebony cabinet, inlaid with plates of ivory, on which the figures from Holbein's Dance of Death had been graved - by the hand, some said, of that famous master himself.

But the little Dwarf cared nothing for all this magnificence. He would not have given his rose for all the pearls on the canopy, nor one white petal of his rose for the throne itself What he wanted was to see the Infanta before she went down to the pavilion, and to ask her to come away with him when he had finished his dance. Here, in the Palace, the air was close and heavy, but in the forest the wind blew free, and the sunlight with wandering hands of gold moved the tremulous leaves aside. There were flowers, too, in the forest, not so splendid, perhaps, as the flowers in the garden, but more sweetly scented for all that; hyacinths in early spring that flooded with waving purple the cool glens, and grassy knolls; yellow primroses that nestled in little clumps round the gnarled roots of the oak-trees; bright celandine, and blue speedwell, and irises lilac and gold. There were grey catkins on the hazels, and the fox-gloves drooped with the weight of their dappled bee-haunted cells. The chestnut had its spires of white stars, and the hawthorn its pallid moons of beauty. Yes: surely she would come if he could only find her! She would come with him to the fair forest, and all day long he would dance for her delight. A smile lit up his eyes at the thought and he passed into the next room.

Of all the rooms this was the brightest and the most beautiful. The walls were covered with a pink-flowered Lucca damask, patterned with birds and dotted with dainty blossoms of silver; the furniture was of massive silver, festooned with florid wreaths, and swinging Cupids; in front of the two large fire-places stood great screens broidered with parrots and peacocks, and the floor, which was of sea-green onyx, seemed to stretch far away into the distance. Nor was he alone. Standing under the shadow of the doorway, at the extreme end of the room, he saw a little figure watching him. His heart trembled, a cry of joy broke from his lips, and he moved out into the sunlight. As he did so, the figure moved out also, and he saw it plainly.

The Infanta! It was a monster, the most grotesque monster he had ever beheld. Not properly shaped, as all other people were, but hunchbacked, and crooked-limbed, with huge lolling head and mane of black hair. The little Dwarf frowned, and the monster frowned also. He laughed, and it laughed with him, and held its hands to its sides, just as he himself was doing. He made it a mocking bow, and it returned him a low reverence. He went towards it, and it came to meet him, copying each step that he made, and stopping when he stopped himself. He shouted with amusement, and ran forward, and reached out his hand, and the hand of the monster touched his, and it was as cold as ice. He grew afraid, and moved his hand across, and the monster's hand followed it quickly. He tried to press on, but something smooth and hard stopped him. The face of the monster was now close to his own, and seemed full of terror. He brushed his hair off his eyes. It imitated him. He struck at it, and it returned blow for blow. He loathed it, and it made hideous faces at him. He drew back, and it retreated.

What is it? He thought for a moment, and looked round at the rest of the room. It was strange, but everything seemed to have its double in this invisible wall of clear water. Yes, picture for picture was repeated, and couch for couch. The sleeping Faun that lay in the alcove by the doorway had its twin brother that slumbered, and the silver Venus that stood in the sunlight held out her arms to a Venus as lovely as herself.

"Was it Echo? He had called to her once in the valley, and she had answered him word for word. Could she mock the eye, as she mocked the voice? Could she make a mimic world just like the real world? Could the shadow of things have color and life and movement? Could it be that - ?

He started, and taking from his breast the beautiful white rose, he turned round, and kissed it. The monster had a rose of its own, petal for petal the same! It kissed it with like kisses, and pressed it to its heart with horrible gestures.

"When the truth dawned upon him, he gave a wild cry of despair, and fell sobbing to the ground. So it was he who was misshapen and hunchbacked, foul to look at and grotesque. He himself was the monster, and it was at him that all the children had been laughing, and the little Princess who he had thought loved him - she too had been merely mocking at his ugliness, and making merry over his twisted limbs. "Why had they not left him in the forest, where there was no mirror to tell him how loathsome he was? "Why had his father not killed hint, rather that sell him to his shame? The hot tears poured down his cheeks, and he tore the white rose to pieces. The sprawling monster did the same, and scattered the faint petals in the air. It grovelled on the ground, and, when he looked at it, it watched him with a face drawn with pain. He crept away, lest he should see it, and covered his eyes with his hands. He crawled, like some wounded thing, into the shadow, and lay there moaning.

And at that moment the Infanta herself came in with her companions through the open window, and when they saw the ugly little dwarf lying on the ground and beating the floor with his clenched hands, in the most fantastic and exaggerated manner, they went off into shouts of happy laughter, and stood all round him and watched him.

"His dancing was funny," said the Infanta; "but his acting is funnier still. Indeed he is almost as good as the puppets, only of course not quite so natural." And she fluttered her big fan, and applauded.

But the little Dwarf never looked up, and his sobs grew fainter and fainter, and suddenly he gave a curious gasp, and clutched his side. And then he fell back again, and lay quite still.

"That is capital," said the Infanta, after a pause; "but now you must dance for me."

"Yes," cried all the children, "you must get up and dance, for you are as clever as the Barbary apes, and much more ridiculous."

But the little Dwarf never moved.

And the Infanta stamped her foot, and called out to her uncle, who was walking on the terrace with the Chamberlain, reading some despatches that had just arrived from Mexico where the Holy Office had recently been established. "My funny little dwarf is sulking," she cried, "you must wake him up, and tell him to dance for me."

They smiled at each other, and sauntered in, and Don Pedro stooped down, and slapped the Dwarf on the cheek with his embroidered glove. "You must dance," he said, "petit monstre. You must dance. The Infanta of Spain and the Indies wishes to be amused."

But the little Dwarf never moved.

"A whipping master should be sent for," said Don Pedro wearily, and he went back to the terrace. But the Chamberlain looked grave, and he knelt beside the little dwarf, and put his hand upon his heart. And after a few moments he shrugged his shoulders, and rose up, and having made a low bow to the Infanta, he said:

"Ma bella Princesa, your funny little dwarf will never dance again. It is a pity, for he is so ugly that he might have made the King smile."

"But why will he not dance again?" asked the Infanta, laughing.

"Because his heart is broken," answered the Chamberlain.

And the Infanta frowned, and her dainty rose-leaf lips curled in pretty disdain. "For the future let those who come to play with me have no hearts," she cried, and she ran out into the garden.

星星男孩

他已經在世界上流浪了三年，

這三年來，

沒有人對他表現過一絲仁慈、憐憫和愛，

然而，這樣的世界卻是當初太過驕傲的他一手造成的。

在很久很久以前，有兩個伐木工人正越過濃密廣袤的松樹林，走在回家的路上。時值冬夜，空氣中激盪著冷冽的寒氣。大雪覆蓋著地面，也停佇在樹枝上；寒霜行經樹林時也不住地扯扯樹枝；當寒霜隨著大雪來到多倫特山時，便靜靜地懸浮在空中，因為雪王親吻了她。

天氣這麼冷，連野獸和鳥兒都不知道該怎麼熬過去。

「嗚！」這是野狼的嗥叫聲，他正夾著尾巴躍過草叢，「這天氣真是可怖極了，政府怎麼不管管呢？」

「啾！啾！啾！」蒼白的紅雀顫抖地叫道，「老邁的大地死了，他們為她穿上白色的壽衣準備下葬啦。」

「大地要結婚了，她穿的是她的新娘禮服。」斑鳩彼此耳語著。他們紫紅色的小腳被寒霜凍得疼痛不堪，但還是覺得以浪漫的眼光來看世界，是他們該守的本份。

「胡說八道！」野狼咆哮著，「我告訴你們，這一切全是政府的錯，如果們不相信我的話，那我只好吃掉你們。」野狼的見解總是非常實際，而且他從不曾在任何一場精采的辯論中嘗過敗績。

「可是，我個人認為，」啄木鳥開口了，他是一位天生的哲學家，「探討事情不必拘泥於旁枝末節。如果事情是這樣，那它就是這樣了，目前嘛，是冷得要命就是了。」

的確是冷得要命。住在高大棕樹裡的小松鼠，必須不斷地彼此摩擦鼻子以保持溫暖；野兔子蜷縮在自己的窩裡，連到門邊上探探頭也不敢。唯一喜歡這種天氣的，好像就只有貓頭鷹了。他們的翅膀都讓霜給凍得硬邦邦的，可是他們一點也不在乎，仍然骨碌碌地轉著黃褐色的大眼睛，在森林裡飛來飛去，互相問候著：「咦唔！咦唔！天氣真好啊！」

那兩個伐木工人繼續向前走去，抖擻著精神，用他們加掛防滑鐵圈的靴子在蛋糕似的雪地上踩出一排排腳印。有一次，他們不小心摔進一個深坑裡，從坑裡爬起來時，兩人活像從麵粉堆走出來似的；還有一次，兩人在結了冰、又硬又滑的湖面上摔了一跤，捆好的柴薪全散開來，兩人只好把地上的柴薪一一拾起，重新捆紮；更有一次，他們以為迷路了，兩人害怕得不得了，因為他們知道，對於在雪地裡打盹的人，大雪會用殘酷的手法對付他們的。還好他們全心信任旅人的守護神馬丁，終於再度找到回家的路，一步一步小心翼翼地繼續前進，後來，他們總算走到森林的盡頭了，兩人俯視著腳下的山谷，看到了村裡明亮的燈火。

對於能夠平安歸來，這兩個伐木工人都欣喜欲狂，此時，他們覺得大地彷彿是一朵銀色的花兒，而月亮則像一朵金色的花兒。

不過，欣喜的情緒退去後，悲哀的思緒隨即湧上心頭，因為他們想起自己家裡是如此清貧，於是其中一個伐木工人開口說道：「我們這麼高興幹嘛？生命之花是為有錢人而綻放，又不是為我們這些窮光蛋而開的。我們倒不如凍死在森林裡頭，或是讓野獸吃掉還來得好過些。」

「沒錯啦，」他的同伴回答道，「有些人比較富裕，有些人比較貧窮。這世界上充滿了不公平的事，只有『煩憂』對所有的人們一視同仁。」

正當這兩人彼此互吐苦水時，怪事發生了。天空中掉下來一顆既亮又美的星星，這顆星星從天邊滾下來，順著自己的航道掠過其他星星，一路下滑，這兩個伐木工人一直看著它，他們覺得，這顆星星應該是掉在不遠處一座羊棚旁的柳樹叢後。

其中一個伐木工人跑得比同伴還快，他穿過柳樹叢，走捷徑出來。哇，看哪！白皚皚的雪地上果真躺著一個金黃閃亮的東西。於是他快步來到它旁邊，蹲下身來用手摸摸它——這是一塊用金線縫成的斗篷，上頭繡著星星，中間彷彿包著什麼物品似的捲了好幾層。於是這個伐木工人大聲呼喚著同伴，說他已經找到從天上掉下來的財寶了，他的同伴一趕過來，兩人便一齊坐在雪地上，打開斗篷包著的東西以便平分財寶。可是，哎，裡頭竟然沒有黃金，也沒有白銀，更別提其他任何值錢的東西了，事實上，斗篷裡頭只裹著一個熟睡中的嬰孩而已。

其中一個伐木工人說道：「這就是我們美好希望的痛苦結局，我們前途無亮了，一個小孩能為一個男人帶來什麼好處呢？把這孩子留在原地好了，我們回家吧，想想我們自己只是窮人，除了養育自己的孩子之外，根本沒有能力再養別人的孩子了。」

然而，他的同伴卻答道：「不，把這孩子留在雪地上凍死，是件罪過。雖然我和你一樣貧窮，而且家裡還有幾張嗷嗷待哺的嘴，但我還是想把這孩子抱回家，我的妻子會照顧他的。」

於是他輕柔小心地抱起孩子，用斗篷將他裹好，免得在這樣寒冷的天氣裡受凍，然後走下山坡，一路走回村裡去；同伴對他的愚蠢和善良感到非常不可思議。

當他們回到村裡時，同伴對他說道：「既然你得到那個小孩，那麼，斗篷就該給我了，因為這是我們共同發現的東西，理當均分才對。」

然而，他卻回答道：「不行，這斗篷不是你的也不是我的，它是那孩子的東西。」說完，他向同伴道聲再見，便往自己的家門口走去。

他敲敲門。

他妻子一打開門，看到自己丈夫平安歸來，立刻高興得摟住他的脖子，親吻他，卸下他揹著的柴薪，還幫他把靴子上的積雪掃掉，叫他快些進屋裡去。

可是他告訴她：「我在森林裡撿到一樣東西，而且我把它帶回來，想讓你照顧它。」他仍然站在門口。

「是什麼東西？」她叫道，「快讓我看看，我們已是家徒四壁，我們需要的東西可多了。」於是伐木工人打開斗篷，露出那個還沒睡醒的孩子。

「啊，天哪！」她喃喃地說道，「我們自己的孩子還不夠多？你非得帶一個回來湊熱鬧不可嗎？而且，這孩子不曉得會不會帶來厄運？況且，我們該怎麼照顧他呢？」她氣得不得了。

「不要生氣了，他是星星男孩哪！」他解釋道，並且將發現這孩子的過程告訴妻子。

然而，他的解釋並不能平息妻子的怒氣，她反而嘲諷他，生氣地哭道：「我們自己的孩子都吃不飽了，怎麼去養另一個孩子？有人會關心我們嗎？有人會給我們食物嗎？」

「不要這麼說，即便是麻雀，上帝不也照顧牠們，給牠們食物吃嗎？」他答道。

「在冬天裡，麻雀不也餓死了嗎？」她反駁道，「眼下正值寒冬，不是嗎？」伐木工人沒有搭腔，只是站在門口。

從森林裡吹過來的寒風透過開著的門，直吹進屋內，她冷得發抖，於是開口道：「你還不把門關上？冷風一直吹進屋裡來，我快冷死了。」

「屋裡有顆硬如鐵石的心，冷風還會吹不進來嗎？」伐木工人說道。可是妻子不說一句話，只是離火爐又更近了些。

過了一會兒，妻子轉過頭來看看他，眼裡飽含著淚水。伐木工人輕快地走進來，把小孩塞進妻子懷裡；婦人親了小孩一下，把小孩放在一張小床上，讓這個撿回來的孩子和他們家最小的孩子一塊兒睡。第二天，伐木工人便將那件華麗的黃金斗篷收到大櫥櫃裡，他的妻子也將那小孩脖子上戴著的琥珀項鍊收進大櫥櫃裡。

於是，星星男孩就此住在伐木工人家中，和他們家的孩子們一起長大，一起吃喝，一起玩耍。而且星星男孩愈長愈漂亮，全村的人都對他的美貌感到不可思議，因為這村裡的人全都長得黑黝黝的，就連頭髮也是黑色的；然而星星男孩的膚色卻又白又細緻，像鋸開的象牙一樣，而他的鬈髮也如花朵般美麗。他的雙唇簡直就像兩片紅色的花瓣，他的雙眼更有如生長在純淨水邊的兩朵紫羅蘭，他的身形更有如田邊的水仙花。

然而，他的美麗卻只讓他成為一個邪惡的人。因為他不但驕傲、殘忍，還很自私。他看不起伐木工人的孩子和村裡其他的孩童，他說他們的血統卑賤，只有他擁有高貴的血統，因為他是星星的後裔，於是，他要所有的小孩子都尊他為王，而且他稱這些小孩子是他的僕役。他從來不憐憫貧窮、眼盲、殘障或任何受病苦的人，反而還拿石頭丟他們，把他們趕到馬路上去，叫他們到別的地方去乞食；所以，除了亡命之徒，再沒有人會到這個村子乞討。

事實上，星星男孩對於美有著近乎癡狂的愛戀，對於貧窮或討厭的人，他總是毫不留情地加以嘲諷、謾罵，甚至拿他們開玩笑，他只愛他自己。夏天裡，當風靜止時，他就會待在神父果園裡的水井旁，低頭俯視自己映在水面上的美麗面容，並因自己的美貌而愉快地笑著。

伐木工人和他的妻子經常責備星星男孩道：「你也是孤單、需要幫助的人，可是我們並沒有用你對待那些上門求助的人的態度，來對待你。你為什麼要對那些需要憐憫的人如此殘酷呢？」

神父經常找他過去，想要教會他愛世界上一切有生命的東西，他告訴星星男孩：「蒼蠅是你的兄弟，不可以傷害它。徜徉在森林裡的野鳥有牠們的自由，不要為了你個人的取樂而設陷阱捕捉牠們。上帝造無腳蜥蜴，也造鼹鼠，而且牠們各有各的生活空間。你憑什麼為上帝所造的世界帶來痛苦？就連草場上的牛犢也要讚美上帝。」

然而，星星男孩卻從來不把他們的教誨當成一回事，他總是皺著眉頭、嘲弄他們一番，就又回到同伴身邊，帶領他們玩樂。他的同伴們當然跟隨著他，因為他長得好看、動作迅捷、還會跳舞、吹笛、唱歌。無論星星男孩吩咐他們做什麼，他們一定照作不誤。當星星男孩拿起一根尖銳的蘆葦刺傷鼹鼠朦朧的眼睛時，他的同伴們便哈哈大笑；當他拿石頭丟麻瘋病患的時候，他們也哈哈大笑。在星星男孩的調教下，這群孩童的心腸也變得愈來愈硬，簡直就快和他一個樣了。

有一天，村子裡來了一個乞丐婆。她身上的衣服既破且爛，雙腳也因走過粗糙路面而血流不止，整個人散發著悲慘的窘況。由於疲累不堪，乞丐婆便坐在一棵栗樹下休息。

星星男孩一看到她，立刻告訴他的同伴們：「看哪！那棵美麗鮮綠的栗樹下，坐了一個又髒又臭的乞丐婆。來吧，我們把她趕走，因為她又醜又討人嫌。」

於是，星星男孩走近乞丐婆，朝她丟擲石塊，還對她冷嘲熱諷。乞丐婆眼中滿是驚懼地看著他，但是她卻沒有走開，也沒有將目光從星星男孩身上移開。正在附近砍柴的伐木工人看到星星男孩的行為，趕緊跑過來斥責他，告訴他：「沒錯，你是鐵石心腸，一點也不知道什麼叫憐憫，這個可憐的女人對你做了什麼，你何以要這麼殘忍的對待她？」

星星男孩卻氣得脹紅了臉，還用力地踩腳，說道：「你有什麼資格干涉我的作為？我又不是你的兒子，根本不必聽你的話。」

「你說得對，」伐木工人答道，「即便如此，我在森林裡發現你的時候，還憐憫你呢。」

那個乞丐婆一聽到這幾句話竟大叫一聲，昏倒在地。於是伐木工人將她帶回自己家中，要妻子照顧她。當她甦醒過來時，他們為她準備了肉和酒，也好好地安慰她。

然而，乞丐婆卻不吃也不喝，只是問著伐木工人：「你說，剛剛那孩子是你在森林裡發現的？是不是十年前的事？」

伐木工人答道：「是啊，我的確是在森林裡發現他的，從那時候到現在也已經過了十年了。」

「你在他身上有沒有發現什麼東西？」乞丐婆急切地問道，「他的脖子上是不是掛了一條琥珀項鍊？他是不是被一件繡著星星的黃金斗篷包裹著？」

「沒錯，」伐木工人答道，「跟妳說的完全吻合。」於是伐木工人從大櫥櫃取出那件斗篷和琥珀項鍊，拿給乞丐婆看。

乞丐婆一看到這兩件東西，高興得流下眼淚來，她說道：「他就是我遺落在森林裡的小兒子，請你們快些把他找回來，我為了找他，幾乎走遍全世界了。」

星星男孩一聽到消息便興高采烈地跑進屋裡。然而，他一看到等著他的竟是那個乞丐婆，不禁刻薄地笑道：「哈，我的母親在哪兒呢？這兒只有一個貧賤的乞丐婆而已啊。」

然而，乞丐婆卻說道：「我就是你的母親。」

「你是瘋了才這麼說。」星星男孩憤怒地叫道，「我不是妳兒子，因為妳是一個乞丐，不但醜陋而且還穿得破破爛爛的。所以，妳走吧，不要讓我再看到妳那張可憎的臉。」

「你錯了，你真的是我的小兒子，我是在森林裡生下你的。」她哭道，跪了下來，伸出雙臂要擁抱星星男孩。「匪徒從我懷裡把你搶了去，留你在森林等死。」她喃喃地說道，「可是我一看到你就認出你了，這些東西我也認得，黃金斗篷和琥珀項鍊都是當初讓你帶在身上的啊。因此，請你跟我一塊兒走吧，為了找你，我已經走遍全世界了。兒子，跟我走吧，我需要你。」

然而，星星男孩卻動也不動，鐵硬著心腸拒絕了乞丐婆的請求，對於她痛苦的悲泣也充耳不聞。

最後，星星男孩終於對乞丐婆說話了，可是他的聲音又冷又澀。「如果妳真是我母親，」他說道，「最好離我遠些，不要再到這兒讓我受窘了，因為我一直認為自己是某顆星星的兒子，而不是像妳所說的，是乞丐的兒子。所以，妳走吧，不要讓我再看到妳了。」

「啊！兒子，」她哭道，「即使在我走之前，你也不親我一下嗎？為了找你，我吃了好多的苦啊。」

「不行，」星星男孩說道，「你實在太醜了，我情願親吻毒蛇或蟾蜍，也不願親吻妳。」

於是乞丐婆站起來，悲傷哭泣著走進森林裡去。星星男孩看她離開了，高興得不得了，立刻跑到他的同伴們那裡，想和他們一起玩耍。

可是他的同伴們一看到他過來，便對他冷嘲熱諷，說道：「嘿，你和蟾蜍一樣醜，和毒蛇一樣噁心。走開吧，我們受不了和你這樣的人一起玩。」於是，他們將星星男孩趕出花園。

星星男孩皺了皺眉，自言自語道：「他們怎麼會這樣說我？我要到井水旁去看看自己的樣子，井水會映出我的美麗的。」

於是，他來到井邊，低頭往下看。天哪！他的臉是一張和蟾蜍一樣的臉，而身軀竟有如毒蛇一般。他嚇了一跳，撲在草地上痛哭，告訴自己：「這一定是上天給我的懲罰，因為我不肯和自己的母親相認，還把她趕走，又那麼傲慢、殘酷地對待她。為此，我要走遍全世界去找她，直到找著她為止。」

那時，伐木工人的小女兒來到星星男孩身邊，將手放在他的肩膀上，說道：「即使你不再美麗又怎麼樣呢？留下來吧，我不會笑你的。」

然而他告訴她：「不行，我是因為殘酷地對待自己的母親，才會受到這麼可怕的懲罰。為此，我必須離開這兒，尋遍全世界，直到我找著她，得到她的寬恕為止。」

於是，他跑進森林裡，呼喊著他的母親，卻沒有人回答他。星星男孩在森林裡找了一整天，當太陽下山、夜幕低垂時，他就睡在落葉堆上，而鳥兒和其他動物都避開他，因為牠們都知道他過往的殘忍作為；他的身邊除了瞪著他的蟾蜍和慢慢爬過他身邊的毒蛇之外，再沒有別人了。

天亮時，他站起身來，從樹上摘了些澀澀的漿果吃，吃完便又趕路，悲傷哭泣著離開大森林。一路上，不論他遇上誰，總要問對方有沒有看見星星男孩的母親。

他告訴鼴鼠：「你有鑽地的本領，請告訴我，我母親在地面下嗎？」

鼴鼠回答道：「你弄瞎了我的眼睛，我怎麼會知道？」

他告訴紅雀：「你可以飛上最高的樹梢，看到全世界。請告訴我，你看得到我母親嗎？」

紅雀回答道：「你為了好坑剪掉我的翅膀，你想，我現在還能飛嗎？」

星星男孩又對那隻住在樅樹樹幹裡的孤獨松鼠說道：「你知道我的母親在哪裡嗎？」

松鼠回答道：「你殺了我的母親。怎麼，你現在要找到你自己的母親，然後殺了她嗎？」

星星男孩哭著低垂下頭，請求這些動物原諒他，然後又繼續趕路，尋找那位乞丐婆。三天後，他來到森林的邊緣，隨即走到了平原地區。

當他走過村莊時，小孩子們不僅嘲笑他，還拿石頭丟他，就連他向村人要求借宿在牛欄裡，人家也不想答應，因為怕他會為收藏積貯的穀物帶來黴菌；而且他長得實在太可怕了，人們都不願意收留他，更沒有人憐憫他。他已經在世界上流浪三年，卻仍然打聽不到那位乞丐婆——也就是他親生母親的消息。有好幾次，他彷彿見到自己母親站在前面的路上，於是他呼喊著她，拚命向前奔跑，一直跑到雙腳被尖銳的石頭磨出血來為止。可是，他卻永遠也追不上母親，他問路旁的人有沒有看到她，他們卻說沒有見過他母親，也未曾看過長得像她的人，他們甚至拿他的悲傷開玩笑。

他已經在世界上流浪了三年，這三年來，沒有人對他表現過一絲仁慈、憐憫和愛，然而，這樣的一個世界，卻是當初太過驕傲的他一手造成的。

有一天晚上，他來到佇立於河畔、一座有著高大堅固城牆的城市門口，雖然他疲累腳疼，卻仍想進城去。然而，守門的衛兵卻用戟攔住入口，粗魯地問他道：「你要進城去做什麼？」

「我要找我母親，」他答道，「請你們讓我過去吧，我母親也許在這個城裡。」

然而衛兵卻嘲笑他，而且其中一個衛兵還摸摸鬍子，放下手中的盾牌，叫道：「說真的，即使你母親看到你，也不會高興的，因為你長得比沼澤旁的蟾蜍還討人嫌，也比在濕地上爬的毒蛇還討人厭。走吧、走吧，你母親不住在這城裡。」

另一個手裡拿著一面黃旗的守衛告訴他：「你母親是誰？你為什麼要找她呢？」

星星男孩答道：「我母親是個和我一樣的乞丐，我曾經用非常惡劣的態度對待她，請你們讓我過去吧。如果我母親住在這座城裡的話，我就可以去見她，請她寬恕我。」可是衛兵們不答應，還用他們的矛刺他。

就在他哭著離去之際，有個甲冑上鑲嵌著金箔花飾、頭盔上蹲著一隻雙翼獅子的人走了過來，詢問守城的衛兵，剛剛是誰想進城來。衛兵答道：「不就是一個乞丐來找他的乞丐母親，我們已經把他趕出去了。」

「真笨，」那個人笑道，「我們可以將那種貨色賣給其他人當奴隸，那乞丐還值一碗甜酒呢。」

此時剛好有個一臉邪惡的老人走過去，他聽見這話便高聲說道：「我出一碗甜酒買他。」老人付了錢之後，隨即拉著星星男孩的手，帶他進城裡去。

老人帶著星星男孩走過好幾條街，來到石榴樹蔭遮蔽的牆邊，這裡有一扇小門。老人用鑲嵌著寶石的戒指敲門，小門隨即打開，他們走下五級青銅製的階梯，來到一座滿是黑色罌粟花和綠色陶土罐的花園。老人從頭巾中抽出一條絲製圍巾，用來蒙住星星男孩的眼睛，並且要星星男孩走在他前面。後來，當老人除去蒙住星星男孩眼睛的圍巾時，星星男孩發覺自己置身在一座土牢裡，唯一的光線來源是一個角形燈籠。

老人將一個盛著硬麵包的木盤擺在星星男孩面前，說道：「吃。」還給了他一杯鹹鹹的水，說道：「喝。」星星男孩吃喝完後，老人便離開土牢，鎖上門，還用一條鐵鍊緊緊鎖住。

第二天，這個老人，也就是全利比亞最狡詐的魔法師（他曾向尼羅河畔一處墓穴裡的魔法師學藝），來到星星男孩面前，對他皺起眉頭，說道：「距城門不遠的一座森林裡藏有三塊金子，分別是白金、黃金和赤金。今天，你得將那塊白金帶回來給我，如果你失敗了，我會抽你一百下鞭子。快去吧，日落時，我在花園門口等你。聽著，你如果不將那塊白金帶回來給我，可就有苦頭吃了，因為你是我的奴隸，是我用一碗甜酒的代價買回來的。」於是老人再度用絲製圍巾蒙住星星男孩的眼睛，將他帶出土牢，走過長滿罌粟花的花園，走上五級青銅製臺階，再用他手上的戒指打開那扇小門，放星星男孩到街上去。

於是星星男孩走出城門，來到魔法師說的那座森林。這森林看起來蓊鬱青翠，真是美極了，而且好像住滿了引吭高歌的鳥兒和長滿了氣味芳香的花朵，星星男孩愉快地走進森林裡去。然而，森林卻不怎麼禮遇他，無論他走到哪裡，尖利的野薔薇和荊棘總是從地上探出頭來圍繞著他，搗蛋的蕁麻老愛黏著他，薊花也以身上那利如短劍的針刺傷他，星星男孩痛得不得了。他也找不到魔法師吩咐要找的那塊白金，他從早晨找到中午，再從中午找到晚上，卻依然遍尋不著。日落時，他望著城裡，眼淚撲簌簌地流下來，因為他知道，一回去會受到什麼樣的懲罰。

　　快要走出樹林時，星星男孩聽到草叢裡傳出痛苦的哭聲，他忘了自己的悲傷，立刻跑到草叢邊。他看到一隻小野兔陷在獵人所設的陷阱中。

　　星星男孩心中充滿憐憫，立刻放了小野兔，對牠說道：「雖然我只是個奴隸，卻可以助你得到自由。」

　　小野兔回答道：「沒錯，是你給了我自由，我該怎麼回報你呢？」

　　於是星星男孩告訴牠：「我正在尋找一塊白金，可是怎麼也找不到，如果我不將那塊白金帶回去，我的主人會用鞭子打我。」

　　「跟我來，」野兔說道，「我帶你去找，因為我知道它藏在哪裡，也知道它為什麼要藏在那裡。」

　　星星男孩便跟在小野兔後面走，看哪！在一棵老橡樹樹幹的裂縫中，藏著一塊白金。星星男孩喜出望外地拿起它，對小野兔說道：「我幫你的忙，你已經數倍奉還；我對你付出的慈愛，你也以百倍的仁慈回饋了。」

　　「沒這回事，」小野兔答道，「你怎麼對我，我就怎麼對你而已。」說完，牠輕快地跑開，星星男孩也往城裡走去。

　　此時，城門口坐了一個痲瘋病患。他臉上罩著一塊灰色亞麻布頭套，只露出一雙像燒紅煤炭似的眼睛。他一看到星星男孩走過來，便遞上一只木碗，搖著鈴，呼喚著星星男孩，對他說道：「給我一點錢吧，我快餓死了。他們把我丟出城來，也沒有人給我一絲同情。」

「唉！」星星男孩難過地說道，「我的錢袋裡只有一塊白金，可是我若不將它交給我的主人，他就會用鞭子抽打我，因為我是他的奴隸。」

然而那個癩瘋病人卻一再地懇求他，拜託他，後來星星男孩因為同情他，便將那塊白金給了他。

星星男孩一回到魔法師的住處，魔法師立刻打開門，一把將他揪進去，問道：「找到白金了嗎？」星星男孩回答：「沒有。」於是魔法師將他推倒，拿了鞭子狠狠地抽打他，再將一只空盤子擺到他面前，說道：「吃。」也把一只空的杯子放到他眼前，說道：「喝。」然後，再次把他扔進地牢裡。

隔天，魔法師又來找他，告訴他：「今天你如果不把黃金帶回來，你就永遠當我的奴隸，而且我還會抽你三百鞭。」

於是，星星男孩又來到森林裡，整天忙著尋找那塊黃金，但是他仍然遍尋不著。日落時，他坐在地上開始哭泣，就在此時，昨天他從陷阱裡救出的那隻小野兔，又來到他身邊。

小野兔告訴他：「你為什麼要哭呢？你在森林裡找些什麼？」星星男孩回答：「我在找一塊藏在森林裡的黃金，如果我找不到那塊黃金帶回去給我的主人，他就要用鞭子抽打我，還要我永遠當他的奴隸。」

「跟我來。」小野兔說道，牠跑過森林，來到一處池塘邊。原來，那塊黃金就藏在池塘下面。

「我該怎麼謝謝你呢？」星星男孩問道，「這已經是你第二次救我了。」

「不必客氣，是你先對我好的。」小野兔答道，然後輕快地跑開了。

於是星星男孩拿起那塊黃金，放進錢袋裡，急急地走向城裡。然而，那個痲瘋病患還是一看到他走過來便又跑到他身邊，跪下來哭道：「給我一點錢吧，我快餓死了。」

星星男孩告訴他：「我的錢袋只有一塊黃金，我如果不把它帶回去交給我的主人，他就會打我，要我永遠當他的奴隸。」

可是那個痲瘋病患一再地懇求他，於是星星男孩又動了惻隱之心，將那塊黃金送給了痲瘋病人。

星星男孩一回到魔法師的住處，魔法師立刻打開門，一把將他揪了進去，問道：「你找到黃金了嗎？」星星男孩回答：「沒有。」於是，魔法師再度推倒他，狠狠地抽打他，還把他用鐵鍊鎖住，扔進地牢裡。

隔天，魔法師又來找他，對他說道：「今天，如果你把赤金帶來給我，我就還你自由，但是，如果你做不到，我就殺了你。」

於是星星男孩第三次來到森林裡，整天忙著找尋赤金，然而他還是遍尋不著。黃昏時，他坐下來痛哭，正當他淚眼婆娑時，小野兔又出現了。

小野兔告訴他，「你要找的那塊赤金，就藏在你身後的洞穴裡。別哭了，高興點吧。」

「我該怎麼報答你呢？」星星男孩叫道，「這是你第三次救我了。」

「不用客氣，是你先對我好的。」小野兔答道，然後輕快地跑開了。

於是星星男孩鑽進洞穴裡，在最遠處的角落找到那塊赤金。他將赤金裝進錢袋裡，急速走向城裡。那個痲瘋病患看到星星男孩走過來，立刻又站到路中央，哭喊道：「給我一點錢吧，否則我死定了。」星星男孩又再一次地憐憫痲瘋病人，將錢袋裡的那塊赤金送給了他，說道：「你比我還需要它。」然而，星星男孩的心情卻無比沉重，因為他知道，殘酷的處罰正等著他。

但是，看哪！當星星男孩走進城門時，守門的衛兵竟向他彎腰鞠躬致敬，並且說道：「我們的國王真是美麗！」星星男孩身後也跟著一大群市民，他們高聲叫道：「那當然，他是全世界最美的人。」於是星星男孩哭了，他自言自語道：「他們在嘲笑我，拿我的痛苦開玩笑。」由於跟在他身旁的人愈來愈多，星星男孩迷失了路，最後竟來到皇宮所在的雄偉廣場上。

皇宮的大門立刻敞開來，城裡的神父和達官顯貴們全都跑出來迎接他，他們向他行禮致敬道：「您就是我們期盼已久的王位繼承人，也就是我們國王的兒子。」

然而星星男孩卻告訴他們：「我不是國王的兒子，我是一位可憐乞丐婆的兒子。你們為什麼要說我很美呢？我知道自己長得其醜無比。」

此時，那個身穿鑲嵌金箔花飾的甲冑、頭戴蹲狀飛獅頭盔的人高舉著盾牌，大聲說道：「我王怎麼可能不美呢？」

星星男孩看著自己那張映照在盾牌上的臉，看哪！他的臉已經恢復原來的面貌了，全身上下也恢復昔日的華美，當他看著自己的雙眼時，看到了自己從來沒有見過的東西。

神父和達官顯貴們在他面前跪下，並且說道：「有一個流傳已久的預言說，我們的統治者將在今天出現。因此，我王，戴上這頂皇冠吧，拿著這柄王杖，成為我們公義仁慈的君王吧。」

可是星星男孩說道：「我不配當你們的君王，因為我曾經不認我的親生母親，在我找到她、求得她的寬恕之前，我仍得繼續流浪。因此，讓我走吧，我得繼續我的旅程，不能留在這兒，即使你們要我當國王，我也不能答應。」正當說這番話時，他看向通往城門口的街道，看哪！在擁擠的人群中，他看到那個乞丐婆，也就是他的母親，在他母親身旁的就是那個坐在路邊的痲瘋病患。

他高興地大叫，立刻跑去母親身旁，跪下來親吻她腳上的每一處傷口，也用他的眼淚濡濕這些傷口。他頭頂著地，哭得像一個心快要碎的人似的，他告訴母親：「媽媽，在我驕橫傲慢的時候，我不認您。而今，在我謙卑的時候，請接受我這個兒子。媽媽，我曾以怨懟回報您對我的關愛。媽媽，過去我拒絕認您，現在，請承認您的兒子。」然而，乞丐婆卻一句話也不說。

於是他伸出雙手緊緊抱住那個痲瘋病患發白的雙腳，對他說道：「我曾三次同情你，請你讓我母親對我說一次話吧。」然而，痲瘋病患也不發一語。

星星男孩再度哭泣道：「媽媽，我再也無法承受心裡的悲傷了。請您寬恕我，好讓我回森林裡去。」乞丐婆伸出手來按著他的頭，說道：「起來。」此時，痲瘋病患也伸出手撫著他的頭，說道：「起來。」

星星男孩於是站起身來，看著他們。看哪！他們竟然是國王和皇后。

皇后對他說道：「這是你的父親，你救了他。」

國王對他說道：「這是你的母親，你用眼淚為她洗了腳。」

然後他們摟住星星男孩的脖子，親吻他，引領他進到皇宮裡，為他換上華服，戴上皇冠，並且把王杖交給他。河流所圍繞的領土全歸他治理，他是這座都城的王。他以公義和慈愛治理人民，放逐邪惡的魔法師；他送給伐木工人和他的妻子許多貴重的禮物，也給伐木工人的孩子們許多賞賜。他不再殘酷地對待鳥兒和其他動物，反而以慈悲、憐憫和關愛為訓誨，賜食物給窮人，賜衣服給赤身露體的人，他的國度裡充滿了祥和及富足。

然而，星星男孩治理都城的期間並不長，只因他受過太大的苦難、太痛苦的試煉；三年之後，他便與世長辭，但繼承他王位的卻是一位暴君。

The Star-Child

Once upon a time two poor Woodcutters were making their way home through a great pine-forest. It was winter, and a night of bitter cold. The snow lay thick upon the ground, and upon the branches of the trees: the frost kept snapping the little twigs on either side of them, as they passed: and when they came to the Mountain-Torrent she was hanging motionless in air, for the Ice-King had kissed her.

So cold was it that even the animals and the birds did not know what to make of it.

"Ugh!" snarled the Wolf as he limped through the brushwood with his tail between his legs, "this is perfectly monstrous weather. Why doesn't the Government look to it?"

"Weet! weet! weet! twittered the green Linnets, "the old Earth is dead, and they have laid her out in her white shroud."

"The Earth is going to be married, and this is her bridal dress," whispered the Turtle-doves to each other. Their little pink feet were quite frost-bitten, but they felt that it was their duty to take a romantic view of the situation.

"Nonsense!" growled the Wolf. "I tell you that it is all the fault of the Government, and if you don't believe me I shall eat you." The Wolf had a thoroughly practical mind, and was never at a loss for a good argument.

"Well, for my own part, said the Woodpecker, who was a born philosopher, "I don't care an atomic theory for explanations. If a thing is so, it is so, and at present it is terribly cold."

Terribly cold it certainly was. The little Squirrels, who lived inside the tall fir-tree, kept rubbing each other's noses to keep themselves warm, and the Rabbits curled themselves up in their holes, and did not venture even to look out of doors. The only people who seemed to enjoy it were the great horned Owls. Their feathers were quite stiff with rime, but they did not mind, and they rolled their large yellow eyes, and called out to each other across the forest, "Tu-whit! Tu-whoo! Tu-whit! Tu-whoo! what delightful weather we are having!"

On and on went the two Woodcutters, blowing lustily upon their fingers, and stamping with their huge iron-shod boots upon the caked snow. Once they sank into a deep drift, and came out as white as millers are, when the stones are grinding; and once they slipped on the hard smooth ice where the marsh-water was frozen, and their faggots tell out of their bundles, and they had to pick them up and bind them together again; and once they thought that they had lost their way, and a great terror seized on them, for they knew that the Snow is cruel to those who sleep in her arms. But they put their trust in the good Saint Martin, who watches over all travellers, and retraced their steps, and went warily, and at last they reached the outskirts of the forest, and saw, far down in the valley beneath them, the lights of the village in which they dwelt.

So overjoyed were they at their deliverance that they laughed aloud, and the Earth seemed to them like a flower of silver, and the Moon like a flower of gold.

Yet, after that they had laughed they became sad, for they remembered their poverty, and one of them said to the other, "Why did we make merry, seeing that life is for the rich, and not for such as we are? Better that we had died of cold in the forest, or that some wild beast had fallen upon us and slain us."

"Truly," answered his companion, much is given to some, and little is given to others. Injustice has parcelled out the world, nor is there equal division of aught save of sorrow."

But as they were bewailing their misery to each other this strange thing happened. There fell from heaven a very bright and beautiful star. It slipped down the side of the sky, passing by the other stars in its course, and, as they watched it wondering, it seemed to them to sink behind a clump of willow-trees that stood hard by a little sheep-fold no more than a stone's throw away.

"Why! there is a crock of gold for whoever finds it," they cried, and they set to and ran, so eager were they for the gold.

And one of them ran faster than his mate, and outstripped him, and forced his way through the willows, and came out on the other side, and lo! there was indeed a thing of gold lying on the white snow. So he hastened towards it, and stooping down placed his hands upon it, and it was a cloak of golden tissue, curiously wrought with stars, and wrapped in many folds. And he cried out to his comrade that he had found the treasure that had fallen from the sky, and when his comrade had come up, they sat them down in the snow, and loosened the folds of the cloak that they might divide the pieces of gold. But, alas! no gold was in it, nor silver, nor, indeed, treasure of any kind, but only a little child who was asleep.

And one of them said to the other: "This is a bitter ending to our hope, nor have we any good fortune, for what doth a child profit to a man? Let us leave it here, and go our way, seeing that we are poor men, and have children of our own whose bread we may not give to another."

But his companion answered him: "Nay, but it were an evil thing to leave the child to perish here in the snow, and though I am as poor as thou art, and have many mouths to feed, and but little in the pot, yet will I bring it home with me, and my wife shall have care of it."

So very tenderly he took up the child, and wrapped the cloak around it to shield it from the harsh cold, and made his way down the hill to the village, his comrade marvelling much at his foolishness and softness of heart.

And when they came to the village, his comrade said to him, "Thou hast the child, therefore give me the cloak, for it is meet that we should share."

But he answered him: "Nay, for the cloak is neither mine nor thine, but the child's only," and he bade him Godspeed, and went to his own house and knocked.

And when his wife opened the door and saw that her husband had returned safe to her, she put her arms round his neck and kissed him, and took front his back the bundle of faggots, and brushed the snow off his boots, and bade him come in.

But he said to her, "I have found something in the forest, and I have brought it to thee to have care of it," and he stirred not from the threshold.

"What is it?" she cried. "Show it to me, for the house is bare, and we have need of many things." And he drew the cloak back, and showed her the sleeping child.

"Alack, goodman!" she murmured, "have we not children enough of our own, that thou must needs bring a changeling to sit by the hearth? And who knows if it will not bring us bad fortune? And how shall we tend it?" And she was wroth against him.

"Nay, but it is a Star-Child," he answered; and he told her the strange manner of the finding of it.

But she would not be appeased, but mocked at him, and spoke angrily, and cried: "Our children lack bread, and shall we feed the child of another? Who is there who careth for us? And who giveth us food?"

"Nay, but God careth for the sparrows even, and feedeth them," he answered.

"Do not the sparrows die of hunger in the winter?" she asked. And is it not winter now?" And the man answered nothing, but stirred not from the threshold.

And a bitter wind from the forest came in through the open door, and made her tremble, and she shivered, and said to him: "Wilt thou not close the door? There cometh a bitter wind into the house, and I am cold."

"Into a house where a heart is hard cometh there not always a bitter wind?" he asked. And the woman answered him nothing, but crept closer to the fire.

And after a time she turned round and looked at him, and her eyes were full of tears. And he came in swiftly, and placed the child in her arms, and she kissed it, and laid it in a little bed where the youngest of their own children was lying. And on the morrow the Woodcutter took the curious cloak of gold and placed it in a great chest, and a chain of amber that was round the child's neck his wife took and set it in the chest also.

So the Star-Child was brought up with the children of the

Woodcutter, and sat at the same board with them, and was their playmate. And every year he became more beautiful to look at, so that all those who dwelt in the village were filled with wonder, for, while they were swarthy and black-haired, he was white and delicate as sawn ivory, and his curls were like the rings of the daffodil. His lips, also, were like the petals of a red flower, and his eyes were like violets by a river of pure water, and his body like the narcissus of a field where the mower comes not.

Yet did his beauty work him evil. For he grew proud, and cruel, and selfish. The children of the Woodcutter, and the other children of the village, he despised, saying that they were of mean parentage, while he was noble, being sprung from a Star, and he made himself master over them, and called them his servants. No pity had he for the poor, or for those who were blind or maimed or in any way afflicted, but would cast stones at them and drive them forth on to the highway, and bid them beg their bread elsewhere, so that none save the outlaws came twice to that village to ask for aims. Indeed, he was as one enamored of beauty, and would mock at the weakly and ill-favored, and make jest of them; and himself he loved, and in summer, when the winds were still, he would lie by the well in the priest's orchard and look down at the marvel of his own face, and laugh for the pleasure he had in his fairness.

Often did the Woodcutter and his wife chide him, and say: "We did not deal with thee as thou dealest with those who are left desolate, and have none to succor them. Wherefore art thou so cruel to all who need pity?"

Often did the old priest send for him, and seek to teach him the love of living things, saying to him: "The fly is thy brother. Do it no harm. The wild birds that roam through the forest have their freedom. Snare them not for thy pleasure. God made the blind-worm and the mole, and each has its place. Who art thou to bring pain into God's world? Even the cattle of the field praise Him."

But the Star-Child heeded not their words, but would frown and flout, and go back to his companions, and lead them. And his companions followed him, for he was fair, and fleet of foot, and could dance, and pipe, and make music. And wherever the Star-Child led them they followed, and whatever the Star-Child bade them do, that did they. And when he pierced with a sharp reed the dim eyes of the mole, they laughed, and when he cast stones at the leper they laughed also. And in all things he ruled them, and they became hard of heart, even as he was.

Now there passed one day through the village a poor beggar-woman. Her garments were torn and ragged, and her feet were bleeding from the rough road on which she had travelled, and she was in very evil plight. And being weary she sat her down under a chestnut-tree to rest.

But when the Star-Child saw her, he said to his companions, "See! There sitteth a foul beggar-woman under that fair and green-leaved tree. Come, let us drive her hence, for she is ugly and ill-favored."

So he came near and threw stones at her, and mocked her, and she looked at him with terror in her eyes, nor did she move her gaze from him. And when the Woodcutter, who was cleaving logs in a haggard hard by, saw what the Star-Child was doing, he ran up and rebuked him, and said to him: "Surely thou art hard of heart and knowest not mercy, for what evil has this poor woman done to thee that thou should'st treat her in this wise?"

And the Star-Child grew red with anger, and stamped his foot upon the ground, and said, "Who art thou to question me what I do? I am no son of thine to do thy bidding."

"Thou speakest truly," answered the Woodcutter, "yet did I show thee pity when I found thee in the forest."

And when the woman heard these words she gave a loud cry, and fell into a swoon. And the Woodcutter carried her to his own house, and his wife had care of her, and when she rose up from the swoon into which she had fallen, they set meat and drink before her, and bade her have comfort.

But she would neither eat nor drink, but said to the Woodcutter, "Did'st thou not say that the child was found in the forest? And was it not ten years from this day?" （譯註： Did'st 意即did，與thou一起使用）

And the Woodcutter answered, "Yea, it was in the forest that I found him, and it is ten years from this day."

"And what signs didst thou find with him?" she cried. "Bare he not upon his neck a chain of amber? Was not round him a cloak of gold tissue broidered with stars?"

"Truly," answered the Woodcutter, "it was even as thou sayest." And he took the cloak and the amber chain from the chest where they lay, and showed them to her.

And when she saw them she wept for joy, and said, "He is my little son whom I lost in the forest. I pray thee send for him quickly, for in search of him have I wandered over the whole world."

So the Woodcutter and his wife went out and called to the Star-Child, and said to him, "Go into the house, and there shalt thou find thy mother, who is waiting for thee."

So he ran in, filled with wonder and great gladness.

But when he saw her who was waiting there, he laughed scornfully and said, "Why, where is my mother? For I see none here but this vile beggar-woman."

And the woman answered him, "I am thy mother."

"Thou art mad to say so," cried the Star-Child angrily. "I am no son of thine, for thou art a beggar, and ugly, and in rags. Therefore get thee hence, and let me see thy foul face no more."

"Nay, but thou art indeed my little son, whom I bare in the forest," she cried, and she fell on her knees, and held out her arms to him. "The robbers stole thee from me, and left thee to die," she murmured, "but I recognized thee when I saw thee, and the signs also have I recognized, the cloak of golden tissue and the amber-chain. Therefore I pray thee come with me, for over the whole world have I wandered in search of thee. Come with me, my son, for I have need of thy love."

But the Star-Child stirred not from his place, but shut the doors of his heart against her, nor was there any sound heard save the sound of the woman weeping for pain.

And at last he spoke to her, and his voice was hard and bitter. "If in very truth thou art my mother," he said, "it had been better hadst thou stayed away, and not come here to bring me to shame, seeing that I thought I was the child of some Star and not a beggar's child, as thou tellest me that I am. Therefore get thee hence, and let me see thee no more."

"Alas! my son," she cried, "wilt thou not kiss me before I go? For I have suffered much to find thee."

"Nay," said the Star-Child, "but thou art too foul to look at and rather would I kiss the adder or the toad than thee."

So the woman rose up, and went away into the forest weeping bitterly, and when the Star-Child saw that she had gone, he was glad, and ran back to his playmates that he might play with them.

But when they beheld him coming, they mocked him and said, "Why, thou art as foul as the toad, and as loathsome as the adder. Get thee hence, for we will not suffer thee to play with us," and they drove him out of the garden.

And the Star-Child frowned and said to himself, "What is this that they say to me? I will go to the well of water and look into it, and it shall tell me of my beauty."

So he went to the well of water and looked into it, and lo! his face was as the face of a toad, and his body was scaled like an adder. And he flung himself down on the grass and wept, and said to himself, "Surely this has come upon me by reason of my sin. For I have denied my mother, and driven her away, and been proud, and cruel to her. Wherefore I will go and seek her through the whole world, nor will I rest till I have found her."

And there came to him the little daughter of the Woodcutter, and she put her hand upon his shoulder and said, "What doth it matter if thou hast lost thy comeliness? Stay with us, and I will not mock at thee."

And he said to her, "Nay, but I have been cruel to my mother, and as a punishment has this evil been sent to me. Wherefore I must go hence, and wander through the world till I find her, and she give me her forgiveness."

So he ran away into the forest and called out to his mother to come to him, but there was no answer. All day long he called to her, and when the sun set he lay down to sleep on a bed of leaves, and the birds and the animals fled from him, as they remembered his cruelty, and he was alone save for the toad that watched him, and the slow adder that crawled past.

And in the morning he rose up, and plucked some bitter berries from the trees and ate them, and took his way through the great wood, weeping sorely. And of everything that he met he made enquiry if perchance they had seen his mother.

He said to the Mole, "Thou canst go beneath the earth. Tell me, is my mother there?"

And the Mole answered, "Thou hast blinded mine eyes. How should I know?"

He said to the Linnet, "Thou canst fly over the tops of the tall trees, and canst see the whole world. Tell me, canst thou see my mother?"

And the Linnet answered, "Thou hast clipt my wings for thy pleasure. How should I fly?"

And to the little Squirrel who lived in the fir-tree, and was lonely, he said, "Where is my mother?"

And the Squirrel answered, "Thou hast slain mine. Dost thou seek to slay thine also?"

And the Star-Child wept and bowed his head, and prayed forgiveness of God's things, and went on through the forest, seeking for the beggar-woman. And on the third day he came to the other side of the forest and went down into the plain.

And when he passed through the villages the children mocked him, and threw stones at him, and the carlots would not suffer him even to sleep in the byres lest he might bring mildew on the stored corn, so foul was he to look at, and their hired men drove him away, and there was none who had pity on him. Nor could he hear anywhere of the beggar-woman who was his mother, though for the space of three years he wandered over the world, and often seemed to see her on the road in front of him, and would call to her, and run after her till the sharp flints made his feet to bleed. But overtake her he could not, and those who dwelt by the way did ever deny that they had seen her, or any like to her, and they made sport of his sorrow.

For the space of three years he wandered over the world, and in the world there was neither love nor loving-kindness nor charity for him, but it was even such a world as he had made for himself in the days of his great pride.

And one evening he came to the gate of a strong-walled city that stood by a river, and, weary and footsore though he was, he made to enter in. But the soldiers who stood on guard dropped their halberts across the entrance, and said roughly to him, "What is thy business in the city?"

"I am seeking for my mother," he answered, "and I pray ye to suffer me to pass, for it may be that she is in this city."

But they mocked at him, and one of them wagged a black beard, and set down his shield and cried, "Of a truth, thy mother will not be merry when she sees thee, for thou art more ill-favored than the toad of the marsh, or the adder that crawls in the fen. Get thee gone. Get thee gone. Thy mother dwells not in this city."

And another, who held a yellow banner in his hand, said to him, "Who is thy mother, and wherefore art thou seeking for her?"

And he answered, "My mother is a beggar even as I am, and I have treated her evilly, and I pray ye to suffer me to pass that she may give me her forgiveness, if it be that she tarrieth in this city." But they would not, and pricked him with their spears.

And, as he turned away weeping, one whose armor was inlaid with gilt flowers, and on whose helmet couched a lion that had wings, came up and made enquiry of the soldiers who it was who had sought entrance. And they said to him, "It is a beggar and the child of a beggar, and we have driven him away."

"Nay," he cried, laughing, "but we will sell the foul thing for a slave, and his price shall be the price of a bowl of sweet wine."

And an old and evil-visaged man who was passing by called out, and said, "I will buy him for that price," and, when he had paid the price, he took the Star-Child by the hand and led him into the city.

And after that they had gone through many streets they came to a little door that was set in a wall that was covered with a pomegranate tree. And the old man touched the door with a ring of graved jasper and it opened, and they went down five steps of brass into a garden filled with black poppies and green jars of burnt clay. And the old man took then from his turban a scarf of figured silk, and bound with it the eyes of the Star-Child, and drove him in front of him. And when the scarf was taken off his eyes, the Star-Child found himself in a dungeon, that was lit by a lantern of horn.

And the old man set before him some mouldy bread on a trencher and said, "Eat," and some brackish water in a cup and said, "Drink," and when he had eaten and drunk, the old man went out, locking the door behind him and fastening it with an iron chain.

And on the morrow the old man, who was indeed the subtlest of the magicians of Libya and had learned his art from one who dwelt in the tombs of the Nile, came in to him and frowned at him, and said, "In a wood that is nigh to the gate of this city of Giaours there are three pieces of gold. One is of white gold, and another is of yellow gold, and the gold of the third one is red. To-day thou shalt bring me the piece of white gold, and if thou bringest it not back, I will beat thee with a hundred stripes. Get thee away quickly, and at sunset I will be waiting for thee at the door of the garden. See that thou bringest the white gold, or it shall go in with thee, for thou art my slave, and I have bought thee for the price of a bowl of sweet wine." And he bound the eyes of the Star-Child with the scarf of figured silk, and led him through the house, and through the garden of poppies, and up the five steps of brass. And having opened the little door with his ring he set him in the street.

And the Star-Child went out of the gate of the city, and came to the wood of which the Magician had spoken to him.

Now this wood was very fair to look at from without, and

seemed full of singing birds and of sweet-scented flowers, and the Star-Child entered it gladly. Yet did its beauty profit him little, for wherever he went harsh briars and thorns shot up from the ground and encompassed him, and evil nettles stung him, and the thistle pierced him with her daggers, so that he was in sore distress. Nor could he anywhere find the piece of white gold of which the Magician had spoken, though he sought for it from morn to noon, and from noon to sunset. And at sunset he set his face towards home, weeping bitterly, for he knew what fate was in store for him.

But when he had reached the outskirts of the wood, he heard front a thicket a cry as of someone in pain. And forgetting his own sorrow he ran back to the place, and saw there a little Hare caught in a trap that some hunter had set for it.

And the Star-Child had pity on it, and released it, and said to it, "I am myself but a slave, yet may I give thee thy freedom."

And the Hare answered him, and said: "Surely thou hast given me freedom, and what shall I give thee in return?"

And the Star-Child said to it, "I am seeking for a piece of white gold, nor can I anywhere find it, and if I bring it not to my master he will beat me."

"Come thou with me," said the Hare, "and I will lead thee to it, for I know where it is hidden, and for what purpose."

So the Star-Child went with the Hare, and lo! in the cleft of a great oak-tree he saw the piece of white gold that he was seeking. And he was filled with joy, and seized it, and said to the Hare, "The service that I did to thee thou hast rendered back again many times over and the kindness that I showed thee thou hast repaid a hundredfold."

"Nay," answered the Hare, "but as thou dealt with me,

so I did deal with thee," and it ran away swiftly, and the Star-Child went towards the city.

Now at the gate of the city there was seated one who was a leper. Over his face hung a cowl of grey linen, and through the eyelets his eyes gleamed like red coals. And when he saw the Star-Child coming, he struck upon a wooden bowl, and clattered his bell, and called out to him, and said, "Give me a piece of money, or I must die of hunger. For they have thrust me out of the city, and there is no one who has pity on rite."

"Alas! cried the Star-Child, "I have but one piece of money in my wallet, and if I bring it not to my master he will beat me for I am his slave."

But the leper entreated him, and prayed of him, till the Star-Child had pity, and gave him the piece of white gold.

And when he came to the Magician's house, the Magician opened to him, and brought him in, and said to him, "Hast thou the piece of white gold?" And the Star-Child answered, "I have it not." So the Magician fell upon him, and beat him, and set before him an empty trencher, and said "Eat," and an empty cup, and said, "Drink," and flung him again into the dungeon.

And on the morrow the Magician came to him, and said, "If to-day thou bringest me not the piece of yellow gold, I will surely keep thee as my slave, and give thee three hundred stripes."

So the Star-Child went to the wood, and all day long he searched for the piece of yellow gold, but nowhere could he find it. And at sunset he sat him down and began to weep, and as he was weeping there came to him the little Hare that he had rescued from the trap.

And the Hare said to him, "Why art thou weeping? And what dost thou seek in the wood?"

And the Star-Child answered, "I am seeking for a piece of yellow gold that is hidden here, and if I find it not my master will beat me, and keep me as a slave."

"Follow me," cried the Hare, and it ran through the wood till it came to a pool of water. And at the bottom of the pool the piece of yellow gold was lying.

"How shall I thank thee?" said the Star-Child, "for lo! this is the second time that you have succored me."

"Nay, but thou hadst pity on me first," said the Hare, and it ran away swiftly.

And the Star-Child took the piece of yellow gold, and put it in his wallet, and hurried to the city. But the leper saw him coming, and ran to meet him and knelt down and cried, "Give me a piece of money or I shall die of hunger."

And the Star-Child said to him, "I have in my wallet but one piece of yellow gold, and if I bring it not to my master he will beat me and keep me as his slave."

But the leper entreated him sore, so that the Star-Child had pity on him, and gave him the piece of yellow gold.

And when he came to the Magician's house, the Magician opened to him, and brought him in, and said to him, "Hast thou the piece of yellow gold?" And the Star-Child said to him, "I have it not." So the Magician fell upon him, and beat him, and loaded him with chains, and cast him again into the dungeon.

And on the morrow the Magician came to him, and said, "If to-day thou bringest me the piece of red gold I will set thee free, but if thou bringest it not I will surely slay thee."

So the Star-Child went to the wood, and all day long he searched for the piece of red gold, but nowhere could he find it. And at evening he sat him down, and wept, and as he was weeping there came to him the little Hare.

And the Hare said to him, "The piece of red gold that thou seekest is in the cavern that is behind thee. Therefore weep no more but be glad."

"How shall I reward thee," cried the Star-Child, "for lo! this is the third time thou hast succored me."

"Nay, but thou hadst pity on me first," said the Hare, and it ran away swiftly.

And the Star-Child entered the cavern, and in its farthest corner he found the piece of red gold. So he put it in his wallet, and hurried to the city. And the leper seeing him coming, stood in the centre of the road, and cried out, and said to him, "Give me the piece of red money, or I must die," and the Star-Child had pity on him again, and gave him the piece of red gold, saying, "Thy need is greater than mine." Yet was his heart heavy, for he knew what evil fate awaited him.

But lo! as he passed through the gate of the city, the guards bowed down and made obeisance to him, saying, "How beautiful is our lord!" and a crowd of citizens followed him, and cried out, "Surely there is none so beautiful in the whole world!" so that the Star-Child wept, and said to himself, "They are mocking me, and making light of my misery." And so large was the concourse of the people, that he lost the threads of his way, and found himself at last in a great square, in which there was a palace of a King.

And the gate of the palace opened, and the priests and the high officers of the city ran forth to meet him, and they abased themselves before him, and said, "Thou art our lord for whom we have been waiting, and the sort of our King."

And the Star-Child answered them and said, "I am no king's son, but the child of a poor beggar-woman. And how say ye that I am beautiful, for I know that I am evil to look at?"

Then he, whose armor was inlaid with gilt flowers, and on whose helmet couched a lion that had wings, held up a shield, and cried, "How saith my lord that he is not beautiful?"

And the Star-Child looked, and lo! his face was even as it had been, and his comeliness had come back to him, and he saw that in his eyes which he had not seen there before.

And the priests and the high officers knelt down and said to him, "It was prophesied of old that on this day should come he who was to rule over us. Therefore, let our lord take this crown and this sceptre, and be in his justice and mercy our King over us."

But he said to them, "I am not worthy, for I have denied the mother who bare me, nor may I rest till I have found her, and known her forgiveness. Therefore, let me go, for I must wander again over the world, and may not tarry here, though ye bring me the crown and the sceptre." And as he spake he turned his face from them towards the street that led to the gate of the city, and lo! amongst the crowd that pressed round the soldiers, he saw the beggar-woman who was his mother, and at her side stood the leper, who had sat by the road.

And a cry of joy broke from his lips, and he ran over, and kneeling down he kissed the wounds on his mother's feet, and wet them with his tears. He bowed his head in the dust, and sobbing, as one whose heart might break, he said to her: "Mother, I denied thee in the hour of my pride. Accept me in the hour of my humility. Mother, I gave thee hatred. Do thou give me love. Mother, I rejected thee. Receive thy child now." But the beggar-woman answered him not a word.

And he reached out his hands, and clasped the white feet of the leper, and said to him: "Thrice did I give thee of my mercy. Bid my mother speak to me once." But the leper answered him not a word.

And he sobbed again, and said: "Mother, my suffering is greater than I can bear. Give me thy forgiveness, and let me go back to the forest." And the beggar-woman put her hand on his head, and said to him, "Rise," and the leper put his hand on his head, and said to him "Rise," also.

And he rose up from his feet, and looked at them, and lo! they were a King and a Queen.

And the Queen said to him, "This is thy father whom thou hast succored."

And the King said, "This is thy mother, whose feet thou hast washed with thy tears."

And they fell on his neck and kissed him, and brought him into the palace, and clothed him in fair raiment, and set the crown upon his head, and the sceptre in his hand, and over the city that stood by the river he ruled, and was its lord. "Much justice and mercy did he show to all, and the evil Magician he banished, and to the Woodcutter and his wife he sent many rich gifts, and to their children he gave high honor. Nor would he suffer any to be cruel to bird or beast, but taught love and loving-kindness and charity, and to the poor he gave bread, and to the naked he gave raiment, and there was peace and plenty in the land.

Yet ruled he not long, so great had been his suffering, and so bitter the fire of his testing, for after the space of three years he died. And he who came after him ruled evilly.

漁夫與他的靈魂

靈魂乃是一個人最高貴的部分，是上帝所賜予，
我們應該發揮它高貴的用途。
世上再也沒有比人類靈魂更高貴的東西了，
世上沒有任何一物能和它相提並論。

　　每天晚上，這名年輕的漁夫都到海邊去，將漁網撒向海中，每當夜風從陸地吹過來時，他什麼也沒法捕到，漁獲寥寥可數；只因這乘著黑色羽翼而來的風滿是苦澀，而洶湧的波濤總趕著來和它相會。然而，當風吹向海岸時，魚兒就會從深處游來，從網眼裡游進漁網中，於是他將這些魚拿到市場上賣。

　　每天晚上，漁夫都到海邊去。有一天晚上，漁網極其沉重，令他幾乎無法將漁網拖上船。於是他笑了，自言自語道：「我肯定是把正游著的魚一網打盡，或者捕獲了什麼會讓人們嘆為觀止的笨怪物，要不然就是抓到偉大的女王陛下會想要的恐怖東西了。」說著，他使盡全力，拚命地拉著粗礪的繩索，有如拉著繫上藍色琺瑯線的銅壺般，手臂逐漸浮現出脈絡分明的青筋，接著他拉住細繩，然後那扁圓的浮塞逐漸冒上來，漁網也終於浮出水面。

　　不過，網中一條魚也沒有，更別提什麼怪物或恐怖的東西了。

網子裡只有一條小美人魚，正沉沉地睡著。

　　她的頭髮彷彿打濕的金線團般，一根根髮絲有如玻璃杯裡的金線。她的身體有如潔白的象牙，尾巴則是亮銀與珍珠的結合。銀與珍珠是她的尾巴，纏繞其上的則是綠色的海草；貝殼似的東西是她的耳朵；她的雙唇則有如海中的珊瑚一般。冰冷的海浪衝擊著她冷冷的胸部，結晶鹽在她眼皮上閃閃發光。

　　她的美麗令漁夫心中充滿了讚嘆，他伸手將漁網拉近，然後傾身向前，將她擁進臂彎裡。就在他碰觸到她時，她卻發出受驚海鷗般的叫聲，醒了過來，並用她那紫水晶般的雙眼害怕地看著他，一邊掙扎著想要逃開去，但是漁夫仍緊緊地抱著她，怎麼也不願意讓她離開。

　　當她明白自己無法脫困時，便開始哭泣著說道：「請你讓我走吧，因為我是國王唯一的女兒，而且我父親年紀大了，他是那麼孤獨無依。」

　　但年輕的漁夫卻答道：「我絕不會讓妳走的，除非妳答應我，只要我一呼喚妳，妳就會來唱歌給我聽。因為魚兒喜歡聽人魚的歌聲，這樣一來，我的漁網就會滿載漁獲。」

　　「如果我答應你這個要求，你真的會讓我走嗎？」小美人魚哭著問道。

　　「我保證會讓妳走。」年輕的漁夫說道。

　　於是她答應了漁夫的要求，還依人魚的誓約發了誓。他便鬆開她的雙臂，美人魚隨即迅速地沉進水裡去，全身還因莫名恐懼不停地顫抖著。

　　每天晚上，這名年輕的漁夫都到海邊去呼喚美人魚，而她也隨即浮出水面，對他歌唱。海豚層層圍繞著她，四處翱翔的海鷗也在她的頭上盤旋。

　　她唱起令人讚嘆的歌。她描述著海中的族類，自一個又一個洞穴穿進穿出，將他們的小仔仔揹在肩上；她提及那有著長長綠色落腮鬚和毛茸茸胸膛的海神，每當祂看到國王經過時總是吹著形狀扭扭曲曲的海螺；還有，以琥珀打造而成的國王王宮，屋頂是翡翠做的，走道是閃亮的珍珠舖的；以及，那座一整天都有著鑲嵌珠寶似的扇狀珊瑚搖曳其間的海中花園，也有那彷彿銀色小鳥般疾馳而過的魚類，更有依戀地附在岩石上的海葵，和在波紋狀黃沙上竄出的嫩芽。

她吟唱著來自北海、魚鰭上黏附著銳利垂冰的大鯨魚。她唱著那善於吟唱的女妖賽倫的故事，來往商旅得用蠟封住耳朵，才不會因為聽到賽倫的歌聲而跳下海淹死。她唱著有著高大桅杆、沉於海底的奴隸船的故事，裡頭的水手抱著裝備，凍僵了身子死去，還有在那開放的舷窗中游進游出的鯖魚群。她唱著不平凡的客旅——小雁鳥群佇立在船隻龍骨上，不停環遊世界的故事。她唱著那住在斷崖兩側的墨魚，牠們伸出長長的黑色手臂，只要牠們想要，隨時可以把白天變成黑夜。她唱著擁有自己船隻的鸚鵡螺，那船是用蛋白石鑿出來的，飄揚其上的是綢緞般的風帆。她唱著那善於彈奏的雄人魚，其琴藝可使大海怪進入夢鄉。她也唱著那抓住滑溜溜海豚、笑著騎在牠們背上的孩童。她唱著那在白色泡沫中載浮載沉、伸手招呼水手們的美人魚，以及那長著彎曲長牙的海獅群，與鬃毛飄飄的海馬。

當她唱歌時，所有奇奇怪怪的魚都會從深海浮上來聽，漁夫便將網撒向魚群，一舉捕獲；至於其他的魚兒，他則用魚叉解決。當漁夫的小船裝滿了魚之後，美人魚便對他一笑，沉入海裡。

然而，她始終不曾靠近他，因為怕他會碰觸自己。許多次，他呼喚她，懇求她，但她仍不肯答應。每逢他試著抓住她時，她就立即像隻海豹般潛進水中，而且那一天他就再也別想見到她了。他愈來愈喜歡聽她的聲音。她的聲音好聽得讓他忘了他的漁網和他的詭詐，甚至也忘了他的船。鮮紅亮眼的鮪魚成群地游過去了，但他一點也不在意。他的魚叉閒置一旁，柳條編成的籃子空空如也。他忘情地張著嘴巴，眼神充滿困惑，失神地坐在小船上傾聽著；直到海上起了霧，霧氣向他聚攏，四處巡行的月亮也將銀色的月光灑滿他古銅色的身體。

有一天晚上他呼喚她，對她說道：「小美人魚，小美人魚，我愛妳。讓我成為妳的新郎吧，我愛妳啊！」

但美人魚搖搖頭。「你擁有屬於人類的靈魂，」她答道，「只有捨棄你的靈魂，我才能愛你。」

年輕的漁夫喃喃自語：「我的靈魂對我有什麼用呢？我看不到它，摸不著它，更不認識它。我當然可以捨棄它，而且這樣一來，我也會快樂得多。」於是他爆出一聲歡呼，從彩繪的船上站直身子，張開雙臂迎向美人魚。「我會捨棄我的靈魂，」他叫道，「妳要當我的新娘喔，我就要當新郎了，我們要一起住在深海裡，而且妳要帶我去看妳曾經吟唱的那些事物。我會盡全力滿足妳的任何渴望，我們再也不分離。」

小美人魚愉快地笑著，把臉埋在雙手中。

「可是我該怎麼捨棄靈魂呢？」年輕的漁夫哭道，「告訴我該怎麼做，唉！這事非做不可。」

「啊！我不知道，」小美人魚說道，「人魚沒有靈魂。」說著她沉入水裡，熱切地看著他。

現在已是第二天清晨，太陽就快要出來了，年輕的漁夫來到神父家門口，在門上敲了三下。

見習修士從窗口往外看，看清楚了門外的人，便拉開門栓說道：「進來吧！」

年輕的漁夫走了進去，跪在飄著甜味的藺草地板上，對著正在讀聖經的神父說道，「神父啊，我愛上了一隻人魚，可是我的靈魂阻擋了我的慾望。請你告訴我，要如何才能拋開我的靈魂，因為我真的不需要它。我的靈魂對我而言有什麼價值呢？我看不到它，摸不著它，更不認識它呀！」

神父一聽，捶打著自己胸膛說道：「悲哀啊！悲哀啊！你是瘋了，還是吃了有毒的藥草？靈魂乃是一個人最高貴的部分，是上帝所賜予，我們應該發揮它高貴的用途。世上再也沒有比人類靈魂更高貴的東西了，世上沒有任何一物能和它相提並論。它有如全世界所有的黃金那麼貴重，還比國王的紅寶石更加可貴。所以，孩子，不要再想這件事了，因為這是一種無法被赦免的罪。至於人魚，那乃是失落的族類，凡與他們相交者也是會失落的。他們如同田間野獸無法分辨善惡，我主並未為他們而死。」

　　年輕漁夫聽著神父說著這些令他痛苦的話語時，眼裡噙滿了淚水。他站起來對祭司說道：「神父，森林裡的半人半獸愉快地生活著，美人魚坐在岩石上彈奏著火紅黃金打造的豎琴。讓我和他們一樣吧，我拜託您，因為他們的年日如同花朵的年日。至於我的靈魂，如果它成了我和我所愛之物之間的阻礙，對我又有何益處呢？」

　　「肉體之愛是貧乏的。」神父叫道，眉頭緊鎖著。「貧乏和邪惡是造物主所苦惱著的，在祂的世界裡，那些四處遊蕩的異教事物，如森林裡的半人半獸是該受詛咒的，海上的歌者也是！我曾在夜裡聽過他們歌唱，他們想誘惑我離開我的念珠，他們笑著輕敲窗戶，他們在我的耳畔低吟著危險的歡愉，他們用試探來誘我犯罪。我祈禱時他們對我皺眉頭。他們不知該何去何從，我告訴你，他們是迷失的一群；對他們而言，既無天堂也無地獄，他們更不會在其中頌讚造物主。」

　　「神父，」年輕漁夫哭道，「您不知道您在說些什麼。我曾在我的漁網中捕到一位國王的女兒。她比早晨的星星更美麗，比月亮更皎潔。為了她的身體，我寧願付出我的靈魂；為了她的愛，我寧願放棄天堂。告訴我問題的答案，然後讓我平安地走吧。」

　　「去！去！」神父叫道，「你的愛人迷失了，你也會和她一起迷失！」他沒有祝福他，只是把他趕了出去。

年輕的漁夫走到菜市場，他走得很慢，頭垂得低低的，像個憂愁難當的人。

商販見他走來，便交頭接耳著，其中一人朝他走了過去，叫喚他的名字，說道：「你有什麼要賣的嗎？」

「我要把我的靈魂賣給你，」年輕的漁夫答道，「我求你把它買去吧！因為我為它煩憂。靈魂對我有何用呢？我看不到，摸不著，更不認識它。」

然而商販們卻取笑他，說道：「人的靈魂對我們有何用呢？可能還值不了能發出清脆響聲的一錠銀子呢。把你自己賣給我們當奴隸吧，我們會讓你穿上藍紫色的衣服，在你手指上戴枚戒指，讓你變成女王的僕役。就是別再提靈魂了，因為對我們而言，它什麼都不是，對我們的買賣一點價值也沒有。」

於是年輕的漁夫對自己說道：「奇怪了！神父告訴我，靈魂值得拿世上所有的黃金來換，商人卻告訴我它連那能發出清脆響聲的一錠銀子都還不值。」他走過市集，直抵海邊，開始思考自己該怎麼做。

就在中午時分，他想起一個採茴香的朋友曾告訴過他，有個年輕的女巫住在海灣口的一個洞穴裡，巫術極為了得。於是他向前跑去，急著想擺脫自己的靈魂。他急奔過沙灘，揚起了一陣塵土。年輕的女巫手掌發癢便知道他來了，於是她笑著，垂放下她的紅髮。她站在洞穴入口處，身上纏繞著垂下的頭髮，手裡握著一小枝綻放著花朵的野毒芹。

「你缺啥？你缺啥？」她叫道。年輕的漁夫正氣喘吁吁地爬上斜坡，向她欠身致意。

「風吹得狂時，網裡就會有魚嗎？我有一支小蘆笛，只要一吹，灰鯔就會游進海灣，可是這得付出代價，小帥哥，要付出代價哪！你缺啥呢？一場毀壞船隻、能把裝滿寶藏的箱子沖上岸的暴風雨？我擁有的暴風雨比風所擁有的還多，因為我所服侍的那一位比風更強大，而且我只需要用一個篩子和一桶水就可以把大戰艦送到海底去。可是這要付出代價的，小帥哥，要付出代價的哪！你缺啥呢？我知道山谷裡長著一種花，除了我之外沒人知道。它有紫色的葉子，心臟裡有一顆星星，它的汁液如同牛奶一樣白。千萬別讓皇后的硬嘴唇碰上這花，否則她會跟你到天涯海角。她會離開國王的床上，跟著你到天涯海角。可是這要付出代價的，小帥哥，要付出代價的哪！你缺啥呢？我可以把一隻蟾蜍搗碎在研缽裡，再把它做成一鍋肉汁，然後用一隻死人的手攪拌這肉汁。在你的敵人睡覺時，只要將這肉汁灑在他身上，他就會變成一條黑色的毒蛇，他的母親會不明所以地殺了他。只需要一個輪子，我就能將月亮摘下來；在水晶球裡，我可以讓你看見死神。你缺啥呢？告訴我，你要的東西，我可以讓你如願，而你，可得付出代價，小帥哥，你可得付我代價呀！」

「我要的不過是個小東西。」年輕的漁夫說道，「但神父卻對我大發雷霆，還把我趕了出來。就連商人也取笑我，並拒絕了我。所以我才來找妳，雖然大家都說妳很邪惡，但不論妳要求的代價是什麼，我都會照付的。」

「你想要什麼？」女巫問道，更加走近他。

「我要我的靈魂離開我。」年輕漁夫答道。

女巫臉色發白，全身抖個不停，還把臉埋進她的藍色斗篷裡。「小帥哥，小帥哥，」她低語，「那可是件恐怖的事啊！」

他甩甩棕色的鬈髮，笑著說：「我的靈魂對我來說一點也不重要。我看不到，摸不著，更不認識它。」

「如果我告訴你怎麼做，你要給我什麼呢？」女巫用她漂亮的眼睛俯看著他，問道。

「五塊金子，」他說道，「我的漁網，我住的小屋，還有我出海用的那艘彩繪小船。只要告訴我如何甩掉靈魂，我就會把我所擁有的一切都給妳。」

女巫嘲笑他，還用手裡的野毒芹枝打他。「我可以把秋天的落葉變成黃金，」她答道，「只要我願意，我也可以將朦朧的月光編成白銀。我服侍的那一位，祂可是比世界上任何國王還富裕，權力更凌駕於他們之上。」

女巫用她纖細潔白的手，撫弄著年輕漁夫的頭髮。「你必須和我跳一支舞，小帥哥。」她微笑著對他喃喃低語。

「就這樣？」年輕漁夫疑惑地問道，站了起來。

「就這樣。」她答道，她再度對他微笑。

「那麼，日落時在某個神祕之處，我們得一塊兒跳舞。」他說道，「跳完舞以後，妳就得把我想知道的事告訴我。」

她搖搖頭。「滿月時，滿月時，」女巫低語道。然後她望了望四周，靜靜傾聽著。一隻青鳥驚叫著飛離鳥巢，在沙丘上盤旋；另外三隻偵察著附近動態的鳥兒急速飛過粗糙的灰白草地，彼此竊竊私語。此外，除了下方那拍打著平滑小鵝卵石的海浪聲外，別無他聲。於是她伸出手，把他拉向自己，又將自己乾燥的嘴唇附在他耳畔。

「今晚，你得到山頂來，」她輕聲說道，「今天是安息日，他會在那裡。」

年輕的漁夫定睛看著她，只見女巫露出潔白的牙齒笑著。「妳所說的他是誰？」他問道。

「那不重要，」她答道，「今晚，站在角樹的樹枝下等我。如果有隻黑狗向你跑去，拿柳樹條打牠，牠就會走開。如果有隻貓頭鷹跟你說話，也別理牠。月圓時分我就會與你同在，然後我們就在草地上共舞。」

「可是妳願意發誓，說妳會告訴我，該如何拋開自己的靈魂嗎？」他問道。

女巫移步至陽光下，紅髮在風中翻飛著。「我以山羊蹄發誓，一定會告訴你。」她答道。

「妳真是最棒的女巫，」年輕的漁夫叫道，「我今晚一定會在山頂上和妳共舞。說真的，我倒寧願妳向我要金子或銀子呢。但妳既已決定妳要的代價，就照妳的意思吧！因為，這真的只是小事一樁。」於是他脫帽，深深地向女巫欠身行禮，便滿心歡喜地跑回城裡去了。

女巫目送著他離去，直到看不見他，才回到洞穴裡去。她從一個雕工精細的杉木盒中拿出鏡子來，放在架上，再於鏡前燃燒著的木炭裡放進馬鞭草，然後在一陣煙霧瀰漫中往前看去。半晌，她生氣地握緊拳頭。「他應該是我的，」她低吼著，「我跟她一樣漂亮。」

那一夜，當月亮升起時，年輕漁夫已爬上山頂，站在角樹樹枝下。渾圓的海洋彷彿一塊放在他腳畔、擦得晶亮的金屬盾牌，海面上的帆影正在小小的海灣裡移動著。一隻有著硫磺色雙眼的大貓頭鷹叫著他的名字，但他沒理會。一隻黑狗向他跑來，對他咆哮，他用柳條打牠，那狗便哀叫著跑開了。

午夜時，女巫們如蝙蝠般凌空而來。「噴，噴！」她們照亮地面時叫道，「這兒有個我們不認識的人！」她們嗅來嗅去，還彼此吱嘎吱嘎地交談，比著手勢。最後到達的是那個年輕女巫，她的紅髮在風中飛舞，有如一道紅色河流。她穿著一套以金線織成的衣服，上面繡有孔雀眼睛，頭上戴著一頂綠色天鵝絨小帽。

「他在哪裡，他在哪裡？」女巫們看到她隨即尖著嗓子問道，然而她只是笑著跑到角樹下。她拉起漁夫的手，領著他到月光下，開始跳舞。

他們一圈又一圈地旋轉著，那年輕的女巫躍動得如此之高，令他看到了她紅色的鞋跟。然後，他們對面忽然傳來奔騰的馬蹄聲，可是卻沒有馬匹出現。他開始覺得害怕了。

「轉快點兒，」女巫叫道，她的雙手抱著他的頸子，她灼熱的呼吸吹在他的臉上。「快點兒，快點兒！」她喊道，地面似乎在他的腳下旋轉，他腦中一片渾沌，極度的恐懼籠罩著他，彷彿某種邪惡之物正看著他似的。最後，他終於注意到就在岩石的陰影處有個人影，是他從沒看過的那種。

那是個穿著黑色天鵝絨套裝的男人，服裝剪裁的樣式是西班牙風格。他的臉異常慘白，嘴唇卻像朵驕傲的紅花。他似乎很疲憊，傾身斜向後靠，漠然地把玩著他短劍上的劍柄。他身旁的草地上躺著一頂飾著羽毛的帽子，還有一雙飾著銀絲花邊的騎馬用長手套，上面以珍珠織成一幅精巧的圖案。他的肩膀上披著一件黑貂皮襯底的短斗篷，而他纖細潔白的雙手則裝飾著戒指，沉重的眼皮覆蓋住他的雙眼。年輕的漁夫看著他，好似一個被咒語定住的人。他們目光交會，不論他跳舞的身子旋轉到哪，那男人的眼睛似乎總是盯著他。他聽到女巫在笑，他的手抓住她的腰，瘋狂地一直讓她轉圈、轉圈。

突然間，森林裡有隻狗咆哮起來，舞者們都停了下來。他們兩兩成雙地走上前，屈膝並親吻那男人的手。當他們這麼做時，一抹淺淺的微笑浮上他驕傲的嘴唇，就像小鳥的羽翼碰觸水面，水面綻放出漣漪般，其中隱隱藏著輕蔑。那人還是盯著年輕漁夫看。

「來吧！我們去致意，」女巫低聲道，引領他向前走去；她熱切地抓住他的手，於是他跟在她後頭。但當他靠近那男人時，不知何故，年輕的漁夫突然在自己胸前畫了個十字，又呼喊著上帝的名字。

他一這麼做，女巫們便立刻像老鷹般尖叫著，朝天空飛去。而那張一直注視著他的蒼白臉孔，也因痙攣而痛苦地扭曲著。那男人走進小森林裡，吹了聲口哨，一匹配著銀質馬具的西班牙小馬便跑出來迎接他。躍上馬鞍時，他轉過身來，哀傷地望著年輕漁夫。

那名紅髮女巫也試著要逃走，但年輕漁夫扣住了她的手腕，緊緊抓著她。「放開我！」她大叫道，「讓我走。因為你呼喊了不該呼喊的名字，畫出了不可以讓人看到的記號。」

「不，」他答道，「我是不會讓妳走的，除非妳把祕密告訴我。」

「什麼祕密？」女巫說道，她像隻野貓緊咬著自己發白的嘴唇，掙扎著想要逃離他。

「妳知道的。」他答道。

她那雙草綠色眸子因淚水盈眶而黯淡了下來，她告訴年輕漁夫：「除了那件事以外，你問我別的事，我都告訴你！」

他笑了，更加使力地抓緊她。

當她明白自己毫無機會脫逃時，便低聲告訴他：「我確信我和那海洋的女兒一樣美，也和那些住在蔚藍海水裡的生物一樣豔麗。」說著，她諂媚地撒嬌，還把自己的臉貼近年輕漁夫的臉。

但他不悅地將她推開，對她說道：「如果妳不信守對我的承諾，我就當妳撒謊，我會殺了妳。」

她的臉死灰得有如洋蘇木上的花朵，她發著抖。「就這樣吧，」她低吼著，「那畢竟是你的靈魂，不是我的靈魂。你愛拿它怎麼辦，就怎麼辦好了。」說著，她從腰帶裡抽出一把刀柄上纏著綠蝮蛇皮的小刀，將這把刀給了年輕漁夫。

「這把刀對我有什麼用？」他疑惑地問她。

女巫靜默了一會兒，然後臉上露出一個恐怖的表情。她將額前的頭髮梳向腦後，怪異地笑著對他說：「人們所說的影子其實並不是身體的影子，乃是靈魂的身體。你只要站在海灘上，背對著月亮，將你的影子，也就是你靈魂的身體，從腳底周圍割掉，並且吩咐它離開你，你的靈魂就會離開了。」

年輕的漁夫顫抖著：「真的嗎？」他喃喃地說道。

「是真的。我真希望，我沒告訴過你這些話。」女巫抱住膝蓋，哭喊了起來。

他推開她，將她留在茂密的草地上，獨自走向山崖，將小刀插進皮帶，開始攀爬下山。

他體內的靈魂呼喊著他，對他說道：「嘿，我在你身體裡住了這麼多年，也一直服侍著你。請你不要捨棄我，我哪裡得罪你了呢？」

年輕的漁夫大笑：「你沒得罪我，只是我不需要你而已。這世界如此寬廣，有天堂也有地獄，還有那介於天堂地獄間的灰色地帶。你愛上哪兒去就上哪兒去，別來煩我就行，因為我的愛正在呼喚我。」

然後，他的靈魂一直不斷地切切懇求他，他卻連聽都不聽。年輕漁夫在峭壁中跳躍著，步履穩健得有如野山羊。最後，他下到了海平面，來到黃色的海岸邊。

他古銅色的身軀，健美的身形，彷彿一尊精工打造的希臘雕像，背對著月光，立於沙灘上。浪花從打出的泡沫中升起白色手臂向他招呼著，海浪中翻騰出的灰暗波濤也朝他致意。躺在他面前的是他的影子，也就是他靈魂的身體；掛在他身後蜂蜜色夜空中的，則是一輪明月。

他的靈魂告訴他：「如果你非得捨棄我不可，那麼請你讓我帶著心一起走。這個世界如此殘酷，把你的心給我，讓我帶著你的心走。」

他搖搖頭，微笑著：「如果我把心給你，那我要用什麼來愛我的愛人呢？」。

「喔，你可憐可憐我吧，」他的靈魂說道，「給我你的心吧，因為這世界太殘酷，我實在很害怕呀！」

「我的心屬於我的愛，」他回答，「所以，別再拖時間了，你快走吧！」

「難道我就不該有愛？」他的靈魂問道。

「你快走吧，因為我不需要你。」年輕漁夫叫嚷著。他拿出那把飾著綠蝮蛇皮刀柄的小刀，從腳邊將他的影子割去。他的影子向上躍起，站在他面前，注視著他，簡直和他一模一樣。

他蹣跚地退後，將刀子收進皮帶，一股恐懼感向他襲來。「你快走吧，」他低聲說道，「別再讓我看見你了。」

「不，不，我們必須再見面，」靈魂說道。它的聲音低沉、有如笛聲，當它說話時，嘴唇彷彿動也不動。

「我們要怎麼見面？」年輕漁夫大聲說道，「你該不會要跟著我到海裡去吧？」

「我每年都會來這裡一次，呼喚你，」靈魂說道，「你可能會需要我。」

「我要你幹嘛？」年輕漁夫叫道，「不過，既然你想這麼做，就這麼辦吧！」接著他跳進了海裡。海神吹起號角，小美人魚立刻浮出海面迎接他，用雙臂抱著他的頸項，並給他深深一吻。

靈魂佇立在孤獨的沙灘上看著他們。當他們一起沉入大海時，它哭泣著穿過沼澤地，離去了。

一年後，靈魂回到沙灘上，呼喚著年輕漁夫。他便浮出海面，說道：「你找我幹嘛？」

靈魂答道：「靠近點嘛，我才好跟你說話啊，我見識了好多奇妙的事呢。」

於是他靠近，在淺水處蹲下，偏著頭聽它說話，還用手撐著頭。

靈魂告訴他：「當我離開你時，就往東方旅行去了。從東方來的每一件事物都深富智慧。我旅行了六天，在第七天早晨來到韃靼境內的一座小山。我在一棵松樹下乘涼。那地方很乾燥，熱得不得了。那兒的人在平原上來來去去，就像一堆蒼蠅在晶亮的銅板上爬來爬去一樣。

「正午時分，一片紅色灰塵形成的雲從地平線上升起。韃靼人一看到它，便拉弓上弦，立刻跳上馬去追它。女人們則尖叫著跳進馬車，躲在毛氈帘幕後頭。

「黃昏時，韃靼人回來了，卻少了五個人，而且回來的人之中有不少受了傷。他們把馬車套上馬，急速地離去了。三隻狐狼從洞穴探出頭來，在他們後頭窺探著；牠們的鼻孔朝上用力吸了吸氣，然後就朝著反方向快步跑走了。

「當月亮升起時，我看到平原上有營火燃燒著，於是我便走了過去。一群商人正圍著營火坐著，屁股底下還墊著絨毯。他們的駱駝都繫在身後的木樁上，黑人僕役正把黃褐色的帳棚搭在沙地上，還用霸王樹搭起一堵高牆。

「當我走近時，商人裡的首領立刻站起來，拔出他的劍，問我是做什麼的。

「我告訴他，我在自己的國家是個王子；才剛從韃靼人手中逃出，因為他們想抓我去當奴隸。那首領笑了起來，叫我看看掛在長竿上的五顆人頭。

「然後他問我，上帝的先知是誰，我答說是穆罕默德。

「當他聽到這個假造的先知名字時，便鞠了個躬，拉著我的手，讓我在他身旁坐下。有個黑人僕役為我送上一大木盤子的騾奶和一塊烤羊排。

「天亮時，我們便開始了旅程。我騎了一匹紅毛駱駝走在首領旁邊，有個聽差的拿著長矛在我們前面跑著。戰士們則排列在我們左右兩側，騾子馱著貨物跟在後面。這個商隊一共有四十匹駱駝和八十四騾子。

「我們從韃靼人的國境走到詛咒月亮之人的國境去。我們看到半獅半鷲的怪獸，守護著牠們在白岩石上的黃金，全身是鱗片的龍則在洞穴裡睡著。而當我們越過山嶺時，大夥全都屏住呼吸以免引起雪崩，每個人還得在自己的眼前綁條薄紗哩。當我們途經山谷時，矮人族從中空的樹幹朝我們射箭；夜晚來臨時，我們聽到野人們在打鼓。來到人猿塔時，我們將水果擺在牠們面前，人猿就沒有傷害我們。當我們走到毒蛇塔時，我們給蛇群送去用銅碗裝著的溫熱牛奶，牠們便讓我們順利通過。旅程中，我們曾三次通過有河馬的河堤，我們靠著加裝了大型獸皮氣囊的木筏過河。河馬很生氣，想要幹掉我們；而駱駝一看到河馬這樣，嚇得腿都軟了。

「每個城市的國王都向我們徵收過路費，卻不願讓我們走進他們的城門裡。他們把麵包扔過城牆來給我們，也給我們沾著蜂蜜烘烤的玉米蛋糕和棗椰蛋糕。他們會用一百個籃子跟我們換一串琥珀念珠。

「村莊裡的居民一看到我們來，就會在井裡下毒，然後逃到山頂上去。我們跟馬革大伊人打仗，這些人出生時老態龍鍾，卻愈活愈年輕，死時就變成孩童的模樣。我們也跟拉克脫伊人打仗；他們說自己是老虎的後代，因此為自己漆上了黑黃相間的色彩。我們還跟奧朗提人打仗，這些人把死人埋在樹梢上，自己則習慣住在黑暗的洞穴裡，只因為怕被他們的神祇──太陽給殺了。然後是克林姆人，他們崇拜一隻鱷魚，不但給牠綠琉璃做成的耳環，還餵牠吃奶油和新鮮的飛禽。還有阿加松貝人，他們是狗臉人身哩！更有長著馬腿的司班人，他們跑起來比馬更快呢！我們的商隊有三分之一的人死於戰爭，三分之一的人死於物資缺乏，剩下的人則喃喃地數落我，說是我為他們帶來了霉運。我從石頭底下翻出一隻毒蛇，讓牠來咬我；當他們見到我被毒蛇咬卻沒什麼事時，他們就開始覺得害怕了。

「我們在旅行的第四個月到達伊萊市。當我們來到城牆外的小叢林時已入夜了，但天氣仍酷熱難當，因為月亮正在天蠍座旅行。我們從樹上摘下成熟的石榴，打破後，吸取它甜美的汁液，然後就在我們的毯子上躺下等待黎明。

「黎明時分我們便起，敲著城門。那門是由紅銅打造而成，門上還雕刻著潛游海中的龍和振翅高飛的龍。衛兵們從城牆牒口往下看，問我們是作什麼的。商隊裡的翻譯答說，我們是從敘利亞海島來的，帶著許多貨物。他們拿了些抵押品，並且告訴我們，他們中午時會來幫我們開門，還要我們別走開。

「中午時分他們開了城門。當我們走進城裡時，那兒的人全都從自己家裡一擁而上到街上來看我們，還有一個傳令兵繞著全城吹號傳訊。我們站在市場上，黑人僕役解開一捆捆圖案華美的服飾，打開用無花果木雕刻的箱子。當他們作完這些工作時，商人們便陳列出奇特的商品——來自埃及的上蠟亞麻布；來自衣索匹亞的彩色亞麻布；來自泰爾的紫海綿；來自西頓的藍門帘，還有琥珀製成的杯子，精緻的玻璃容器和稀奇的陶器。一群女人從屋頂上盯著我們看，其中一個戴著飾有金箔的皮面具。

「第一天，一群祭司過來和我們交換貨物；第二天是一些貴族；第三天則是工匠和奴隸群。他們對所有到城裡來做生意的商旅都保有這習慣。

「我們停留了一個月。開始月缺時，我覺得百無聊賴，便在城裡逛來逛去，來到了他們祭拜的神殿。身穿黃袍的祭司安靜地在綠色的樹木間穿梭，黑色大理石走道旁矗立著一棟玫瑰紅色澤的房子，那就是神殿了。神殿的門上塗著瓷漆，還裝飾著精金浮雕的公牛和孔雀；屋頂是深綠色的瓷磚，飛簷則飾以小鈴鐺做成的花綵，白鴿飛掠此處時總會拿翅膀碰一下鈴鐺，讓它們叮噹作響。

「神殿前有個乾淨的水池，鋪設著紋理清晰的縞瑪瑙。我在一旁躺了下來，用蒼白的手指觸摸著寬闊的金屬池面。有個祭司朝我走來，站在我身後。他足蹬涼鞋，一隻鞋是軟蛇皮作的，另一隻則是鳥羽毛作的。他頭上戴著一頂黑氈禮冠，上頭鑲一只半月形銀飾。他的袍子上有七種不同的黃色，他的鬈髮則是用銻染色的。

「半晌，他開始和我交談，並問我想要些什麼。我告訴他，我想要見到神。

「『神正在打獵。』那祭司說道，又用他那雙細小的斜眼狐疑地看著我。

「『那就告訴我，祂在哪個森林裡，我可以跟祂一塊兒騎馬。』我回答道。

「祭司用他那又尖又長的指甲，梳理著外袍上柔軟的流蘇。『神正在睡覺哪。』他低語道。

「『那就告訴我，祂在哪個躺椅上，我會在旁邊看。』我又說。

「『神正在飲酒哪。』他叫道。

「『假使酒是甜的，我會和他一塊兒喝；如果酒是苦的，我也會和他一塊兒喝。』我又這麼回答他。

「他驚訝地低下頭，握住我的手，將我拉了起來，然後領我走進神殿。

「在第一個房間裡，我看到一個人偶坐在一個碧玉打造、以東方珍珠鑲邊的王座上。那人偶以黑檀木雕成，樣子看來像人。它的前額有一顆紅寶石，濃稠的油從它的髮間直淌到大腿；它的雙腳讓一個不久前才被殺害的孩子鮮血給染紅了；它的腰上束著一條銅腰帶，其上繫著七片綠柱玉。

「我對祭司說：『這就是神嗎？』他答道：『這就是神。』

「『帶我去見神，』我大叫，『要不然我就殺了你。』我碰觸他的手，沒想到他的手竟枯乾了。

「那祭司哀求我：『求我主治癒他的僕人吧，我會帶我主去見神的。』

「於是我在他手上吹了一口氣，他的手立刻恢復原貌。他發著抖，帶我到第二個房間去。在那兒，我又看到另一個人偶站在玉蓮花上，精美的翡翠在四周垂掛著。那人偶是用象牙雕成，樣子有真人兩倍大。前額有顆昂貴的橄欖石；胸部塗著沒藥和肉桂。它的一隻手握著一根玉作的彎曲權杖，另一隻手則握著一顆圓形水晶。它穿著黃銅製的短靴，粗脖子上圍裹著一圈透明石膏。

「於是我對祭司說道：『這就是神嗎？』他答道：『這就是神。』

「『帶我去見神，』我大叫，『要不然我就殺了你。』於是我摸了摸他的眼睛，他就失明了。

「那祭司哀求我：『求我主治癒他的僕人吧，我會帶我主去見神的。』」

「於是我在他眼睛上吹了一口氣，他的視力就恢復了。他再次發著抖，帶我到第三個房間裡去，啊！房間裡沒有人偶，眼前也沒有任何景象，只有一面架在石祭壇上的金屬圓鏡。

「我對祭司說道：『神在哪裡？』」

「他回答道：『除了你見到的這面鏡子外，並沒有神。因為這是智慧之鏡，會映照出所有在天堂或人間發生的事，唯一不會映照出的是窺視它的人的臉。若它不會映照出這個人的臉，那人就可能是有智慧的。這裡還有許多別的鏡子，不過都是意見之鏡，只有這面是智慧之鏡。擁有這面鏡子的人能夠知道每一件事，世上沒有任何一件事能瞞得過這人的耳目。所以，沒有這面鏡子的人也沒有智慧。它就是神，因此我們才敬拜它。』我聞言看了鏡子，結果就如他所說的一樣。

「然後我做了件奇怪的事，儘管我做了些什麼並不重要。在離此地僅一天路程的地方，有個小村莊，我把智慧之鏡藏在那兒。讓我回到你身體，當你的僕人吧！你會比任何一位智者更有智慧，完完全全地擁有智慧。讓我回到你身體吧，這世上沒有人會跟你一樣有智慧的！」

但年輕漁的夫笑了起來。「愛情好過智慧，」他叫道，「小美人魚愛我的！」

「不，沒有任何事情能夠好過智慧。」靈魂說道。

「愛情比較好。」年輕漁夫答完，便潛進海裡去了。靈魂哭著走過了沼澤地。

第二年過去了，靈魂來到海岸邊，呼喚年輕漁夫。他浮上海面，說道：「你叫我幹嘛？」

靈魂答道：「過來點嘛，我好跟你說話啊，我見識了好多奇妙的事呢。」

於是他靠近些，並且在淺水處蹲了下來，偏著頭聽它說話，還用手撐著頭。

靈魂告訴他：「在離開你之後，我就往南方旅行去了。從南方來的東西可都珍貴得很哪。我沿著大馬路走了六天，來到艾斯特城。那條路是朝聖者常常走的漫天塵沙路呢！第七天早晨我睜開眼睛一看，那座位在山谷裡的城市，就躺在我腳下！

「那城市有九個城門，每道城門都立著一匹青銅駿馬。每當貝都因人從山上下來時，馬兒就會嘶嘶作響。城牆鑲著銅框，城牆上的瞭望臺則以紅銅為屋頂。每座瞭望臺都站著一個持弓的弓箭手。日出時，他以箭擊打銅鑼；日落時，他則吹響號角。

「當我想要進城時，衛兵們把我攔下來，問我是誰。我答稱，我是個回教的托缽僧，正在前往麥加的路上，麥加這城市有塊綠色的面紗，天使親自將可蘭經以銀製的字母繡在面紗上。他們一聽，心中充滿驚奇，便請我進去。

「城裡就像個市集，你真該和我一塊兒去的。窄窄的街道上掛著色彩炫麗的紙燈籠，看起來就像翩翩飛舞的大蝴蝶；當風吹過屋頂時，它們彷彿彩色泡泡般上下搖動著。商人們坐在各家攤位前的絲質坐墊上，蓄著直直長長的黑鬍子；他們的頭巾上裝飾著一層小金幣；長串的琥珀與雕工精緻的美麗寶石，在他們淡漠的手指間流轉著。他們之中有人販賣白松香、甘松香，還有來自印度洋海島上奇特的香水，濃郁的紅玫瑰油、沒藥與小小的指甲狀丁香。一旦有人停下腳步攀談，他們就會把一小撮乳香丟進炭火裡，讓空氣變得香甜。我看到一個敘利亞人手裡拿著一根蘆葦般細薄的枝條，一縷灰煙從枝條上冒起，燃燒的香氣有如春天裡燃燒桃色杏仁的香氣。其他人則販賣浮雕著色澤柔和土耳其玉的銀手鐲，珍珠鑲邊的紅銅腳環，黃金鑲邊的虎爪，金絲貓爪，豹爪等也都是黃金鑲邊的；還有打洞的翡翠耳環與中空的玉戒指。茶館裡傳來吉他聲，抽鴉片的人們帶著蒼白笑臉，看著屋外的路人。

「你真該跟我一塊兒去的。酒販將黑色的大酒囊扛在肩上，穿梭在擁擠的人群中。他們大部分人都賣舒瓦茲酒，一種香甜如蜂蜜的酒；他們將酒倒在小金屬杯中，再灑上玫瑰花瓣。市場上賣水果的人什麼貨都賣──果肉呈深紫色的成熟無花果；味道有如麝香、色澤彷彿黃玉的香瓜；香櫞和玫瑰蘋果；也有一串串白葡萄，橙黃渾圓的柑橘，以及綠色黃金般的橢圓形檸檬。有一次我還看到有隻大象經過，牠的鼻子被漆成鮮紅色與薑黃色，耳朵上方有一個用深紅絲線編成的網子。牠在一個攤位前停了下來，開始吃柑橘，那人卻只是笑著。你實在無法想像那些人有多奇怪。他們高興的時候就走到賣鳥人的攤位去，買隻鳥，然後把鳥放出籠子；這樣做似乎讓他們更高興。他們悲傷的時候就用荊棘鞭打自己，免得自己的悲傷減損。

「有天傍晚，我遇到幾個扛著沉重轎子經過市集的黑人僕役。轎子是用鍍金的竹子作成，轎桿則上了朱紅色的漆，並飾以黃銅作的孔雀。窗口掛著的薄帘以回教刺繡的方式，繡上了昆蟲翅膀和小顆珍珠。轎子經過我面前時，一個臉色蒼白的塞設西人從窗口往外望，還對我微笑。我跟在他們後面，黑人僕役們卻加快腳步，並皺起了眉頭。不過我不在乎，只覺得強烈的好奇心正籠罩著我。

「最後他們停在一棟白色的四方形屋子前頭。那房子並沒有窗戶，只有一個墓門似的小門。他們放下轎子，用一根銅槌敲了三下門。一個身穿綠皮長袍的亞美尼亞人，微開小門，往外張看。當他一見是他們，便立即開門，還在地上鋪上地毯，轎裡的女人便走了出來。就在她進屋時，她轉過身，再次對我微笑；我從未見過臉色這麼蒼白的人。

「當月亮升起時，我回到剛才那地方要找那房子，但房子已失去蹤影了。我當即明白過來那女人是誰，又為何要對我微笑。

「你實在應該和我一起去的。在月初時，年輕的皇帝從他的皇宮走了出來，進到清真寺裡祈禱。他的頭髮和鬍子都以玫瑰花瓣做成的染料來染色；雙頰則抹上細緻的金粉；他的腳掌和手掌則是以番紅花染成黃色。

「日出時，他穿著一件銀袍從皇宮裡出來；日落時，他穿著一件金袍返回皇宮。人們遮住臉俯伏在地，我卻沒這麼做，只是站在一個賣棗椰的攤位旁等著。當皇帝看到我時，揚起他那上了顏色的眉毛，停下腳步。我直挺挺地站著，沒有向他行禮。人們因我的大膽而詫異，還好心地勸我逃離此地，我卻完全不予理會，只是自顧自地走到販賣怪異神像的攤販那兒去，和他們一起坐著；那些神像因雕工之故看起來十分面目可憎。當我告訴攤販我的行為之後，他們每個人都給了我一尊神像，還拜託我快快離開他們。

「那天晚上，當我在石榴街上一家茶館的靠墊躺下來時，皇帝的侍衛進來，帶我到皇宮裡去。我一進去，他們立即將我身後每一扇門關起，還上了閂。這裡頭是一座有著通往四面八方迴廊的皇宮內院，牆面以白色的雪花石膏為底，再穿插飾以藍色與綠色的瓷磚；柱子是以綠色的大理石做成；人行道則是某種桃花色大理石，我從未見過這樣的東西。

「當我走過院子時，有兩個蒙著面紗的女人從陽臺上往下看著我，開始咒罵我。衛兵用槍托敲著光滑的地板，催促我快點走。他們打開一扇象牙雕成的門，讓我進到一個有著七層臺階、流水環繞的花園中。花園裡種植著鬱金香、瓢葫蘆，和有著銀絲邊的蘆薈。噴泉中噴灑出來的水，有如一支纖細的水晶懸掛在幽暗的空中。絲柏彷如燃燒著的火把，夜鶯則駐足其中唱著歌。

「花園盡頭佇立著一座小樓閣。當我們走進時，兩個太監出來迎接我們，他們肥胖的身軀在行走時搖來晃去，又好奇地用那有著黃色眼瞼的雙眼偷看我。其中一人將侍衛隊長拉到一旁低聲交談，另一人則裝模作樣地從一個淡紫色的橢圓搪瓷盒中，拿出氣味清香的嚼片使勁嚼了起來。

「不一會兒，侍衛隊長讓士兵先回宮裡去，兩個太監則緩步跟在後頭，經過桑椹樹時，他們摘了些甜美的果實。有一回，那個比較年長的太監還轉過身，給了我一抹邪惡的笑容。

「然後侍衛隊長比了一個叫我到小樓閣入口去的手勢，我便無所畏懼地往前走去，伸手拉開厚重的帘幕，走了進去。

「年輕的皇帝斜倚在彩色的獅皮靠墊上，一隻鷹隼停在他的手腕上。他後頭還站著一個努比亞人，那人包著黃銅色的頭巾，打赤膊，裂開的耳垂上掛著重重的耳環。躺椅旁的桌子上，還擺著一把巨大的半月形鋼質彎刀。

「當皇帝看到我時，皺起了眉頭，對我說道：『你叫什麼名字？你不知道我是這裡的皇帝嗎？』但我一語未發。

「他用手指指那把彎刀，努比亞人便掄起那刀，狂暴地向我襲來。刀鋒咻咻咻地劈過我，卻沒傷到我。那努比亞人跌坐在地板上，爬起來時，神情恐懼得牙齒喀搭喀搭作響，然後便躲到躺椅後頭去了。

「那皇帝跳起來，伸手到武器架上抽了枝矛，朝我扔來。我接住那拋過來的矛，對半折斷。他又拿了枝箭射我，但我舉起手，箭便停在半空中。然後他從白色皮革做的皮帶中抽出短劍，刺向那努比亞人的咽喉，免得他將皇帝吃癟的事傳出去。那人痛苦地蜷縮著，彷彿一條被人用力踐踏在地的蛇，嘴唇不斷冒出紅色的泡沫。

「那努比亞人一死，皇帝立即轉向我。他用一條鑲著紫絲綢花邊的手巾，拭去他額頭上晶亮的汗珠時，對我說道：『你是先知嗎？所以我傷不了你。或者，你是先知之子嗎？是以我無法傷你。拜託你，今夜就離開我的城市吧，因為只要有你在，我就不再是本城之主了。』

「於是我答道：『要我走，就把你一半的財寶分給我。給我你一半的財寶，我就走。』

「他拉著我的手，帶我到花園去。當侍衛隊長看到我時滿臉狐疑，太監看到我則立刻雙膝發顫，嚇得摔倒在地。

「皇宮裡有個八角形房子，牆壁是用紅色斑岩做的，黃銅做的藻井上垂掛著燈。皇帝碰觸了其中一堵牆，那牆隨即打開。我們走下一條點著許多火把的迴廊，迴廊兩邊的壁龕上擺著裝滿銀塊的酒缸。當我們來到迴廊中央時，皇帝說了一個不該說的字，然後一道由隱形彈簧控制的花崗岩門便往後旋開。皇帝用雙手遮住自己的臉，以免眼睛因強光而睜不開。

　　「你可能無法相信那是一個多麼令人讚嘆的地方。那裡有極大的海龜殼，殼裡滿是珍珠；中空的大型月長石和大顆紅寶石成堆地堆積著。黃金則存放在可容得下一隻大象的箱子裡，還有用皮製酒壺盛裝著的砂金。那裡也有蛋白石和藍寶石，前者裝在水晶杯裡，後者放在玉杯中。渾圓的碧綠翡翠依序排列在象牙托盤中，角落一隅則有鼓鼓的絲綢袋子，有些裝的是土耳其玉，其他的則是綠柱玉。象牙號角和紫水晶堆積成堆，此外還有黃銅號角與紅玉髓。用杉木做成的柱上垂掛著成串的黃色貓眼石。在橢圓盾牌上有著紅玉，酒紅色的、草綠色的兼而有之。然而，我告訴你的這些，還只是寶藏的十分之一而已。

　　「那皇帝把手從自己的臉上挪開時告訴我：『這是我的藏寶屋，如之前約定的，這裡頭有一半的寶物是你的了。我還會給你駱駝和駕駱駝的人。他們會聽從你的吩咐，帶著你的寶藏，到任何你想要的地方去。而這事今晚就得辦妥，因為我不想讓我父親，也就是太陽知道，在這城裡竟有個我殺不死的人。』

　　「然而，我答道：『這裡的黃金是你的，白銀也是你的，貴重的珠寶和價值不菲的寶物也都是你的。至於我，我一點寶藏也不需要，除了你手上戴的那枚小戒指外，你的東西我什麼也不想拿。』

　　「皇帝皺起了眉頭。『這不過是個鉛作的戒指而已。』他叫道，『沒什麼價值，你還是拿走這屋裡的一半寶藏，離開我的城市吧！』

　　「『不，』我答道，『除了那個鉛戒指外，我什麼都不帶走，因為我知道戒指上寫了些什麼、有什麼用處。』

「皇帝開始顫抖起來，懇求我：『原本歸我的那一半也給你，你把全部的寶藏都拿走，只要離開我的城市。』

「然後我作了一件奇怪的事，不過也沒什麼啦，只是我把那個寶藏之戒藏在離此地約一天路程的某個山洞裡，僅僅離這裡一天的路程而已嘣，就等著你去拿。任何一個擁有這戒指的人，將會比世上任何一個君王都還要富裕。所以，來吧，去拿這戒指吧！全世界的財富就會變成你的了。」

但年輕的漁夫笑了：「愛情比財富重要，」他大聲說道，「而且小美人魚愛我。」

「不，不，沒有任何東西會比財富重要。」靈魂說道。

「愛情比較重要，」年輕漁夫說道，然後潛入海裡，靈魂又哭泣著走過沼澤地去了。

第三年過去了，靈魂來到海岸邊，呼喚年輕漁夫、漁夫又浮上海面，說道：「你找我幹嘛？」

靈魂答道：「過來點嘣，我好跟你說話呀，我見識了好多奇妙的事哪。」

於是漁夫走近了點、在淺水處蹲了下來，用手撐著斜倚的頭，聽靈魂說話。

於是靈魂告訴他：「在我知道的一座城市裡，有個小酒館就位在一條小河旁邊。我跟水手們一塊兒在那兒坐著，他們喝著兩種不同顏色的酒，吃著大麥麵包，和放在月桂葉上必須沾醋吃的小鹹魚。就在我們快樂吃喝時，酒館裡來了一個帶著一條皮毯，和一把有著兩個翡翠琴頭琵琶的老頭子。當他用翎毛敲著琵琶上的琴弦時，有個蒙著面紗的女孩便跑進來，開始在我們面前跳舞。她蒙著一塊薄薄的金屬面紗，腳上沒穿鞋。雖是赤足，但在地板上卻像隻鴿子般移動靈活。我從來沒見過這麼讓人神魂顛倒的奇景，而那女孩跳舞的城市距離此地不過一天的路程而已。」

當年輕漁夫聽著他的靈魂訴說的故事時，他忽然想起美人魚並沒有腳，無法跳舞。一股熱切的慾望湧上了心頭，於是他告訴自己：「不過就是一天的路程而已，而且我還是可以回到我的愛人身邊去啊，」他笑著，從淺水處站起身來，大步朝岸邊走去。

當他的腳踏上乾燥的岸邊，他又笑了，還向他的靈魂伸出了雙手。他的靈魂欣喜地大叫一聲，奔向他，進入他的身體。年輕漁夫看到，平坦的沙地上映射著自己身體的影子，也就是靈魂的身軀。

他的靈魂對他說道：「我們別耽擱時間，儘速啟程吧，因為海神會相當嫉妒，而且他們可是有供其差使的海怪呢！」

於是他們快步離開，整個夜裡都在月色下趕著路，第二天他們在陽光下趕了一天路，終於，在傍晚時分來到一個城市。

年輕漁夫對他的靈魂說道：「這就是你說的，那女孩跳舞的城市嗎？」

他的靈魂答道：「不是這個城市，是另一個。不過，不管了，我們進去吧。」

於是他們走進城裡，在街上逛著。當他們逛著珠寶商人擺攤的街道時，年輕漁夫在一個攤位上看到一只美麗的銀杯。此時，他的靈魂告訴他：「拿那個銀杯，藏起來。」

於是他拿起那個銀杯，把它藏在自己長袍的褶縫裡，然後急急地走出城去。

在他們離城約三哩遠時，年輕漁夫皺起眉頭，扔掉銀杯，對靈魂說道：「你為什麼要我拿那銀杯，還要我把它藏起來？這是壞事哪！」

但他的靈魂答道：「別生氣，別生氣。」

第二天傍晚，他們又來到另一座城市。年輕漁夫問著他的靈魂：「這是你說的那個女孩跳舞的城市嗎？」

可是他的靈魂回答道：「不是這一個，是另一個。不過，不管了，我們進去吧。」

於是他們走進城裡，在街上逛著。當他們逛著涼鞋商擺攤的街道時，年輕漁夫看到一個小孩站在水缸旁。他的靈魂對他說：「用力打那小孩。」於是他用力打了那小孩，打到小孩都哭了。他們作了這件事後，隨即匆忙出城去了。

在他們離城約三哩遠時，年輕漁夫更生氣了，他告訴他的靈魂：「為什麼叫我打那個小孩？這是壞事哪！」

但他的靈魂只答道：「別生氣，別生氣。」

第三天傍晚，他們來到了某個城市。年輕漁夫對他的靈魂說道：「這就是你所說的那個女孩跳舞的城市嗎？」

靈魂只答道：「可能是這個城市，我們進去吧！」

於是他們走進城裡，在街上逛著，但是年輕漁夫逛來逛去就是找不到那條河，或那家位在小河邊的酒館。而且城裡的人都好奇地看著他，他害怕起來，便對靈魂說道：「我們離開這裡吧，因為那個用一雙白皙赤足跳舞的女孩不在這兒。」

但他的靈魂答道：「不，我們多留一會兒吧，天黑了，路上會有盜匪呢！」

於是年輕漁夫在市集上坐著休息了一下。不久，來了個裹著頭巾的商人，他穿著一件韃靼布料作的斗篷，手裡提著一根連接起來的蘆笛，那蘆笛另一端掛了個穿著孔的號角，好當作燈籠用。商人對他說道：「你為什麼在市集上坐著啊？是因為看到攤位都收了，貨物都打包了嗎？」

年輕漁夫答道：「我在這城裡找不到可以歇息的酒館，而且這裡也沒有可供我一宿的親戚。」

「我們不都是親戚嗎？」那商人說道，「我們不都是同一位上帝所創造的嗎？所以，跟我來吧。我有一間客房。」

於是年輕漁夫站起身，跟著那商人回家。當他走過一個石榴園，進到屋子裡時，商人給了他一個銅盤，裡頭盛著要給他淨手的玫瑰水；又拿出讓他解渴的香瓜；又在他面前擺了一碗飯和一塊烤山羊肉。

　　他吃完後，商人領他到客房去，吩咐他好好睡覺、休息。年輕漁夫向商人道謝，親吻著他戴在手上的戒指，然後便舒服地躺在彩色的山羊毛地毯上。當他蓋上黑羊毛毯時，便沉沉入睡了。

　　破曉前三小時，仍是深夜，他的靈魂喚醒他，對他說道：「起來，到那商人的房間去，就是那個他睡覺的房間，快去把他給殺了。把他的金子拿來，因為我們用得著。」

　　於是年輕漁夫便起身，躡手躡腳地走到那商人的房間去。商人腳邊擺著一把彎刀，他身旁的托盤裡排著九袋金子。年輕漁夫伸出手碰了碰彎刀，當他碰到彎刀時，商人醒了過來，一躍而起握住彎刀，對著年輕漁夫叫道：「你要以惡報善嗎？還是要以流血回報我對你的仁慈？」

　　然而漁夫的靈魂卻對漁夫說：「打他！」漁夫便打了商人，還把人家打暈了過去，之後便抓起那九袋金子，飛快地逃出石榴園，又抬頭仰望星空，此時晨星已經出現。

　　在他們離城約三哩遠時，年輕漁夫捶著胸，對靈魂說道：「你為什麼叫我殺了商人，還拿走他的金子啊？你真的很邪惡！」

　　然而他的靈魂只是說：「別生氣，別生氣。」

　　「不，」年輕漁夫叫道，「我不能不生氣，因為我厭惡你叫我做的每一件事，而且我也厭惡你。現在我要你告訴我，為什麼要讓我扯進這一切陰謀裡？」

　　他的靈魂答道：「當初你打發我走進這世界時，並未把心給我啊，所以我才會學到這些事情，而且非常喜歡這麼做。」

　　「你在說什麼啊？」年輕漁夫低語。

　　「你知道的啊，」他的靈魂答道，「你清楚得很。我不信你忘了當初沒把心給我。所以，別因我而煩惱了，不要生氣了。因為世上沒有你忘不掉的痛苦，也沒有你接受不了的快樂呀。」

　　年輕漁夫聽到這些話，頓時打了個寒顫，對他的靈魂說道：

「不，你太邪惡了，而且還讓我忘了我的愛人。你引誘我到許多試探裡去，還讓我的腳走在罪惡的道路上。」

然而他的靈魂答道：「你沒有忘記自己當初打發我走時，並沒有把心給我。來吧，我們到另一個城市去找些樂子吧，我們手上有九袋金子呢！」

但年輕漁夫把九袋金子拿出來丟在地上，還用腳踐踏。

「不，」他叫道，「我和你不會再有什麼瓜葛了，我也不會和你一起到任何地方去了，就像我以前打發你走那樣，我現在也要打發你走，因為你對我一點好處也沒有。」於是他轉身背向月亮，拿出那把刀柄上包著綠蝮蛇皮的小刀，努力地想從自己腳邊割去他身體的影子，也就是他靈魂的身體。

然而，靈魂並未被割開，也毫不在意年輕漁夫的命令，只是告訴他：「那女巫告訴你的咒語已經不靈了。我不會離開你，你也不能叫我走。一個人一生中只能讓靈魂離開一次，一旦那人接回自己的靈魂，就得永遠跟它在一起了。這是他的懲罰，也是他的報償。」

年輕漁夫臉色蒼白、握緊拳頭大叫：「那女巫說謊，她告訴我的事是假的。」

「不，」他的靈魂答道，「她對她所敬拜的那人是真誠的，她永遠都會是他的僕役。」

當年輕漁夫知道自己永遠也擺脫不掉這個邪惡的靈魂，而且靈魂還會永遠住在他體內時，他伏在地上傷心地哭了起來。

天亮時，年輕漁夫站了起來，對他的靈魂說道：「我要把我的手捆起來，這樣我就不會去作你叫我作的事了。我要把嘴巴閉起來，這樣我就不會說你叫我說的話了。而且，我要回到我愛人居住的地方去。我要回到大海裡，回到她經常唱歌的小海灣，呼喚她，並且告訴她那些你要我做的惡事，你設計陷害我作的事。」

他的靈魂想試探他，便說道：「誰是那個你該回去尋找的愛人啊？這世上比她美的人多得是。撒瑪利亞的歌舞女郎會跳各種鳥類與獸類姿態的舞蹈。她們的腳趾頭塗著指甲花作成的染料，手腕上戴著小小的銅鈴。她們舞蹈時綻放著笑容，她們的笑聲有如潺潺的流水聲。跟我來吧！我帶你去找她們。這什麼罪不罪的有什麼好困擾你的呢？人生的樂趣不就在享受嗎？烈酒才有味道，不是嗎？別再庸人自擾了，跟我到另一個城市去吧。這附近就有一個小城，城裡有一個種滿鬱金香的花園。這個美麗的花園裡住著白孔雀和藍胸孔雀。當牠們在陽光下展開尾巴時，看起來就像一排鑲著金箔的象牙小圓碟。那負責餵食牠們的女孩，常為了娛樂孔雀而跳舞；有時她用手跳舞，有時也用腳跳舞。她的眼睛塗抹著銻的顏色，她的鼻孔形狀有如燕子的羽翼，她的鼻環垂掛著一朵珍珠雕成的小花。她一跳舞就笑，腳踝上的銀環會因跳動而相互碰撞，發出銀鈴般的清脆聲響。所以，別再煩惱了，跟我到這個城市去吧。」

然而年輕漁夫並不答腔，只是沉默地緊閉雙唇，用繩索緊縛自己的雙手，朝著來時的方向走，走向他愛人以前常在那兒唱歌的小海灣。但他的靈魂還是一路不斷地引誘他，而他就是不肯理它，也不作任何它要自己作的壞事。因為，他心中愛的力量是如此強大。

抵達海邊時，他鬆開捆著自己雙手的繩索，解除封在自己雙唇的沉默——他呼喚著小美人魚。然而，小美人魚並未出現，儘管他整天呼喊哀求著她。

於是他的靈魂嘲笑道：「顯然，你在你愛人的心目中沒什麼地位喔，你不過是曾被舀進一只破瓶裡的一滴珍貴之水而已。放棄了擁有的一切，卻得不到任何回報。你最好還是跟我走吧，我知道歡樂谷在哪裡，也知道那裡有什麼好東西。」

然而年輕漁夫並不理會它，只是在一個斷崖上用樹枝編了一間小屋，作為自己的棲身之所，還在那裡住了一年。每天早晨他呼喚她，每天中午又呼喚她，夜幕低垂時還是呼喊著她的名字。但她卻從未浮出水面與他相見；他無法在大海中找到她，也無法在任何一個水穴或任何一個綠水地、潟湖，或任一個水井深處找到她。

　　他的靈魂邪惡地誘惑他，低聲說些可怕的事。但這一切都無法動搖年輕漁夫，因為，他心中愛的力量是如此強大。

　　一年過去了，靈魂自忖：「我以邪惡誘惑我的主人，但他的愛卻超越了我。現在，我要以善良來誘惑他，也許他就會跟從我了。」

　　於是它對年輕漁夫說道：「我把世上的歡樂告訴你，你卻不理不睬。現在，我要告訴你這世上的痛苦，也許你會有興趣一聽！說實在的，痛苦才是這世界的主宰，因為沒有任何人可以逃離它的天羅地網。在這世上，不是有人缺衣就是有人欠糧。王侯之家有寡婦，貧寒之家也有寡婦。癩瘋病人在沼澤地帶徘徊，卻仍彼此傷害。乞丐在大馬路上遊走，錢囊裡一毛錢也沒有。飢餓在城市街道上漫遊，疫病坐在他們家門口。來吧，我們去改善這情形，讓這些事情不要再發生。你為什麼還停留在這兒呼喚你的愛呢？你明知她不會回應你。況且，愛是什麼，你貯存那麼多的愛要幹嘛？」

　　但是年輕漁夫仍不回答，因為，他心中愛的力量是如此強大。

　　每天早晨他呼喚著小美人魚，每天中午又呼喚著她，夜幕低垂時仍舊呼喊著她。但她卻從未浮出水面與他相見，雖然他試圖在海底水道、浪濤下的幽谷、夜空下的紫色海洋與晨曦下的銀色大海尋找她，仍舊無法在大海的任一角落找到她。

　　第二年過去了。靈魂在一個夜裡對獨坐小屋的漁夫說道：「嘿，我用邪惡誘惑你，也用善良誘惑你，不過都被你的愛打敗了。我不要再誘惑你了，只請求你讓我進入你心裡，這樣我就可以跟你合而為一，跟以前一樣。」

　　「你當然可以進來，」年輕漁夫說道，「因為你在那些沒有心而浪跡天涯的日子裡，一定吃了不少苦。」

　　「哎呀！」他的靈魂大叫了一聲，「我找不到路進去，你的這顆心被愛團團圍繞住了。」

「但我還是願意幫你的。」年輕漁夫說道。

他說話時，一聲巨大的哀泣從大海中傳出。人們聽到這種哭聲就知道有人魚死了。年輕漁夫立刻跳了起來，跑出他的小屋，衝到海邊去。黑色的浪花急速湧向岸邊，載著一個比白銀更白的事物。那東西幾乎和浪花一樣白，看似一朵被拋在浪頭上的白花。浪頭將它從海浪那兒接過來，泡沫又將它從浪頭那兒接過來，海岸承接了那事物。年輕漁夫看到，自己腳邊躺著的是小美人魚的屍體，她就躺在他腳邊，毫無生息。

被痛苦重擊而忍不住悲泣的他，哭倒在小美人魚身旁，親吻著那冰冷的紅唇，撫弄著濕髮上的琥珀。他倒在小美人魚身旁的沙灘上，哭得像一個因喜悅而顫抖的人。他用古銅色的雙手將她抱在自己懷裡。雖然雙唇是那樣冰冷，但他仍熱切地親吻著；鹽巴是濕髮上的結晶，但他卻帶著苦澀的歡喜品嚐；他親吻著她那緊閉的眼瞼，蓄積在那眼窩裡的海水都不及他的眼淚鹹。

他對著懷中的小美人魚屍體懺悔，將那劣酒般的故事注入她的耳朵。他拉起那纖纖雙臂，環繞在自己頸項間；他用指頭輕觸她單薄如蘆草的咽喉。苦澀，苦澀是他的歡欣，而充滿著異樣歡愉的是他的痛苦。

黑色的大海愈來愈近，白色的浪花泡沫像個瘋瘋病人般哀泣。大海用它那白沫形成的指爪攫住海岸，海洋之王的宮殿再度傳出痛哭聲，在海底深處，偉大的海神吹出了低啞的號角聲。

「快逃吧，」他的靈魂說道，「大海愈來愈近了，你再不走，它會殺了你的。快逃吧，我看到你的心被愛的力量所封閉因而拒絕了我，我感到很害怕。快逃到安全的地方去吧，你一定不會將沒有心的我送進另一個世界去吧？」

但年輕漁夫根本不理會他的靈魂，只是對著小美人魚說話，他說道：「愛情遠勝智慧，比財富寶貴，也比人類女子的雙腳更美，是火無法燒毀，水無法澆熄的。我在晨曦中呼喚妳，妳不回應。月亮都聽見了我的呼喊，妳卻不理我。我邪惡地離開了妳，帶著我對妳的傷害徘徊流浪。然而妳的愛將住在我心裡，它將永遠強大，不管是邪惡或善良，任何事物都無法超越它。現在妳既已死去，我當然也將追隨妳而去。」

他的靈魂求他離開，但他不為所動，因為，他心中愛的力量是如此強大。大海愈來愈近，試圖以海浪掩蓋他，當他知道結局將近時，他瘋狂地親吻著小美人魚冰冷的雙唇，他的心在體內裂開了。雖然他的心被愛塞得滿滿的，卻還是裂開了。他的靈魂終於找著了空隙，進到他的心裡，與他合而為一，就像從前一樣。此時，大海用它的浪濤掩蓋了年輕漁夫。

早晨，因為大海很不安寧，神父便前往海邊為之祝禱。隨神父前往的還有修士、樂師、執燭者、端香爐者和一大群人。

當神父來到海邊，看到溺死的年輕漁夫，和他雙手環抱著的小美人魚屍體時，他緊皺眉頭，往後退去，用手畫著十字，大聲哭叫道：「我不祝禱這海和其中的任何生物。人魚理應受詛咒，所有和他們交往的人也一樣。為了愛情而拋卻上帝，並因此遭受處罰，把死在這裡的年輕人與他愛人的屍體搬上來，葬在漂布場角落，不要在上頭立下任何記號，也不要留下任何標誌，這樣就沒有人知道他們的安息之地。因為，他們生前受詛咒，死後也該受詛咒。」

於是人們按照他的吩咐去作，在那個寸草不生的漂布場角落處，挖了個深坑，將死屍放了進去。

第三年過去了。這一天是個聖日，神父起身到教堂去，以便教導眾人認識救世主身上所受之傷的意義，並告訴眾人上帝的震怒。

當他穿好袍子走進去，在祭壇面前屈身敬拜時，他看到祭壇上滿是奇異的花朵，是他前所未見的。這些花看起來很不尋常，有著怪異的美。他忍不住注意到這些花，花的甜美香氣鑽進他的鼻間，讓他無由地開心了起來。

半晌，他打開聖龕，讓香爐的香氣裊繞在聖體匣上，將美好的聖餅分發給眾人，然後再將聖龕藏在帷幕之中。他開始對眾人說話，本來是想傳達上帝的震怒，卻不禁被那些白花的美干擾。那甜美的香氣鑽進他的鼻孔，嘴唇傳送出了其他的訊息。他講的不是上帝的震怒，而是名之為愛的上帝旨意，他也不知道自己為何要講述這個。

他講完後，人們都哭了。當神父回到聖器收藏室時，他的眼裡也滿溢著淚水。執事們來幫他解下身上的袍子，脫下白麻布聖職衣與腰帶、飾帶、聖帶等等。神父站在那兒，彷如置身夢境。

他們幫他更換完衣飾後，他看著他們，問道：「祭壇上那些花是什麼花？打哪兒來的？」

他們答道：「我們不知道那些是什麼花。不過，它們是從漂布場來的。」神父一聽，打了個寒顫，馬上返回自己家禱告。

清晨，天剛破曉，他隨同修士、樂師、執燭者、端香爐者和一大群人來到海邊，為大海祝禱，也為所有海中的生物祝禱，並為人面羊身的獸類祝禱，還有在森林裡跳舞的小動物，那躲在葉間偷看、眼睛晶亮的小東西，以及上帝世界中的一切都受到了祝福。人們的心裡充滿了喜悅與驚奇，漂布場上的角落也不再長出花朵，恢復了往日的寸草不生。人魚也不再去過往常去的海灣，因為他們往大海另一邊去了。

The Fisherman
and his Soul

Every evening the young Fisherman went out upon the sea, and threw his nets into the water.

When the wind blew from the land he caught nothing, or but little at best, for it was a bitter and black-winged wind, and rough waves rose up to meet it. But when the wind blew to the shore, the fish came in from the deep, and swam into the meshes of his nets, and he took them to the market-place and sold them.

Every evening he went out upon the sea, and one evening the net was so heavy that hardly could he draw it into the boat. And he laughed, and said to himself "Surely I have caught all the fish that swim, or snared some dull monster that will be a marvel to men, or some thing of horror that the great Queen will desire," and putting forth all his strength, he tugged at the coarse ropes till, like lines of blue enamel round a vase of bronze, the long veins rose up on his arms. He tugged at the thin ropes, and nearer and nearer came the circle of flat corks, and the net rose at last to the top of the water.

But no fish at all was in it, nor any monster or thing of horror, but only a little Mermaid lying fast asleep.

Her hair was as a wet fleece of gold, and each separate hair as a thread of line gold in a cup of glass. Her body was as white ivory, and her tail was of silver and pearl. Silver and pearl was her tail, and the green weeds of the sea coiled round it; and like sea-shells were her ears, and her lips were like sea-coral. The cold waves dashed over her cold breasts, and the salt glistened upon her eyelids.

So beautiful was she that when the young Fisherman saw her he was filled with wonder, and he put out his hand and drew the net close to him, and leaning over the side he clasped her in his arms. And when he touched her, she gave a cry like a startled sea-gull and woke, and looked at him in terror with her mauve-amethyst eyes, and struggled that she might escape. But he held her tightly to him, and would not suffer her to depart.

And when she saw that she could in no way escape from him, she began to weep, and said, "I pray thee let me go, for I am the only daughter of a King, and my father is aged and alone."

But the young Fisherman answered, "I will not let thee go save thou makest me a promise that whenever I call thee, thou wilt come and sing to me, for the fish delight to listen to the song of the Sea-folk, and so shall my nets be full."

"<u>Wilt thou</u>in very truth let me go, if I promise thee this?" cried the Mermaid. （譯註：Wilt thou 意即 will you）

"In very truth I will let thee go," said the young Fisherman.

So she made him the promise he desired, and swore it by the oath of the Sea-folk. And he loosened his arms from about her, and she sank down into the water, trembling with a strange fear.

Every evening the young Fisherman went out upon the sea, and called to the Mermaid, and she rose out of the water and sang to him. Round and round her swam the dolphins, and the wild gulls wheeled above her head.

And she sang a marvellous song. For she sang of the Sea-folk who drive their flocks from cave to cave, and carry the little calves on their shoulders; of the Tritons who have long green beards, and hairy breasts, and blow through twisted conchs when the King passes by; of the palace of the King which is all of amber, with a roof of clear emerald, and a pavement of bright pearl; and of the gardens of the sea where the great filigrane fans of coral wave all day long, and the fish dart about like silver birds, and the anemones cling to the rocks, and the pinks bourgeon in the ribbed yellow sand. She sang of the big whales that come down from the north seas and have sharp icicles hanging to their fins; of the Sirens who tell of such wonderful things that the merchants have to stop their ears with wax lest they should hear them, and leap into the water and be drowned; of the sunken galleys with their tall masts, and the frozen sailors clinging to the rigging, and the mackerel swimming in and out of the open portholes; of the little barnacles who are great travellers, and cling to the keels of the ships and go round and round the world; and of the cuttlefish who live in the sides of the cliffs and stretch out their long black arms, and can make night come when they will it. She sang of the nautilus who has a boat of her own that is carved out of an opal and steered with a silken sail; of the happy Mermen who play upon harps and can charm the great Kraken to sleep; of the little children who catch hold of the slippery porpoises and ride laughing upon their backs; of the Mermaids who lie in the white foam and hold out their arms to the mariners; and of the sea-lions with their curved tusks, and the sea-horses with their floating manes.

And as she sang, all the funny-fish came in from the deep to listen to her, and the young Fisherman threw his nets round them and caught them, and others he took with a spear. And when his boat was well-laden, the Mermaid would sink down into the sea, smiling at him.

Yet would she never come near him that he might touch her. Often times he called to her and prayed of her, but she would not; and when he sought to seize her she dived into the water as a seal might dive, nor did he see her again that day. And each day the sound of her voice became sweeter to his ears. So sweet was her voice that he forgot his nets and his cunning, and had no care of his craft. Vermilion-finned and with eyes of bossy gold, the tunnies went by in shoals, but he heeded them not. His spear lay by his side unused, and his baskets of plaited osier were empty. With lips parted, and eyes dim with wonder, he sat idle in his boat and listened, listening till the sea-mists crept round him, and the wandering moon stained his brown limbs with silver.

And one evening he called to her, and said: "Little Mermaid, little Mermaid, I love thee. Take me for thy bridegroom, for I love thee."

But the Mermaid shook her head. "Thou hast a human soul," she answered. "If only thou <u>would'st</u> send away thy soul, then could I love thee." （譯註：would'st 意即 would）

And the young Fisherman said to himself "Of what use is my soul to me? I cannot see it. I may not touch it. I do not know it. Surely I will send it away from me, and much gladness shall be mine." And a cry of joy broke from his lips, and standing up in the painted boat, he held out his arms to the Mermaid. "I will send my soul away," he cried, "and you shall be my bride, and I will be the bridegroom, and in the depth of the sea we will dwell together, and all that thou hast sung of thou shalt show me, and all that thou desirest I will do, nor shall our lives be divided."

And the little Mermaid laughed for pleasure, and hid her face in her hands.

"But how shall I send my soul from me?" cried the young Fisherman. "Tell me how I may do it, and lo! it shall be done."

"Alas! I know not," said the little Mermaid: "the Sea-folk have no souls." And she sank down into the deep, looking wistfully at him.

Now early on the next morning, before the sun was the span of a man's hand above the hill, the young Fisherman went to the house of the Priest and knocked three times at the door.

The novice looked out through the wicket, and where he saw who it was, he drew back the latch and said to him, "Enter."

And the young Fisherman passed in, and knelt down on the sweet-smelling rushes of the floor, and cried to the Priest who was reading out of the Holy Book and said to him, "Father, I am in love with one of the Sea-folk, and my soul hindereth me from having my desire. Tell me how I can send my soul away from me, for in truth I have no need of it. Of what value is my soul to me? I cannot see it. I may not touch it. I do not know it."

And the Priest beat his breast, and answered, "Alack, Alack, thou art mad, or hast eaten of poisonous herb, for the soul is the noblest part of man, and was given to us by God that we should nobly use it. There is no thing more precious than a human soul, nor any earthly thing that can be weighed with it. It is worth all the gold that is in the world, and is more precious than the rubies of the kings. Therefore, my son, think not any more of this matter, for it is a sin that may not be forgiven. And as for the Sea-folk, they are lost, and they who would traffic with them are lost also. They are as the beasts of the field that know not good from evil, and for them the Lord has not died."

The young Fisherman's eyes filled with tears when he heard the bitter words of the Priest, and he rose up from his knees and said to him, "Father, the Fauns (譯註：此為羅馬神話中，半人半羊之獸) live in the forest and are glad, and on the rocks sit the Mermen with their harps of red gold. Let me be as they are, I beseech thee, for their days are as the days of flowers. And as for my soul, what doth my soul profit me, if it stand between me and the thing that I love?"

"The love of the body is vile," cried the Priest, knitting his brows, "and vile and evil are the pagan things God suffers to wander through His world. Accursed be the Fauns of the woodland, and accursed be the singers of the sea! I have heard them at night-time, and they have sought to lure me from my beads. They tap at the window, and laugh. They whisper into my ears the tale of their perilous joys. They tempt me with temptations, and when I would pray they make mouth at me. They are lost, I tell thee, they are lost. For them there is no heaven nor hell, and in neither shall they praise God's name."

"Father," cried the young Fisherman, "thou knowest not what thou sayest. Once in my net I snared the daughter of a King. She is fairer than the morning star, and whiter than the moon. For her body I would give my soul, and for her love I would surrender heaven. Tell me what I ask of thee, and let me go in peace." （譯註：knowest意即know；sayest 意即say）

"Away! Away!" cried the Priest: "thy leman is lost, and thou shalt be lost with her." And he gave him no blessing, but drove him from his door.

And the young Fisherman went down into the market-place, and he walked slowly, and with bowed head, as one who is in sorrow.

And when the merchants saw him coming, they began to whisper to each other, and one of them came forth to meet him, and called him by name, and said to him, "What hast thou to sell?"

"I will sell thee my soul," he answered: "I pray thee buy

it off me, for I am weary of it. Of what use is my soul to me? I cannot see it. I may not touch it. I do not know it."

But the merchants mocked at him, and said, "Of what use is a man's soul to us? It is not worth a clipped piece of silver. Sell us thy body for a slave, and we will clothe thee in sea-purple, and put a ring upon thy finger, and make thee the minion of the great Queen. But talk not of the soul, for to us it is <u>nought</u>, nor has it any value for our service." （譯註：nought 也可拼做naught，為「零」之意）

And the young Fisherman said to himself: "How strange a thing this is! The Priest telleth me that the soul is worth all the gold in the world, and the merchants say that it is not worth a clipped piece of silver." And he passed out of the market-place, and went down to the shore of the sea, and began to ponder on what he should do.

And at noon he remembered how one of his companions, who was a gatherer of samphire, had told him of a certain young Witch who dwelt in a cave at the head of the bay and was very cunning in her witcheries. And he set to and ran, so eager was he to get rid of his soul, and a cloud of dust followed him as he sped round the sand of the shore. By the itching of her palm the young Witch knew his coming, and she laughed and let down her red hair. With her red hair falling around her, she stood at the opening of the cave, and in her hand she had a spray of wild hemlock that was blossoming.

"What <u>d'ye</u> lack? What <u>d'ye</u> lack?" （譯註：d'ye意為do you） she cried, as he came panting up the steep, and bent down before her. "Fish for thy net, when the wind is foul? I have a little reed-pipe, and when I blow on it the mullet come sailing into the bay. But it has a price, pretty boy, it has a price. What d'ye lack? What d'ye lack? A storm to wreck the ships, and wash the chests of rich treasure ashore? I have more storms than the wind has, for I serve one who is stronger than the wind, and with a sieve and a pail of water I can send the great galleys to the bottom of the sea. But I have a price, pretty boy, I have a price. What d'ye lack? What d'ye lack? I know a flower that grows in the valley, none knows it but I. It has purple leaves, and a star in its heart, and its juice is as white as milk. <u>Should'st</u> （譯註：Should'st意即should）thou touch with this flower the hard lips of the Queen, she would follow thee all over the world. Out of the bed of the King she would rise, and over the whole world she would follow thee. And it has a price, pretty boy, it has a price. What d'ye lack? What d'ye lack? I can pound a toad in a mortar, and make broth of it, and stir the broth with a dead man's hand. Sprinkle it on thine enemy while he sleeps, and he will turn into a black viper, and his own mother will slay him. With a wheel I can draw the Moon from heaven, and in a crystal I can show thee Death. What d'ye lack? What d'ye lack? Tell me thy desire, and I will give it thee, and thou shalt pay me a price, pretty boy, thou shalt pay me a price."

"My desire is but for a little thing," said the young Fisherman, "yet hath the Priest been wroth with me, and driven me forth. It is but for a little thing, and the merchants have mocked at me, and denied me. Therefore am I come to thee, though men call thee evil, and whatever be thy price I shall pay it."

"What would'st thou?" asked the Witch, coming near to him.

"I would send my soul away from me," answered the young Fisherman.

The Witch grew pale, and shuddered, and hid her face in her blue mantle. "Pretty boy, pretty boy," she muttered, "that is a terrible thing to do."

He tossed his brown curls and laughed. "My soul is nought to me," he answered. "I cannot see it. I may not touch it. I do not know it."

"What wilt thou give me if I tell thee?" asked the Witch looking down at him with her beautiful eyes.

"Five pieces of gold," he said, "and my nets, and the wattled house where I live, and the painted boat in which I sail. Only tell me how to get rid of my soul, and I will give thee all that I possess."

She laughed mockingly at him, and struck him with the spray of hemlock. "I can turn the autumn leaves into gold," she answered, "and I can weave the pale moonbeams into silver if I will it. He whom I serve is richer than all the kings of this world and has their dominions."

"What then shall I give thee," he cried, "if thy price be neither gold nor silver?"

The Witch stroked his hair with her thin white hand. "Thou must dance with me, pretty boy," she murmured, and she smiled at him as she spoke.

"Nought but that?" cried the young Fisherman in wonder, and he rose to his feet.

"Nought but that," she answered, and she smiled at him again.

"Then at sunset in some secret place we shall dance together," he said, "and after that we have danced thou shalt tell me the thing which I desire to know."

She shook her head. "When the moon is full, when the moon is full," she muttered. Then she peered all round, and listened. A blue bird rose screaming from its nest and circled over the dunes, and three spotted birds rustled through the coarse grey grass and whistled to each other. There was no other sound save the sound of a wave fretting the smooth pebbles below. So she reached out her hand, and drew him near to her and put her dry lips close to his ear.

"To-night thou must come to the top of the mountain," she whispered. "It is a Sabbath, and He will be there."

The young Fisherman started and looked at her, and she showed her white teeth and laughed. "Who is He of whom thou speakest?" he asked.

"It matters not," she answered. "Go thou to-night, and stand under the branches of the hornbeam, and wait for my coming. If a black dog run towards thee, strike it with a rod of willow, and it will go away. If an owl speak to thee, make it no answer. When the moon is full I shall be with thee, and we will dance together on the grass."

"But wilt thou swear to me to tell me how I may send my soul from me?" he made question.

She moved out into the sunlight, and through her red hair rippled the wind. "By the hoofs of the goat I swear it," she made answer.

"Thou art the best of the witches," cried the young Fisherman, "and I will surely dance with thee to-night on the top of the mountain. I would indeed that thou hadst (had) asked of me either gold or silver. But such as thy price is thou shalt have it, for it is but a little thing." And he <u>doffed</u> his cap to her, and bent his head low, and ran back to the town filled with a great joy. （譯註：doffed 為do + off的簡寫，為脫帽、丟棄、廢除之意）

And the Witch watched him as he went, and when he had passed from her sight she entered her cave, and having taken a mirror from a box of carved cedarwood, she set it up on a frame, and burned vervain on lighted charcoal before it, and peered through the coils of the smoke. And after a time she clenched her hands in anger. "He should have been mine," she muttered, "I am as fair as she is."

And that evening, when the moon had risen, the young Fisherman climbed up to the top of the mountain, and stood under the branches of the hornbeam. Like a targe of polished metal the round sea lay at his feet, and the shadows of the fishing boats moved in the little bay. A great owl, with yellow sulphurous eyes, called to him by his name, but he made it no answer. A black dog ran towards him and snarled. He struck it with a rod of willow, and it went away whining.

At midnight the witches came flying through the air like bats. "Phew!" they cried, as they lit upon the ground, "there is someone here we know not!" and they sniffed about, and chattered to each other, and made signs. Last of all came the young Witch, with her red hair streaming in the wind. She wore a dress of gold tissue embroidered with peacocks' eyes, and a little cap of green velvet was on her head.

"Where is he, where is he?" shrieked the witches when they saw her, but she only laughed, and ran to the hornbeam, and taking the Fisherman by the hand she led him out into the moonlight and began to dance.

Round and round they whirled, and the young Witch jumped so high that he could see the scarlet heels of her shoes. Then right across the dancers came the sound of the galloping of a horse, but no horse was to be seen, and he felt afraid.

"Faster," cried the Witch, and she threw her arms about his neck, and her breath was hot upon his face. "Faster, faster!" she cried, and the earth seemed to spin beneath his feet, and his brain grew troubled, and a great terror fell on him, as of some evil thing that was watching him, and at last he became aware that under the shadow of a rock there was a figure that had not been there before.

It was a man dressed in a suit of black velvet, cut in the Spanish fashion. His face was strangely pale, but his lips were like a proud red flower. He seemed weary, and was leaning back toying in a listless manner with the pommel of his dagger. On the grass beside him lay a plumed hat, and a pair of riding gloves gauntleted with gilt lace, and sewn with seed-pearls wrought into a curious device. A short cloak lined with sables hung from his shoulder, and his delicate white hands were gemmed with rings. Heavy eyelids drooped over his eyes. The young Fisherman watched him, as one snared in a spell. At last their eyes met, and wherever he danced it seemed to him that the eyes of the man were upon him. He heard the Witch laugh, and caught her by the waist, and whirled her madly round and round.

Suddenly a dog bayed in the wood, and the dancers stopped, and going up two by two, knelt down, and kissed the man's hands. As they did so, a little smile touched his proud lips, as a bird's wing touches the water and makes it laugh. But there was disdain in it. He kept looking at the young Fisherman.

"Come! let us worship," whispered the Witch, and she led him up, and a great desire to do as she besought him seized on him, and he followed her. But when he came close, and without knowing why he did it, he made on his breast the sign of the Cross, and called upon the holy name.

No sooner had he done so than the witches screamed like hawks and flew away, and the pallid face that had been watching him twitched with a spasm of pain. The man went over to a little wood, and whistled. A jennet with silver trappings came running to meet him. As he leapt upon the saddle he turned round, and looked at the young Fisherman sadly.

And the Witch with the red hair tried to fly away also, but the Fisherman caught her by her wrists, and held her fast. "Loose me," she cried, "and let me go. For thou hast named what should not be named, and shown the sign that may not be looked at."

"Nay," he answered, "but I will not let thee go till thou hast told me the secret."

"What secret?" said the Witch, wrestling with him like a wild cat, and biting her foam-flecked lips.

"Thou knowest," he made answer.

Her grass-green eyes grew dim with tears, and she said to the Fisherman, "Ask me anything but that!"

He laughed, and held her all the more tightly.

And when she saw that she could not free herself she whispered to him, "Surely I am as fair as the daughters of the sea, and as comely as those that dwell in the blue waters," and she fawned on him and put her face close to his.

But he thrust her back frowning, and said to her, "If thou keepest not the promise that thou madest to me I will slay thee for a false witch."

She grew grey as a blossom of the Judas tree, and shuddered. "Be it so," she muttered. "It is thy soul and not mine. Do with it as thou wilt." And she took from her girdle a little knife that had a handle of green viper's skin, and gave it to him.

"What shall this serve me?" he asked of her wondering.

She was silent for a few moments, and a look of terror came over her face. Then she brushed her hair back from her forehead, and smiling strangely she said to him, "What men call the shadow of the body is not the shadow of the body, but is the body of the soul. Stand on the sea-shore with thy back to the moon, and cut away from around thy feet thy shadow, which is thy soul's body, and bid thy soul leave thee, and it will do so."

The young Fisherman trembled. "Is this true?" he murmured.

"It is true, and I would that I had not told thee of it," she cried, and she clung to his knees weeping.

He put her from him and left her in the rank grass, and going to the edge of the mountain he placed the knife in his belt, and began to climb down.

And his soul that was within him called out to him and said, "Lo! I have dwelt with thee for all these years, and have been thy servant. Send me not away from thee now, for what evil have I done thee?"

And the young Fisherman laughed. "Thou has done me no evil, but I have no need of thee," he answered. "The world is wide, and there is Heaven also, and Hell, and that dim twilight house that lies between. Go wherever thou wilt, but trouble me not, for my love is calling to me."

And his soul besought him piteously, but he heeded it not, but leapt from crag to crag, being sure-footed as a wild goat, and at last he reached the level ground and the yellow shore of the sea.

Bronze-limbed and well-knit, like a statue wrought by a Grecian, he stood on the sand with his back to the moon, and out of the foam came white arms that beckoned to him, and out of the waves rose dim forms that did him homage. Before him lay his shadow, which was the body of his soul, and behind him hung the moon in the honey-colored air.

And his soul said to him, "If indeed thou must drive me from thee, send me not forth without a heart. The world is cruel, give me thy heart to take with me."

He tossed his head and smiled. "With what should I love my love if I gave thee my heart?" he cried.

"Nay, but be merciful," said his soul: "give me thy heart, for the world is very cruel, and I am afraid."

"My heart is my love's," he answered, "therefore tarry not, but get thee gone."

"Should I not love also?" asked his soul.

"Get thee gone, for I have no need of thee," cried the young Fisherman, and he took the little knife with its handle of green viper's skin, and cut away his shadow from around his feet, and it rose up and stood before him, and looked at him, and it was even as himself.

He crept back, and thrust the knife into his belt, and a feeling of awe came over him. "Get thee gone," he murmured, "and let me see thy face no more."

"Nay, but we must meet again," said the soul. Its voice was low and flute-like, and its lips hardly moved while it spake.

"How shall we meet?" cried the young Fisherman. "Thou wilt not follow me into the depths of the sea?"

"Once every year I will come to this place, and call to thee," said the soul. "It may be that thou wilt have need of me."

"What need should I have of thee?" cried the young Fisherman, "but be it as thou wilt," and he plunged into the water, and the Tritons blew their horns, and the little Mermaid rose up to meet him, and put her arms around his neck and kissed him on the mouth.

And the soul stood on the lonely beach and watched them. And when they had sunk down into the sea, it went weeping away over the marshes.

And after a year was over the soul came down to the shore of the sea and called to the young Fisherman, and he rose out of the deep, and said, "Why <u>dost</u> thou call to me?" （譯註：dost 意 即 do）

And the soul answered, "Come nearer, that I may speak with thee, for I have seen marvellous things."

So he came nearer, and couched in the shallow water, and

leaned his head upon his hand and listened.

And the soul said to him, "When I left thee I turned my face to the East and journeyed. From the East cometh everything that is wise. Six days I journeyed, and on the morning of the seventh day I came to a hill that is in the country of the Tartars. I sat down under the shade of a tamarisk tree to shelter myself from the sun. The land was dry, and burnt up with the heat. The people went to and fro over the plain like flies crawling upon a disk of polished copper.

"When it was noon a cloud of red dust rose up from the flat rim of the land. When the Tartars saw it, they strung their painted bows, and having leapt upon their little horses they galloped to meet it. The women fled screaming to the wagons, and hid themselves behind the felt curtains.

"At twilight the Tartars returned, but five of them were missing, and of those that came back not a few had been wounded. They harnessed their horses to the wagons and drove hastily away. Three jackals came out of a cave and peered after them. Then they sniffed up the air with their nostrils, and trotted off in the opposite direction.

"When the moon rose I saw a camp-fire burning on the plain, and went towards it. A company of merchants were seated round it on carpets. Their camels were picketed behind them, and the negroes who were their servants were pitching tents of tanned skin upon the sand, and making a high wall of the prickly pear.

"As I came near them, the chief of the merchants rose up and drew his sword, and asked me my business.

"I answered that I was a Prince in my own land, and that I had escaped from the Tartars, who had sought to make me their slave. The chief smiled, and showed me five heads fixed upon long reeds of bamboo.

"Then he asked me who was the prophet of God, and I answered him Mohammed.

"When he heard the name of the false prophet, he bowed and took me by the hand, and placed me by his side. A negro brought me some mare's milk in a wooden-dish, and a piece of lamb's flesh roasted.

"At daybreak we started on our journey. I rode on a red-haired camel by the side of the chief, and a runner ran before us carrying a spear. The men of war were on either hand, and the mules followed with the merchandise. There were forty camels in the caravan, and the mules were twice forty in number.

"We went from the country of the Tartars into the country of those who curse the Moon. We saw the gryphons guarding their gold on the white rocks, and the scaled Dragons sleeping in their caves. As we passed over the mountains we held our breath lest the snows might fall on us, and each man tied a veil of gauze before his eyes. As we passed through the valleys the Pygmies shot arrows at us from the hollows of the trees, and at night time we heard the wild men beating on their drums. When we came to the Tower of Apes we set fruits before them, and they did not harm us. When we came to the Tower of Serpents we gave them warm milk in bowls of brass, and they let us go by. Three times in our journey we came to the banks of the Oxus. We crossed it on rafts of wood with great bladders of blown hide. The river-horses raged against us and sought to slay us. When the camels saw them they trembled.

"The kings of each city levied tolls on us, but would not suffer us to enter their gates. They threw us bread over the walls, little maize-cakes baked in honey and cakes of fine flour filled with dates. For every hundred baskets we gave them a bead of amber.

"When the dwellers in the villages saw us coming, they poisoned the wells and fled to the hill-summits. We fought with the Magadae who are born old, and grow younger and younger every year, and die when they are little children; and with the Laktroi who say that they are the sons of tigers, and paint themselves yellow and black; and with the Aurantes who bury their dead on the tops of trees, and themselves live in dark caverns lest the Sun, who is their god, should slay them; and with the Krimnians who worship a crocodile, and give it earrings of green glass, and feed it with butter and fresh fowls; and with the Agazonbae, who are dog-faced; and with the Sibans, who have horses' feet, and run more swiftly than horses. A third of our company died in battle, and a third died of want. The rest murmured against me, and said that I had brought them an evil fortune. I took a horned adder from beneath a stone and let it sting me. When they saw that I did not sicken they grew afraid.

"In the fourth month we reached the city of Illel. It was night time when we came to the grove that is outside the walls, and the air was sultry, for the Moon was travelling in Scorpion. We took the ripe pomegranates from the trees, and broke them and drank their sweet juices. Then we lay down on our carpets and waited for the dawn.

"And at dawn we rose and knocked at the gate of the city. It was wrought out of red bronze, and carved with sea-dragons and dragons that have wings. The guards looked down from the battlements and asked us our business. The interpreter of the caravan answered that we had come from the island of Syria with much merchandise. They took hostages, and told us that they would open the gate to us at noon, and bade us tarry till then.

"When it was noon they opened the gate, and as we entered in the people came crowding out of the houses to look at us, and a crier went round the city crying through a shell. We stood in the market-place, and the negroes uncorded the bales of figured cloths and opened the carved chests of sycamore. And when they had ended their task, the merchants set forth their strange wares, the waxed linen from Egypt and the painted linen from the country of the Ethiops, the purple sponges from

Tyre and the blue hangings from Sidon, the cups of cold amber and the fine vessels of glass and the curious vessels of burnt clay. From the roof of a house a company of women watched us. One of them wore a mask of gilded leather.

"And on the first day the priests came and bartered with us, and on the second day came the nobles, and on the third day came the craftsmen and the slaves. And this is their custom with all merchants as long as they tarry in the city.

"And we tarried for a moon, and when the moon was waning, I wearied and wandered away through the streets of the city and came to the garden of its god. The priests in their yellow robes moved silently through the green trees, and on a pavement of black marble stood the rose-red house in which the god had his dwelling. Its doors were of powdered lacquer, and bulls and peacocks were wrought on them in raised and polished gold. The tiled roof was of sea-green porcelain, and the jutting eaves were festooned with little bells. When the white doves flew past, they struck the bells with their wings and made them tinkle.

"In front of the temple was a pool of clear water paved with veined onyx. I lay down beside it, and with my pale fingers I touched the broad leaves. One of the priests came towards me and stood behind me. He had sandals on his feet, one of soft serpent-skin and the other of birds' plumage. On his head was a mitre of black felt decorated with silver crescents. Seven yellows were woven into his robe, and his frizzed hair was stained with antimony.

"After a little while he spoke to me, and asked me my desire. I told him that my desire was to see the god.

" 'The god is hunting,' said the priest, looking strangely at me with his small slanting eyes.

" 'Tell me in what forest, and I will ride with him,' I answered.

"He combed out the soft fringes of his tunic with his long pointed nails. 'The god is asleep,' he murmured.

" 'Tell me on what couch, and I will watch by him,' I answered.

" 'The god is at the feast,' he cried.

" 'If the wine be sweet I will drink it with him, and if it be bitter I will drink it with him also,' was my answer.

"He bowed his head in wonder, and, taking me by the hand, he raised me up, and led me into the temple.

"And in the first chamber I saw an idol seated on a throne of jasper bordered with great orient pearls. It was carved out of ebony, and in stature was of the stature of a man. On its forehead was a ruby, and thick oil dripped from its hair on to its thighs. Its feet were red with the blood of a newly-slain kid, and its loins girt with a copper belt that was studded with seven beryls.

"And I said to the priest, 'Is this the god?' And he answered me, 'This is the god.'

" 'Show me the god,' I cried, 'or I will surely slay thee.' And I touched his hand, and it became withered.

"And the priest besought me, saying, 'Let my lord heal his servant, and I will show him the god.'

"So I breathed with my breath upon his hand, and it became whole again, and he trembled and led me into the second chamber, and I saw an idol standing on a lotus of jade hung with great emeralds. It was carved out of ivory, and in stature was twice the stature of a man. On its forehead was a chrysolite, and its breasts were smeared with myrrh and cinnamon. In one hand it held a crooked sceptre of jade, and in the other a round crystal. It ware buskins of brass, and its thick neck was circled with a circle of selenites.

"And I said to the priest, 'Is this the god?'And he answered me. 'This is the god.'

" 'Show me the god,' I cried, 'or I will surely slay thee. ' And I touched his eyes, and they became blind.

"And the priest besought me, saying, 'Let my lord heal his servant, and I will show him the god.'

"So I breathed with my breath upon his eyes, and the sight came back to them, and he trembled again, and led me into the third chamber, and lo! there was no idol in it, nor image of any kind, but only a mirror of round metal set on an altar of stone.

"And I said to the priest, 'Where is the god?'

"And he answered me: 'There is no god but this mirror that thou seest, for this is the Mirror of Wisdom. And it reflecteth all things that are in heaven and on earth, save only the face of him who looketh into it. This it reflecteth not, so that he who looketh into it may be wise. Many other mirrors are there, but they are mirrors of Opinion. This only is the Mirror of Wisdom. And they who possess this mirror know everything, nor is there anything hidden from them. And they who possess it not have not Wisdom. Therefore is it the god, and we worship it.'And I looked into the mirror, and it was even as I he had said to me.

"And I did a strange thing, but what I did matters not, for in a valley that is but a day's journey from this place have I hidden the Mirror of Wisdom. Do but suffer me to enter into thee again and be thy servant, and thou shalt be wiser than all the wise men, and Wisdom shall be thine. Suffer me to enter into thee, and none will be as wise as thou." But the young Fisherman laughed. "Love is better than Wisdom," he cried, "and the little Mermaid loves me."

"Nay, but there is nothing better than Wisdom," said the soul.

"Love is better," answered the young Fisherman, and he plunged into the deep, and the soul went weeping away over the marshes.

And after the second year was over the soul came down to the shore of the sea, and called to the young Fisherman, and he rose out of the deep and said, "Why dost thou call to me?"

And the soul answered, "Come nearer that I may speak with thee, for I have seen marvellous things."

So he came nearer, and couched in the shallow water, and leaned his head upon his hand and listened.

And the soul said to him, "When I left thee, I turned my face to the South and journeyed. From the South cometh every thing that is precious. Six days I journeyed along the highways that lead to the city of Ashter, along the dusty red-dyed highways by which the pilgrims are <u>wont</u> to go did I journey, and on the morning of the seventh day I lifted up my eyes, and lo! the city lay at my feet, for it is in a valley. (譯註：wont為形容詞,意指：往往會做的、習慣於的)

"There are nine gates to this city, and in front of each gate stands a bronze horse that neighs when the Bedouins come down from the mountains. The walls are cased with copper, and the watch-towers on the walls are roofed with brass. In every tower stands an archer with a bow in his hand. At sunrise he strikes with an arrow on a gong, and at sunset he blows through a horn of horn.

"When I sought to enter, the guards stopped me and asked of me who I was. I made answer that I was a Dervish and on my way to the city of Mecca, where there was a green veil on which the Koran was embroidered in silver letters by the hands of the angels. They were filled with wonder, and entreated me to pass in.

"Inside it is even as a bazaar. Surely thou should'st have been with me. Across the narrow streets the gay lanterns of paper flutter like large butterflies. When the wind blows over the roofs they rise and fall as painted bubbles do. In front of their booths sit the merchants on silken carpets. They have straight black beards, and their turbans are covered with golden sequins, and long strings of amber and carved peach-stones glide through their cool fingers. Some of them sell galbanum and nard, and curious perfumes from the islands of the Indian Sea, and the thick oil of red roses and myrrh and little nail-shaped cloves. When one stops to speak to them, they throw pinches of frankincense upon a charcoal brazier and make the air sweet. I saw a Syrian who held in his hands a thin rod like a reed. Grey threads of smoke came from it, and its odor as it burned was as the odor of the pink almond in spring. Others sell silver bracelets embossed all over with creamy blue turquoise stones, and anklets of brass wire fringed with little pearls, and tigers" claws set in gold, and the claws of that gilt cat, the leopard, set in gold also, and earrings of pierced emerald, and finger-rings of hollowed jade. From the tea-houses comes the sound of the guitar, and the opium-smokers with their white smiling faces look out at the passers-by.

"Of a truth thou should'st have been with me. The wine-sellers elbow their way through the crowd with great black skins on their shoulders. Most of them sell the wine of Shiraz, which is as sweet as honey. They serve it in little metal cups and strew rose leaves upon it. In the market-place stand the fruitsellers, who sell all kinds of fruit: ripe figs, with their bruised purple flesh, melons, smelling of musk and yellow as topazes, citrons and rose-apples and clusters of white grapes, round red-gold oranges, and oval lemons of green gold. Once I saw an elephant go by. Its trunk was painted with vermilion and turmeric, and over its ears it had a net of crimson silk cord. It stopped opposite one of the booths and began eating the oranges, and the man only laughed. <u>Thou canst</u> not think how strange a people they are. (譯註：canst意即can，用於主詞為thou

時）When they are glad they go to the bird-sellers and buy of them a caged bird, and set it free that their joy may be greater, and when they are sad they scourge themselves with thorns that their sorrow may not grow less.

"One evening I met some negroes carrying a heavy palanquin through the bazaar. It was made of gilded bamboo, and the poles were of vermilion lacquer studded with brass peacocks. Across the windows hung thin curtains of muslin embroidered with beetles' wings and with tiny seed-pearls, and as it passed by a pale-faced Circassian looked out and smiled at me. I followed behind, and the negroes hurried their steps and scowled. But I did not care. I felt a great curiosity come over me.

"At last they stopped at a square white house. There were no windows to it, only a little door like the door of a tomb. They set down the palanquin and knocked three times with a copper hammer. An Armenian in a caftan of green leather peered through the wicket, and when he saw them he opened, and spread a carpet on the ground, and the woman stepped out. As she went in, she turned round and smiled at me again. I had never seen anyone so pale.

"When the moon rose I returned to the same place and sought for the house, but it was no longer there. When I saw that, I knew who the woman was, and wherefore she had smiled at me.

"Certainly thou should'st have been with me. On the feast of the New Moon the young Emperor came forth from his palace and went into the mosque to pray. His hair and beard were dyed with rose-leaves, and his cheeks were powdered with a fine gold dust. The palms of his feet and hands were yellow with saffron.

"At sunrise he went forth from his palace in a robe of silver, and at sunset he returned to it again in a robe of gold. The people flung themselves on the ground and hid their faces, but I would not do so. I stood by the stall of a seller of dates and waited. When the Emperor saw me, he raised his painted eyebrows and stopped. I stood quite still, and made him no obeisance. The people marvelled at my boldness, and counselled me to flee from the city. I paid no heed to them, but went and sat with the sellers of strange gods, who by reason of their craft are abominated. When I told them what I had done, each of them gave me a god and prayed me to leave them.

"That night, as I lay on a cushion in the tea-house that is in the Street of Pomegranates, the guards of the Emperor entered and led me to the palace. As I went in they closed each door behind me, and put a chain across it. Inside was a great court with an arcade running all round. The walls were of white alabaster, set here and there with blue and green tiles. The pillars were of green marble, and the pavement of a kind of peach-blossom marble. I had never seen anything like it before.

"As I passed across the court two veiled women looked down from a balcony and cursed me. The guards hastened on, and the butts of the lances rang upon the polished floor. They opened a gate of wrought ivory, and I found myself in a watered garden of seven terraces. It was planted with tulip-cups and moonflowers, and silver-studded aloes. Like a slim reed of crystal a fountain hung in the dusky air. The cypress-trees were like burnt-out torches. From one of them a nightingale was singing.

"At the end of the garden stood a little pavilion. As we approached it two eunuchs came out to meet us. Their fat bodies swayed as they walked, and they glanced curiously at me with their yellow-lidded eyes. One of them drew aside the captain of the guard, and in a low voice whispered to him. The other kept munching scented pastilles, which he took with an affected gesture out of an oval box of lilac enamel.

"After a few moments the captain of the guard dismissed the soldiers. They went back to the palace, the eunuchs following slowly behind and plucking the sweet mulberries from the trees as they passed. Once the elder of the two turned round, and smiled at me with an evil smile.

"Then the captain of the guard motioned me towards the entrance of the pavilion. I walked on without trembling, and drawing the heavy curtain aside I entered in.

"The young Emperor was stretched on a couch of dyed lion skins, and a gerfalcon perched upon his wrist. Behind him stood a brass-turbaned Nubian, naked down to the waist, and with heavy earrings in his split ears. On a table by the side of the couch lay a mighty scimitar of steel.

"When the Emperor saw me he frowned, and said to me, 'What is thy name? Knowest thou not that I am Emperor of this city?' But I made him no answer.

"He pointed with his finger at the scimitar, and the Nubian seized it, and rushing forward struck at me with great violence. The blade whizzed through me, and did me no hurt. The man fell sprawling on the floor, and, when he rose up, his teeth chattered with terror and he hid himself behind the couch.

"The Emperor leapt to his feet, and taking a lance from a stand of arms, he threw it at me. I caught it in its flight, and brake the shaft into two pieces. He shot at me with an arrow, but I held up my hands and it stopped in mid-air. Then he drew a dagger from a belt of white leather, and stabbed the Nubian in the throat lest the slave should tell of his dishonor. The man writhed like a trampled snake, and a red foam bubbled from his lips.

"As soon as he was dead the Emperor turned to me, and when he had wiped away the bright sweat from his brow with a little napkin of purfled and purple silk, he said to me, 'Art thou a prophet, that I may not harm thee, or the son of a prophet that I can do thee no hurt? I pray thee leave my city to night, for while thou art in it I am no longer its lord.'

"And I answered him, 'I will go for half of thy treasure. Give me half of thy treasure, and I will go away.'

"He took me by the hand, and led me out into the garden. When the captain of the guard saw me, he wondered. When the eunuchs saw me, their knees shook and they fell upon the ground in fear.

"There is a chamber in the palace that has eight walls of red porphyry, and a brass-scaled ceiling hung with lamps. The Emperor touched one of the walls and it opened, and we passed down a corridor that was lit with many torches. In niches upon each side stood great wine-jars filled to the brim with silver pieces. When we reached the centre of the corridor the Emperor spake the word that may not be spoken, and a granite door swung back on a secret spring, and he put his hands before his face lest his eyes should be dazzled.

"Thou could'st not believe how marvellous a place it was. There were huge tortoise-shells full of pearls, and hollowed moonstones of great size piled up with red rubies. The gold was stored in coffers of elephant-hide, and the gold-dust in leather bottles. There were opals and sapphires, the former in cups of crystal, and the latter in cups of jade. Round green emeralds were ranged in order upon thin plates of ivory, and in one corner were silk bags filled, some with turquoise-stones and others with beryls. The ivory horns were heaped with purple amethysts, and the horns of brass with chalcedonies and sards. The pillars, which were of cedar, were hung with strings of yellow lynx-stones. In the flat oval shields there were carbuncles, both wine-colored and colored like grass. And yet I have told thee but a tithe of what was there.

"And when the Emperor had taken away his hands from before his face he said to me: 'This is my house of treasure, and half that is in it is thine, even as I promised to thee. And I will give thee camels and camel drivers, and they shall do thy bidding and take thy share of the treasure to whatever part of the world thou desirest to go. And the thing shall be done to night, for I would not that the Sun, who is my father, should see that there is in my city a man whom I cannot slay.'

"But I answered him, 'The gold that is here is thine, and the silver also is thine, and thine are the precious jewels and the things of price. As for me, I have no need of these. Nor shall I take aught from thee but that little ring that thou <u>wearest</u> on the finger of thy hand.' (譯註：wearest意即wear)

"And the Emperor frowned. 'It is but a ring of lead,'he cried,   'nor has it any value. Therefore take thy half of the treasure and go from my city.'

" 'Nay,' I answered,   'but I will take nought but that leaden ring, for I know what is written within it, and for what purpose.'

"And the Emperor trembled, and besought me and said, 'Take all the treasure and go from my city. The half that is mine shall be thine also.'

"And I did a strange thing, but what I did matters not, for in a cave that is but a day's journey from this place have I hidden the Ring of Riches. It is but a day's journey from this place, and it waits for thy coming. He who has this Ring is richer than all the kings of the world. Come therefore and take it, and the world's riches shall be thine."

But the young Fisherman laughed. "Love is better than Riches," he cried, "and the little Mermaid loves me."

"Nay, but there is nothing better than Riches," said the soul.

"Love is better," answered the young Fisherman, and he plunged into the deep, and the soul went weeping away over the marshes.

And after the third year was over, the soul came down to

the shore of the sea, and called to the young Fisherman, and he rose out of the deep and said, "Why dost thou call to me?"

And the soul answered, "Come nearer, that I may speak with thee, for I have seen marvellous things."

So he came nearer, and couched in the shallow water, and leaned his head upon his hand and listened.

And the soul said to him, "In a city that I know of there is an inn that standeth by a river. I sat there with sailors who drank of two different colored wines, and ate bread made of barley, and little salt fish served in bay leaves with vinegar. And as we sat and made merry, there entered to us an old man bearing a leathern carpet and a lute that had two horns of amber. And when he had laid out the carpet on the floor, he struck with a quill on the wire strings of his lute, and a girl whose face was veiled ran in and began to dance before us. Her face was veiled with a veil of gauze, but her feet were naked. Naked were her feet, and they moved over the carpet like little white pigeons. Never have I seen anything so marvellous, and the city in which she dances is but a day's journey from this place."

Now when the young Fisherman heard the words of his soul, he remembered that the little Mermaid had no feet and could not dance. And a great desire came over him, and he said to himself, "It is but a day's journey, and I can return to my love," and he laughed, and stood up in the shallow water, and strode towards the shore.

And when he had reached the dry shore he laughed again, and held out his arms to his soul. And his soul gave a great cry of joy and ran to meet him, and entered into him, and the young Fisherman saw stretched before him upon the sand that shadow of the body that is the body of the soul.

And his soul said to him, "Let us not tarry, but get hence at once, for the Sea-gods are jealous, and have monsters that do their bidding."

So they made haste, and all that night they journeyed beneath the moon, and all the next day they journeyed beneath the sun, and on the evening of the day they came to a city.

And the young Fisherman said to his soul, "Is this the city in which she dances of whom thou <u>did'st</u> speak to me?" （譯註：did'st意即did）

And his soul answered him, "It is not this city, but another. Nevertheless let us enter in."

So they entered in and passed through the streets, and as they passed through the Street of the Jewellers the young fisherman saw a fair silver cup set forth in a booth. And his soul said to him, "Take that silver cup and hide it."

So he took the cup and hid it in the fold of his tunic, and they went hurriedly out of the city.

And after that they had gone a league from the city, the young Fisherman frowned, and flung the cup away, and said to his soul, "Why didst thou tell me to take this cup and hide it, for it was an evil thing to do?"

But his soul answered him, "Be at peace, be at peace."

And on the evening of the second day they came to a city, and the young Fisherman said to his soul, "Is this the city in which she dances of whom thou didst speak to me?"

And his soul answered him, "It is not this city, but another. Nevertheless let us enter in."

So they entered in and passed through the streets, and as they passed through the Street of the Sellers of Sandals, the young Fisherman saw a child standing by a jar of water. And his soul said to him, "Smite that child." So he smote the child till it wept, and when he had done this they went hurriedly out of the city.

And after that they had gone a league from the city the young Fisherman grew wroth, and said to his soul, "Why did'st thou tell me to smite the child, for it was an evil thing to do?"

But his soul answered him, "Be at peace, be at peace."

And on the evening of the third day they came to a city, and the young Fisherman said to his soul, "Is this the city in which she dances of whom thou did'st speak to me?"

And his soul answered him, "It may be that it is this city, therefore let us enter in."

So they entered in and passed through the streets, but nowhere could the young Fisherman find the river or the inn that stood by its side. And the people of the city looked curiously at him, and he grew afraid and said to his soul, "Let us go hence, for she who dances with white feet is not here."

But his soul answered, "Nay, but let us tarry, for the night is dark and there will be robbers on the way."

So he sat him down in the market-place and rested, and after a time there went by a hooded merchant who had a cloak of cloth of Tartary, and bare a lantern of pierced horn at the end of a jointed reed. And the merchant said to him, "Why dost thou sit in the market-place, seeing that the booths are closed and the bales corded?"

And the young Fisherman answered him, "I can find no inn in this city, nor have I any kinsman who might give me shelter."

"Are we not all kinsmen?" said the merchant. "And did not one God make us? Therefore come with me, for I have a guest-chamber."

So the young Fisherman rose up and followed the merchant to his house. And when he had passed through a garden of pomegranates and entered into the house, the merchant brought him rose-water in a copper dish that he might wash his hands, and ripe melons that he might quench his thirst, and set a bowl of rice and a piece of roasted kid before him.

And after that he had finished, the merchant led him to the guestchamber, bade him sleep and be at rest. And the young Fisherman gave him thanks, and kissed the ring that was on his hand, and flung himself down on the carpets of dyed goat's hair. And when he had covered himself with a covering of black lambs-wool he fell asleep.

And three hours before dawn, and while it was still night, his soul waked him, and said to him, "Rise up and go to the room of the merchant, even to the room in which he sleepeth, and slay him, and take from him his gold, for we have need of it."

And the young Fisherman rose up and crept towards the room of the merchant, and over the feet of the merchant there was lying a curved sword, and the tray by the side of the merchant held nine purses of gold. And he reached out his hand and touched the sword, and when he touched it the merchant started and awoke, and leaping up seized himself the sword and cried to the young Fisherman, "Dost thou return evil for good, and pay with the shedding of blood for the kindness that I have shown thee?"

And his soul said to the young Fisherman, "Strike him," and he struck him so that he swooned, and he seized then the nine purses of gold, and fled hastily through the garden of pomegranates, and set his face to the star that is the star of morning.

And when they had gone a league from the city, the young Fisherman beat his breast, and said to his soul, "Why didst thou bid me slay the merchant and take his gold? Surely thou art evil."

But his soul answered him, "Be at peace, be at peace."

"Nay," cried the young Fisherman, "I may not be at peace, for all that thou hast made me to do I hate. Thee also I hate, and I bid thee tell me wherefore thou hast wrought with me in this wise."

And his soul answered him, "When thou didst send me forth into the world thou gavest me no heart, so I learned to do all these things and love them."

"What sayest thou?" murmured the young Fisherman.

"Thou knowest," answered his soul, "thou knowest it well. Hast thou forgotten that thou gavest me no heart? I trow not. And so trouble not thyself nor me, but be at peace, for there is no pain that thou shalt not give away, nor any pleasure that thou shalt not receive."

And when the young Fisherman heard these words he trembled and said to his soul, "Nay, but thou art evil, and hast made me forget my love, and hast tempted me with temptations, and hast set my feet in the ways of sin." And his soul answered him, "Thou hast not forgotten that when thou didst send me forth into the world thou gavest me no heart. Come, let us go to another city, and make merry, for we have nine purses of gold."

But the young Fisherman took the nine purses of gold, and flung them down, and trampled on them.

"Nay," he cried, "but I will have nought to do with thee, nor will I journey with thee anywhere, but even as I sent thee away before, so will I send thee away now, for thou hast wrought me no good." And he turned his back to the moon, and with the little knife that had the handle of green viper's skin he strove to cut from his feet that shadow of the body which is the body of the soul.

Yet his soul stirred not from him, nor paid heed to his command, but said to him, "The spell that the Witch told thee avails thee no more, for I may not leave thee, nor mayest thou drive me forth. Once in his life may a man send his soul away, but he who receiveth back his soul must keep it with him for ever, and this is his punishment and his reward."

And the young Fisherman grew pale and clenched his hands and cried, "She was a false Witch in that she told me not that."

"Nay," answered his soul, "but she was true to Him she worships, and whose servant she will be ever."

And when the young Fisherman knew that he could no longer get rid of his soul, and that it was an evil soul and would abide with him always, he fell upon the ground weeping bitterly.

And when it was day the young Fisherman rose up and said to his soul, "I will bind my hands that I may not do thy bidding, and close my lips that I may not speak thy words, and I will return to the place where she whom I love has her dwelling. Even to the sea will I return, and to the little bay where she is wont to sing, and I will call to her and tell her the evil I have done and the evil thou hast wrought on me."

And his soul tempted him and said, "Who is thy love that thou should'st return to her? The world has many fairer than she is. There are the dancing-girls of Samaris who dance in the manner of all kinds of birds and beasts. Their feet are painted with henna, and in their hands they have little copper bells. They laugh while they dance, and their laughter is as clear as the laughter of water. Come with me and I will show them to thee. For what is this trouble of thine about the things of sin? Is that which is pleasant to eat not made for the eater? Is there poison in that which is sweet to drink? Trouble not thyself, but come with me to another city. There is a little city hard by in which there is a garden of tulip-trees. And there dwell in this comely garden white peacocks and peacocks that have blue breasts. Their tails when they spread them to the sun are like disks of ivory and like gilt disks. And she who feeds them dances for their pleasure, and sometimes she dances on her hands and at other times she dances with her feet. Her eyes are colored with stibium, and her nostrils are shaped like the wings of a swallow. From a hook in one of her nostrils hangs a flower that is carved out of a pearl. She laughs while she dances, and the silver rings that are about her ankles tinkle like bells of silver. And so trouble not thyself any more, but come with me to this city."

But the young Fisherman answered not his soul, but closed his lips with the seal of silence and with a tight cord bound his hands, and journeyed back to the place from which he had come, even to the little bay where his love had been wont to sing. And ever did his soul tempt him by the way, but he made it no answer, nor would he do any of the wickedness that it sought to make him to do, so great was the power of the love that was within him.

And when he had reached the shore of the sea, he loosed the cord from his hands, and took the seal of silence from his lips, and called to the little Mermaid. But she came not to his call, though he called to her all day long and besought her.

And his soul mocked him and said, "Surely thou hast but little joy out of thy love. Thou art as one who in time of dearth pours water into a broken vessel. Thou givest away what thou hast, and nought is given to thee in return. It were better for thee to come with me, for I know where the Valley of Pleasure lies, and what things are wrought there."

But the young Fisherman answered not his soul, but in a cleft of the rock he built himself a house of wattles, and abode there for the space of a year. And every morning he called to the Mermaid, and every noon he called to her again and at night-time he spake her name. Yet never did she rise out of the sea to meet him, nor in any place of the sea could he find her, though he sought for her in the caves and in the green water, in the pools of the tide and in the wells that are at the bottom of the deep.

And ever did his soul tempt him with evil, and whisper of terrible things. Yet did it not prevail against him, so great was the power of his love.

And after the year was over, the soul thought within himself, "I have tempted my master with evil, and his love is stronger than I am. I will tempt him now with good, and it may be that he will come with me."

So he spake to the young Fisherman and said, "I have told thee of the joy of the world, and thou hast turned a deaf ear to me. Suffer me now to tell thee of the world's pain, and it may be that thou wilt hearken. For of a truth, pain is the Lord of this world, nor is there anyone who escapes from its net. There be some who lack raiment, and others who lack bread. There be widows who sit in purple, and widows who sit in rags. To and fro over the fens go the lepers, and they are cruel to each other. The beggars go up and down on the highways, and their wallets are empty. Through the streets of the cities walks Famine, and the Plague sits at their gates. Come, let us go forth and mend these things, and make them not to be. Wherefore should'st thou tarry here calling to thy love, seeing she comes not to thy call? And what is love, that thou should'st set this high store upon it?"

But the young Fisherman answered it nought, so great was the power of his love. And every morning he called to the Mermaid, and every noon he called to her again, and at night-time he spake her name. Yet never did she rise out of the sea to meet him, nor in any place of the sea could he find her, though he sought for her in the rivers of the sea, and in the valleys that are under the waves, in the sea that the night makes purple, and in the sea that the dawn leaves grey.

And after the second year was over, the soul said to the young Fisherman at night-time, and as he sat in the wattled house alone, "Lo! now I have tempted thee with evil, and I have tempted thee with good, and thy love is stronger than I am. Wherefore will I tempt thee no longer, but I pray thee to suffer me to enter thy heart, that I may be one with thee even as before."

"Surely thou mayest enter," said the young Fisherman, "for in the days when with no heart thou didst go through the world thou must have much suffered."

"Alas!" cried his soul, "I can find no place of entrance, so compassed about with love is this heart of thine."

"Yet I would that I could help thee," said the young Fisherman.

And as he spake there came a great cry of mourning from the sea, even the cry that men hear when one of the Sea-folk is dead. And the young Fisherman leapt up, and left his wattled house, and ran down to the shore. And the black waves came hurrying to the shore, bearing with them a burden that was whiter than silver. White as the surf it was, and like a flower it tossed on the waves. And the surf took it from the waves, and the foam took it from the surf, and the shore received it, and lying at his feet the young Fisherman saw the body of the little Mermaid. Dead at his feet it was lying.

Weeping as one smitten with pain he flung himself down beside it, and he kissed the cold red of the mouth, and toyed with the wet amber of the hair. He flung himself down beside it on the sand, weeping as one trembling with joy, and in his brown arms he held it to his breast. Cold were the lips, yet he kissed them. Salt was the honey of the hair, yet he tasted it with a bitter joy. He kissed the closed eyelids, and the wild spray that lay upon their cups was less salt than his tears.

And to the dead thing he made confession. Into the shells

of its ears he poured the harsh wine of his tale. He put the little hands round his neck, and with his fingers he touched the thin reed of the throat. Bitter, bitter was his joy, and full of strange gladness was his pain.

The black sea came nearer, and the white foam moaned like a leper. With white claws of foam the sea grabbled at the shore. From the palace of the Sea-King came the cry of mourning again, and far out upon the sea the great Tritons blew hoarsely upon their horns.

"Flee away," said his soul, "for ever doth the sea come higher, and if thou tarriest it will slay thee. Flee away, for I am afraid, seeing that thy heart is closed against me by reason of the greatness of thy love. Flee away to a place of safety. Surely thou wilt not send me without a heart into another world?"

But the young Fisherman listened not to his soul, but called on the little Mermaid and said, "Love is better than wisdom, and more precious than riches, and fairer than the feet of the daughters of men. The fires cannot destroy it, nor can the waters quench it. I called on thee at dawn, and thou didst not come to my call. The moon heard thy name, yet hadst thou no heed of me. For evilly had I left thee, and to my own hurt had I wandered away. Yet ever did thy love abide with me, and ever was it strong, nor did aught prevail against it, though I have looked upon evil and looked upon good. And now that thou art dead, surely I will die with thee also."

And his soul besought him to depart, but he would not, so great was his love. And the sea came nearer, and sought to cover him with its waves, and when he knew that the end was at hand he kissed with mad lips the cold lips of the Mermaid and the heart that was within him brake. And as through the fullness of his love his heart did break, the soul found an entrance and entered in, and was one with him even as before. And the sea covered the young Fisherman with its waves.

And in the morning the Priest went forth to bless the sea,

for it had been troubled. And with him went the monks and the musicians, and the candle-bearers, and the swingers of censers, and a great company.

And when the Priest reached the shore he saw the young Fisherman lying drowned in the surf, and clasped in his arms was the body of the little Mermaid. And he drew back frowning, and having made the sign of the cross, he cried aloud and said, "I will not bless the sea nor anything that is in it. Accursed be the Sea-folk, and accursed be all they who traffic with them. And as for him who for love's sake forsook God, and so lieth here with his leman slain by God's judgment, take up his body and the body of his leman, and bury them in the corner of the Field of the Fullers, and set no mark above them, nor sign of any kind, that none may know the place of their resting. For accursed were they in their lives, and accursed shall they be in their deaths also."

And the people did as he commanded them, and in the corner of the Field of the Fullers, where no sweet herbs grew, they dug a deep pit, and laid the dead things within it.

And when the third year was over, and on a day that was a holy day, the Priest went up to the chapel, that he might show to the people the wounds of the Lord, and speak to them about the wrath of God.

And when he had robed himself with his robes, and entered in and bowed himself before the altar, he saw that the altar was covered with strange flowers that never had he seen before. Strange were they to look at, and of curious beauty, and their beauty troubled him, and their odor was sweet in his nostrils. And he felt glad, and understood not why he was glad.

And after that he had opened the tabernacle, and incensed the monstrance that was in it, and shown the fair wafer to the people, and hid it again behind the veil of veils, he began to speak to the people, desiring to speak to them of the wrath of God. But the beauty of the white flowers troubled him, and their odor was sweet in his nostrils, and there came another word into his lips, and he spake not of the wrath of God, but of the God whose name is Love. And why he so spake, he knew not.

And when he had finished his word the people wept, and the Priest went back to the sacristy, and his eyes were full of tears. And the deacons came in and began to unrobe him, and took from him the alb and the girdle, the maniple and the stole. And he stood as one in a dream.

And after that they had unrobed him, he looked at them and said, "What are the flowers that stand on the altar, and whence do they come?"

And they answered him, "What flowers they are we cannot tell, but they come from the corner of the Fullers' Field." And the Priest trembled, and returned to his own house and prayed.

And in the morning, while it was still dawn, he went forth with the monks and the musicians, and the candle-bearers and the swingers of censers, and a great company, and came to the shore of the sea, and blessed the sea, and all the wild things that are in it. The Fauns also he blessed, and the little things that dance in the woodland, and the bright-eyed things that peer through the leaves. All the things in God's world he blessed, and the people were filled with joy and wonder. Yet never again in the corner of the Fullers' Field grew flowers of any kind, but the field remained barren even as before. Nor came the Sea-folk into the bay as they had been wont to do, for they went to another part of the sea.

為藝術而藝術的王爾德

一八五四年出生於愛爾蘭都柏林的王爾德（Oscar Wilde），集詩人、小說家、劇作家、說故事高手與美學主義者於一身。其絢爛多彩卻也命運多舛的一生，真讓人有不勝唏噓之嘆。早在他進入牛津大學就讀時，他就以獨樹一幟的言行和異於他人的服飾裝扮，引起眾人注意；然而，他的天分才是他最引以為傲的得意。他曾經公開在眾人面前說道：「除了我的天才，我沒什麼好說的。」

早在牛津大學求學時期，王爾德就以詩作〈拉溫納〉（Ravenna）拔得校際紐迪蓋特獎（Newdigate prize）詩作比賽獎頭籌。也是在牛津大學時期，他深受唯美主義大師約翰·羅斯金（John Ruskin）與華特·佩特（Walter Pater）的影響。在一八七八年拿到學位離開牛津大學時，他決定當個徹底的美學主義者。不但在文學創作或是日常生活中，他都要為藝術而藝術。

王爾德於一八八二年到美國展開為期一年的巡迴演說，他機智詼諧的談吐、優雅的外表讓他在美國很受歡迎。一八八四年時他與康斯坦絲結婚，而在往後兩年，他的兩個兒子相繼出世。一八八八年，他為兒子們寫了一系列童話故事——《快樂王子與其他故事》，奠定了他說故事高手的地位。在這些童話故事中，他用淺顯的文字，略嫌傷感的筆調，闡述「愛」的重要——或是朋友間的愛，或是戀人間的愛，或是造物主對世人的愛，都令人感動不已。

這張快樂王子畫像出自知名的英國插畫家沃爾特‧克蘭（Walter Crane, 1845～1915）之手。克蘭的畫風筆觸十分古典，他亦曾為許多經典童話故事繪製充滿線條感的美哉插畫，如《睡美人》《小紅帽》《美女與野獸》等等。

在童話故事之後，他的長篇小說《格雷的畫像》更以其極具神秘性的故事架構吸引了眾多讀者。此外，他的喜劇作品如《溫德美爾夫人的扇子》、《一個不重要的女人》、《一個理想的丈夫》與《不可兒戲》等也都獲得社會大眾青睞。其實，王爾德的戲劇作品除了上述四部較為人所熟知的喜劇劇本，還有一個以《聖經》中的故事為藍本寫成的悲劇劇本《沙樂美》，但此劇並不像其他喜劇作品那麼受歡迎。

　　文學成就之外，王爾德在現實生活中與一位侯爵之子的情誼，掀起了他生命的狂濤。昆士貝里侯爵在一八九五年控告王爾德與其子有同性戀關係。雖然王爾德也反控侯爵誹謗，但被控為同性戀的罪名成立，他被判刑兩年，並被送往瑞丁監獄服刑。一八九七年，他結束了牢獄生活，重獲自由，但此時的他，真可說是既窮困又潦倒。他旅居法國、義大利和瑞士等地，後來在法國定居。但在重獲自由三年之後，他就被死神接走了，留下的是令人百讀不厭的文學作品和似是而非、發人深思的「王爾德珠璣語」。以下列出數則從王爾德作品中摘錄出來的語句，與讀者共賞：

◎ 關於男人

· 男人會變老，但絕不會變好。Men become old, but they never become good.

——《溫德美爾夫人的扇子》Lady Windermere's Fan

· 愛說教的男人常是偽君子，而愛說教的女人必然平庸。A man who moralizes is usually a hypocrite, and a woman who moralizes is invariably plain.

——《溫德美爾夫人的扇子》Lady Windermere's Fan

· 現今的已婚男人都活得像單身漢，而單身漢都活得像已婚男人。Nowadays all the married men live like bachelors and all the bachelors live like married men.

——《格雷的畫像》 The Picture of Dorian Gray

◎ 關於女人

· 絕不能相信那種會說出自己實際年齡的女人，這樣的女人，肯定什麼事都會說出來。One should never trust a woman who tells one her real age. A woman who would tell one that, would tell one anything.

——《一個不重要的女人》A Woman of No Importance

· 哭是平庸女人的避難所，卻是美女的致命傷。Crying is the refuge of plain women but the ruin of pretty ones.

——《溫德美爾夫人的扇子》Lady Windermere's Fan

· 男人太早理解人生，女人太晚理解人生。這就是男女之間的差異。Men know life too early. Women know life too late. That is the difference between men and women.

——《一個不重要的女人》A Woman of No Importance

延伸閱讀 為藝術而藝術的王爾德

◎ 關於世人

· 除了該知道的事情,大家對每一件事都有著無盡的好奇心。The public have an insatiable curiosity to know everything, except what is worth knowing.

———《社會主義下人的靈魂》The Soul of Man Under Socialism

· 大部分的世間男女都被迫扮演著不適合的角色。Most men and women are forced to perform parts for which they have no qualification.

———〈亞瑟·沙維爾爵士之罪〉Lord Arthur Savile's Crime

◎ 關於人生

· 人生太重要,故無法認真討論它。Life is much too important a thing ever to talk seriously about it.

———《薇拉》Vera, or The Nihilists

◎ 關於愛情

· 年輕男人想忠實卻做不到;老男人想不忠實,卻也做不到。Young men want to be faithful and are not; old men want to be faithless and cannot.

———《格雷的畫像》 The Picture of Dorian Gray

· 人應該永保戀愛的狀態才是,那正是人們不該結婚的理由。One should always be in love. That is the reason one should never marry.

———《一個不重要的女人》A Woman of No Importance

王爾德生平事略 · 作品年表

1854 年	十月十六日出生於愛爾蘭都柏林 本名為奧斯卡・芬格・歐佛蘭第・威斯・王爾德（Oscar Fingal O'Flahertie Wills Wilde）
1871 年	於都柏林三一學院開始學習古典文學
1874 年	進入英國牛津大學瑪格德蘭學院
1878 年	獲得學位，並以詩作〈Ravenna〉獲得校際Newdigate獎
1879 年	定居倫敦
1881 年	作品——詩集（Poems）
1882 年	在北美展開為期一年的巡迴演說
1884 年	與康斯坦絲・洛伊德（Constance Lloyd）結婚
1885 年	長子西瑞爾（Cyril）出生
1886 年	次子維維安（Vyvyan）出生
1888 年	作品——快樂王子與其他故事（The Happy Prince and Other Tales）
1889 年	作品——說謊的腐敗（The Decay of Lying）
1890 年	作品——格雷的畫像（The Picture of Dorian Gray）
1891 年	作品——石榴屋（The House of Pomegranates） 作品——亞瑟・沙維爾爵士之罪與其他故事（Lord Arthur Savile's Crime and Other Stories） 作品——意圖（Intentions） 作品——沙樂美（Salome）
1893 年	作品——溫德美爾夫人的扇子（Lady Windermere's Fan）
1894 年	作品——一個不重要的女人（A Woman of No Importance）
1895 年	控告昆士里侯爵（Marquess of Queensberry）誹謗名譽；被昆士里侯爵控告與其子的同性戀關係罪名成立，遂被送往瑞丁監獄（Reading Gaol）服刑
1897 年	結束牢獄生活。流浪法國、義大利與瑞士等地，化名為希巴斯坦・梅爾默斯（Sebastian Melmoth）
1898 年	妻子康斯坦絲去世。 作品——瑞丁監獄之歌（The Ballad of Reading Gaol）
1899 年	作品——一個理想的丈夫（An Ideal Husband） 作品——不可兒戲（The Importance of Being Earnest）
1900 年	十一月三十日死於法國，葬於巴黎拉雪茲神父國家公墓

國家圖書館出版品預行編目資料

王爾德短篇小說集 I ／王爾德（Oscar Wilde）著；劉珮芳譯
——四版——臺中市：好讀，2024.08
冊；　公分，——（典藏經典；56）
〔中英雙語新版〕
ISBN 978-986-178-731-2（平裝）
873.57　　　　　　　　　　　　　　　　　113009722

好讀出版

典藏經典 56

王爾德短篇小說集 I

作　　者／王爾德 Oscar Wilde
譯　　者／劉珮芳
總 編 輯／鄧茵茵
文字編輯／簡伊婕、鄧語荸
美術編輯／廖勁智
發行所／好讀出版有限公司
　　　　台中市 407 西屯區工業 30 路 1 號
　　　　台中市 407 西屯區大有街 13 號（編輯部）
TEL:04-23157795 FAX:04-23144188 http://howdo.morningstar.com.tw
（如對本書編輯或內容有意見，請來電或上網告訴我們）
法律顧問　陳思成律師

讀者服務專線／ TEL：02-23672044 / 04-23595819#212
讀者傳真專線／ FAX：02-23635741 / 04-23595493
讀者專用信箱／ E-mail：service@morningstar.com.tw
網路書店／ http：//www.morningstar.com.tw
郵政劃撥／ 15060393（知己圖書股份有限公司）
印刷／上好印刷股份有限公司
如有破損或裝訂錯誤，請寄回知己圖書更換

四　　版／西元 2024 年 8 月 1 日
定　　價／ 250 元

線上讀者回函
好讀新書資訊